SERGEANT BACK AGAIN

SERGEANT
BACK AGAIN

Charles Coleman

HARPER & ROW, PUBLISHERS, New York
Cambridge, Hagerstown, Philadelphia, San Francisco
London, Mexico City, São Paulo, Sydney

1817

Grateful acknowledgment is made for permission to reprint the following lyrics:

"The Ballad of Davy Crockett," words and music by Tom Blackburn and George Bruns. Copyright © 1954 by Wonderland Music Co., Inc. Reprinted by permission.

"The Ballad of the Green Berets" by Barry Sadler and Robin Moore. Copyright © 1963, 1965, 1966 by Music, Music, Music Inc.

"Crystal Blue Persuasion" by Tommy James, Mike Vale, and Ed Gray. Copyright © 1969 by Big Seven Music Corp.

"I Shall Be Released" by Bob Dylan. Copyright © 1967 by Dwarf Music. Used by permission. All rights reserved.

A portion of this work originally appeared in somewhat different form in *Tri-Quarterly.*

FIRST EDITION

Designer: Sidney Feinberg

Library of Congress Cataloging in Publication Data

Coleman, Charles.
   Sergeant back again.
   1. Vietnamese Conflict, 1961–1975—Fiction. I.
Title.
PZ4.C689667Se   [PS3553.04738]   813'.54   80-7601
ISBN 0-06-010864-9

80 81 82 83 84 10 9 8 7 6 5 4 3 2 1

ACKNOWLEDGMENTS

Lynne, Edna, and Chester Burwell
Elaine and Charles Coleman
Debra Coleman-Hyde
Holbrook Hyde
Sherilyn Newman-Driscoll
William Stein

Elliott Anderson
Betty Anne Clarke
Paul Freemeyer
Judy Graham
Robert Kroetsch
John Leonard
Robert Piper
Ted Solotaroff
Philip Sullivan

David Headley
John Robiola
Nasty-Jack Watson

FOREWORD

I would like to think that this book is finished now—but having lived with it and the lives which populate it for over a decade, I know it isn't, just as the repercussions of the war in Vietnam will continue to reverberate through our thoughts, feelings, and actions for decades to come.

I did not *make* this story: it came that way, ready-made, defined by historical circumstances, generated by the soldiers who have had to fight the most insidious and intimate battle: the one with yourself. That battle, which has become part of a new consciousness in the American mind, has—one hopes—just commenced. Indeed, the lessons for us to learn are not on the vacant battlefields of South Vietnam or Cambodia; not within the reams of statistical data being gathered even now by analysts in the Pentagon who ask, What happened? How? Why?; not gained by staring at graduation pictures, rereading letters, or standing solemnly before headstones: the lessons are within us the living . . . if we would only look.

But who wants to look back at, to understand, to share responsibility for a war so botched, so contradictory, so riddled with accusations as this one? Who wants to revive a period in American history when fathers stood against sons, brothers against brothers, men against themselves? But we must try, lest the tragedy of Vietnam be repeated tomorrow, or the day after.

In writing this book, I am mainly a chronicler who was left no choice but to try to speak for the inarticulate, the psychically scarred, and the wasted. This book, therefore, is neither a defense nor a prosecution of the events which occurred in Vietnam. Rather it is a synthesis of personal experiences, observations, interviews, and journals here woven together into a narrative which, I trust, will be accepted with compassion, will be understood and heeded: because these men are your own.

January 1980

SERGEANT BACK AGAIN

CHAPTER 1

Collins stood in front of the door, staring at the black-and-white plastic name plaque:

GEORGE W. NIELAND, M.D.

"Go ahead, Collins. Knock again. He's in there," said the ward supervisor, Specialist Hinckley. "Go ahead."

"Come in," said Nieland after the second knock.

"Andrew Collins, sir," he said, extending his hand.

"Yes. Yes. How are you feeling this morning, Collins?"

"Fine," he replied, looking back into the psychiatrist's jet-black eyes.

"Good. . . . Sit down over here. . . . I took your records home with me this past weekend. I must say, Collins, it's certainly an unusual assortment of information. There are your diaries and notebooks," he said, pointing to a stack of worn, soiled composition books on his desk. "This one begins on the first day of your enlistment in the Medical Corps back in January 1969. And this one here ends on 15 March 1970—your last entry. And here are the reports from the field units to which you were attached: the Eighty-third, the One-o-first, the Fifth, and then the Fortieth Field Surgical Hospital. Mostly routine evaluations, but they add up to a very fine service record.

"And here, Collins . . ." Dr. Nieland held up two affidavits on U.S.

Army Intelligence stationery. The psychiatrist waited for a reaction from his patient: a hint of anger, or fear, or even curiosity. But Collins stared through the signatures.

"The one in my left hand is for your participation in the Underground—the ESR, as it's called. The other one is for unauthorized release of classified documents to civilians employed in Vietnam by the major news media, namely CBS. You were pending trial before Major Jennings, Chief of Psychiatric Services at MacArthur's Hospital in Tokyo, had you transferred here, to Chambers Pavilion. You do know where you are now, don't you, Collins? . . . Good. . . . Where are you?"

"I'm in the hospital."

"In what hospital?"

"Brooke Army Medical Center, Fort Sam Houston, Texas."

"Yes, but what kind of hospital is *this?*"

"It's a hospital for cripples."

"That's right, in part, Collins. But the cripples occupy only the fourth and one half of the third floor. You're on one of the third-floor wards, Collins, and you're not a cripple."

"Haven't we been through all this once before, Dr. Nieland?"

"That's right, Collins. The day you came out of the isolation cell. But you're not a cripple, are you?"

"No. Not like the others. And I have ninety days to get better."

Dr. Nieland gathered together a pile of papers from inside his desk drawer.

"And, Collins," he said, rising, "here are a dozen or so rather . . . bizarre letters mailed—apparently—to you by some individual or persons. All of them have one thing in common: they're all written by soldiers who were either seriously wounded or crippled in action—and who never signed their names. It's these letters which I find most disturbing, Collins. And I would like to begin with them this morning. Can you tell me anything about the person or persons who wrote these?"

"No!"

"You can tell me nothing about them at all?"

"No. Nothing."

"Because you can't recall or because you just don't want to tell me about it?"

"No. Nothing."

"O.K. But let me tell *you* something. You're going to waste a lot

"What in hell are you talking about?"

"No. Nothing."

"I'm talking to you about these notebooks. Your notebooks. What are you talking about?"

"No. Nothing."

"Let's get back to what happened before you shipped to Vietnam, before you were a line medic with the Eighty-third. Let's get back to these notebooks of yours. There're progressions of sorts in your descriptions of people and things that I noticed while reading them over. The words you use—the labels you've become accustomed to using—bring things out there very close to you. And occasionally you try to push them back, but generally you pull living and *nonliving*—or should I say no longer living—things very close to you. And I would guess that that's the beginning of the problem right there. In the distancing. Even before you bent over to treat your first field casualty. Even before you landed at Tan Son Nhut on . . . let me see. On April 30, 1969.

"So the problem is really one of identification. See that pine tree out there? Tell me, do you feel more affinity with that pine tree than —say—that bayonet plant over there?"

"I suppose so." Then Collins began to sing:

> "Look over yonder
> What do you see?
> The sun is arisin'
> Most definitely.
> A new day is dawnin'—"

"Collins!"

> "The sun is arisin'
> Most defin—"

"Collins!" shouted Dr. Nieland, slamming his fist down on the desk.

"What!" Collins shouted back at the psychiatrist. "What do you want of me!"

"You seem to forget that I've read your notebooks. I've read all the reports, including Captain Marks's from MacArthur Hospital. And I've read *all* the letters. Remember, Collins? Remember how Army Intelligence confiscated them while you were in MacArthur Hospital, and you didn't have time to destroy a word? Not one word.

4

of extremely valuable time if you persist in remaining withdrawn and above it all. You know that already, I think. And your journals, your field notes, the type of work you did for the Underground, and your background are a hell of a lot more revealing than I think you realize. That, and your service record, tell me how easily you could defeat my attempts to help you leave this hospital for civilian life rather than rot in a VA hospital."

Collins had stopped staring. His gaze was vacant except for an intermittent tremor of his eyes, as though he were watching or heeding something disturbing.

". . . You arrived in this hospital on April eighth. You were in seclusion for eight days and then dropped to the third floor on the fifteenth. Since then you've shown yourself to be the sort of person who can fake cooperation and make everyone here think that you really didn't need treatment. But—"

"Untouchable," said Collins.

"What? What did you just say?" insisted Nieland, leaning across his desk.

"No. Nothing."

"Collins, you just said something. What was it? . . . Untouchable? Isn't that what you just said?"

"Me?"

"Yes, you! Who the hell else is in this room?"

"No. Nothing."

"O.K., Collins. You have it your way. It's curious, though . . . that's exactly what I was—you listening to me, Collins?—that's exactly what I'm getting at. Sooner or later, it seems to me, you'll see, or accept, that nothing living is untouchable. In your world, right now, perhaps there is such a thing as the *untouchable* part of you. But, Collins, it's not really a living thing. It has no life, no emotion. Except the fantasy life which you lend to it. But *it's* not really alive. And if you keep on thinking that you can be reached in some respects while holding yourself untouchable in others, you'll become . . . well, Collins, you *became* the embodiment of just that, didn't you? It's all right here in black and white. In your own notebooks. The whole picture is here in your own language written in your own hand. And—"

"Nain So Pa. Sergeant Back Again. Captain Sarkofsky. Colonel—"

"Andrew? Andrew!"

"Yes."

Remember the first notebook, the one you wrote in basic at Fort Dix? How you described—to use your own words—the 'butchering of a tree'?"

"It doesn't matter."

"Doesn't matter? Oh, so now it doesn't matter. Is that right? Collins, don't play with me, don't play with who you really are and what you've come to believe in. You . . . in fact, you predicted what would happen right here on . . . page twenty of the first notebook. *You*, Collins, *you* wrote—and I quote—'In their blind killing of such a—' "

"In their blind killing of such a low, innocent form of life they are killing themselves. We are killing ourselves in our obsession and hatred of what we are becoming."

"Good memory, Collins. I thought so. But it goes on, doesn't it: ". . . of what we are here for . . . what we are on our way to becoming is less than what we began with.' You wrote that, Collins. And you became . . . less too. Less than whole. You lost something too, Collins. You mismanaged a sense of space for yourself. You speak of the 'amputation,' the 'dismemberment,' the 'murder.' You talk here of the tree's sap as 'blood.' "

"So what?"

"You were describing the deliberate trampling of a small pine tree by a platoon of trainees back at Fort Dix, who went out of their way just to destroy this tree. . . . Isn't that right, Collins?"

"Nothing."

"Nothing? Nothing, Collins? . . . I'll let you in on my theory right from the start. Even before you were on the field, you managed to narrow that fundamental gap between yourself—your consciousness, your sensitivity—and that which exists out there. Whether trees or people, you embraced them. You pulled them closer to you than they really should be. Then—"

"Any suckers?"

"Collins, what's that supposed to mean? When you make these incoherent remarks, these non sequiturs, with that distant gaze, what are you seeing? What do you feel?"

"No. Nothing."

"You're a disturbed man, all right, Collins. And you have reason to be. But you're sure as hell not that sick. You've got me puzzled right now, but . . . I know far more than you think I do."

"The bluff."

5

"Is that right? Well, we'll see. You've got a tough skin, Andrew Collins. Real tough. You couldn't have made it this far if you didn't. And I understand that. But inside? Inside you're as soft as a marshmallow. I'm going to find that soft spot—and you're going to help me."

"Andrew."

"That's right. Andrew Collins is going to find Andrew Collins. O.K. I'll see you a week from today. That's Friday, May first. I'm not going to play the friendly family physician with you, Collins. No. You're too far above that routine. But I am going to work right on to the very end with you. You have my word on it. And you know where I think it all leads? Take a guess, Collins."

"Choose one from column A and one from column B."

"Very funny. . . . It leads back to those letters, Collins. Right back to those anonymous letters. And that's not funny at all. I think I know who—"

" '. . . blue persuasion. When I look down . . .' "

"You can go now, Collins. Hinckley's just outside the door. Do you know how to open doors yet, Collins?"

Collins stood up, turned, and then stopped, his arms held rigidly at his sides.

"Collins. Turn around and face me," said Nieland quietly. He studied the quivering jaw of his new patient. Voices rose in disembodied waves from the wards and were swept into the silence by the fan in the air conditioner, as though it were a wall speaker.

"What are you thinking about, Collins?" asked the psychiatrist as he put his hand on Collins's shoulder.

"In case something happens to me. Which is not unlikely at this point. You understand the risks, don't you?"

"Nothing's going to happen to you here, Collins. You're back. I won't say you're home yet. But you're back. . . . And you're safe here, even from the court-martial, for the time being."

Collins turned toward the door.

"Oh, Andrew, would you please turn off the air conditioner on your way out the door? The room's a bit too cold."

"High card, Andy? . . . He's yours. Pull the plugs. I'll write him up DOA and tag 'm for Graves."

"Thank you, Andrew," said Nieland with a friendly smile. "You're going to blow your cover if you keep that up. How did you know enough to pull the plugs?"

6

"S-O-P."

"S-O-P?"

"No. Nothing."

"That's right, Collins. No thing. . . . Specialist Hinckley," Dr. Nieland called out.

"Sir?" came the answer.

"Come in and take Collins back up to the ward."

"Yes, sir," responded Hinckley, opening the door. As he poked his head into the office, he was startled by the patient's face directly in front of his.

"Well, that didn't take long, now did it?" began Hinckley in his cheerful whine as he took Collins firmly by the arm. "Everything copacetic? . . . Nieland's a good man, you know. He's the hardest-workin' M.D. I've ever met in the service. And I've met a lot of 'em."

"He's all right."

"He's worked some real wonders with Captain—I mean Mister—Pollard. . . . You know, the loud-mouth wise guy who bunks next to you."

"Wonders."

"You feelin' O.K., Collins?"

"No. Nothing," Collins replied.

"I have a buddy who was in your company when you were with the Hundred-and-first. He's over at Beach Pavilion now with two busted legs. Got hit by a transport. When I read you were in the same company together at the same time, I asked him about you. He said you probably wouldn't remember him, but his name's Courtland. Ron Courtland. He was treated at the Fortieth Field when his ear got blown off. Ring a bell?"

"I remember him," whispered Collins as the two turned into the third-floor ward.

CHAPTER 2

Collins remembers him well enough. He remembers the concussion of a mortar round exploding outside the dugout hospital. He stepped on an ear as he knelt beside Corporal Courtland. He recalls working over Courtland with Captain Todd and Major Hepburn. It looked as though the graft would take, but they cut the infected ear off two days later. If a chopper could have got in . . . maybe.

Collins was an extraordinary surgical specialist. He had worked in the operating room of a hospital outside Concord before going to medical school, and trauma procedures were second nature to him. He was quick to anticipate, and his assistance was precise. Occasionally he offered a unique reconstructive approach in his desire to see flesh restored to its normal place and function. When it occurred to him that their efforts amounted to little more than pinning the tail on the donkey, he was more sane than usual. But as the offensives during the rainy season of 1969–70 increased, he began to lose touch with the realities of warfare, wounds, and death.

Major Hepburn, company commander of the Fortieth Field Surgical Hospital, had taken a liking to Collins the first time he observed him under pressure. The man's got a good eye and a cool head, thought the major. Collins could assume a greater share of the load than some of the others. Even in the most depressing situations

8

there was a pluck about him, and his rejuvenating spirit often provoked a psychic second wind in the other surgical specialists. It was his sprints of energy, either in the guise of a joke or in a sudden acceleration of technical proficiency, that so often made the difference for the wounded soldier beneath their hands. The major admired that application of energy, the assumed trust and insistent professionalism, which constituted the aura of Collins. Hepburn had read Collins's records when he was transferred to the Fortieth Field. He was surprised to see that Collins had dropped out of Tufts Medical School in his third year, but was delighted to find that his practical skills were in trauma medicine.

The major was aware of how sensitive Collins was becoming while working over these living or dying soldiers. Perhaps he was oversensitive. The specialist saw hope and potential in the most hopeless cases. Often he envisioned rotation or peduncular flaps in anticipation of reconstruction when amputation was in order. To prune and close, or to conjunct and graft? Collins believed in the former only when there was absolutely nothing more to do. Many recoveries were indeed phenomenal. And as news came back from the sophisticated hospital complexes in Tokyo, Manila, and the States concerning patients initially treated at the Fortieth Field Hospital, the word "impossible" was used by members of the unit less and less frequently.

But by the fourth month of his assignment to the Fortieth Field, Collins was uttering disjointed words and phrases, until little remained of his coherency. The staff members were not especially concerned about Collins back then: it wasn't unusual to talk out loud senselessly while under the intense pressure. And often they comprehended Collins's bits of speech as his mind thinking ahead to what remained to be completed, or the issues of one approach against those of another. But a few of the members began to gain an inkling that Specialist Collins was talking as though he were the very patient being rejoined. At first they assumed that Collins was experiencing a heightened empathy. And that was part of his animating spirit: it served as a reminder to the other staff members that the thing beneath them was human, was alive, had feelings and an identity worthy of restoration. But then it began to register even on the less aware staff members that Collins, despite his skills and his unflagging efforts, was not exactly in his right mind. Dr. Hepburn watched the expressions on his colleagues' faces as those

9

strange, disembodied phrases floated above the operating table, begging for some sense to be made of them.

As it grew worse, Collins couldn't fall asleep during the slack hours the way he used to; he had trouble keeping down any food except coffee and cheese sandwiches; and his eyes seemed to retreat farther into his head, leaving two small dark caverns there. As soon as a surgical procedure was completed, he fell into a motionless stupor which left him numb and drained until the next flock of casualties descended on the unit, when once again he would spring into action with boundless energy.

Dr. Hepburn watched him one night standing alone above a captain whose left arm had been nearly severed just above the shoulder, the upper-left-hand side of his back a mere flap of tissue, and his neck exposed along the base of the skull. Earlier, after they had lost the captain on the table, the other members of the team threw off their gloves, lit cigarettes, and walked silently out of the underground hospital, rubbing their eyes and shaking sweat from their arms. Collins resumed working, unaware that his colleagues had left. He talked to the vanished surgeons as though they were still pitted shoulder to shoulder against the cyanotic reality sweeping in from atrophying extremities. When Major Hepburn stepped into Station Two that night and realized that Collins was working on a corpse, suturing the severed nerves at the base of the skull, it didn't surprise him.

And out of pity—or guilt—he walked over to Collins, who was just asking the imaginary anesthesiologist to post the captain's vital signs. Major Hepburn sat on the stool between the regulators at the head of the table. He knew the decision he was about to make could propel them into an unpredictable, hideous relationship. The major lied then: Pulse 62; pressure 90 over 50; RPM 40; MUA 110; thiopent level 4. He helped Collins finish the piece, and after removing the row of traction sutures they walked out together into the pre-dawn haze.

Well satisfied with his performance and hopeful for the dead captain's full recovery, Collins sat down to write a letter. Often he wrote to surgeons he had known or worked with in Concord to cite problems in technique and to ask for their suggestions. But this wasn't one of those letters. Instead he wrote a letter to himself. And he wrote it from the hand of Captain Arnold Sarkofsky, who had received the fragments of VC artillery that resulted in a four-fifths

sever of his left arm along the neck of the scapula. Captain Sarkofsky's arm was flour-colored and his blue fingers were rigid on the
table in the hootch. But Collins had recalled the life's spirit through
his own hand to let the captain speak for himself of his reflections
and his recovery. He mentioned his friends, how he missed his
family; recalled an act of bravery which made him reconsider a man
he had thought a coward; wrote about how it felt to be wounded,
his hopes for recovery, and when he expected to return to the
States. And as his hand moved across the lined pages in his notebook, the letters he formed bore little resemblance to his normal
penmanship. His hand shook, his fingers strained, and the pen
jerked spastically, creating words that would appear to have been
written by an eighty-year-old.

But before he could finish Captain Sarkofsky's letter, four skin-
ships set down in rapid succession from the northeast. He hadn't
heard the squawk-box alert. He wasn't even aware of their arrival
until the rotor wash blinded him with dust and he turned his face
to rub his eyes. And in flowed the wounded, moaning and groaning.
Some had died in transit: the slight purple discoloration at the tip
of the I.V. tubes revealed that the troopers' hearts had stopped.
Major Hepburn had seen to the removal of the captain's body
through the east tunnel before Collins reentered the hootch. The
major knew he couldn't take the slightest chance with Collins. Not
now. Collins was the best specialist he had. But now there were
problems of an insidious and haunting nature.

The major decided to intervene by assigning the basket cases
directly to Colonel Shied or Major Todd. This way, reasoned Dr.
Hepburn, Collins's skills could be applied more effectively, while he
was also being protected from the more pathological aspect of his
obsession. When an M-60 gunner was brought in with the pilot of
a chopper downed by ground fire, Major Hepburn ordered the
bearers to carry the pilot, who was badly burned, to Colonel Todd's
station. The gunner, whose leg had been nearly severed at the knee,
was taken to Northcross's station, where Collins was assigned as
assistant.

This delicately engineered triage seemed to be effective for a
while. The specialist worked as hard as he always did, but was more
sociable and buoyant. He smiled for the first time in weeks. He
visited the patients in the recovery bunker for longer periods because they were, for the most part, conscious and grateful for the

prospects of their recovery. He began taking walks before sunrise and ate breakfast in the mess hall—the first meals he had eaten with the staff in over two months.

But then the fragmented remarks became more pronounced again, confirming what Dr. Hepburn had feared might happen. Collins's metabolism was responding to the brighter side of the situation, but his mind had moved beyond the point of an easy recovery. With increasing frequency, Collins would clutch that part of his own body which corresponded with the shattered anatomy beneath him. Specialist Collins's identity was no longer his own— it belonged to whomever he was engaged in working over.

Early on the morning of March 16, the field hospital and the adjoining support base were attacked by VC regulars. The first-line defenses crumpled almost instantly. The lights in the surgical hootches flickered and went out before they heard the jarring thunder of two explosions to the west. The power plant was gone. The auxiliary lighting came on a second later, casting monstrous shadows on the walls and ceiling. Sand accumulated in the plastic sheets that were stretched above the operating tables. With each concussion, the sagging pockets moved closer to the patients lying beneath them. The staff operated bent over, to avoid hitting their heads on the suspended bellies of sand. Instruments and chemicals fell to the floor. The oxygen was discontinued and the tanks dropped into holes along the wall. Casualties were piled along both sides of the steep tunnel leading to the six stations in the underground hospital. Smoke and dust swept in through the entrance, depositing dirt on the drop cloths, instruments, and open wounds. Utensils left a white silhouette on a gray background as they were snatched into play.

But aside from the inconveniences and the changes in procedure, it was not unusual for them to work knowing that thirty or forty criticals were lying in the tunnel. Major Hepburn and Specialist Esplaier treated the chest wounds. Major Thurston packed a satchel with morphine and Sodium Pentothal to knock out the wounded for surgery or holdover. Northcross and Collins went after the bleeders. Colonel Shied and Specialist Dorst concentrated on the tracheotomies.

As Collins moved ahead of Northcross and into the pale light at the mouth of the tunnel, he came upon a wounded sergeant who hadn't yet been tagged with a time-and-dosage card by Major Thurston. Nevertheless, Collins went to work on the soldier who had a superficial wound in the face and a shattered left hand. Collins packed the anterior facial vein, tied a tourniquet around the brachial artery, and packed the ulnar with Surgicel at the point of perforation. Then he lifted the trooper's right hand and turned it over to check that wrist. But the arm rotated without the slightest resistance: Collins had that feeling of knowing without actually seeing. He dropped the hand and slit open the trooper's sleeve. A large bandage at the elbow was absorbing the blood of a concealed wound. As Collins unraveled the last few spans of gauze, he didn't even glance at the sergeant's face. He knew who it was. He had assisted Northcross the previous morning reconnecting the soldier's elbow. There was their workmanship exposed before his own eyes. The neat tension sutures hooked around the circumference of the brachial artery on either side of the sever, the reconstructions of the radial and ulnar arteries, the median nerve graft that was sure to take, the repairs to the brachioradialis and the biceps brachia . . . all of it, the whole piece of reunited flesh, torn apart once again. The sutures were ripped out of the articulators, spilling blood stupidly over the olecranon.

There it was undone, Collins's best resolutions, the stamp of his skill. The only reason he had for going on had turned against him. He dropped his pack on the trooper's chest and stepped across the body. He looked once more at the sergeant's elbow and walked out of the tunnel into the rainy gray light. As he emerged from the entrance, he didn't turn to look at the long dugout bunker used as a pre-evacuation recovery room. He knew it had been blown to bits along with the men awaiting medevac to the hospital ship anchored off Saigon. They were all he had had to keep himself together, all there was to confirm that he must keep working against the tide of mutilation. Now there was nothing. Nothing inside and nothing outside.

U.S. and ARVN regulars had retaken the west perimeter from the VC and were sweeping north as Collins walked aimlessly into the sheets of light rain blown down off the mountains. He was unaware of the tears on his cheeks; he didn't know that he kept shaking his head with disgust; he didn't notice that the roll of Surgicel oozing between his fingers had turned to paste with the pressure of his clenched fist. When he came to a section of wooden fence and

13

rested his hands on the rail, he couldn't recall what he was doing with a scalpel. But there it was, the dull stainless-steel handle clutched in his right hand. He leaned against the upper rail and looked across the misty terrain. It was perfectly quiet to his mind. Not even the bodies littering the landscape caught his eye. The scalpel blade came to rest on his cheek. He moved his hand. He could feel nothing. He did it again. Nothing. He pressed the blade harder and moved it across his face. Nothing but a thin stream of blood mixed with water running down his neck and arm. It swirled along the railing and trickled onto his bloodied pants. Blood to blood. And again: nothing. The senselessness had never occurred to him before. Not like this. Now *he* couldn't feel anything.

He wiped the remaining globs of Surgicel on the fence post and laid his arm against the rotted rail, wrist up. He positioned the blade over his ulnar artery. More pressure. The skin resisted imperceptibly. Then the scalpel fell from his hand.

Captain Northcross had come upon the same sergeant lying in the tunnel and guessed at Collins's reaction. He saw the exposed elbow, the pulled sutures, and the compresses scattered across the trooper's chest. Northcross finished the criticals and alerted Major Hepburn that Collins had finally freaked and was probably wandering somewhere in the camp.

The major's first inclination was to have Northcross take his place and to search for Collins himself, but he thought twice about it. Hepburn knew he couldn't bear the sight of coming upon the face of this shattered man: not with what he knew and had foreseen. He asked Northcross to find Collins and to keep the matter quiet. "Find him fast," the major ordered as he slipped a suction tube into a trooper's lung.

When Captain Northcross found Collins staring into the sky, his face bloody and a scalpel at his feet, he knew that the specialist was wasted. Northcross saw the bleeding wrist but realized that whatever Collins had done, he hadn't severed his artery.

For a moment or two, the captain leaned against the fence post and cupped his face in his hands. Then he took Collins by the arm and began leading him back to the remains of the surgical hootch. The specialist's eyes never looked down at the ground. After he stumbled on a sandbag, nearly pulling them both into the mud, the captain placed his arms around Collins's waist and half-carried him to the outpatient hootch. He ordered a passing grunt to bring Major

Hepburn back with a plastics tray. Northcross laid Collins on a bench and watched his fixed eyes staring up at the sky.

When the major arrived, they set to work closing the deep gashes in the specialist's face. They worked slowly, running their sutures so close together along the lacerations that no skin showed between stitches. They readjusted the tension on the ties so that flesh just touched flesh without gap or buckle. When the wounds healed, only the faintest thin lines would show.

After they finished, Northcross eased morphine into Collins's vein. Major Hepburn knelt down to talk, but his new patient closed his eyes in the middle of the first sentence. Hepburn rose and looked over the battle-scarred landscape, drenched with rain. He had to make a fast decision. Falsify the incident in Collins's records, or lay the whole thing open? State that Collins had experienced his injuries during the assault and gone into shock, or try to explain the history of his breakdown? The major decided to help Collins reach a positive environment and remain there as long as possible. That ruled out a psychiatric hospital. The major hoped that with rest in a place that had nothing to do with Vietnam, Collins's psychological condition would begin to cure itself. But was that acting in Collins's best interests or in the major's own self-interest? The major searched his soul. Why overreact and set up a whole slew of obstacles to Collins's recovery by involving himself, his own perceptions, and his sense of guilt as a third party? Who could possibly understand this situation who wasn't part of it? Or the subtle and insidious nature of the specialist's problem? Or even the major's own feelings and role?

He turned to Captain Northcross and ordered him to report that Collins's injuries were "sustained by frags to the face and wrist, precipitating acute systemic shock." The captain looked into the major's eyes: What good would that do now? The major only replied that he would countersign the report and accept all responsibility. He ordered the captain never to mention the cause of Collins's injuries, or what led to the breakdown. In fact, he said he never wanted to hear the captain mention Collins's name again. Then the captain understood that there were personal issues between the major and the specialist. Captain Northcross began to argue that the major should have relieved Collins of duty as soon as he noticed the first signs of a breakdown. But the major insisted that wasn't the issue now; he wanted Collins on a priority

15

airlift to Tokyo immediately, and the records in this case were to be written his way.

When Captain Northcross had left to find the dispatcher and arrange for Collins's evacuation, Major Hepburn looked down at the specialist, lying expressionless on the bench. He knew it was useless to let himself slide into the complex tangle of responsibility. Not now anyway. The major signaled to two stretcher bearers and ordered them to carry Collins to the makeshift evacuation tent. Then he ordered a lineman to break the lock off Collins's footlocker and pack his belongings into a shipping bag, and to place the bag under Collins's cot in the recovery tent. Late that afternoon, Major Hepburn signed Collins's medical report and his evacuation orders. He hesitated for only a moment.

CHAPTER 3

Collins arrived in Tokyo twenty-one hours later. They placed him on an ambulatory ward in a sunny room which looked out over a manicured garden. Brightly painted pagodas were surrounded by dwarf trees and radiant flowers. There was a three-tiered fountain, and two small, artificial streams spanned by footbridges with low railings.

It was exactly what the major had envisioned for Collins.

But Collins never saw the pagodas or the footbridges. He only stared at the ceiling tiles above him. He didn't hear the conversations, or the music in the ward. He heard nothing. He saw nothing.

After the second day it was obvious to the attending physician that there was more wrong with Specialist Andrew B. Collins than field shock and a few frag lacerations on the face and wrist. He was unresponsive. He muttered a few disjointed phrases once in a while, but they were addressed to no one. The other men in his room began to ridicule Collins, calling him Fruitcake or telling him to tighten down his screws.

On the third morning, Collins's physician, Captain Rodney Marks, called Major Jennings at Psychiatric Services to ask for advice. The major suggested that Captain Marks keep Collins where he was and observe him more carefully than usual. After all, the patient had been in the field for eleven months. He required rest, peace, and quiet.

On the ninth day of Collins's hospitalization, Captain Marks prepared to pull the stitches. As he removed the gauze compresses from the wounds, he was startled to see the extraordinary work done on the patient's face. Strange that a field unit would use plastic technique on a man who had a few frag lacerations. Strange indeed, thought Captain Marks: for the lacerations couldn't possibly have been caused by frags. The edges of the wounds were too sharp and straight. When he unwrapped the bandage on Collins's wrist, he was surprised to see twelve sutures on a wound that was only half an inch long. And the edges of that wound as well were too sharp to have been caused by a frag. He entered his observations in Collins's folder.

Late that afternoon, Captain Marks was called out of the doctors' lounge. Two officers were standing at the ward station. They told him they were from Intelligence and requested that Collins's shipping bag be brought up to the ward and opened in Captain Marks's presence. They removed everything except Collins's clothes and a large wooden case with assorted surgical instruments. Captain Marks's suspicions increased. The officers refused to explain, but said that they would return the following morning. Captain Marks pulled Collins's medical file again, as well as the large manila envelope with his field record, and carried them back into the lounge. It was a distinguished record, no doubt about that. And there seemed to be no reason to be suspicious. But those lacerations couldn't have been caused by frags. . . . No, said the captain to himself, certainly not. And there was no mention of hysteria, malaise, or the usual indications of stress and breakdown. And yet the patient was obviously catatonic. No one snaps like that without some sign or warning. Captain Marks knew how closely the members of a field hospital worked. Surely someone would have noticed a change in the man.

The next morning, Colonel Demming from the Intelligence Division met Captain Marks in the cafeteria. He had two court-martial warrants with him. One was already in effect against Specialist Collins, the other was pending corroborating evidence. The colonel felt that it would be another day or two before the second charge would be posted. Captain Marks, at first shocked, then confused, opened Collins's file and read aloud to Demming from his patient's field record: Major Tackman stated that Collins's transfer to a field surgical group be expedited immediately, that the man's capabilities far exceeded his current classification as a line medic. And a Major Hepburn with the Fortieth Field Surgical Unit called him the best reconstructive surgical and trauma specialist he had ever observed. And the other comments said much the same. No one had the slightest idea of these subversive acts? No one noted the signs of mental collapse?

"Are you certain you have the right man?" he asked.

"Yes, Captain, we're certain," replied Colonel Demming, planting his elbows firmly on the table. "It's been a waiting game—for the indictments to come up from Saigon."

The two officers looked at each other for a few moments before the colonel reached into his attaché case.

"You've heard of the ESR—Every Soldier's Responsibility—*the* Underground, haven't you, Captain?"

"No."

"Well, you probably will. They seem especially gung ho for sympathetic, well-educated professionals like yourself. The ESR began as just another anti-war, anti-regs, anti-Army group at Fort Benning in 1967. The members of the organization began their tours in Nam early in 1968 and by the fall of '69 they had infiltrated Army and Air Force Intelligence, Air America, HQ Command, the ARVN, and maybe even the VC. The membership went from about two thousand to eighteen thousand in less than two years. From privates to major generals. And in all divisions."

"But what exactly—"

"These men violate military security. They've already uncovered and disclosed classified information and they'll eventually undermine the credibility of our mission in Vietnam. Their contacts are so good that they've got their own lines to CBS and NBC. They've gotten through to congressmen. Legislators. Even the damn Supreme Court. And what's worse is that they feed dissension back in the States, and we cannot tolerate that. We have our orders, Captain."

Colonel Demming slid a stack of xeroxed papers across the table.

"What's all this?"

"They're pages copied from Collins's notebooks. The ones we impounded yesterday. In your presence. This is your signature, is it not, Captain?"

"Yes, but I don't understand what this—"

"Here. This is part of what's known as an AL-6. An Area of Operations Locater. It accounts for all of the non-allied troops and other miscellaneous persons killed, wounded, or captured. This AL-6 is for wounded prisoners who died following interrogation, transfer, or detainment after routine sweeps in specific regions and are so recorded in the enemy body count for the week. What Collins did was to check the official field report against eyewitness accounts. Here, and here. See, he's got a column for what he calls 'Actual Cause of Death' next to the officially reported cause of death. In other words, Captain, he's got documented accounts here in these notebooks of his of torture, fraud, and murder committed by U.S. and ARVN troops."

"How serious is all this?" Marks asked, looking up from the evidence.

"How serious? If this war in Vietnam was a declared war rather than a covered-up war, he would have been shot."

When Captain Marks returned to his ward, he did another neurological examination on Collins. There were still no reflexes, only weak delayed contractions. It was as if Collins were in a coma. The doctor ran the needle along the inside of his patient's palm. No reaction. Not even a flutter. He pressed the needle into Collins's arm. No response. Captain Marks touched his finger to the corner of Collins's eye: it closed slowly but without a blink.

When he closed his eyes, Collins saw the form of a cloud enclosing a sound echoing from within a dense jungle. Hot and damp. He crouches over a soldier bleeding from the head, moaning. He hears a twig snap and another noise off to the left. A Cong suddenly appears above him on a fallen tree trunk. Collins is frozen as he watches the young VC pulling around his shiny AK-47. It looks like a toy rifle sprayed with metallic paint. The scene in Collins's mind abruptly slows down. Very slow now. The Cong's eyes spread wider in surprise after his finger has already slid to the trigger, after he has begun to brace himself against the recoil, after his arm is already taut from the weight of the weapon. The barrel flickers in shafts of sunlight above the patrol of Americans. The Cong's jaws slowly lock together, teeth grating teeth, his torso coming around after the rifle, exposing his naked chest, neck straining, veins bulging. In slow motion the VC slides into a crouch. Rip! The bounce of an M-16

20

from behind Collins's shoulder. The blur of the AK-47 catapulted into the air as the Cong's body jerks on the impact of an entire magazine. The VC is thrown into the air backward, twists, falls over, and disappears.

Captain Marks felt the irritation of having a sick man in front of him whom he was at a loss to treat. He washed the fine lines on Collins's face and wrist with alcohol. . . . But now what? He called Collins by his first name, his last name, rank, serial number, blood type. He read off his father's name, mother's name, place of birth, tours, units, battalions, more names, dates, places, battles. Anything to get some bearing on the man. He screamed out Collins's name again and then "Medic! Medic!" so loud it brought a nurse running into the room.

There is a flickering in the cloud inside Collins's mind as layers and scenes open to more scenes. It stops. Collins is bent over, running through a rice paddy. Shirt open, sleeves cut off at the shoulders like a vest. Jets of water pop into the air around his ankles. He falls in the marsh. Gets up. Trips again. Lurches forward pawing the surface of the water, running on all fours. He reaches the trooper lying face down in the water, a tripod still clutched in his hand, his legs still kicking frantically in a shallow pool. Collins drags him out of the water and under cover. He begins to roll the soldier over on his back.

"Oh, my God! My God! It's the same face as the other face as the other face!"

Captain Marks was just at the threshold when he heard Collins utter those words. They were shockingly clear and distinct. The captain saw a marked difference in his patient's expression. The dead stare had been replaced by a sharpening focus as Collins's pupils narrowed. His rate of respiration had increased, his pulse was up, his lips quivered slightly. Captain Marks grabbed Collins's hand and bent over the man eye to eye. He squeezed the limp hand as hard as he could and repeated the patient's name over and over again.

But the misty cloud of scenes and recollections in Collins's mind suddenly changed form. Words emerged on a notebook page. Collins sees himself sitting on a hilltop above a two-lane highway in An Loc Valley, on patrol. There were casualties from the early-morning raid and the S2 has detained one young and two middle-aged civilians he suspects of collaboration. The three prisoners have government-issue ID cards and plead their innocence to the ARVN interpreter assigned to the patrol. An argument breaks out between the translator and one of the middle-aged men. The ARVN tears up the man's pass and yells, *"Ði-di-mau, di-di-mau,"* pushing the one prisoner down the slope of the hill. The man turns and begins to run for the highway. A single shot from a grunt with a scope-mounted rifle . . . Collins feels it.

Captain Marks felt his patient's fingers tighten down slowly on his wrist. It wasn't a tenacious grasp; in fact, it was hardly perceptible. But it was enough to suggest to the captain that Collins was reacting to something there in his world.

The next time the physician was to see a change in his patient was during a violent electrical storm in the early-morning hours. Because of the ear-piercing bursts of thunder and the intense flashes of light, he had found it impossible to sleep soundly. He was awake when he received the call from the night supervisor. His wife switched on the lamp, but the bulb didn't light; the power plant had been knocked out. The captain dressed hurriedly, surrounded by blue-white flashes.

When he entered his ward it was obvious that something serious had indeed occurred. Broken glass was scattered down the length of the corridor. Chairs and stretchers were overturned. The picture window at the far end of the wing was smashed. The door to the bathrooms across from Collins's room hung into the hallway on one hinge.

Collins was lying face up, his wrists and ankles anchored to the bedrails with straps. He was still struggling against the restraints, even though Dr. Beckman had given him forty milligrams of Taractan ten minutes earlier. Deep scratches on his patient's shoulders and across his chest marked the aides' attempts to subdue him.

It was clear now that Collins must be transferred to the psychiatric unit. No more observation, no more waiting, no more bullshit from Major Jennings. Captain Marks had reached his wits' end: how do you treat something you can't touch? And he wanted no part of the violent and unpredictable disorders of another man's mind.

Major Jennings was not receptive to Captain Marks's insistence that his patient be admitted to the psychiatric unit. What in Collins's record—aside from this one incident—could possibly warrant such an admission? There wasn't even the suggestion of depression, instability, lack of cooperation, mental fatigue, psychotic episodes.

22

. . . In fact, the record showed just the opposite. Besides, Major Jennings reiterated, the psychiatric facility could only admit psychotic and psychoneurotic cases directly from NP units attached to the major field hospitals. The facility was jam-packed anyway. They were too overcrowded to even consider treating soldiers with mild neurosis. Major Jennings reminded the captain that the man in question was in *his* ward and was *his* responsibility. There were other options open. The major recommended that Collins be shipped to the Philippines or, even better, to the psychiatric center in San Francisco, if the captain felt certain that dealing with Collins was beyond his competence. But before he did anything with his patient, he'd have to clear it with Tokyo Intelligence.

CHAPTER 4

On the morning of April 7, Collins found himself sitting in the waiting room of Psychiatric Services at the U.S. Army Intake and Referral Center in San Francisco. A black MP sat beside him on a small couch. They were handcuffed together.

When Major Parkinson, one of the senior psychiatrists at the facility, entered his office, the MP was standing by the desk and Collins was animating the patterns of water stains beneath the window sill. He made them move again in his mind, plummeting down the wall little by little.

"Yes, Sergeant, you can go now. Send Lieutenant Edmunds over," said Major Parkinson as he dismissed the MP, who twirled his handcuffs around his index finger. The major turned then to another subordinate, a captain, who was also on the way out the door.

"No, Captain. I'd like you to stay for this observation. It will familiarize you with a serious psychological problem complicated by the legalities you just brought to my attention. . . . Specialist Collins," began the major, squatting beside Collins, "my name is Major Parkinson. Specialist, why don't you take a seat over by my desk?" He slid his hand under Collins's armpit and walked him to a chair.

Seating himself in his swivel chair, the major leaned forward over his desk. "I've studied your records very carefully, the entire re-

24

cord, very thoroughly. And I've communicated with Major Jennings and Captain Marks at MEO Tokyo shortly after your departure. I think I do understand what's been going on." He leaned far back in his chair, which squealed in protest.

"You've had a hand in a great number of things, haven't you?" He patted a stack of papers and then drummed his fingers across the fat composition books like the sound of hoofs. The covers were warped and bloodstained. Collins knew what was in them, all right.

"And it's on the basis of this material primarily, Specialist . . ."— he straightened in his chair and folded his hands—"this material, and a number of supplementary reports on your *other* activities . . . that I must commit you to the custody of an Army psychiatric facility. Captain Marks also informed me, by the way, that the lacerations on your face and wrist were not caused by frags."

The major's face twitched in minute spasms between eye and nose. He rose to his feet and moved from behind the scratched steel desk.

"I hope you understand, Specialist, that the decision to have you officially committed was mine alone, and that I feel I have acted in behalf of the Army with respect to *everyone's* best interests, primarily your own in a therapeutic sense. I have specified that you will undergo treatment at the neuro-psych facility at Fort Sam. Chambers, as it's known, is the finest hospital of its kind the Army has to offer. Perhaps the best mental hospital in the entire armed services."

He walked toward a long row of gigantic olive-colored file cabinets. The drawers were secured by thick flat steel bars running from ceiling to floor. At the base of each tier was a cylindrical combination lock. The major turned with his hands behind his back and leaned against the files.

"I do have some important questions I must now ask you, Specialist, for the records, before you leave my custody."

The major reached under his jacket and fished out a cigarette. He took a long drag and blew the smoke from his nostrils like a dragon.

"As I'm sure you know, Sergeant William P. Wentworth was arrested in Dong Bien on 14 March. Among a number of other confidential documents, he had a copy of the Group Medical Unit's count and cause for Sector 4-PRC during the period 15 January through 15 February. It was an AL-6 form for *your* area, Specialist, and listed VC killed, wounded, or captured. But as you know, it listed the names, ranks, and serial numbers of those prisoners who expired during interrogation or in transit to prisoner processing terminals. Wentworth was apprehended delivering this information to that CBS stooge whose code name was Black Eye. His real identity was . . . ah, Captain?"

The captain removed a brown folder from Parkinson's desk and referred to a paper inside it.

"Ming Chien Lo, sir. Captain, second grade, Second RVN Brigade, Intelligence. Born 7 November 1941 in the village of Song Wei. Father's name: Paul Loug. Mother's: Cho Lif. Moved to Nha Trang at the age of eight and—"

"Thank you, Captain. . . . Do you know, Specialist, *how* this information came out of *your* medical battalion and into *his* hands? . . . Captain, refresh Specialist Collins's memory a bit about what that report contained, about the so-called additional information."

"Yes, sir. You mean the so-called actual causes column?"

"That's correct."

"Area of Operations Locater. Form Six. Regional for MBCD, Sector 4-C. Determin—"

"No, no, Captain. Just the prisoners who have actual causes of death written in next to their names."

"Yes, sir. O.K. 'Number eight. Dej, Lo Sei-Mai. Private. Sixth Regiment. 646326-C. Condition at Capture: Frags in left lower leg, left ankle, displaced femur at hip. Cause of Death: Acute loss of blood.' And then written in as a third column, the 'Actual Cause' column: 'Prisoner beaten and left untreated. Refused to comply with S2 interrog. Shot in the head by Second Lieutenant Robert Johnson.'

" 'Number fourteen. Lai, Pau. Private. Second Regimental Division. 862-B-916. Condition at Capture: Left medial skull fracture, probable left temporal lobe lesions. Cause of Death: Severe hematoma D-L-D. Actual Cause: Shoved out of chopper 416-S six clicks north-northwest of LZ Baker Six over coordinate N-I-D 16-46.'

" 'Number sixteen. Nain, So Pa. Private. Sixth Regiment. 616467-B. Condition at Capture: Compound fracture left humerus, left tibia; near sever right leg BK, fully displaced femur. Cause of Death: Acute hematoma, convulsive shock. Actual Cause: Prisoner surrendered with broken arm only, clipped by frag. Later hung upside down and beaten by an S2 and an ARVN interpreter, later shot in the head by ARVN, name unknown.'

26

" 'Number twenty-two—' "

"That's enough, Captain. . . . Well, Specialist, you know full well what I'm talking about now, don't you."

Glimpses of faces in shock, pieces of anatomy, flickered in Collins's mind.

"Well, Collins? . . . Ah, what's the use. Captain, order the MP outside the door to place Specialist Collins in Medical Holding, Departmental Arrest, under clock supervision until the transport leaves this evening."

"Yes, sir."

The captain closed the brown folder and placed it in front of the major as he left the room. Major Parkinson sat in his squealing swivel chair. He leaned forward and looked up at Collins, who was studying the scarred bark of a tree through the window.

"You realize, Specialist," he began in a low voice, "what you've done to yourself? The responsibility for all this—since you seem so concerned where it rests—does not rest with the Army. The Army, as such, is merely a four-letter word for a very specific reality. The reality of humanity, Specialist, of man's relationship to man, of one culture's trespass on another's freedom. Men, Specialist, make up the massive body of the Army, of any army. It is the life-and-death conflict of one human in a green uniform with a creature in black pajamas. I'm sorry you never came to understand this. It's really very simple.

"It may well be that 'every man's hand is against his neighbor's,' as you say in your notebook. But that, Specialist, *is* our present reality. Yes, our 'inheritance,' as you chose to call it. Almost by the genes, instead of the numbers.

"Why not call it survival, Specialist? Why not call it life? You were responsible for treating U.S. soldiers, and you were very good, according to your records. Are you meeting that responsibility now?"

There was a knock at the door. The major rocked back in his chair and then leaned forward again.

"Well, Specialist, regardless of your immediate predicament, I've temporarily superseded the order for your court-martial, on medical grounds. The final decision as to trial will rest with your attending physician at Chambers Pavilion. . . . Come in."

"Lieutenant Edmunds reporting, sir."

"Lieutenant. Captain Longfield briefed you on the disposition of this prisoner?"

"Yes, he did, sir."

"What time does the transport leave for San Antonio?"

"Nineteen hundred hours, sir."

"Fine. You, Lieutenant, are responsible for this . . . this prisoner —his condition, his whereabouts, and his behavior—until you can no longer see his plane in the air. He is to see no one, speak to no one, nor is he to leave his room, or to read or write.

"Do you understand what's going on here, Collins? I've committed you to the Attended Seclusion Ward at Chambers Pavilion, Fort Sam Houston, Texas. A corpsman has been assigned to escort you to San Antonio. He'll meet you at the plane."

The major methodically arranged Collins's records to deliver to the MP. After sliding the Army history into a large brown envelope, he rose slowly and placed his palms on either side of the incriminating package.

"Goodbye . . . Mister Collins. Your active career is officially terminated."

CHAPTER 5

Collins watched Captain Pollard, the man who slept in the bunk next to his own. "The Professor," as he was known among the patients and staff on Neuro-Psych 3-East, was leaning with his face almost touching the wall behind their bunks. He seemed to be arranging something on the surface of the wall.

Collins looked at the side of Pollard's face. He had high, sharp cheekbones, an absolutely straight nose which looked as though it had been machined, and narrow lips. Profiled against the wall, his face revealed a haggard, intense look that reminded Collins of the expressions on the faces of his team back at the Fortieth Field Hospital. The Professor's hands were long and fine, and he manipulated them in the quick, decisive way a surgeon would handle a hemostat or forceps.

Captain Pollard's blue hospital-issue bathrobe slid off his shoulder, and Collins was stunned by his cadaverous complexion: it was so white that it seemed iridescent, with the faintest blue hue as though his body were glowing with a cyanosis from a cold, deadly source within.

"Hey, you. Collins," the Professor called out, without turning his eyes from the wall. "Have you moved your stand or bunk in the past twenty-four hours?"

"No," replied Collins, still lost in the ice-blue aureole emanating from Pollard's shoulder.

"Here. Hold this," ordered the Professor, reaching back a spool of pale-yellow thread.

"Now, Collins, push your bedstand tight against the wall to block that damned draft. . . . Yes. There now. There," said Pollard, stepping back to admire his work. "See. It goes tick-tock but without the tick-tocks. You stand where I am. Come on. We don't have all morning. O.K. Now signal to me like a surveyor would with your hands when the shadow of the hand is darkest."

"Hand? Shadow?"

"Yes. Yes. The hand, Specialist. The toothpick to you. See. Right here!" he insisted, pointing irritably at a toothpick.

Collins looked at the toothpick dangling from a thread about a half inch from the wall. Then he saw that the thread was attached to a pin stuck into the grout between the pale-yellow wall tiles. Six faint lines etched into the wall in a half circle behind the toothpick suddenly jumped into focus. Then a thin shadow appeared between two of the lines, which grew fainter as it bounced to the left of the half circle. Collins pointed to the right. And to the right again. Then the shadow was sharp like a pencil line. Collins held out both hands.

"Outstanding," confirmed the Professor, as he, too, studied the shadow. "It's zero nine fifty hours, Specialist Collins. And I can prove it to you." He yelled across the ward: "Hey, Hinckley! Hinckley!"

"Yes." The weary voice of the ward supervisor came over the intercom. Hinckley stood up in his glass-enclosed station to look down the aisle between the two rows of beds. "What is it, Pollard?"

"Aren't you going for some spiritual refreshment today?"

"Yes, Pollard, I am. What's it to you?"

"Which of the Dorothea Dixes is relieving you?"

"One of your favorites—Corpsman Barrett."

"And when may I expect his angelic form?"

"In ten minutes, Pollard."

"Perfect," announced the Professor proudly as he looked back to the wall again.

"What is that thing?"

"To you, Collins, it probably looks like a taper needle and gut. To you. But no. . . . Time, Collins, time. . . . It's a sundial! It's good for six hours, when the sun's rays reflect off that air-conditioner cover

onto this exact spot on the wall. The angle of incidence equals
. . . Oh, never mind. This first mark's eight hundred hours, and the
last, thirteen hundred. It's good for six hours. . . . How do you tell
time, Specialist?" concluded Pollard condescendingly.

"I don't," replied Collins, sitting back down on his bunk. "There
aren't any clocks, or watches, or radios—"

"Precisely. Nor TVs, nor newspapers, nor telephones, nor magazines, on this ward. They even strip the envelopes off your mail so
you can't tell from the postmark. . . . But you may use my clock,
Collins," offered the Professor, with a formal bow of the head.

Collins noticed a small bald spot.

"And when it's past thirteen hundred hours, you can tell fourteen
hundred through seventeen hundred by looking out from that window over there if you sit up on the casement. You can read it
according to how the uprights of the backstop fall across home
plate. It's simple. . . . Time, Collins, is recognized by the higher
civilized forms of life."

"Why do you need to know what time it is in here, especially
when it's so hard to get?"

"Ah, Collins," began the Professor with a sigh as he swept the
disheveled hair out of his face. "First, because we must work to find
our way back to civilization. And second, we have been deprived
of a most fundamental given. And third, because like an hourglass,
the sand runs out. From the moment you enter this . . . this *casa gris*
you have two thousand one hundred and sixty hours to walk out on
your own. Ninety days from the isolation ward and . . . let's see: You
arrived in the iso bin on the afternoon of 8 April. Today it's 26 April
1970. That's eighteen days gone already."

"How long have you been in here?"

"Well . . . I'm over the halfway mark." The Professor dropped his
lusterless gray eyes to the floor and sat on his bunk facing Collins.

Collins looked up at the Professor's sundial, and then spoke again:
"How did you end up in here?"

"How? You, after you've been in here for only eighteen days, ask
me how!" he shouted. Then he suddenly pulled his head in like a
turtle, crouched over, and scanned the ward nervously from side to
side, as though someone might be listening.

"How? . . . Yes . . . How? Now, just what happened? Isn't that what
you're really asking, Collins? Now, what happened to me?"

His agitated whispering seemed to erupt from some dark cavern in his soul. "It's not what happened just to me. It's what happened to all of us in Vietnam. I am one of a million like myself. We are only minutely different from the killed, wounded, missing, and even those who have returned or will return home. We are all the products . . . the results . . . of a crimson parallax. That's what happened." He spoke so rapidly and quietly that Collins had to strain to hear him. "The burning red . . . white . . . and blue parallax. An absolute freak—an impossible coincidence—of history. . . . A fatal split in the evolution of the American mind. You see . . . we were supposed to be the living embodiment, the torchbearers, of a concept, an idea, an ideal, a splinter of something so absurdly American that only we have a chance of understanding it. And only *this* war, in *that* country, under *these* exact circumstances, and *this* precise moment in the evolution of *this* country, could have produced a displacement of *this* magnitude. And . . ."

The Professor stopped speaking, or so it seemed to Collins, who couldn't tell if Pollard was still whispering or whether he had ceased altogether. It was the first time that Collins consciously thought of himself as one of hundreds of thousands of Americans—one who, like the others, like the objects of speculation, had indeed suffered a displacement.

Collins felt the numbness creeping into his spirit again as he looked at the forehead of the slumped figure before him. A numbness of sensation, of spirit, of energy, of life itself.

"And," resumed the Professor abruptly, "we will pay dearly for this chance coalescence in history. This fated rendezvous with ourselves past and present. America will pay. . . . No, not in blood and bodies. No. The ultimate fee, the hidden toll yet to be paid, will be extracted for decades to come—slowly! painfully! torturously!" he suddenly shouted, rising up from his bunk, "by *what we were before Vietnam!* All of us," he screamed, throwing his hand open toward the ward. "Look! You fool! It's right in front of you! Think! And never, ever bother me again. I thought you might be a worthy friend. But you're just like the rest!"

The Professor disappeared into the day room, followed swiftly by Corpsman Barrett. Collins could hear Pollard's deafening voice echoing through the ward: "He must solve it for himself! He is the answer to the riddle! We're all answers! We were America! We are America!"

After what seemed like a long while, Collins moved. He shifted his back against the headboard of his hospital bed and looked down the row of bunks to his right, in the direction of the day room. He could still hear a muffled exchange between Pollard and Barrett. Collins felt somehow responsible for the Professor's outburst: he had seemed so proud of his clock and even offered to let Collins use it. It occurred to Collins that he might never be any good to anyone again, perhaps not even to himself.

"A displaced person. No better off than a refugee. Worse."

He recalled pondering the question of responsibility when he decided to drop out of med school in his fifth semester.

At Thanksgiving dinner, he had told his parents that he was taking a few months off. "I feel like I'm becoming nothing more than a robot. And I don't like that feeling. I don't know anything about people, except what I hear or read. I know nothing about what the world is really like. I live in a laboratory and a hospital. I don't even know anything about myself. And they keep talking about 'a professional responsibility.' I have no idea what they're talking about. . . . Anyway, I've already sent my withdrawal to the registrar."

Little did he know how desperate the Army was for competent medical specialists. He received his "Greetings" three days before Christmas and was freezing his ass off in below-zero weather at Fort Dix by the second week in January.

Collins emerged from his reveries shivering from the draft of the air conditioners. He stared out across the ward, moving his eyes slowly from bunk to bunk, patient to patient, watching other patients staring at other patients. He knew only a few of them by name. Alexander, one of the twelve blacks in his ward, was lying face up, with his eyelids opening and closing like a mechanical shutter while he hummed some soft, sonorous tune. He was so tall that his feet hung over the end of his bunk, swaying in time with his song. And Sergeant Sailor, considered a "senior" patient because he had remained on the third floor for more than forty-five days, was sitting bolt upright on his bunk, meticulously tearing his bathrobe to pieces thread by thread. His blond hair was cut very close to his head and he reminded Collins of a schoolboy waiting patiently for his mother.

Sergeant Franklin, one of the latest admissions to Chambers, was slugging his pillow and mumbling something about gooks and a particular ambush over and over again. He had the build of an NFL guard and the bathrobe fit him like a shrunken T-shirt. With each easy punch thrown into his pillow, his bed smashed into the wall. A pile of fine masonry dust had accumulated under his headboard.

Lieutenant Williams, who was pacing the floor behind Franklin, jumped each time the bed crashed into the wall. His eyes closely followed every movement in the ward, as though he expected to be assassinated at any minute.

"I know. I know," he said aloud, arguing with himself. "I know what I've seen. And McCafferty knows I saw him do it. O.K. So that means I'm dangerous. O.K. Now, any one of these nuts could snuff me. O.K. So . . . now what do I do?" He threw his hands over his head. "Christ, if I was back in Eau Claire, I'd know just how to croak him. . . ." His face was swollen, his cheeks puffed out as though his blood, under tremendous pressure, was about to gush through his pores.

"The crimson parallax," Collins muttered. He turned and looked down at the other end of the ward. Sergeant Wright, tall, lanky, and amiable, was slouched in a chair playing Hanoi Hearts. Collins chuckled to himself as he listened to Wright trying to explain the rules to a patient whose medication had turned him into a somnambulant. Wright looked like a rooster disciplining a hen. His dark-brown hair grew straight out from his thin head with a swath running down the center.

"Once more, you dummy. Spades is the highest suit. Right? They represent the forces of nature. You know? Like water, wind, storms, floods, earthquakes, and the like. Right? Right. Then comes hearts and diamonds. They're equal. Hearts represents the forces of emotion. Like anger, fear, love, hate, and the like. Diamonds means reason, thinking, planning, cool calm calculations. Now, you're my partner, right? And you just went and played a club after I played a spade. Now, you know clubs is the lowest, uh? They stand for man-made creations. By that I mean buildings, bridges, villages, tanks, planes, trucks, and so on. So now, like in this case, you put our choppers against their ground forces when I just laid a typhoon on 'em. And what did you say when you put that club down? Something like: 'Many birds make the skies grow dark.' Right? The only reason the skies are going to get dark is from all our choppers crashing and burning all through the mountains. . . .

"You left us wide open for that ace of diamonds off the board. See it there, idiot? I'll bet you six kilos of jade that the VC use the cover of the storm to move to a new location. Uh? . . . See, Grimes just played the ace of diamonds. Right? What he did is called tactics, strategy. Ya know? Now, there's . . ."

Collins was distracted by Corporal Rodriguez, who began running up and down the aisle between the row of bunks, jumping in midair as he played quarterback and receiver simultaneously. The imaginary pigskin flew from one end of the ward to the other as he hopped over bunks and patients, chairs and tables, in his mad pursuit. Two patients sat cemented to the floor like stone lions. Another belly-crawled in some perpetual maneuver. But most lay lifeless on their bunks, tranquilized out of this world.

It suddenly struck Collins, as his eyes completed their survey of the ward and returned to stare at his body, that he must be in very rough shape to be locked away with this group.

But I've already served my sentence, he thought. He knew he'd been wounded, but he didn't know where, or how seriously. He touched his arms and legs to confirm that they weren't illusions.

Well, he said to himself, at least I have a chance. . . . A chance for what? To find it again. To find that lost peace of my mind. Yes, it's my mind that's missing in action, lost in a field hospital thirteen thousand miles from here. Nieland's right. I lost it piece by piece. Piece by piece I must find it.

"Now I understand what you tried to say to me!" Collins shouted, leaping off his bunk. The ward was momentarily silenced by Collins's outburst: the vacant gazes turned toward him to acknowledge the thin, blue-eyed medic as one of their own.

Collins, startled by his own behavior, slowly sat back down on his bunk.

But I do understand what you were trying to say, he repeated to himself. You had to come back. Sergeant Back Again came back to find something too. . . . I know. I know. We lost more than arms and legs over there. We lost the faith, in ourselves and in each other. And you came back to find the faith because you knew you couldn't go home without it.

Collins thought about going home to Concord, but that seemed to him to be another figment of his imagination, for which he felt no familiarity nor even a desire to return. He felt ashamed of himself, his home, and his homeland. In a fit of despair, Collins threw himself off his bunk and climbed onto the marble window sill where Pollard had said you could tell time.

Collins peered out through the thick black iron bars welded across the window. From his perch he could see the four-lane Boulevard pulsating past the post as it rushed into the heart of San Antonio. At the intersection of Schofield St. and Boulevard, cars were backed up at the bank of traffic signals, waiting to enter the military reservation. The light changed. In they came, to witness in sadness or with elation the conditions of their sons, husbands, friends, or lovers. An endless procession connected by one thread running through all their minds: diagnosis, prognosis, progress, discharge—what, when, and how?

Some automobiles displayed minute American flags, unfurled from antennas, flickering in the noon sun. The interspersion of MP cruisers with orange numbers on their roofs suggested the pomp and circumstance of a visit from high-ranking officials come to inspect the installation—or for the weekly decorations ceremony. But no, not today—Sunday is visitors' day.

Most of the vehicles were headed for Beach Pavilion, the sprawling surgical facility which runs the length of the central quadrangle. But a number of cars flowed into the parking slots opposite the main entrance to Chambers. An elderly man and a small gray-haired woman walked arm in arm across the road. They glanced up at the gray structure, covered with ivy. An MP marched out tall and proud to meet the old folks halfway across the road. The old woman hesitated for a moment—as the MP slid his arm through hers—to watch a chopper bank off the roof. She raised her hand—the one clutching her gloves or a Kleenex—to cover her ear against the pounding turbos. The MP patted her shoulder and smiled. In they went, as black flakes of rubber from the neoprene landing pad and clouds of blue-black smoke eddied down.

A man in a coat and tie, two women, and three little girls in their Sunday finery piled out of a Chevy station wagon. They rubbed their eyes. The man held a thick pile of newspapers under his arm. The children raced to the edge of the parking strip, waiting to cross over. They pointed to the building, perhaps to the very floor. The younger woman kept raising a handkerchief to her eyes so compulsively she seemed to wear it like a wedding veil. She walked slowly, almost painfully, in the direction of the double doors. Someone's wife? She dropped one of the presents she was carrying on her shoes. The man bent down and picked it up. He smoothed the wrapping and stuffed it under his armpit.

36

The parking lot was full and still they tried to squeeze one more and then one more onto the asphalt strip, overgrown with weeds at the edges. At one end was a black Buick, Georgia plates, with a "Permanent Visitor" decal on the bumper. Next to it was a faded bumper sticker: "AMERICA: LOVE IT OR LEAVE IT." And at the other end of the lot was a Volvo. The driver had parked on the grass strip claimed by the post's legal offices. The car had a Massachusetts plate with a "Restricted Pass" marker next to "BRING THE BOYS HOME: NOW."

Laughter and loud voices came from the cripples' ward on the other side of the thick steel double doors. Collins turned for a moment to stare at the doors and listen to the music. He felt like a kid put away before bedtime because of the coming of parents' friends. He could imagine handshakes, glowing faces in spite of missing limbs, the smell of bourbon, onion dip, cigarettes.

And on the first and second floors of the psychiatric unit patients being prepared for "reentry" were undergoing another trial run with their friends, parents, women. The entire complex—except for the closed third-floor wards—seemed to be laughing.

Collins walked over to enter the chain-link-enclosed deck off the day room. But the door was locked. He looked out through the wired glass, beyond the chain-link enclosure, down at the pit. Patients and visitors were strolling across the asphalt. Some sat on benches along the sidelines, in the shade created by the cantilevered decks. People emerged with plates of sandwiches and drinks from the mess hall. Some patients sat reading by themselves or were stretched out asleep beneath the healing sun.

Farther out, past the softball field, under the shade of the pines and cottonwoods, men in blue bathrobes sat with their friends and families at the redwood picnic tables. Hibachis on posts spouted lines of gray smoke. A tall veteran moved his crutches carefully across the outfield toward the picnic area, an elderly person walking on either side. He stumbled and fell on the grass, breaking the fall with his hands. A crutch had caught along the fringe of the picnic area. He rolled over onto his back and began laughing and laughing. His father bent over to help him up, his mother gathered up the aluminum crutches. But no, he waved off his father's gesture, waved off his mother, offering the crutches to him tip first, upside down. Still seizures of laughter. The picnickers sitting on the benches in the grove turned their heads to concentrate on their paper plates. Now they smiled or laughed themselves. A few children pointed at the fallen trooper, laughing; one child reenacted the scene, to the amusement of his brothers and sisters.

Finally the soldier's parents smiled too. The father spoke to another parent in the grove, pointing at his fallen son as if to say, "I don't know what's wrong with him. He's never acted like this before, but he sure thinks it's the funniest thing that ever happened." The mother put down the crutches to wipe tears from her eyes. The father offered his hand again to his son. The patient clasped his arm and managed to pull himself to his feet—his foot—once again. With one hand on his father's shoulder, he bent over and picked up his artificial leg and tucked it under his arm like a loaf of Italian bread. He took the crutches in one hand. The hospital slipper that had been pulled over the plastic foot was left behind as the three headed for a table. The cripple popped up and down like a jack-in-the-box between his father and mother.

The stand of pines swayed gently in the breeze, turning shafts of smoke into snakelike undulations. Small bits of trash from across the road were swept up and pressed against the chain-link fences with barbed wire across the top. Only tiny pieces could pass through the steel mesh. There was a picture-book cleanliness and order within the fenced-off perimeter of Chambers. The grounds crew worked around the clock, trimming and cutting, planting and watering, sweeping and painting.

Collins wondered, as his eyes followed the long line of chain-link fence, whether the barrier had been constructed to keep the reality of Chambers in, or the reality of the world out. Which reality is the real one? he mused as he compared the lush grounds of Chambers with the shaggy, overgrown, and burned-out landscaping of the legal offices and the Fourth Army Photographic Division across the street.

Collins's eyes sought a place to rest his mind, where his own thoughts and feelings would be at ease with the world again. He searched for his private sanctuary among the gardens and grass below him. Some spot out there to which he could return and find his peace of mind . . . anything to confirm, to return his lost spirit. But he could find nothing. Nothing outside, nothing inside. Instead he found his doubt, which, like a saprophyte, had infiltrated his spirit. It came and it went, but the place of doubt was always reserved there among the other cells in his mind. It causes the gray pallor of consciousness turned in upon itself among the psychos like himself. The cripples have lost their will too. They know what most combat veterans know: that the spirit of survival began to destroy itself from within before they ever saw a rubber plantation, a rice paddy, a napalm strike, a gook, or another American blown away. Why? Because you can't live in the shadow of a doubt when it's kill or be killed: and the doubt about who they were and why they were in Vietnam had already spread through their nerves and muscles.

The cripples feel those false stimuli returning from something severed, that missing piece, to haunt them forever. As though the parted limb were still in some mystical communication with the brain, it tingles, begs to be scratched, or asks to have its position changed. And some cripples absent-mindedly scratch their mattress or paw in the air to rub that vacant space where the limb should have been. A few are so convinced that they have not lost the missing limb that they will be assigned a bunk in the closed third-floor ward of Chambers as soon as their prosthesis has been fitted. But there's a big difference between a simple psycho and a crazy cripple: you can't scratch a limb rotting in a jungle thousands of miles away.

When the will has finally withered and died, enmity springs from its dry, rotting tubers. Enmity grows, a powerful vine that spreads slowly through the gray rooming house of the mind, slithers up walls, silently creeps under doorjambs, infiltrates even the spirit, finally clouding the eye, distorting whatever peace and beauty might be left outside, blooming. And then come the nightmares outraged by the spirit's demise, by a lost limb, by a mind missing in action.

And so they come back again, the faces and limbs, voices and cries, gathered together in Collins's recurrent nightmare. It begins with a fly dissected in a bar in Saigon, on Tu' Do Street, opposite the Café Delaronge. That was during his first break in forty-one days—but for him the revulsion had been going on longer than that. He saw it again while he sat on a rickety bamboo stool in that sleazy bar, staring into the depths of varnished mahogany and listening to an old piano solo, slightly distorted as the music floated through the damp evening air from a distant place.

In burst an American captain and a *dai-uy,* a South Vietnamese captain. The bamboo chairs creak and fibers pop as they settle down at the bar, on Collins's left. The American is on his way to Tan Son

Nhut, the main airstrip. A quick drink with his buddy before the airlift to the Philippines and then Stateside. He's "short"—his tour in Vietnam at an end.

They talk the usual line: the petty botches; the costly screw-ups; the "sorry communications man that got his signals crossed and called in for an illuminary over the perim," rather than to the west, during the siege of Base Camp Mad Hatter. That took place around the end of July. And a poorly sighted nape run that landed "right in the middle of our unit. Jesus. What a mess. . . ." And So-and-so "was a fine trooper"; and So-and-so was the "best damn plastics man over here. We called him Shape-Shifter Sam. Remember him, Lo Chan?"

The captain orders another double Scotch, and pays extra for a separate glass filled with ice. Pieces of dirt settle to the bottom as the ice melts. The edge of a thin air letter hangs limply out of his breast pocket like soggy toilet paper. He fingers the letter.

Collins listens to them, and then to the piano melody again, the only thing to cool off with. The heat is intense. The captain orders another round of drinks. Two more glasses of ice on the side. Eight hundred piasters cross the bar. The ice costs as much as the drink. A fat fly buzzes overhead and then lands on the shrinking pile of ice. He takes off before the captain's hand covers the glass to trap and then drown him. The *dai-uy* asks the American about "the testimony on Allerton." The piano music stops, and then a light, unimpassioned applause: an intermission at Café Delaronge.

"I'm not sure about that yet," says the American, stirring his drink with a bamboo swizzle stick.

"You know him before then?" asks the *dai-uy*.

"Yeah. We were in ROTC together. In college. In Missouri. We came over at the same time. Ended up in the same battalion, even in the same company. I was best man at his wedding."

"What did really happen?" asks the *dai-uy*.

"Pretty much what you heard then, Lo Chan. Except it was a premeditated thing. There's a technicality there. Was he together or not? Did he *mat tri,* as you would say?" The fly inches across the bar in the direction of the American captain. He notices it coming closer.

"Before you and your strikers rendezvoused with us, Allerton and I were walking the perimeter. We wandered off toward the river. To watch the sunset. Beautiful setting in that light. Soft and quiet.

40

With a mist steaming up off the water. When we came out of the thickets along the river, there was this young chick. Taking off her clothes to bathe.

"There was something unusual. It was the light, I think. I mean, you could feel it through your skin. Warm, serene. It made you kinda forget where you were. And what was going on. . . . We grinned at each other for a second and shook our heads. You'd pay a lot of dough back in the States for a vacation to such a place."

The captain continues shaking his head. A tight smile comes across his face as though he were suppressing a fit of laughter. He downs the remaining Scotch, drinks the ice water in a gulp, and orders two more drinks, two more sidecars of ice. The *dai-uy* pays, pushes only six hundred piasters across the bar. The bartender nods, says nothing. Collins watches the fly jump on the American's hand. The captain watches it crawl across his knuckles, and then flicks his wrist. The fly zooms off.

"Anyway," continues the captain, raising the glass to his lips, "she strips naked at the water's edge. The sun had just sunk beneath the trees. She was pretty. In her late teens, I'd guess. And she stood on the bank for a while, watching the river. . . . What was that river, Lo Chan?"

"Song Ba."

"Yeah. There was this pink glow reflecting off the water. It flickered on her body." The fly begins to approach the captain's hand, from the same angle as before.

"Then Allerton hands me his rifle. Shrugs his shoulders. And says, 'Why not?' And walks over toward the girl. I was going to stop him. But somehow it didn't seem to matter much. It was his affair. I sat down against a tree and checked his clip. It was about half expended, so I popped in a fresh load. We weren't very well secured then. As you remember. It was risky business all the way around. Very risky. We knew Charlie was around, but we hadn't gotten a fix on him."

The fly creeps cautiously within range of the captain now. He has a swizzle stick in his hand. Without even being aware of it, he nails that fat, pesty fly with a snap of the stick on the bar. The carcass just lies there, in front of his drink, until he begins playing with it, pushing it an inch this way, and an inch that way. The fly is still alive, revived by the prodding of the stick. He plants it on the fly's body, severs one wing, and sweeps it off to the right, toward Collins.

"The next thing I heard was Allerton screaming. At the top of his lungs. It made a weird echo in the valley. His voice came back in a long scream: 'Jees-us Kee-rist. . . . What the hell's go-in' on? . . . What the fu-ck?' I jumped to my feet and ran toward them. He was screaming and shouting"—the other wing slides off to the left —"and running around in circles. He kept falling down 'cause his pants were wrapped around his ankles. He held his arms up to the sky, yelling." The head comes off, goes to the right. "He kept shouting and screaming. Ghastly situation. I grabbed him just as he was about to fall into the river"—the chest to the left. "I shook him, and tried to pull him to the ground, but he was rigid. The muscles all over his body had gone hard. And he was still shouting. Finally I came around in back of him. And kicked him as hard as I could right in back of his knees. Down he came then on his knees, looking up at the sky. Pitiful. . . .

"Then Evans came running over. And Lieutenant Baker. And a few grunts from a nearby fireteam. And then the doc came over and jabbed Allerton with a needle. In a few seconds he began to sway and then leaned over on the ground." The legs and abdomen go to the right, legs still kicking.

"The doc checked out the girl. She lay there bleeding from the crotch. She never moved. Not a sound outa her, either. No wonder Allerton flipped out. Weird, all right.

"And you know the rest, *Dai-uy.* Man, you saved our asses that time, Lo Chan. We were cut down hard on that first assault. And then sniped at. Jesus. None of us could have handled a second wave. Allerton, thank God, may never know what he did to that girl. I don't think so, anyway. Just as well. What difference does it make now?"

"She die from shrapnel already in her back?"

"Yeah, according to the doc. There was a piece of shrapnel lodged in her backbone. Been there a while, he said. It was barely visible coming through the skin. I saw it. When Allerton came down on her with his weight, the steel must have hit her spinal cord. And, I don't know, either severed it . . . or something. Anyway, she was paralyzed. She died before a skinship could get in."

"What condition is Allerton now?"

"Well, you saw him after he was hit in that ambush. They patched up his head after that attack. It put him into a coma and he hasn't come out of it yet. At least not that I've heard. I got a letter here from his wife. She says he's the same as before. No progress. I'll go and see him when I get Stateside."

The piano began again, with the same drifting melody. There was a whitish mark on the mahogany surface from the guts, in Collins's field of vision. He stared into the captain's method of dissection. With each move of the stick, precise and neat like a scalpel, it ran through his mind like a high-speed movie—the best way to hemostat, cauterize, begin reconstruction of the severed appendages: and plasma, dextrose, pints of blood. . . . Preposterous. A wound is workable: but dismemberment . . . ? Like a limb dropped off a tree in a storm. Something violent came over him, a mixture of panic and rage.

". . . over and over again. Now, Captain, let's see you put it back together again. Come on, Captain, reassemble it."

"What's that, Specialist? What did you say? You talking to me?" asked the captain, addressing Collins.

"You did a nice job of taking that apart, sir. Think you can put it back together again? Put it back in the air, where it belongs? Make it fly again?"

"Hey, medic, you got a problem? You got a problem, soldier? What the hell are you talkin' about? What do you mean?"

"Make it fly, Captain! Make it fly!" shouted Collins.

"Hey, you all right, trooper? Are you drunk? Sick?"

The captain looked at *Dai-uy* Lo Chan with a get-a-load-of-him flick of his head. They rose, pushed their unfinished drinks across the bar, and walked between the rows of tables. The captain turned twice to look at Collins.

He stared back at the fly on the bar. . . . It was gone. The bartender had begun mopping up. There was nothing left: no limbs, no corpse, no evidence that anything had occurred.

In less than forty-eight hours he was back in the field. Four hundred kilometers from the dismembered fly that disappeared, the distorted piano music from the Café Delaronge, and the captain with the disintegrating letter from his best friend's wife.

The wounded he had treated, the faces, bodies of Americans, clothing, the boot with someone's foot still laced inside, bits and pieces of expression, inaudible words, and then screams streamed through his mind. As he sat in the window casement, a fly appeared and then disappeared. It whispered in his ear: "Reconstruct. Reconstruct. Reconstruct what you can." Suddenly the picture show sped up to compensate for the instantaneous and conclusive injuries sustained by the flesh in combat. The faces of the men who had looked up at Collins as the last living thing they would ever see were assembled in a whirling montage of afterimages.

Some of the casualties' last words weren't even in English. A few cried out to Collins in Vietnamese but with a Southern accent. A few let go mumbling ghetto gibberish.

"Shidt, man. . . . Now look whadt dey gone an' done ta dis boy. . . ."

But they all asked the same thing, over and over again. A voice spoke in their behalf, echoing through Collins's mind, some reduced to a smear of nerves, tendons, and arteries in glistening color. The voice spoke for them all.

"But you're dead! You're all dead!" shouted Collins.

For the fly on the bar, for a brown dog in a ditch on the side of Thunder Road, picked off by a bored grunt, for the unconscious trooper lying in a heap on the ground, the comatose, the wounded, and the dead . . . the voice begins. . . .

SMASH

"Has it really gone this far!"

SMASH

"Christ, Collins, I didn't mean to scare you like that. You know —" The Professor broke off to dodge Collins's fist.

SMASH

"Easy, Collins. Now easy. Relax. Get a hold of yourself. I didn't mean to upset you like that. I only—" He ducked again.

"Collins? Collins? Now get a hold of yourself. What's the matter? Collins! Collins! For Christ's sake, stop it!" Captain Pollard grabbed Collins's wrists and yanked him off the window sill.

"What in hell's gotten a hold of you? Calm down. What were you doing? I didn't intend anything. Is your hand all right? . . ." The Professor turned Collins's hand over. Blood ran from a small cut at the base of his palm.

"Look what you've done to yourself. You. Even you're a damned masochist. Do you have any idea what will happen to you if any of the staff sees that? Or sees your hand?"

Pollard glanced nervously from side to side as he pulled Collins over to an unoccupied bunk.

"You've got to be more aware, my friend. For your own well-

44

being, Collins. This isn't some exclusive neighborhood nursery school. For heaven's sake. They're going to notice that cracked pane and the blood smears. They'll attempt to find out who did this.

"How's your hand now? Here, let me see it. . . . Well, could be worse."

Hinckley appeared through the doorway at the far end of the ward.

"Punctual bastard. He didn't get enough of the blessed body and blood at the communion rail, so he's back for more. I knew he was a vampire. Relax now, Collins. I'll take care of this," whispered the captain.

". . . and then she said, 'You will go to Bangkok for rest. You need rest. There you will meet Thai woman in most unlikely place. She will be part French and part Thai.' This is a loose translation, you understand, Collins. 'Has much education in Europe. You will fall in love. You will not want to go back to your unit. You will go AWOL and leave . . .' "

"You two gettin' pretty chummy around here, holding each other's hands. How nice. You enjoying yourself now, Pollard?" said Hinckley, hoisting a bunch of keys out of his pocket.

"Hinckley, have you no appreciation for verisimilitude, for a dramatic reenactment of a very amusing scene? I was just now attempting to convey the hilarious circumstances of what transpired between myself and a fortuneteller I met in Saigon. A very brief tête-à-tête it was. She was a VC sympathizer, Hinckley, trying—I might add, quite successfully—to woo men away from their units to go play Romeo and Juliet in Thailand. I doubt that any of the star-crossed romantics made it—but it was amusing being in their shoes for a while," said Pollard, laughing.

"And what did you do with her, Pollard? Slide toothpicks under her fingernails or steal her dragon's teeth?" goaded Hinckley as he bent over the air conditioner.

"No, Specialist," fired the performer. "I had her *shot* the next morning. You cretin!" Captain Pollard began laughing again. Hinckley lost his grin and absorbed himself in the wiring of the air conditioner.

"That should keep him occupied for a while," whispered this man of many talents.

". . . And then she went on, after I appeared engrossed in her tempting mysticism. I can assure you, my friend, I looked the epitome of the newly enlightened. She held my wrists, leaned over her twenty-five-cent crystal-ball paperweight with her eyes closed, and pressed my hands firmly to her warm breasts." Pollard closed his eyes in the intensity of telepathy:

" 'I see you a handsome man. . . .' To this day I have no idea why she found it necessary to close her eyes to disclose that bit of privileged information. 'I see you a handsome man. You young man. You not want to die in jungle. One man not make any difference anyway. Not when hundreds like you die every day. I see you dead. You smart man, Captain. A man with passion. You want life. You not want to die.'

"So I encouraged her," continued the captain, opening his eyes, "by toying with her nipples. I mentioned that I had a lot of buddies in my unit—you know the line—that I had a responsibility to my men and that I wouldn't feel right walking out on them. Especially now, I told her, since we were about to be transferred to establish a new base camp just south of the DMZ. Well, that did it. She took the bait.

" 'Oh, Captain,' she moaned like Circe, 'I see death waiting you —for you in this mission. I feel deep inside me, I feel your death,' she groaned, rubbing my hands across her tits. 'There are places for you not to be. . . . Oh, Captain, where is this place you go? I have visions of your death.'

"So I told her we were being shipped out to Ban Me Thuot: ETD, twenty-four hours. She drew back aghast—very fine acting, you know, first rate—and said, 'Oh, no, Captain! No! . . . No! You die there! Many of you die there! No. You go to Bangkok. You leave tonight. Believe me!'

"I hesitated, playing on the degree of conviction and compassion she exhibited. 'Captain, I like you,'" resumed Captain Pollard in his mock female voice. " 'I not want to see you die. I can help you.' "

Hinckley had finished with the air conditioner and was pretending that it required further assistance. He shut off the machine to listen to the Professor's story.

"So I squirmed in nervous anticipation, becoming myself moved with the prospects of her proposal, and encouraged her to reveal how she might help me—like this. . . ." The Professor's eyes enlarged as he opened his mouth and leaned forward holding his breath, spellbound.

"She said that she had hands that were skilled in moving Americans secretly into southern Cambodia and others who could work the miracle—for a nominal fee, of course—as far as Bangkok, where I was destined to fall in love with the beautiful Thai woman, in a most unlikely place." Pollard laughed. "It was just too much, too much. I had to twist an ankle under my chair to create enough pain to suppress my laughter. I was on the brink of cracking up . . . really. So I asked her how this affair might be arranged. First she said to give her two thousand piasters for something in her mind which must have corresponded with earnest money. I shoved the bills into her hand. She picked up her crystal-ball paperweight and withdrew a small slip of homemade paper. There was an address scrawled on it. The location was in the old dock section on the south side of Saigon. I was to present this passport, she called it reverently, fork over another two thousand piasters to a man with a white belt who would meet me at that place. I asked her when. She said immediately; that it was nearly too late as it was to assure safe passage for the day.

"I took my passport and headed for the door. 'You want life. You smart man. You think how I help you. Yes?' Oh, yes, of course, yes I will, I responded as I walked out of her decrepit apartment. The pig.

"Of course I had requisitioned secret police to stake out her place before I entered." Pollard stopped and whispered in Collins's ear: "Slide your foot over the blood on the floor." Collins looked down at the ring of blood spots that had oozed out of his hand. He slid his slipper across the stains.

"And a few minutes after I had departed the dwelling," resumed Pollard, reviving his stage presence, "out came a Vietnamese male suspected of collaboration—I had figured correctly, of course. One of the plainclothesmen tailed him to the Hotel Sway. He made two calls—one undoubtedly to a contact in the VC underground to alert their intelligence of the impending build-up outside Ban Me Thuot. Actually, of course, Collins, the maneuver was already well under way by then. The other call surely went to a contact waiting near the warehouse section. Before I left to rendezvous with the man in a white belt, I ordered the arrest of Madame Dupey. Then I phoned MPH-6 for more police and drove to the warehouse. When I arrived, the MPs were in a semicircle about two blocks from the site. We moved in. Sure enough, Madame Dupey was our setup lady. . . .

"We killed two gooks perched in the scaffolding above the entrance to the warehouse. They were armed with recent-issue U.S. forty-fives. We found two dead GIs down in a mechanic's pit. In the next bay—four more. All had forty-five slugs in their bodies. . . .

"Now, isn't that a hilarious story of my first intelligence assignment in Saigon? Know what I mean, Collins? Even funnier was the look on the face of that guard assigned to the security section where Madame Dupey was jailed. He discovered her dead in her cell on one of his hourly rounds early the next A.M. She had a forty-five in her hand, one slug fired through her temple. And don't you know? It was the same identical pistol we took off one of those assassins in the warehouse. Now, how do you suppose she committed suicide in a guarded cell, in security sector, the guard never hearing a shot fired, with a pistol belonging to a dead VC henchman killed twelve miles away?

"And that's it! That's the story of the bitch who said, 'You smart man, Captain. You want life.' Actually, she was wrong about everything, including that Thai woman I was to fall in love with in an unlikely place.

"You're smiling. You think I made that up, Collins?" Collins shook his head no. "Well, I can assure you that's exactly what happened. And I'll let you in on another bit of classified info, Collins," said the Professor, lowering his voice. "I still have enough influential contacts right here in this very hospital to . . . well, let us say remove —yes, to remove certain individuals who perpetrate various impostures, such as air-conditioning maintenance men who eavesdrop on privileged communication. Now, I—"

"All right, Pollard, that's enough!" bellowed Hinckley. He slammed the heavy steel enclosure over the machine.

As Hinckley stomped past them with his business-as-usual manner, Captain Pollard, smiling, said, "Ah . . . Hinckley? Specialist? It seems to me that you failed to reactivate the refrigeration, so engrossed were you in trying to shut it off. You wouldn't want to be held responsible for accelerating our metabolisms, now would you?" Hinckley stopped, muttered something, and retraced his steps to the air-conditioning unit.

"What do they call that, Collins?"

"Call what?"

"What's the technical name for refrigeration therapy?"

"Hypothermia?"

48

"Yes. Yes, that's it. They have it all figured out, don't you see. There's more to their methods than simply keeping us comfortable. . . . Isn't that right, Hinckley?"

Without warning, the Professor's composure reverted to its former state. He looked over his shoulder as though someone had awkwardly excused himself at the mention of some embarrassing topic. Captain Pollard swung his head to look at Collins.

"Now you listen to me, Specialist Collins," he ordered. "Put your hands in your pockets, go to the control room, and ask Barrett for escort to the latrine. Clean up that hand. You must learn discretion! If they see blood on your person, it could go . . . go . . . very badly for . . ."

The Professor hesitated, and his voice trailed off to a whisper. He squinted harder as though chasing something across his mind. He jumped to his feet. The most horrific face emerged, distorted with secret pain.

"Oh, my God! Oh, my God!" shouted the captain in anguish. He looked at the blood pooled in Collins's open palm and then at his own hand, streaked with blood. He held his bloody hand in front of his face and began clawing with his other hand. His fingernails scraped flesh off the back of his hand. He stared at the gouges, repulsed by his own flesh.

Slowly his distant gaze returned to the opened hand. He brought it closer. As the limp hand was about to close over his face, he suddenly gasped, glanced at Collins, and then surveyed the empty barracks, his head bouncing like a ball in spasms of writhing disorientation. Short gasps of breath became more urgent, the gasp louder and heavier. His estranged hand was no longer functionally connected to the rest of his body. It hung there lifelessly in the grasp of his other hand. Gasping arrhythmically, he strained, head twitching at the neck, to avoid the very object of his own self-torture. His lips began forming words to address the pale shape.

"How came you to go so far beyond me? That which was less perverted to carry out you passed over," he groaned. "You signed orders. You signaled the extreme to be executed. You saluted in obedience to the others' call to action. And then you resigned my commission at their insistence. Why? But why? And who but Satan could read between your deranged lines? Who could know the hidden motives concealed in your maze of impulses? And what have you done to *me?*" The Professor's rage began to choke off his words. "How came you . . . then . . . to be so out of reach of . . . of what I wanted you to grasp? You held yourself above me. You thought that by pointing you could remain clean of the touch. Aaaha! Then where did this blood come from? You, in your double-dealing dexterity. How could you so loosen yourself from my grasp? . . . Everyone thought they were right, over there. Everyone was right, in theory. My God," he cried, closing his eyes. His strangled hand fell to his lap, changing from chalk white to vermilion.

Collins left for the latrine to clean his hand. He didn't feel anything.

CHAPTER 6

"Alexander. Collins. Holbrook. Pollard. Wright. Come to the control station. And I mean now!" sputtered Hinckley over the intercom.

"What does that jerkoff want now?" said Wright, without looking up from his cards. "Two clubs. Or maybe three dia—"

"Don't you dare!" shouted the Professor. "Why don't you just tell Collins what's in your damn hand? Christ, Wright, assigning you to a top-secret project would be like putting it on national TV. Back in my outfit, we had our ways of getting rid of mouths. . . . Three hearts."

"Pass," said Collins. "What do you suppose Hinckley wants this late? It's almost lights-out."

"Let's go, Kimmell. The war's waitin' on you," Wright said, turning to Pollard's partner. But Kimmell was barely able to focus on the cards. His head kept nodding as though he was about to pass out momentarily.

"Come on, Kimmell," said Wright, giving him a jab in the ribs. "I wanna finish this Tet of Hanoi Hearts. Do somethin', will ya?"

"Why . . . Why am I . . ." groaned Kimmell, fighting back the effects of his medication. "Why the fuck is I the . . . dummy again? Why," he muttered, wiping the saliva running down his chin, "does I even sit here with you weirdos? Why am I here at all? Why is—"

"'Cause there's a war going on right in your hands," snapped Pollard angrily. "Yours, Kimmell, is not to reason why."

"But why am I the dummy again?"

"Because," began Wright, fanning his cards for the fiftieth time, "you're Mr. Intelligence's partner, which means you gotta be dumb 'cause he's gotta be smart. Right? Right. Second, because you're not back in some Latrobe steel mill punching rivets. And third—"

"O.K., you space cadets. You all deaf?" shouted Hinckley as he whirled into the day room. "Let's go! Chop-chop! Come on. . . . What happened, Wright? You forget your name or somethin'? Put those cards away, Pollard. Jesus, Kimmell, aren't you a little outa your league, playin' with these heavies? . . . O.K., the three of you follow me. Kimmell, you sit right where you are."

Kimmell tried to raise himself out of the chair, but he was too weak and unsteady. He fell back down and raised his hand lethargically toward Hinckley and moaned:

"What am I gonna do now . . . gonna do now . . . to be with . . . but where am I going to be going to do now. . . ."

"Christ, Hinckley, aren't you ashamed of yourself, shooting him so full of Thorazine he can't even remember his name?" said Pollard, keeping up with Hinckley as they walked swiftly toward the control station.

"Shut up, Pollard, or I'll see that your name gets on the shock roster. . . . Now," said Hinckley, closing the door after the patients were assembled in the station, "I have a line order for the five of you to go up to the fourth floor. Barrett and Davis will escort you, and will remain with you. . . . No, Collins, don't freak out. You're not going back into isolation. Relax and listen."

"Well, then, what is it, Hinckley?" demanded Pollard.

"Major Penderspot and Captain Nieland have given you five the *privilege* of watching TV for a while with the cripples."

"What's so *privileged* about that?" Wright asked, running his hand back and forth across his rooster-like forelock.

"You'll see. An' don't go messin' with the cripples. And that's an order," Hinckley insisted sternly. He turned and faced Holbrook: "Now look, Holbrook, this little outing to the fourth floor is gonna determine whether or not you get dropped to the second floor. So keep cool, man. Keep cool."

Holbrook, whose face was contorted with deep grooves like a

walnut shell, looked suspiciously at Hinckley. He was much taller than the ward supervisor and stared down like a scarecrow trying to cry out that a blackbird was nibbling the corn at his feet.

"I know," said Hinckley compassionately. "You don't think you're ready yet. But you've got to try, Holbrook, you've *got* to try. Just do the best you can. If anythin' does happen, I'll do the best I can to play it down. A deal?"

Holbrook didn't answer. He just sighed.

"O.K. I'll tell ya what. Alexander will look out for you. That O.K. with you, uh, Alexander?"

"Shidt, Hinckley, I can't eben look out fo' my own ass never min' baby-sidden sum fucked-up whidt boy from my own stadt. Shiiiidt, mo'fucker!"

"Come on, Alexander. If you can't overcome, then who can?"

"Hohoho," laughed Alexander. "Da good Lor' Jees-us Chris' bes be lookin' down on dis boy if *I's* gonna be lookin' out fo' whidty."

The five patients and the two neuro-psych corpsmen made their way up the worn marble steps to the electronically controlled doors separating the third floor from the fourth. Then past the two dozen eight-by-ten-foot isolation chambers, with translucent windows the size of a postcard. They could hear the cries, whispers, and rambling monologues of the latest arrivals to Chambers Pavilion echoing eerily in the corridor like a phantom chorus of lost souls.

Collins, who had the sudden sensation of being in a haunted house, walked uneasily past the narrow doors. He turned his head from side to side, frightened that someone might sneak up on him. It was the first time he'd been back up on the fourth floor, and the recollection of his thoughts and feelings during his isolation spread before him like the gates of Hell. And the voices behind the doors seemed to be talking in his ears.

"God. Stop it! Stop it!" he moaned, slamming his hands over his ears. But they continued on in his mind.

"That's not surprising, is it, Collins?" stated Captain Pollard as he took Collins by the arm.

"What?"

"The voices. Isn't that what's bothering you? Odd, isn't it. I mean—"

"You're hearing them too?" Collins asked with amazement.

"Why, of course. It's odd, though. This place. A mansion of many rooms, of many disorders. . . . Yes, but who would have thought that I, Jack . . . son Pol . . ."

Collins saw the Professor's eyes fill with tears.

"This is my immediate past," resumed Pollard, forcing himself back under control. "Our past. *We*—yes, we, Collins—were one of *those* behind *these* very doors. How many of us do you suppose there are? How many more in hospitals and asylums across this country? . . . How many more before this is all over?"

They walked in silence toward the steel doors to the cripples' ward.

Corpsman Barrett held up his hand. "One. Two. Three. Four. Five. Fine. O.K. Now, we're gonna sit on the far left in two groups. Collins, Holbrook, and Alexander will sit in a row with me. Wright and Pollard will sit in front of us with Davis. Remember one thing. These here cripples ain't in Chambers just 'cause Beach Pavilion is full. Get my message? Think about that before you go an' open your fool mouths. Any questions?" Barrett was already perspiring across the forehead at the mere thought of what could happen in the TV room.

Inside, Collins sat looking across the top of Captain Pollard's thin head at a telephone commercial. He could smell the cigarettes, grass, beer, and aftershave lotion coming from the cripples' ward even before hearing the patients' loud arguments and forced laughter. And then they suddenly crashed in. One-armed. One-legged. No legs. In wheelchairs, only stranger. With bed parts and coat hangers clamped or taped on their armrests, weird devices to hold cigarettes for no-arms; one with an ice chest secured with adhesive tape to his footrest, where his feet should have been; another with a steel milkshake container screwed to his crutch, the neck of a Budweiser sticking out of it. Another on a crutch without his prosthesis, a black patch slung over one eye and a brightly painted papier-mâché parrot perched on his shoulder. Most of the cripples were still dressed in bits and pieces of their old fatigues. Some with chrome elbow hooks. With stainless-steel wire braces in arching loops coming out of their heads, their ears, their mouths, fingers, shoulders, and backs. Another sandwiched between two sheets of steel in a Foster bed, watching the floor. An orthopedic specialist pushed him into a corner of the room. And the whine of squealing rubber. Wheelchairs smashed into the rows of folding chairs. Steel hitting steel hitting plastic hands and legs or the casts of those who

54

had managed to hang on to their appendages. Laughing. Cursing. Shouting across the room to each other in a bizarre frenzy of commotion.

"Well, mothers, looky what we got us here. I do declare! I swear! Now Lordy be, I swear I see psychos!" "Psychos! Psychos! Psychos!" they chanted. "The Deranged Rangers." "The Cong's Fools." "You yellow-bellied balls-busted battered-brained mother-fuckers!" "What the fuck they doin' on our floor?" "Psycho killer. Psycho killer. Psycho . . ."

Only the face of the President, suddenly appearing on the TV, quieted them down.

"Good evening, my fellow Americans. Ten days ago, in my report to the nation on Vietnam, I announced the decision to withdraw an additional 150,000 Americans from Vietnam. . . ."

"Ah, leave 'em there. Let 'em fight."

"Whose idea of a sick joke is *this?*" mumbled Holbrook. Alexander turned and whispered something in his ear.

". . . increased enemy activity in Laos, Cambodia, and in South Vietnam. And at that time I warned . . ."

"He's gonna do it." The Professor smiled. "He's gonna do it! God, it's about time. Just in time. I knew it. We've officially invaded Cambodia at last! At last! Bravo!" He turned around to Collins and said, "Now what are you peaceniks going to do?"

"Ah, shut up, Pollard!" shouted Wright. "Why is it every time we see a movie you gotta start runnin' off at the mouth?"

". . . the continued success of our withdrawal and Vietnamization program."

"Dadt way yo' all don't go an' knock 'em up. Jus' pull it on out, man. Every boy done knowd dadt already. It's call' *now come on da thigh!*" yelled Alexander. "Ah, fuck it. We done bin Viet-nam-ized an' Viet-nam-ized to curse dis boy's black-ass soul. We done bin dere—"

"Shut up, you fuckin' psycho." A beer bottle smashed to the floor. A cripple picked up the jagged piece of glass and waved it threateningly toward the five mental patients.

"Unless you wanna mess with us. . . ."

" 'I was a corporal, but I've come back a sergeant. See,' " Collins muttered.

"Let us go to the map again. Here is South Vietnam. Here is North Vietnam. . . ."

"Why, I think he could teach geography at Berkeley. We could be colleagues," pronounced Pollard eagerly.

"Our third choice is to go to the heart of the trouble. . . ."

"Sergeant Back Again has come back again," said Collins distinctly. "But look, Major, they blew away his heart! 'How could you expect him to live, Collins?' "

". . . these sanctuaries which serve as the bases for attacks on both Cambodia and American and South Vietnamese forces in South Vietnam. Some of these, incidentally, are as close to Saigon as Baltimore is to Washington. This one, for example, is called the Parrot's Beak—it's only thirty-three miles from Saigon. . . ."

"My last assignment," stated Pollard with schoolboy exuberance.

"Jibe-talkin' whidty. Jus' jibe-talkin' his way on down da line. Oh, op-er-a-tor, gimme Jesus. Gimme Jees-us on da line. Gim—"

"O.K., you two. Pollard. Alexander. Knock it off," ordered Barrett, tapping Pollard on the shoulder and shaking Alexander.

"My fellow Americans, we live in an age of anarchy, both abroad and at home. We see mindless attacks on all the great institutions which have been created by free civilizations in the last five hundred years. Even here in the United States, great universities are being systematically destroyed."

"I got a feelin' you haven't seen anything yet," whispered Pollard. "God. This speech alone will blow this country apart. And then—"

"Barrett! Barrett!" shouted Holbrook at the top of his lungs. His face was scarlet and his body shook in lightning-bolt spasms from head to foot. "Get me outa here! Get me outa here! Get me—"

"O.K. O.K.," snapped Barrett, rising. "Davis. Take Holbrook to Hinckley and report back here on the double."

"Does the richest and strongest nation in the history of the world have the character to meet a direct challenge by a group—"

"Shut up! Shut him up! Shut him up!" screamed Holbrook, breaking loose from Davis and running out into the cripples' ward. An orthopedic specialist tackled him and pinned him to the floor, amid cries of "Kill! Kill! Kill!" from the cripples.

"I promised to win a just peace. I shall keep that promise."

And then a depressing silence, punctuated with short, enthusiastic outbursts from the cripples. They tried to cheer. To applaud. To support their fellow Americans' invasion of Cambodia. But as a few of them began a spontaneous cheer, others drifted further into self-absorbed reflections on how they came to be cripples in Chambers Pavilion. Collins watched them as they shouted some line jargon while picking at their bandages, artificial limbs, wires, and braces.

He leaned forward and said in Pollard's ear, "This is our war of nothingness. We fought for nothing. We die for nothing. It will win us nothing."

Pollard didn't respond at first.

Collins looked back up at the worn and weary face on the screen. The somber, sad expression of a doomed cause reminded him suddenly of Major Hepburn's face toward the end of a long, repetitious round of slicing, splicing, and suturing.

"Wasted, Pollard," he mumbled to the back of the Professor's head. "Wasted on the surgical assembly line. Or the disassembly line. . . . Depends on where you begin and what you have left when it's finished, Pollard. . . .

"I remember that one, Major," said Collins, lost in his time warp. "The one whose arm and eye we saved. And then he died on us just at the end, when you noticed that tiny nick above his liver. Shrapnel, you guessed, and you went in after it. 'Goddamn hopeless approximations,' you said then. And his abdomen burst open like a bloated tick. 'The Fortieth Field Butcher Shop!' you cried out. And then you disappeared for a whole day, Major. And Northcross said, 'Hey, Collins, where's Major Hepburn?' Where did you go, Major? Why? . . . Why?" he said loudly in Pollard's ear.

Pollard spun around in his chair. His cold gray eyes glared in the half-light of the TV room.

"What the hell's going on with you, Collins?" he said angrily. "Don't you realize that you're talking to me?"

Collins, visibly stunned and confused by what Pollard had said, sank back into his chair.

"I ask for your support for our brave men fighting tonight halfway around the world—not for territory, not for glory, but so that their younger brothers and their sons and your sons can have a chance to grow up in a world of peace and freedom and justice. Thank you and good night."

"O.K. Collins. Wright. Alexander. Pollard. On your feet. Let's go. Pollard. . . . Pollard, I said let's go," ordered Barrett, with nervous irritation.

"He's right, of course," affirmed the Professor. "He's right on the mark. The Domino Theory is absolutely, one-hundred-percent accurate."

"Yeah, sure, Pollard. Just keep movin' toward them doors."

The cripples never made a sound as the psychos left the TV room: rather, they sat there like mummies, nursing their beers and biting their nails as they listened to the follow-up commentary.

Hinckley met the returnees at the door to the ward. His light-brown complexion seemed to glow with pleasure as he ushered the remainder of his flock back under lock and key.

"You know," he said softly to the group of four patients, "I know I'm not supposed to say nothin' about what goes on on the outside, but I wondered . . . what didya think of that speech? . . . Collins, that was your first reentry. How did it feel to you?"

"I don't know. We've been runnin' sorties in and out of Cambodia for months. I don't know why he went to all that trouble to pretend that we're just this minute moving across that border. I don't know."

"Well, I do," stated Captain Pollard. "And history will bear me out. People like you, Hinckley, will just have to wait to see, because that culture is as foreign to you as the Harvard Club. Vietnamization is absurd, it's a foolish idealistic and condescending front. Vietnamization is just another term for Americanization, or Westernization. And that won't work with those people. But, Hinckley," the Professor continued, raising his hand, "the so-called Domino Theory isn't a theory at all. If we retreat or back off now, it'll be your children who will be talking about some theory in the fifties and sixties that became the reality in the eighties and nineties. Thank you and good night."

"Wait," said Hinckley. "Don't forget your sleepers. All of you."

"Collins. Collins?" whispered Wright from the next bunk. "You awake?"

"Yes."

"You didn't swallow those pills neither."

"Nope."

"Good."

"Good?"

"Yes, good," repeated Wright. He rolled onto his side and propped his head against his arm. "I got a lot of thoughts goin' through my head. That's all. . . ."

Collins lay motionless on his back, staring into the darkness.

"You . . . ah . . ." Wright began again, unsure of Collins's mood. "You got someone, Andy? I mean, you got a girlfriend, or a wife?"

"I think I still have a girlfriend," Collins replied quietly. He was the more receptive to Wright's question because it was a welcome diversion from analyzing why he had confused Major Hepburn with the Professor in the TV room.

"Of course, I haven't seen her in over a year now. But she . . ." He hesitated, recalling a photograph of her which was lying in a locker with his other personal belongings in the control station. He had taken it in May, just after they met. She was dressed in jeans and a yellow shirt, and stood on the bank of the Charles River across from MIT. Holding a skull she'd signed out from the anthropology department, she had been reciting Hamlet's lines to Yorick's remains.

"She still writes," he resumed. "Most recently about her concern for her brother, who was shipped over last month. Of course, all she gets back now are those postcards they send out acknowledging receipt of the letter and saying I'm hospitalized and unable to reply just now. But she's called here and spoken to Nieland, and I guess he's filled her in, along with my parents."

"Yeah, he's done the same thing for me. Do you feel . . . afraid to see her again, your girlfriend, now? I mean, after all that's happened?"

Collins noticed that Wright's voice, which usually had a lively and optimistic ring, was somber and hesitant. Perhaps that was because of the unwritten law among the patients that no one asked personal questions or discussed their "outside" lives except in the group sessions, and seldom even there. As Collins reflected on this, it occurred to him that of all the patients on his ward, he had gradually come to trust only Wright and Pollard, and only a little.

"I don't know. I honestly don't know what I feel, if anything, anymore. Arty, I don't have the faintest notion of what's *out there*. Maybe I'm just scared a little, but I know I'm not ready to think about her yet."

"Well, maybe that's best," said Wright, considering the differences between his relationship and Collins's. "I've been thinkin'— right?—about how I'd ever try to, like, explain all this to my wife. How I'd ever put it all together. The changes. . . . The changes. Wow."

Collins turned to face Wright. The thought of "putting it all together" had never occurred to him before, and the idea of having to explain or justify himself made him weak.

"I don't think I could put it all together for anyone," Wright went on. "I mean, shit, I can't even get it together for myself. Right? I can't even convince people that assigning that last defoliation sortie was perfectly logical. Uh? So how can I begin to put it all together for anyone? But I mean, I gotta say *something*, right? Something that makes sense to someone else, someone out there. Like my wife. But I get dizzy just thinkin' about thinkin' about it. You know what I mean, Andy?"

"I don't know. . . . Keep going."

"Well, look what I got to go back to," said Wright, beginning to laugh, "assuming I get outa here at all." Collins could see his head as he raised himself up farther on his pillow.

"We—I mean, she lives alone in our apartment in Columbus, Ohio. How do I come back now? Right? I was raised there, Andy. My folks still live there. I went to high school there. How do I come home after this? Uh? I mean, a hero? An asshole? A psycho? A son? . . .

"Or maybe I don't go back at all," he whispered excitedly. "Maybe I don't go back at all. I could get a buddy in Internal to make me up a whole new set of papers. Yeah. New name. New numbers. New identity. An' when I get out, I'll just disappear somewhere—like the Grand Canyon—an' just hang out. Just hang out there in the mountains. And can't you see the sunsets? The peace and quiet? Maybe I'll get me one of them Injun women off one of those reservations out there. And I could teach her how to be a woman instead of an animal. Yeah, instead of an animal. . . ."

Collins heard the Professor turning in his bunk. And then Pollard cleared his throat. So he's overheard all this, Collins thought.

"Wright," whispered Pollard, leaning out of his bunk. "Wright? You there?"

"Yeah. What?" replied Wright cautiously.

"You keep talking like that and you'll never even see a traffic cop again, never mind your wife or the Grand Canyon. Look, why do you think they singled out the five of us to see that speech? Why us? Because they want us to assimilate in order to be eventually assimilated ourselves. Because maybe we're the only ones who can —or at least attempt to—make some sense out of it all.

60

"Look at the three of us: a thirty-year-old Asian-history prof who left Berkeley and joined up—yes, I volunteered for Intelligence—just to find out if what was in the books and what I'd been teaching for the past eight years was right, was the truth, only to end up supervising the torture of the very people whose culture I most revere.

"And Collins here. A med-school dropout. A surgical specialist who, unknowingly, created even more casualties by working for the ESR, and . . . Now, easy, Collins. Don't pull a freak-out. I knew about the busts coming down on the field hospitals for security violations even before they caught up with you. Now, relax, Collins, it's not important how I found out about you. Just listen to me."

"You were in the ESR?" said Wright with surprise.

Collins, who had spun around in his bunk at the mention of the ESR, felt a nauseating revulsion for Pollard, a violent anger directed at the Intelligence officer.

"I'm not bringing this up to be malicious, Collins. You must believe me," pleaded Pollard sincerely. "Just hear me out, O.K.? Then you can say and do what you want. . . .

"And you, Wright, a college graduate with a degree in chemistry; and they drafted you and made you into a bio-chem tech who spent —what?—just over a year in chemical warfare training, only to end up plotting out your days, weeks, and months by the number of square kilometers you could burn with Agent Orange.

"The point of this is that we, gentlemen, we *have* to make some sense of this. We have to make some sense of ourselves. The only—"

"Why?" demanded Collins angrily.

"Why? Think, Collins, think. Who else *can* now? Everyone in here snapped for a reason. Or a coalescence of reasons. But reasons nonetheless. Think of the hundreds of thousands who didn't snap, but nearly did. Or maybe they did snap inside, only it didn't show. And maybe it won't show on the outside for months, or years, to come. You think they're going to try and figure it all out? Hell, no. They'd be crazy to try, or else would end up crazy trying. But therein, gentlemen, lies our advantage."

"Advantage!" Collins cried out.

"We're branded for life. Don't you see? We can't repress it. We can't forget about it. We can't escape from it like all the others. Yes, we're like lepers, Collins. Once we passed through these doors, we were committed. Yes, committed in the clinical and legal sense. But beyond that, we are committed to the question: Why? Committed to the question by the question.

"What's the matter?" said Pollard as he watched Collins clamp his pillow over his head. "See, Wright, that's what you were doing before, only with your escapist fantasy about not going home. Don't you understand? There is no escape for us."

Captain Pollard sat up in his bunk and waited for Collins to take the pillow off his head. But Collins was embroiled in a battle within himself. With an acceptance of the truth he knew was inherent in Pollard's statements came the frightening realization of how miserably he had failed to quell the voices in his mind, voices from the recent past, the sounds of wasted men.

"Look at Collins. It won't work, Collins. It won't work. I've tried it myself." The Professor's words echoed in the darkness and through the pillow. "And look at me. I helped to create the casualties that you later tried to bring back to life while you were out gathering evidence against men like me while other jokers were running around trying to find evidence against you. The circle jerk. All of which creates more dissension, more casualties, more psychosis, more atrocities, more trials, more insanity—which brings us back to Chambers Pavilion and maybe even to Building Six. Now, how did all this happen? And remember, I'm not talking about what happened in Nazi Germany. I'm talking about us in the United States. . . .

"If all this were easy to figure out," continued the Professor as he walked hunched over and sat on the edge of Wright's bunk, "either there would have been a declared war in Nam, or we wouldn't have been there at all. If this were easy to figure out, you wouldn't see such a horrific split in this country. You wouldn't see the demonstrations, the riots, the fire bombings, and the immolation scenes around the world. God knows where it may all lead. Maybe we'll end up shooting each other before this is all over. And you wouldn't see token troopers tried for war crimes when there isn't even a real war going on, so to speak. If this were easy to figure out, you wouldn't be talking about the Grand Canyon."

"O.K. O.K.," said Wright impatiently. "I see what you're saying. But what the hell are we supposed to do? How do we *get* it together now so we *got* it together by the time we get out, if we ever do? Right?"

"I have only one solution, one long shot. . . ."

"What's that, Pollard?"

"We make a pact. A pact between—"

"A pact?" shouted Collins, throwing his pillow across the ward and sitting bolt upright in his bunk.

"Get away from me, McCafferty!" shouted Williams as he strangled Collins's pillow.

"Lie down and shut up, Collins," ordered Captain Pollard. "You want to get the night super out here? . . . Yes, I said a pact. A pact made on the Eve of the Invasion of Cambodia, somewhere around twenty-three hundred hours, 30 April 1970. Yes, we *need* a reason for getting out of here." He was intent, his tone of voice nearly pleading for agreement. But all he heard was a few patients talking in their sleep.

"The pact is the reason. . . . We need something more than living with some squaw in a lean-to perched over the Grand Canyon, more than another year of med school to finish, and more than standing in front of twenty-five squeaky-clean cherubic faces and lecturing on the political significance of Zen. You said it first, Wright: we need to say something that makes sense to someone out there. And that begins with us in here."

"I'm with you, Pollard. I want to. I *have* to. . . . But what about you, Collins, uh?"

Collins saw Wright's eyes flickering in the darkness when he turned his head to ask the question. In the silence that followed, Collins felt his thoughts accelerate, creating the sort of nervous high he used to get from drinking ten cups of coffee. Was that because he hadn't swallowed his sleeping pills, or because Pollard was on to something, some way to turn an utterly destructive experience into a constructive product?

"If I take you seriously, which I'm not sure I do, Pollard, why a pact? Why the three of us?" Collins asked.

"For a number of reasons. The most important are: We need a kind of checks-and-balances among us, so that one or the other doesn't go completely berserk probing deeper and deeper back into what happened, and why. If we're going to dive into dangerous, uncharted waters, we'd better be able to keep an eye on each other. And . . ." Pollard hesitated. He thought for a few moments, and then proceeded:

"And, well, I don't have to tell you this, you already know it; but if you have an urgent dispatch that must get through, you don't send out just one man. You send out a bunch. You do that knowing most of them won't make it through enemy lines: but all you need is for that one to get through. And—"

"Get through to what? Get what through to whom?" Collins asked bitterly. "Just what is it we're supposed to get through to whom, Pollard?"

"We can decide on that together," the Professor answered, avoiding the directness of Collins's questions. "We can figure out what we're going to say and for whom it's meant once we get to that point. Then—"

"Pollard. Answer my questions first."

"The reason for a pact in the first place is to give us a mutual goal. And the pact and the goal will give us purpose and strength."

"To do exactly what?" demanded Collins angrily.

"To tell the truth about what happened, and why it happened, to our fellow Americans. Then—"

"You *are* insane," said Collins, laughing sarcastically. "Let me see if I can follow this demented brainchild of yours: We're going to make a pact to work our way back to the sources of our problems, determine why and how we cracked up, why we're failing in Vietnam, why the country's so screwed up, and then put together something that makes all of that intelligible to the rest of the world. Is that what you're saying?"

"Yes."

"Impossible. . . . What can possibly be gained by going back into . . . the source, the reasons why?" But Collins's voice had faltered, and he knew that Wright and Pollard sensed his fear and loathing at the thought of such a hellish undertaking.

"Go on, Collins," said Wright calmly.

"The last thing we need is to go back. Who needs more of *this?*" he said, pointing into the darkness of the ward. For a moment he was too choked up to go on. "Even if we could answer some of the questions—make some sense of all this—" he resumed with the confidence of a logical rebuttal, "who the hell's going to listen? Who wants to listen? The American public? Ha. That's preposterous and you know damn well it is. . . . And how do you propose to tell them, anyway? Bring a TV camera in here? Put the three of us on radio and tell our fellow Americans that *they*—not the VC, not Nixon, not you and me—are responsible for what's happening here and over

64

there? Tell them that their most affluent, well-educated, baby-faced sons are being blown to pieces for nothing, for absolutely nothing? Tell them—"

"Quiet down, Collins!" interjected Pollard nervously. "You'll have all these psychos going off the wall if they hear what you're saying."

"I just don't see what's to be gained. What good it'll do for anyone," said Collins, resigning from the discussion.

Pollard rose quietly from Wright's bunk. He stood between the two men lying in their hospital beds. It was too dark to see the expressions on their faces.

"I'm not saying we have to slit our palms and play blood brothers," he said in the darkness. "I only ask that you think about what's been said here. That's all . . . for now."

CHAPTER 7

"O.K. Good morning and get up! Good morning and get up! Let's go!" shouted Hinckley, walking swiftly up and down between the rows of bunks and slapping a ruler against the palm of his hand. "Today is Monday, May 4, 1970. The temperature at Lackland is fifty-eight degrees. Wind out of the northeast at fifteen miles per hour. The time is zero six hundred hours. Good morning and get your asses out of them bunks. Let's go! Medications. Latrine. Showers. Mess at zero eight fifteen. Those of you in the Monday group sessions will meet at . . . Collins! Where the hell's Collins?"

Hinckley's eyes instinctively scanned the large, barred windows. Then the crash bar on the fire door. Then the door to the back staircase and the deck.

"Barrett. Hit the floodlights and call security. Collins! . . . Pollard! Pollard! Wake up. Where in hell's Collins gone to?"

"The way of all flesh. What are you asking me for? I don't sleep with him. . . . What are you insinuating, Hinckley? You better—"

"Hinckley," came a wavering voice. "You looking for me, Hinckley?"

"Collins!" called back Hinckley as he spotted his patient curled up under the medications cart just outside the control station. "Collins," he sighed with relief. "Just what do you think you're doin'?" Hinckley stood over Collins now.

66

"Just that."

"Just what?"

"Thinking," replied Collins, crawling out from under the cart. "I was thinking."

"Thinking," repeated Hinckley, with feigned deliberation. "That sounds serious. . . . What's been goin' on with you, anyways? You've been acting mighty peculiar for the past four days or so. . . . Yeah, since you saw that speech last Thursday night." Hinckley looked searchingly at Collins. "I read over the weekend report on you. Mighty peculiar change in your behavior. That speech bother you that much?"

Collins looked into Hinckley's alert brown eyes.

"No," he said, embarrassed at having been discovered somewhere other than his bunk again. "No, not the speech."

"So what's up with you?"

"Look," said Collins angrily. "When I'm asleep, I can't think. And when I'm awake, which is when most people think, there's too much confusion and noise in this zoo of yours to think. So I try to think at night by forcing myself to stay awake. O.K.?"

"Well, look at it this way. You give a man a good bed, you give him sleeping pills so he can get a good night's rest, and you just about tuck him in and give him a kiss good night, and what does he do? He crawls outa his bunk and sleeps on the floor like an animal so he can think. Now, how do you think that looks in your record, mmmm? . . . All clear! False alarm!" Hinckley shouted suddenly, waving off MPs who had appeared on the fire escape, searching for the escapee.

"Collins, get it together, man, or you'll never go home," said Hinckley, before turning to face the other patients in the ward, who were trying to wake up. "Let's go, men. Let's go!" He marched down between the rows of bunks.

At ten-thirty that morning, Collins walked with Pollard and Wright toward the day room for Monday group session. They walked quietly, without saying a word, but they had developed a tacit connection with each other since Pollard had sprung his idea of the pact. Pollard was reluctant to press the idea for fear of scaring off the other two; Wright remained circumspect and silent, because he wanted to see where Collins stood before he committed himself; and Collins was still asking himself the questions he had asked Pollard on the night of the proposition.

67

Having to take part in the group sessions was difficult for Collins. Not because of what was said by any one patient, but rather by the shocking revelation that "I am one of *them*," as he had repeated over and over to himself during the first encounter. And so when he spotted Lieutenant Cummings—the group leader and the only female staff member he had seen since his commitment to Chambers—he lowered his head to avoid her eyes. He was stunned by the intensity of self-hate he felt at that moment, the piercing sense of having degraded his manhood that followed his imagining what he must look like to a normal female.

"A man's no good once he's broken," he muttered, again unaware that he was talking aloud.

Lieutenant Cummings, a dark, pretty young woman, took a step toward him and said, "Why don't you bring that up this morning, Collins?"

But he ignored her and took a seat in the semicircle.

"This morning," she began brightly, setting her coffee cup on the floor next to her stack of patient files, "I'd like for us to start with a comment made by Mr. McCafferty. Does anyone recall what he said at the end of our last session?" She scanned the room for a spark of response, any response. "No one remembers?" She shifted uneasily in her chair.

"Guess you . . . got us . . . with that one," said Holbrook in the slow, arrhythmic speech that made him seem suddenly retarded. The deep lines engraved in his face were pink, a slight allergic reaction to the increase in his Thorazine dosage since his freak-out in the cripples' TV room. The regression frightened Collins.

"Well," she responded, locking eyes with Holbrook. He smiled back like a moron and stared at the inside of her exposed knee.

"Well," she began again, "Mr. McCafferty said that there were at least two sides to every story. . . ."

"My, how very perceptive," interjected the Professor.

"Uh oh," whispered Wright. "Pollard's in one of his moods."

". . . face the problem of confronting the facts of your individual case. Have I expressed your sentiments correctly, Mr. McCafferty?"

Colonel McCafferty finally broke the silence of her hanging question. "I don't care. I am an officer—"

"Were," corrected Lieutenant Cummings from the center of the semicircle of patients. "Otherwise I would have addressed you as Colonel, or Sir."

68

"Goddamn it! I don't care what's in those files," McCafferty shouted. "I don't give a goddamn what the hell they say about me. Goddamn it. Who the hell do they think they are, anyway? . . . Bunch of cowards." He was nearly in tears. "Undisciplined cowering bastards. There is a war going on! Where are the men! Where are the men!" he suddenly shouted at his fellow patients.

"Dead," Williams said, staring with his large, glimmering eyes at McCafferty. "Dead," he said again, with more emphasis. He had the look of unmoving patience, like a cat waiting for the mouse to scurry an inch too far from its hole.

"This is nonsense," continued McCafferty, turning his eyes away from Williams. "These fictitious reports and briefs—don't you know it's a conspiracy, a fraud to get at me! You fools. This is all trumped up by a bunch of traitors and cowards. They're out for *me!*

"Look." McCafferty pointed at Lieutenant Cummings. "I don't give a goddamn what's in those reports. Figures lie and liars figure. It's all a hoax dreamed up by some bunch of sick bastard sympathizers. All those reports. They're all phony. Forgeries of the truth. I know who put them together, too. . . . I know who they are, goddamn it. Your staff here is just plain stupid. Stupid and gullible. I was too damn efficient for them. I nailed the cowards in my command time and again. And if I was over there right now I'd do it . . ."

He stopped and looked with irritable distraction at his index finger, pointed at Lieutenant Cummings. He realized, as he was talking, that he had been pointing at Cummings as though he were holding a pistol at her. He was sighting down his extended arm, squeezing off rounds from his imaginary .45. His hand remained raised in silence, its finger protruding stiffly from his loose fist, still pointing, held suspended and alienated. The colonel loosened his scrutiny as the taut lines left his emaciated face. His hand fell slowly to his side. He glanced at Williams. McCafferty's lips began quivering as though he were struggling to ask Williams if he might help decipher this curious pantomime. Williams smiled at the colonel, who grinned slightly. Then their smiles changed suddenly to snarls. There was murder in their eyes.

"Listen," began McCafferty again. "I have been framed by a group of subversive cowards. They testified that I was—me!—that I murdered men under my own command. Me! Colonel James McCafferty. And these assholes—these doctors—believe them. But you're not so stupid, are you," he stated, appealing to the other

69

patients. "No. And you're in the same foxhole with me. Aren't you? Aren't you!"

"Yes, Mr. McCafferty, and how do you relate all of what you've just told us to why you are here?" inquired Lieutenant Cummings, screwing her bright black eyes down on Colonel McCafferty.

"What the hell does that mean?" he retorted.

"I mean, simply, what does what you've just said and the way you held your hand at me have to do with why you're here?"

McCafferty opened his mouth, about to answer, but the words "Colonel McCafferty sucks . . . his trigger finger!" came from Williams, whose flushed face pulsated with hatred like a red neon sign.

McCafferty clenched his teeth, raised his imaginary pistol, and moved toward Williams, as the Professor rose and stepped between them.

"Not bad, Williams! Not bad at all!" stated the Professor, pushing the colonel back into his chair.

"Honorable Senators and Supreme Council," began Captain Pollard, looking at the other patients with deliberation and then grinning with a paste-up smile at Cummings, acknowledging her personally—with a slight bow of the head—as Supreme Council. Feet shuffled, a cough or two and a yawn, and most of the patients settled back for some long-winded entertainment.

"I humbly beseech this most honored and esteemed body," continued the orator slowly, drawing out in lengthy vowels the more important words in each phrase, "to weigh carefully the means by which we here allow ourselves to sit in judgment of our fellow member Colonel McCafferty. Surely I need not take the time to remind this revered body of intelligence of our responsibility to the State, our duty to our Forefathers, and to the Higher Laws to which we have affixed our honor, pondering as we often do our commitment to *Liberté, Égalité, Fraternité,* and the dictates of our highest consciousness.

"Our noble and wise colleague Lieutenant Williams has, I believe, already trespassed into that vague swamp of noxious prejudice, exhaling vapors of bias so potent as to turn this marble floor into a mephitic quagmire from which none can be extricated." The Professor stopped to ponder the transformation of stone beneath his feet.

"*Recht und Gesetz! Recht und Gesetz!* Law and order!" shouted out the Professor, slamming his hand down.

"Who is to be judge and jury? Prosecutor and accused? Criminal or saint? We await. Yes. Difficult to be judged while judging oneself. Who will listen to whom? *Keiner!* Colonel McCafferty, no one will hear you," asserted the Professor, staring at the colonel.

Corporal Hassley—nicknamed "Gunner" by his fellow patients—was taken by the Professor's address. Collins watched him slowly mouth "No one will hear you." The impact of the phrase seemed to strike deeper into the ex-M-60 gunner's brain with each repetition. As the threads of his stability dissolved, it was all he could manage to lurch spastically out of the day room.

Alexander, too, leaped up, seeking relief, and then grabbed his chair and flung it full force across the length of the room, though well above their heads. The steel chair clipped the lights and smashed the glass in the north window. He stomped past the startled Professor, whose torso wavered back and forth as though his feet were stuck in mud.

The aides galloped out of the control room to quell the uproar. Alexander's ebony face glistened with sweat. He started crying; stopped, forced himself back under control, and then spun on his heel to face the Professor eye to eye. With a trembling black finger jabbed into the Professor's throat, he spoke from behind clenched teeth.

"I did my job, whidt man. I kill your fuckin' gooks. An' for all your shidt-ass jive in the classroom, for all this country's bullshidt, my brothers too, who kill and was killed for all that bullshidt. An' you know too, whidt brains, I ain't tellin' you no godtdamn lies. Why do you . . . how does you have eyes there and talk bullshidt from here?" screamed Alexander, jabbing the Professor repeatedly in the Adam's apple.

The aides were at Alex, pawing their restraints over his arms and hands. But he paid them no attention this time, offered no resistance, so intent was he on making this point.

"How does you have eyes and nodt see that my people is controlled by you . . . you . . ." He began to stammer, losing control, and slammed his elbow into the ribs of a corpsman, then slugged the other under the ear.

"You mean you couldn't see, boy? That us black men wen' over there and kildt those other people, your gooks, when they's just as black as we are to you. Whide man in your fuckin' whide house! Now whatda we do over there? Whatda we go an' do now? Jesus.

71

We kill really black people, people made black ta the eyes of this country by people like you. An' we gone an' kildt them and was kill by them an' really all the time we was killin' each other. . . . Black people killin' more black peoples.

"Whidty's smart. Yeh. He godt us to be his niggers again. Goin' off an' kill them other niggers. Yeah, dat's the truth. We shouldta, shidt man, we shouldta . . . give . . . whid . . . ee . . ."

They dragged him away.

The Professor stood there with a big red mark pulsating on his throat, his eyes rigidly fixed on what a few seconds before had been Alexander's pupils in front of him.

Silence.

So quiet that the air conditioners made the room feel like a wind tunnel. Wind howled all around. It tugged at their arms and legs.

"Rhe-tor-ic," whispered the Professor. "Yes." He spoke out distinctly, folding himself awkwardly into his chair. "Yeah"—he sighed, looking over at Williams—"the colonel sucks his trigger finger." Williams grinned.

No one moved, not even Lieutenant Cummings. She just sat there paralyzed, clutching all her pads and notes and colored pencils (red for relapse and blue for progress). She had pressed down the pencils with such force that the points had snapped off.

"Well, they're broken now, Miss Cummings," muttered Williams in a low monotone. "There wasn't anything to report anyway."

Dr. Penderspot danced in then, looked at the glass on the table, the smashed window hanging by a few steel strands.

"Mr. Hickok's had another seizure on the floor—in *your* ward, Lieutenant Cummings. I suggest you up the Dilantin, drop his fluids, and *do something* otherwise intelligent with him. See Captain Moseby. He's in OP-6 with Hickok now. Go."

Lieutenant Cummings jumped unsteadily to her feet, like a robot running on too few circuits. She snapped to, looking Penderspot in the eyes, tacitly pleading for compassion. He looked down at the superimposed colored circles swarming on his tie.

"This group getting to be too much for you, Lieutenant?" he said, with his bald head under her nose.

"No, sir." And she stumbled off to attend old Bill Hickok, the syphilitic master sergeant, with her broken pencils and one untied shoe.

"The rest of you," snapped out the chief of psychiatry, "can

72

straighten up this pigpen before mess call." And he vanished through the wide, arched door.

The members of the Monday group did nothing of the sort. They straggled out through the maze of bunks in the long barracks, heading for the large deck overlooking the volleyball court below. Collins turned to look at Alexander. He was lying flat out, his arms and legs tied to the bedposts, face up. It looked as though it had just rained on him. A spring shower to cool him down, thought Collins as he passed Alex's bunk. Drops of water glistened over his body, his pajamas were soaked a dark blue, and two little pools of water floated on his closed eyelids.

Next to his pillow was a letter he had started, partially wrinkled:

> Dear Ma,
> You tell JP for me I'll kick his ass
> from here to Atlanta if he go an drop
> out a school. And you

Up in the right-hand corner was printed:

> Sp4c A
> 101st 4-3-86
> RA 88106664
> APO 363
> Da Nang, S.V.

CHAPTER **8**

Collins leaned against the heavy steel mesh and looked down at the people from his ward who were playing volleyball, or something akin to it. The aides were playing too; in fact, the game was played more between the corpsmen than the patients. The usual litter was strewn around the periphery of the court: a few magazines, a book, odd sneakers, a crutch, part of a brace, all tossed down by the cripples to show their disgust and contempt, along with their hoots, howls, and obscenities. Someone from NP-4 had been knocked even dizzier a couple of days earlier by a flying crutch.

The Professor sauntered out onto the deck and sat in an aluminum lawn chair. He gazed out through the heavy chain-link mesh. Flies and grasshoppers, leaves, and occasionally even a small bird could penetrate the openings in the screen. It was possible to press one's face hard against the sieve in such a way as to free the eyes from this wall of wire diamonds. But the eye is too accustomed to seeking out familiar structures and configurations. Inevitably it would come to rest on the volleyball net or the chain-link mesh enclosing an identical deck across the court, or on the three strands of barbed wire atop the towering fences which form the perimeter of Chambers.

"You asked me the other day," the Professor began seriously, motioning Collins to take a seat next to him, "how it was that I ended up in here. It occurred to me a few minutes ago. No, long before. To share impressions, thoughts, ideas, case histories—or what have you—with some others so that no one of us would feel . . . well, alienated or isolated. Alone enough to carry into action some desperate impulse. So I think I'm ready now, more or less, to brief you on my state of affairs. That is, if you're still interested. You being a relative neophyte to our third level of Chambers, there's a chance that my own evaluation of how I perceive my situation may help you to understand—I think you'll discover this to be true—the similarities of disposition which warrant this *intra nos* treatment." He stared down at the concrete floor then and lightly touched his fingertips together.

Collins didn't respond at first. Instead he rose and walked to the fence. He looked out over the grounds and the other patients below playing volleyball and softball, or wandering through the gardens under the colossal magnolias. He recalled that the Professor had described all the mental casualties as lepers that night when he first proposed the pact. He remembered something else from that discussion: Committed to the question by the question.

"Are we the worst of them, Pollard?" asked Collins, his back to the Professor.

"The worst of what?"

"The mentally wounded? The psychos?"

"Everyone coming out of a war is wounded. But especially this war. No exceptions. It's a fine line between the physically wounded and the psychos."

"Answer my question. Are we the worst?"

"For this time in this place, yes. We're still on the closed ward. But the real Waterloo is yet to come. There's still the medical board. And there's the court-martial for me and for you. The worst on this post is Building Six. But the worst of all is Leavenworth, or a VA torture chamber."

"Can't you get released to a private clinic, or into the custody of a civilian psychiatrist?"

"Most get out that way. Not right away, though; it's not that easy. The Army has become increasingly paranoid about veterans who turn into junkies, alcoholics, criminals, and murderers on the streets of their home towns. So they're holding them longer. But it all depends on two things: your psychological-profile classification and the board.

"But, Collins, for me it really doesn't matter anymore. I have undertaken my own inquest," he said proudly. "Which is a quest in the truest sense of the word. I will see it through no matter where I end up."

"Committed to the question by the question?"

"Precisely."

"What's the question?" asked Collins, turning suddenly to face the Professor.

"How . . . ? Why . . . ? Why me? Why you? Why those others down there? Why this hospital? Why Vietnam? Why America in Vietnam? Why Chase Manhattan Bank in Saigon? Why this chance coalescence of Fate? Why did thousands of grunts just give up over there? Why that meaningless sacrifice? Why the lies, the dissension, the cover-ups, the campus riots? Why are we losing? What in the name of Truth is happening? What in God's name is going down?"

"Why a pact?" asked Collins, holding back his anger.

"I know why that bothered you the other night. I know why."

"Why!" he shouted.

"See, Collins?" responded Pollard. "You've started. The whys. Now, if—"

"Just tell me why."

"Because you're scared shitless of anything that requires you to ever put anything on the line again. Especially yourself. Your sanity. Like a private commitment to a very unpopular, very lonely, very sacrificial, very insane goal: to find out what happened to you and to me and to our fellow crazies down there, and why it happened. And then to shout it out to whoever will listen to you. To make some sense out of this nonsense. And get it out. Get it out. That's the pact. Get it out to our fellow Americans," he concluded bitterly.

"Why me? Why Wright? Why the two of *us?*" Collins asked. The phrase "No one will hear you" echoed in his mind. He turned his back to the Professor.

"Don't flatter yourself, Collins," Pollard replied with a laugh. "I've even asked Nieland to join this cause. You and Wright are certainly not the first two. There were others. But the attrition rate is very high in here, Collins, in case you haven't noticed. And I'm not talking about bodies. You watch the troopers in here as the days tick by. The last thing they want to do is scrape open what appear to be healing wounds. On the contrary. All they want is to get out of here, at any price. And that 'any price' just happens to cost them

76

themselves. All they try to do is perform a lobotomy on the last two years of their lives or Tinker-Toy together their brains into some Rube Goldberg rendition of the resurrected, rehabilitated Vietnam veteran—a goddamn walking time bomb.

"Look, Collins," continued the Professor as he walked over to the fence and peered down at the end of an inning. "The reality is this: the Vietnam War, for all of us, is fought in our minds, not south of the DMZ. And for that reason it will never end."

"Why a pact? Tell me again."

"Because I can't do it alone. I may be too far gone myself. We have no real control over our destinies in here. But there's strength in numbers—I think. Someone has *got* to get through. So that the travesty of Vietnam doesn't happen to this country again, to people like you and me, and the rest of us. . . . That's why the pact must be made at this time and in this place: so we don't forget once we're out, if we ever do get out."

In the long silence that followed, Collins paced the length of the deck, running his hand along the fence, stepping in an arc as he passed in back of the Professor.

"I recall"—Pollard began emphatically, and then lowered his voice, directing his eyes to the gray concrete slab of the deck— "the airlift to Fort Sam, to this *hacienda.* I had been confined even before being shipped Stateside. . . . To tell it the way it was, I was arrested. Arrested!" He began to bang his head against the steel fence. "By my company commander on Highway One, just east of Prasaut. He said only three things to me. . . ." The Professor's voice wavered. He cleared his throat. "Only three things. 'Just what happened, Jack?' But it wasn't a question. He already knew what had happened, since I learned everything I knew from him. So he knew what had . . . gone haywire. And then he said, 'Remember what I've always said about protecting yourself? I told you never to *order* someone to perform your unnatural acts'—that was his term for aggressive interrogation. Then he smiled at me: 'You forgot, didn't you, Jack.' He snapped the cuffs on me and we headed for Saigon.

"Oh, Collins!" he cried out suddenly, clamping his thin, angular fingers over his head. "What a fool! What a fool! I had given myself to getting information by *any* means. Any means. Because *that was the job!* And . . . I loved it.

"Then he had *me* locked away in the same jail where *I* had locked away drug traffickers, murders, enemy agents—like Madame Dupey—and hit men. You name it. . . . Ah, the irony of it all. The bitter irony. Do you understand me, Collins?"

Collins nodded. But he was only half listening, and began mumbling again:

" 'We hereby sentence you, Andrew B. Collins, to the Fortieth Field Hospital Division in Bien Hoa. You will serve your sentence not as a member of the surgical group, but as a casualty. You've been promoted from line medic. Congratulations, stiff. Now we—' "

"Collins! Collins! You're doing it again," Pollard said, as he took him by the arm. "It's one thing to realize that you're a prisoner of the past, and another to be the unwitting victim of it. Don't you see the difference? That's why the pact is so important. It will force you to focus, to distinguish. That's why I'm telling you this about me, explaining what happened to me, so you'll know, so you'll understand why I'm the way I am. Committed to the question by the question, remember?"

Collins nodded. "Go on, Pollard. Tell me."

"So my company commander arrested me and locked me up with all the other criminals. And then it really began. All those gooks I had investigated, tracked down, apprehended, worked over—yes, tortured, killed . . . They appeared in the cells next to mine, across from mine, down from mine, up from mine. In my sleep. Then in broad daylight! Can you imagine that? In a light so bright I thought I must be looking into God's own face. They crowd into *my* cell, these gone-mad, garbage gooks. In *my* chair. On *my* cot! They scream out their secrets and then whisper in my ear, 'Just what happened, Jack?' smiling at me as they cry out over and over and—"

"Stop it! Stop it!" shouted Collins, pounding his fists against the chain-link fence. "Stop it! No more, Pollard. . . . No . . . more."

"Why not?" the Professor screamed back. "Why not, Collins? You think you're in some private, exclusive hell? . . . Then may I welcome you and yours," he said, bowing like a rag doll, "to the seventh circle, whence no shade has ever returned."

"Now, what the hell's goin' on out here?" Hinckley yelled, going straight for Pollard. "I leave the two of you out here to enjoy the copacetic view an' look what you go and do. For Christ's sake, Pollard. And you too, Collins. Collins? . . ."

Hinckley put his arm around the specialist's shoulders. "You O.K., my man?" Hinckley glanced up suspiciously at Pollard. "The captain—I mean Mr. Pollard—been on your case again, Collins?"

"'Hey, Collins, tell Northcross we got two more burn cases comin' in. And a suicide. . . . Yeah, this one tried to croak himself by walkin' through a field of Claymores he'd just rigged. . . . Hey, Collins, how's things flowin' through your station?' Like a river, Major."

"Collins," said Hinckley, turning him by the shoulders. "Look at me, Collins. Raise your head up and look at me. Where are you now?"

"Chambers Pavilion. Brooke Army Medical Center. Fort Sam Houston. San Antonio. Texas. America," replied Collins like a robot.

"And who am I?"

"Specialist Santo Hinckley."

"And who's this joker?"

"Captain Jackson Pollard." Collins turned his eyes toward the Professor, who winked back.

"It's my fault," stated Pollard with dignity.

"Pollard," sighed Hinckley, dropping his arms from Collins's shoulders, "everythin's your damn fault. From runnin' outa hot water in the mornin's to dudes freaking out in here who you don't even know. When you gonna stop playin' whipping post? . . . Now, Collins," he said, resuming his weary yet buoyant manner, "you O.K., my man?"

"Yeah," answered Collins, with a half smile, half frown.

"It's from sleepin' on the floor. Gets ya every time. Oh! We got OT before mess. Why don't ya get ready. . . . I'm comin', Barrett! I'm comin'!" Hinckley bounded off the deck.

"I'm sorry, Collins," the Professor moaned as he leaned into the fence. "I know too much. I know too much for anyone's good," he whispered, shaking his head back and forth.

"It's not your fault. Hinckley was right. It's not your fault. I just . . ."

"I know. I know what happened. Remember, I have prophetic pow—"

"What happened, then?" demanded Collins.

"There; that's better. You keep asking why."

"Well, I asked. What do you *think* just happened?"

"Hot flashes."

"Hot flashes? You are nuts, Pollard. Just plain crazy. . . . Hot flashes," repeated Collins, laughing.

"Look, you idiot," snapped Pollard. "Hot flashes. Think about it. Hot . . . flashes. Your displacement. That's why Hinckley gave you the reality test. You were talking about something back on the field. About a major, and Northcross, and flowing like a river."

"I did?" stammered Collins. "I said something about . . . Major Hepburn and Captain Northcross? And . . ."

"Yes, Collins," he pronounced solemnly. "Let it go, man. Let it out. And you'll find that there's more to say that may help you to see beyond yourself, beyond your own reflection in here—here in the windows, the polished floors, the stainless-steel covers over the air conditioners, the mirror when you're shaving—to see beyond the faces here that give you back a reflection of yourself. Like my face in front of yours. And you must, of course, greet all the faces in here as . . . well, in the spirit of receiving a *hoi chan.* You understand—open-armed. Yes, open-armed in appearance, but always beware of the bastard because he can do you in in an instant. You have to get past them all, including the staff, to the truth that there is no one here who can do your work for you—no one to care for you as you can care for yourself. Doctor, heal yourself. If you're lucky, you'll get out.

"The real problem, don't you see—I call it the Charybdis syndrome in my case, having watched others drown here—is to keep to yourself as much as you can stand, on your own two feet. Don't succumb to the culture growing in this place, to the insanity of your bedfellows, their disease. That's the only—"

"Well, well, well. I hope you realize you've detained the whole ward from OT," said Hinckley, who had perched next to them again. He was staring at the Professor as at some pitiful creature. The Professor began to walk off the deck, and a strange sense of abandonment crept over Collins, as though Pollard had taken a serious interest in him—in all of them—and then, without warning or provocation, simply turned his back.

Like a *hoi chan,* he thought. That doesn't make any sense. Like a *hoi chan?* They were defectors. VC who willfully surrendered. Yes, the *chieu hoi* program. And the flyboys dropped leaflets into VC strongholds. They were promised safe passage and good treatment. We shot most of them, leaflet or not. And the ones we received with "open arms" usually shot us.

80

"In the spirit of receiving a *hoi chan?*" Collins said.

"Come on, Collins. Let's get with the program." Hinckley took him by the arm. "Come along now."

Down came the patients from the third floor, some staggering and babbling, others trying to maintain their composure. It looked like a medieval pageant: a parade of the botched and brilliant, the weak and strong, the sensitive and brutal—all in limbo. They walked out into a sunlight so bright that their world turned chalky white, down past "Miracle Sound" (over by the Coke machine where a legendary patient had suddenly begun talking coherently one day) and along the walkway that overlooks a pool without water.

Specialist Barrett, one of the two new neuro-psych personnel assigned to the closed wards of Chambers, was in charge. Attentively he led his patients onto the court, or the Pit, as it was often called by the patients—a square patch of asphalt surrounded on three sides by the wards of the psychiatric hospital, with the mess hall completing the enclosed recreational area.

Residents of the ward adjacent to Collins's were playing volleyball in the center of the court amid shouts of "Hot potato!" or "Live grenade!" as the ball passed from one side to the other. Corporal Rodriguez, the smallest and most agile of the veterans on Collins's ward, suddenly detached himself from the line of patients following Barrett and ran to the sideline of the court, where he performed a series of accomplished gymnastic stunts in rapid-fire succession: flips, twirls, somersaults, and cartwheels in midair, his feet and hands seeming never to touch the ground, his body following the line along the side of the court but never touching it.

Specialist Barrett stood motionless. He tilted his head to one side and then the other, like a dog hearing a curious pitch, as he became more absorbed in Rodriguez's stunts. The volleyball players tried to retain their concentration, but one after another they forgot about their game to watch the performer as he whirled like a gyro. Some looked at him with curiosity, or contempt; a few envied Rodriguez's unself-conscious freedom and supple flight, reminders of their own entrapment.

Rodriguez had not yet faltered—perhaps he never would. But there was a volleyball game at stake, and a few of the stronger patients tried to coerce their distracted teammates back to the sense of order the game lent them. It finally dawned on Barrett, who had stopped to watch Rodriguez, that his charges were scattering aimlessly throughout the compound. Some were walking through the volleyball court. Others yanked desperately at the steel enclosure protecting the Coke machine, the only thing they could immediately associate with the lives they had once lived.

Barrett was flustered, and further unnerved at the growing irritation in the sweaty faces of the four corpsmen who had struggled so diligently to establish the modest workings of a simple group game. Barrett gathered his courage and clumsily jerked his chrome-plated whistle to his mouth. He squeezed out two shrill, prepubescent squeaks. Those patients who were well conditioned stopped dead in their tracks and turned their heads in the direction of the unprofessional peeps.

But order was already lost, the scales of stability having tipped out of control. The volleyball court had been infiltrated by too many semiconscious psychos. Corpsmen and patients alike shouted, pushed, and pointed in a self-defeating effort to get the game going again. Orders were issued, more whistles blown, additional staff called out.

"O.K. That's it, boys. Shut it down and steady 'em up," came the voice of Master Sergeant Morris over the PA system. A few minutes later, he emerged through the narrow door which opened onto the Pit. He made his way slowly across the volleyball court with that manner of assertive control which comes from experience tempered by resignation. He passed close by Rodriguez, who remained perfectly still.

Master Sergeant Morris calmly placed his pale, paternal hand on Barrett's shoulder, looked the massive hulk in the eyes, and quietly said, "O.K., trainee, relax for a second. And think." The compound had fallen silent, except for the hum of insults, jokes, and laughter that fell in an incessant stream from the amputees' sun deck on the roof of the hospital. It was at times like this that the patients from the third-floor wards became aware of the cripples always above them.

"You've got to stay alert, soldier. You just can't afford to be going 'round here playing Little Bo-Peep or something when you're the corpsman runnin' these here dummies across buildings. What's your name?"

82

"Barrett, Specialist Barrett, Master Sergeant."

"Well, now, boy, let's get your shit together and stop messing up this here circus. Got that?"

"Yes, Master Sergeant," replied Barrett.

With a wave of his hand, the master sergeant signaled the ward to leave the Pit.

The Professor, who was standing off to one side, chuckled to himself. He was leaning against the heavy chain-link doors that led to the mess hall. His arms were folded across his chest, his right leg was bent at the knee, with his foot pushing hard against the barricade behind him. He looked well pleased with the performers passing in review as Barrett led the patients toward OT.

But as the last few stragglers, including Collins, passed, Pollard turned his back and slumped forward into the steel barrier, arms above his head, as if surrendering to the wire mesh.

It was pitch black as Collins entered the telescoping corridor and began his descent to the occupational therapy section. As he continued down the enclosed, arched passageway, he suddenly thought of the Queens Midtown Tunnel. How a friend of his father's had turned off the ignition one morning in the middle of the commuter rush. Just shut it off, then opened the door and walked away from his car. Left it there in a line of traffic and walked away. The cops finally caught up with him a few blocks away. They had to keep stride with him, talk to him as he wove between people and cars. He walked right out into the traffic. The cops asked him about motor trouble. Out of gas? Flat tire? Emergency? "No." "Well, then. What the hell's your problem?" "I quit," he said, and just kept right on walking. "What do you mean, you quit?" "I quit. You understand English? I'm through with this nonsense. The whole thing's absurd. My life's absurd. I've been driving this same route to work for eight years, five days a week, three hours a day, sitting like a jerk in this traffic. So today I made up my mind to quit. I'm through, O.K.?" And he handed one officer his briefcase, and the other the keys to his car, house, office, boat, and kept right on walking.

"Where do you think you're goin', Collins? . . . Collins! Collins! Come back here. It's this way," shouted Hinckley, running after him. He grabbed Collins by the shoulder and swung him around one hundred and eighty degrees.

"You don't want to go down *there*. That's the shock clinic, man.

83

Stay the hell away from there . . . if you can. Now march right through there. . . . Where's Pollard, Collins?"

Collins shrugged his shoulders.

"You were just with him! Is he still out there? . . . The Professor!" he shouted, with increasing irritation.

"The Professor? Yes, he was outside the last I saw of him."

"O.K. Follow Barrett into the OT room." Then Hinckley turned and ran to find Pollard.

"Over there, now, we have Specialist Jamison. He's our metalsmith. And very good too, I hear," said Barrett, leading Collins into a small room.

"Yes. Hi. I'm Jamison. I'll be happy to instruct—I mean, to help you make a copper ashtray, or a silver ring. Think of that! Or we can cast a chess set for you out of bronze, like we did for Maste. You've heard about his beautiful chess set up on the ward, haven't you? Well, of course, we have to keep it here for him; he can't take it up on the floor, of course; against the rules. We'll be happy to store anything you make right here for you in tiptop condition, and then when you're boarded and on your way, why, you can pick up your things, or we'll even send them out to your next location. By the way, Barrett, I haven't see Maste for some time now. Isn't he still in your unit?"

"No," replied Specialist Barrett. "He's been transferred to the Arlington VA, I guess a week ago. NTR. Check with Hinckley."

"Never to return, uh? Well, he didn't even ask for his chess set. Must have slipped his mind. I'll have to look at his disposition papers. Oh. Would you . . . what's your name?"

"His name's Collins."

"Yes. Collins. Wouldn't you like to see this beautiful chess set? I poured it from a blend I came up with a few years ago."

The metalwork specialist headed toward a reinforced-steel locker, producing a crooked smile and, from his pocket, three heavily laden key rings. He picked out a key from the tangle and thrust it into the lock, opening both doors simultaneously. Rows of shelves were packed with projects, as they were called—pieces of rugs, half-finished ship models, a dozen or so chess sets, identical in shape and hue, one king sitting out in front with a grotesque crown, the metal scabbed over his head and face like the knobby scars of a healed stump.

Paintings, pieces of stained glass—or rather colored plastic—one propped up in the back: a recognizable form of Christ, the mouth comically twisted open too wide, arms held out stiffly as if embracing the world, open-armed like a scarecrow, standing on one leg, the other left incomplete. And a pistol—a .45, carved out of wood and painted black—hanging in the back. Endless stacks of potholders sagging to one side, shabby, done without care. And two lengths of string stretching the width of the locker and supporting rings, of different shapes and sizes. A bracelet looking more like a medieval shackle, with "LBA 1ST AIR CAV" carved in chicken scratch on the tarnished silver. Some plaster of Paris castings of hands and feet, most missing digits; a plaster face with the eyes closed in old Roman style. Junk, each piece carefully tied to a printed tag containing information relevant to its creator; a line at the bottom that read "DISPOSITION"—most of them blank—and a small caduceus crossed by a sword in red at the bottom, with "BROOKE ARMY MEDICAL CENTER/CHAMBERS PAVILION" across the side.

"So you can see right here what we do here. Nice stuff. Yip. So just let me know what you're interested in."

With a big yellow-toothed grin, he slammed the doors of the enormous steel cabinet so forcefully that a few projects fell off the shelves and crashed. The metalwork specialist was apparently deaf to his destruction, for his wide, thoughtless grin seemed to grow across his face as more pieces crashed to the floor.

"Over here," said Barrett, tugging at Collins's sleeve. "As you can see, it's the woodcraft facility." And there was the Professor, sitting by himself in the corner, near the window facing the garden. A shaft of sunlight cut across his work. Looking over his shoulder, Collins could see a few vertical sticks of wood with white paper or cloth hanging between them. The Professor, shaggy hair hanging over his blue collar, tipped his head a few times with a sort of childish curiosity. He ran his hand slowly over the line of white material, up and over the shorter stick, out across another span of whiteness, touching the tip of the highest post, then on across the white edge to the third shaft, and down. As he repeated this, a maze of fine thread came suddenly into focus as though a dewy spiderweb sparkled in an early-morning sun. A fine crisscross mesh held his construction together. Complex.

". . . from the Philippines, I think, and there's some walnut and cherry and, of course, soft pine. And . . ."

And then Collins knew: The Professor had taken rigid posts and spans of barbed wire and put them on the deck of a ship. How delicately he touched his therapy; with reverence.

"I wanted to look at that ship over there," said Collins.

"Why—ah, yes," replied Barrett, flustered at his directness. "As I understand, though, they would like to permit the patients here some—ah—privacy in their work. But if you want to build a boat or something, why, I'm sure you can work in that craft," he said, accelerating his speech. "And the specialist in charge is . . . Zu . . . Zuber—yes, Specialist Zuber—and I'm sure he'd be willing to instruct you. I mean, well, you know, he has to cut all the pieces and, you know, I guess you can't handle any of the tools," said Barrett with a twinge of embarrassment. "But you can plan, and fit, and glue—you can make your thing, at least. Which is more than I can say for most, Collins." He was whispering now.

"Could I take a look at Pollard's ship?" Collins asked Zuber.

"You mean Pollard's brigantine? I guess so. He's funny about his work. Keeps the whole thing very much to himself. Interesting job, though. He's done a cutaway. Sure, take a quick peek . . . but keep your distance."

The Professor's ship was magnificent. Not a seam showed, not a crude joint was to be found anywhere, nothing to detract from the polished surface of his creation. Even the cloth sails had tiny grommets, made from the minute black beads that the others used for necklaces. He was stringing monofilament from the aft mast to the stern plate. Collins moved in closer, staring over Pollard's shoulder as he pivoted the vessel in its cradle to get a better working angle on the stern. Collins peered into the levels below decks, into a skeleton of inner compartments: cloth hammocks in miniature, a potbellied stove in the galley, metal pulleys and drive chains to the rudder—all exposed in amazing faithfulness.

"What! Get away! What do you want of me *now?* Get back!" Pollard snapped, jumping off his stool. "Who the hell do you think you are?" Collins reeled back and fell across another patient's finger painting, covering his hand with red tempera. He stared dumbly back at the Professor. Suddenly Colonel McCafferty's face was directly in front of his own, bearing the look of a hell-scarred demon, his rigid, teeth-clenched muscles sprung hard through the skin, and blood rage in his eyes. He growled like a bear, seized Collins's wrist, and smashed his hand on the workbench; and again.

Barrett and Zuber quickly pinned the colonel against the narrow window. Williams, hearing McCafferty's voice, came out of the metal shop.

"Traitor!" screamed the colonel. He sighted down his index finger at Williams. "You fucking traitor!"

Williams yelled back, "Murderer! . . . Murderer! . . . Murderer! . . ."

"You fuckin' gook traitor!"

"Assassin!" screamed Williams as he went for Colonel McCafferty. Zuber sprang at Williams, throwing him headlong into the treasure chest of projects. More icons tumbled off the shelves.

"What the hell is going on in here?" Dr. Penderspot shouted, throwing open the door with such force that the handle smashed into the wall. White chips of plaster fell like snowflakes on his black dress shoes. Behind him was Lieutenant Cummings.

"Jesus! . . . Where the hell's Hinckley? Goddamn it, Barrett, what's going on in here? Every time I turn my back there's . . ."

"Yes, well . . ."

"Get these patients to the mess hall. Get 'em out of here! . . . Hinckley! Hinck—leeeee!"

"Sir?" shouted the specialist as he flew into the room. He stood at attention in front of Penderspot, trying to catch his breath.

"I want a green sheet on this for the board. I take it that Mr. McCafferty and Mr. Williams have been at it again."

"Well, sir, I wasn't in . . ."

"Isn't that right, Williams? You two were at it again."

Williams merely stared at Penderspot, who fixed his eyes momentarily on the gash in Williams's forehead and then dropped his eyes to stare at the colored circles on his tie. Williams winked at Lieutenant Cummings and, perhaps finding a compassionate twinkle in her eyes, said distinctly:

"Those armored-personnel hacks would turn their faces from the Pearly Gates for one last look at their colonel now." He turned and again faced McCafferty, who was still squeezing off imaginary rounds with his red trigger finger. A thin smile parted Williams's lips as he relished the pitiful state of his former commanding officer.

"Mother-fucker! You coward bastard! You framed me!" McCafferty screamed.

Williams's smile broadened. "Bang. Bang. You shot 'em down, now didn't you? Shot down five of your own men. Bang. Bang. Bang. Bang. Bang. Murdered five of your own. Bang. Bang—"

"Stop it!" cried out McCafferty, burying his face in his hands.

The patients from the third-floor ward left Colonel McCafferty crying into his red hands and walked through the dark tunnel. At the end of one of many underground corridors, a bright light shone over an enameled door, with a sign to one side:

BROCA-WERNICKE RESEARCH CENTER
BAMC C-1106

And another passageway, like the previous one, ended in:

A phonic phasic **GROUP SPECIALISTS**

BAMC C-1105

"Never seen an unspoken confession before, Collins? . . . Beautiful maneuver on Williams's part. A classic," said the Professor in the darkness. They looked down the next tunnel. The door was marked simply:

ECT
DO NOT ENTER WITHOUT GREEN

The green light suddenly went out and a red one came on.

"This whole complex operates in darkness. It turns back on itself like a huge snake. . . . Hey, listen, Collins. I'm sorry about how I turned on you back in OT."

CHAPTER 9

"Herr Nieland," announced the Professor as the young psychiatrist entered the ward for morning rounds. Because of his height—or because of Dr. Penderspot's lack of it—Nieland walked through the inner door stooped at the neck. His eyes followed the polished floor while he listened to Penderspot advance psychological theories of behavior that had been popular in the early part of the century. Nieland concentrated on what his superior said in the hope of learning how the ranking psychiatrist had survived thirty-one years of service-related disorders.

Nieland was lean and well built. He had played varsity basketball and tennis in his undergraduate years at Penn State, continued on the teams at Johns Hopkins, and even through his residency at Grace–New Haven. He still had a slightly bouncing stride, and not only did he appear energetic, but his eyes glowed with a piercing warmth as he raised his head to glance at his patients, slouched over their bunks. Seductively calm yet somehow irritated and, in contrast to Penderspot's boredom, concerned. For Nieland, treating these war-related mental illnesses and working with these patients remained challenging; in part because he had uncovered a cluster of rare and often contradictory syndromes, seldom seen in military hospitals to date, and strangely absent from the voluminous archives of military psychiatry. His discoveries had gradually led him into an intense search for a common denominator, some subtle precipitating strain, which he pursued to the consternation of the chief of psychiatry, Dr. Thermon Penderspot.

Hinckley slid out of the control station and approached both psychiatrists with a stack of aluminum clipboards. Neither doctor looked at Hinckley as he came to a formal halt. He saluted and held out a pile of records for Dr. Penderspot, who fumbled the mass of histories, lab reports, therapeutic sessions, diagnoses, specialized treatments, revised prognoses, and opinions like a clumsy busboy. And another set of records for Nieland, who slapped them under his arm. The two psychiatrists walked into the control station and closed the door.

"Suppose we do apply Pick's definition of reduplicative paramnesia to parts of the body," said the junior psychiatrist. "What do we have? We end up with fictionalized anatomy, which is either added to or subtracted from the patient's own body by his own mind. But there is still—"

"You're referring to that Specialist Collins from the Fortieth Field Surgical Hospital? Well, we have another staff officer coming in from that unit."

"But don't you see, Therm," continued Nieland, "that his condition is at one end of the continuum. He's symbolic—albeit bizarre—of every patient in here. . . ."

"In what sense?" asked the elder psychiatrist, playing with his pop-art tie.

"They're all compensating for losses," replied Nieland, growing more serious and animated. "They do that in a variety of ways. Only in his case, he developed an anthropomorphic obsession by trying to compensate in behalf of *other* soldiers in the most tangible terms. With arms, legs, hearts, and heads. . . . What do you do with a loss, any loss? You either compensate or substitute. He compensated for the others' losses by substituting his own fictionalized anatomy until there was nothing left of his own identity. And so when he finally collapsed, there was nothing left to fall back on, just like the rest of these men: they have nothing left to support their identities."

Dr. Penderspot tapped the crystal on his wristwatch.

"But that's only the superficial manifestation of a far more insidious and lethal disintegration of person, from which the majority of our younger patients suffer," urged Nieland.

90

"And what might that be?"

"What we're dealing with in this time and place, Therm, is a crisis of personal morality. Of right and wrong in the most intimate, private sense. Of clashing values, of contradictory roles, of conflicting beliefs and responsibilities, which we see reflected daily in the tumultuous confrontations right here in our own country. What happened two weeks ago—"

"Two weeks ago?"

"Kent State."

"Oh . . . yes," acknowledged Penderspot with nonchalance.

"The massacre at Kent State is symptomatic of a national neurosis. It's a disorder of conscience, a conflict inherent in the very bones of this country's spiritual, ethical, and moral framework. That's why we must treat these patients not as an isolated group of veterans suffering from battle fatigue, trench trauma, and Deutsch disease, not as survivors of an error in military strategy, but as the victims of a moral catastrophe.

"We must remember, too, that these men, unlike other generations of American troops, were raised in an atmosphere of radical social reform based on one primary principle: respect for one's fellow man regardless of race, color, or creed. An atmosphere of idealism unprecedented in modern times, which their culture imparted to them in the late fifties and early sixties: 'I have a dream . . .' 'Ask not what your country can do for you . . .' 'Flower Power . . .' 'Make love, not war. . . .' "

"And so the foundation of your therapeutic approach to these psychotic patients is based on the sociological significance of a few stoned sayings tacked to a light pole at the corner of Haight and Ashbury, Dr. Nieland?" A sarcastic grin orchestrated Penderspot's remark.

Nieland, frustrated with his failure to reach his commanding officer, shook his head in weary resignation. Penderspot turned and began walking toward the door of the control station. His hand on the knob, he hesitated, then turned around.

"Give me reason four hundred and eighty-six why I should treat these men any differently than the GIs who fought in World War Two and Korea."

Nieland sighed and ran his hand swiftly through his neatly combed black hair.

"How many times are we going to go back over the differences? Of the hundreds of reasons we've discussed, it all boils down to one crucial fact."

"Which is?"

"Never," replied Nieland, raising his voice and staring straight into Penderspot's faded green eyes, "never in the history of this country has the American fighting man ever felt that he had to justify his presence in a foreign country to *himself,* as well as to his peers when he came home."

"Specialist Hinckley," called out Dr. Penderspot as he opened the door to the ward. "Dr. Nieland will make his rounds first this morning."

"Yes, sir. Dr. Nieland's patients, take two steps forward."

A few of Nieland's twenty-eight charges lurched to the yellow parallel lines that ran the length of the long barracks. He addressed each of his patients, including those who didn't know that they were patients, or that Nieland was their doctor, or where they were. Lieutenant Cummings, glowing with her usual flush, followed Dr. Nieland, one pace behind. She stopped in a businesslike manner whenever he paused. He said only a few words to each man, sometimes in a whisper, other times loudly. Smiling easily, he followed up the exchange with a handshake or a pat on the back.

The Professor, his hands behind his back and his feet spread apart rather unnaturally, seemed to tremble. He had assumed an unsolicited parade rest—the only one on the ward whose body had assumed the resurrected posture. As Nieland approached, a smile broke over the Professor's face.

"You've brought it!"

"Well, Pollard, as you got yourself into this mess so you can get yourself out of here. You're no pedestrian, and it's time you were on your way again. Time you went ahead with your teaching. I want you to finish this book somewhere other than in here. Is that clear, Professor?" The Professor nodded. The book was *Moby Dick.* Dr. Nieland had placed himself above the law of Chambers. Printed matter was not allowed in the closed wards.

"Let's see now," began Nieland, thumbing through Collins's file. "Six incident reports in the past week. . . . Why do you prefer sleeping on the floor rather than in a bed?" Nieland looked abruptly into his patient's pale-blue eyes. "And I see you've refused to eat some of your meals. . . . Specialist Hinckley?"

"Sir?"

"Did I carry that shirt of Collins's back up here?"

"Yes, sir."

"Would you bring it here, Specialist."

Hinckley went into the control station and unlocked the file cabinet. He emerged with a bulky envelope with Collins's name and ID number stamped on the front. Nieland pulled out a white hospital-issue jersey and held it up in front of Collins. It was covered with the graphic detail of a right knee-joint reconstruction. Each anatomical component was shaded in a different color ink, its nomenclature neatly printed in black along the sides of the shirt.

"This is your work, isn't it?"

Collins hesitated, then nodded.

"It's perfect, Andrew." Nieland smiled. "I checked it against *Gray's*. You know your anatomy. Someday you'll tell me why you quit med school. But why did you leave out the patella?"

"There wasn't any."

"I see. Well, we've been finding these illustrations on the mess-hall tables, on the walls of the latrine. And here," said Nieland, pointing to Collins's bedstand. "You've drawn all over that too, haven't you. . . . Hinckley?"

"Sir?"

"Enter an authorization for Collins to have one regular—civilian-issue—notebook and a pencil. They're to be kept in the control box except when he wants to use them. I want them accounted for every P.M. Maybe we can teach him not to draw on the walls and his clothes."

Nieland winked at Collins. "May I keep this?" asked the psychiatrist, holding up the shirt again.

"Sure."

"Now," continued Nieland, turning to Cummings, "I want to see Collins again this coming Monday. That would be the twenty-fifth. Two o'clock open there on the twenty-fifth, Lieutenant?"

"Fourteen-thirty, sir. And you meet with the board at fifteen hundred hours."

"O.K. Then I'll see Collins at two-thirty."

Collins caught a waft of Old Spice as Nieland turned and walked over to his next patient.

"Well, Sailor, you've come a long way, haven't you? The Medical Boarding and Dispensations Committee will meet with you for the last time. . . . I hope it's the final boarding for you. It's scheduled for this afternoon. It'll be the same procedure as before. I'll present your disposition and prognosis, enter a rating, and then the members will ask you some questions. But, Eddie, I intend to play a tape recording RQ'ed from your friend Ross, which I want you to hear before the meeting."

"Ross?"

"Why, yes. I think it's in your best interest, Eddie. It's going to be difficult, I suspect, for you to sit through. It may bother you to know what I've known all along. But some aspects of your past will make more sense to you when you hear his report. You've got to get over your . . . your impasse, let's call it. And you have the strength. It's your strength of accepting and surmounting that they'll be looking for. And you can overcome this one, Eddie."

Sailor began to stutter. As the stuttering became louder and as his impatience grew to anger at his lack of coherency, his hands clutched the folds of his bathrobe until he was about to pull the seams apart. Dr. Nieland extended his arms and slammed them down on Sailor's quivering shoulders. The doctor held him in that vise grip as though he were performing a transfusion of strength and control. "Relax, Sailor. Stop now for a moment. Remember what we said about the expressway, the lanes? How, when we're out moving, we wait to read the signs before we take this exit or that entrance? How we have to pay attention and read ahead? We wait until we can read those directional signs and we often have to slow down a bit. We lay off the accelerator of speech until we know for sure what our next move is. Right?" Dr. Nieland again pressed Sailor firmly on the shoulders.

"YYess   Doctor. I do know." Sailor sighed, shaking his head slowly from side to side. He looked at his feet.

Nieland took his hands away from Sailor's body like a stagehand steadying a prop. Sailor's form swayed while the doctor watched for the return of his patient's self-control.

"I   I guess   I be some a bit ah   It's my   don't you   you understand I keep see seeing o oo only the blurs. And I   "

"I understand, Eddie, I understand. Look, why don't we talk for a while before the board meeting? We'll go over it all again. O.K.? Think that's a good idea?"

"Y Ye sss."

"Cummings."

94

"Yes, sir."

"Have Eddie in my office at two o'clock."

"You already have an appointment with Dr. So Ming from RVN-FMP Battalion at fourteen hundred hours, sir."

"Well, then, get it changed to one o'clock," ordered Nieland.

"Now, Eddie, we—"

"But, sir, you see Major Drumsdee at thirteen hundred hours to review VA disability steps, and then at thirteen thirty you're—"

"Now, Cummings. I don't care how you do it, but I will see Sailor between two and three this afternoon."

"But, Captain . . ."

"But, Lieutenant!"

"Yes, sir."

"And no more DC medication for Edward here. Nothing except Mellaril ten mg's when and if he asks for it. Four tabs daily maximum." The doctor turned to address his patient. "Within a week you'll be on the second floor. Just don't get stopped for speeding!" Dr. Nieland grinned. Sailor, initially still confused, suddenly relaxed into an easy smile and then nodded and stuck out his hand.

The doctor met Sailor's hand in a firm shake, as though a negotiated agreement had reached conclusion except for the formality of passing papers. One representative with neatly combed black hair and black eyes, dressed in a fresh uniform, his face just shaved, belt buckle gleaming, light reflecting from his black shoes. The other agent bent at the waist, his blond hair hanging above his blue eyes, dressed in a flimsy striped bathrobe over discolored blue pajamas and white slippers. Yet an exchange of realities was being negotiated. Yes, thought Collins, a peddler of possibilities, this Nieland.

"It's a big world out there, Sailor. Time you were back in it, uh? . . . Cummings."

"Sir."

"Call Sailor's wife and tell her she can visit her husband beginning two weeks from today."

"Yes, sir."

"See you in a few hours, Eddie."

He turned in haste to continue his rounds. Turned again, and in the mimic of a drill instructor, shouted:

"Sailor, hit yourself a home run today!"

Sailor, his muscles recoiling again, felt the force of a message from out of the past. His fingers curled in a closed fist. But then he suddenly relaxed and brought himself under control. The sparked response had run its course and gone out of him in a second. That threshold of violent reaction met and transcended by the patient was acknowledged by the physician.

As Dr. Nieland was completing the rounds for this ward, soldiers on stretchers in net beds were being unhinged from medevac choppers that had landed on the roof. Within the silence of the ward came the sharp vibrations, the impact of syncopated compressions. New patients were being made from soldiers. Undressed. Showered. Issued blue pajamas and bathrobes. Shaved. Stripped of rings, dog tags, money, watches; photographs and letters slid out of their pockets; cigarettes stacked in drawers. Some of them would be debriefed again by an S2 and a shrink to discover their awareness. A glass of warm orange juice, a ham sandwich. "Go ahead. Eat the Saran Wrap, dummy." Then into the padded cubicles of the isolation ward—the Big House—for a period of close observation. They, too, would trickle down from the roof, slide through the sluice, with bits and pieces extracted, to the third level—to stand with their toes in silly white slippers along a pale-yellow line and to ask themselves questions never conceived of at the front. To ask if this yellow line was not somehow symbolic of another combat yet to come, even to ask if they shared something of its color. To wonder again and again, now swaying on their feet, if it was merely a slight flaw that had run out of control, been pushed unnaturally.

"But why me and not all the others?" mumbled Collins as he looked down the row of patients.

Or was it something else altogether. Maybe a freak coincidence. Many of those hovering above, just beginning the descent, were seventy-two hours out of Nam.

"Oh, yes, there would be questions."

"Collins. Collins. What's the problem with you? We're goin' out now; come on now. We're goin' to play softball. Now let's get that bedstand secured. Put your toothbrush here, in the second drawer, out of the way. Pull this tray out—see, Collins—and then put the utensils on this plastic plate and slide it in. It's a disinfector. Understand? Fine. Now come along." Hinckley was growing impatient.

"Where?"

"Oh, it's all right. You'll really enjoy this. Everybody has just a copacetic time playin' ball. You'll see. It's really pretty—"

"Where is everyone?"

"They're outside playin' ball."

It seemed peaceful and orderly to Collins, passing down the stairs to the second floor. As they rounded the corner he could hear music playing in the corridors. Music, for the first time in nearly two months.

"What strange sounds," he muttered.

"Yes," said Hinckley. "There's plenty of entertainment on this floor, and more on the first. TV, tapes, dances, outings to San Antonio, picnics, field trips to the Alamo . . . well, you name it, Collins."

"How about a subscription to *Stars and Stripes?*"

The music grew louder as the elevator doors parted in front of them. A stretcher bearing Colonel McCafferty emerged from the elevator, toes first, as pale as the sheet covering his body. He was breathing slowly in deep, nasal respirations. His temples were smeared with globs of white grease. It oozed down his head and dripped off his chin, making dark stains on the pillowcase. Then the stench of ammonia caught in Collins's nostrils as two corpsmen pivoted the stretcher and passed through the dim corridor. A black stick pitted with teeth marks hung from the colonel's mouth.

". . . they had him up to eleven hundred milliamps at four-tenths duration and he went into cardiac failure."

"Blew his damn vagus, eh?" replied the other.

"Yeah, but he's got a history of cardiac failure. . . ."

"Wasn't that Colonel McCafferty?" asked Collins of Hinckley.

"Yes, so it was," Hinckley replied, tightening his fingers around Collins's arm.

He led Collins through the main lobby, toward the massive doors with black rods running top to bottom. On either side stood a guard in double-laced boots. Forty-fives in black holsters, the brass of their rank twinkling in the bright sunlight, and two maroon letters on their white helmets—MP—the tailor's horse and sword on their sleeves: the Crazy Horse, First Air Cavalry. As Hinckley and Collins came closer, the two guards moved like figures on a mechanical clock to open the doors.

"Cuckoo. Cuck-koo. Cuck-koo."

"Shut up, Collins. You'll loose your teeth pullin' that," said Hinckley, glancing up at the black MP.

"Pulling what?"

"Careful now. Watch your step." Hinckley's voice boomed in

Collins's ear. His body shivered from the radical temperature change as he struggled to open his eyes against the bright sunlight. Bits and pieces of the surroundings flicked into focus as though projected on a kinescope.

"Over here, Collins."

The familiar sounds of a baseball team at bat grew louder as they approached the backstop. Three sections of chain link curved skyward like an enormous oyster shell. The steel mesh carved the field into thousands of diamond-shaped blue-green fragments.

Specialist Barrett turned around to greet them as they came to the batters' bench. Hinckley loosened his grip and wiped his forehead with the back of his hand.

"Oh, good!" yelled Barrett with childlike enthusiasm. "Can he play?"

"Sure. He can play," answered Hinckley in Collins's behalf.

"Great. He can stand in for McCafferty. I doubt he'll make it for this game."

"Roger on that," said Hinckley abruptly. "He went into a CF on the table. But he'll be O.K. in a couple of days."

"Well, he usually plays center field. That's right in the middle, Collins, so . . . what do you say? Want to play the field?"

"Sure. Sure, he'll play center, won't you?" Collins nodded passively to Hinckley's usurpation of slow tongues.

"Hey! White Tornado! You gonna pitch or play goddamn Florence Nightingale all fucking day? For Christ's sake," yelled Sergeant Wright from the field.

"O.K., Collins, take a seat on the bench. You'll bat eighth, then," said Barrett, hurrying back to the mound.

Collins walked in front of the bench, stepping through a pile of mitts with "BAMC-CP US GOVT PROPERTY" burned black into the wrist straps. Both batter seven and batter nine were fast asleep.

Collins sat on the grass by the mound of bats. Adirondack. Louisville Slugger.

CRACK

Someone managed to hit the ball. But the batter remained motionless at home plate, frightened by the shouts and obscenities. Then he began to run for first, still clutching the bat. He bore down on Williams, who was shouting to center field to get the ball to first. But the batter dodged Williams on first, cut across in front of Barrett at the mound, and slid into third. The center fielder threw the ball to Williams, and Williams fired it to the third baseman, but after the batter had begun running back to first. The third baseman chucked the ball back to Williams, but it sailed over his reach, and the runner slid headlong into first.

When the dust cleared, the batter was perched on the bag, knees drawn up against his chest and both arms locked around his legs, his face registering indifference.

"Hey, Barrett! This turkey won't move for shit," screamed Williams, aiming his mitt at the body beneath him. The batter refused to move a muscle, or to do anything but sit there safe and sound at first. Williams threw his mitt and ball at the runner.

Hinckley carried out another base and set it to the left of the real one. He calmed Williams by picking up his glove and the ball and explaining that runners would bypass the regular base and use this other one. Williams shrugged his shoulders and said, "What the fuck difference does it make in this bullshit game anyway? FTA all the way!"

"You're out!" yelled umpire Hinckley, calling a third strike.

"You wanna make somethin' outa it, Hinckley? You asshole," belched Franklin. He outweighed the neuro-psych specialist by a hundred pounds. Franklin's bathrobe had separated along the seams around his shoulders and up the midline of his back, which gave him the appearance of Popeye moments after he had swallowed his spinach. Franklin held the bat high up on his shoulder and then waved it in Hinckley's face like a stick. The umpire backed away from Franklin until he was against the backstop.

"Now, that could have been a ball, I suppose. I'm sure. So go ahead an' swing at a few more, Franklin. Everythin's copacetic. Take it easy now, Franklin. Easy does it! Franklin!"

"Ya know, Hinckley, you look like a fuckin' gook in that black thing. You oughta be more careful goin' around here like that. You could get yourself killed like that, especially with that mouth of yours. . . ." Franklin brought the bat off his shoulder and turned around for another pitch from Barrett, who was coming off the mound to help Hinckley.

"Get back there an' pitch, you stiff!"

He swung clumsily at four more balls, and then threw his bat against the backstop, missing Hinckley's skull by a foot.

Collins managed to hit a slow pitch toward Sailor in center field. Sailor did a good job of cutting off the ball. So good in contrast to the others that Collins slowed down en route to first to watch him scoop up the ball and throw it in a powerful line.

Suddenly Collins's legs felt heavy and numb. He moved in slow motion. Everything seemed to be slowing down. Very slow. And then the ball beat him to the base. Williams held out the evidence between them.

"You're out, man. Might as well just turn 'round an' head back ta where ya came from. You run like a papa-san. And you a medic? I sure as Christ wouldn't want you in my squad. You, a lineman?"

"Alpha team at bat! All you sleepers hit the turf," shouted Barrett.

The Professor came in from second base and handed Collins his glove.

"They really ought to televise these spectacles," he said, sitting on the bench. "They could show it after the *Wide World of War*— you know, equal time." He was pale and looked dissipated rather than exhausted. "I'll be glad when all this is over one way or the other," he said quietly. "One way or the other. I don't care anymore."

The first batter seemed a long way off to Collins when he reached center field and turned around. He looked out over the well-kept, lush grounds of the psychiatric compound. From center field the diamond appeared filleted in strips of green and red, the grass and clay alternating in bands from the backstop to the outer fringes of the field.

Surrounding the perimeter of the grounds were trees, shrubs, and flowers. Most were bright in their blossoming, partially hiding the chain-link fences. And behind the field, a rolling expanse of grass and pine trees dotted with redwood picnic tables. And two narrow roads, just wide enough for one truck to carry provisions into the facility: food from the main commissary, linen and uniforms from central exchange, and sometimes a drab Army hearse.

The sudden sharp pulsations of a chopper assailed the air. A red-and-white medevac swooped in over the ball field and landed on the roof of Chambers. Its rotor wash spun pebbles and flakes of tar over the edge. The debris pelted patients and staff sitting behind the third base line. One patient held out his hand, thinking it had begun to rain.

The side panel of the skinship slid open. Two medics leaped from the belly and pulled out two in-trans stretchers. A magazine tumbled off one stretcher and plummeted into the bushes behind third base. And then two more corpsmen. Two more stretchers. An officer. A Navy doctor. Then an Intelligence escort with an attaché case. Crouching, they ran along the edge of the roof and disappeared. Then a trooper in torn fatigues, his head in bandages. Then an Army colonel. The colonel turned back and nodded to the pilot. The chopper banked off the roof in a cloud of whirling black vapor and vanished.

Silence, except for the screeches of the cicadas, tuned by some phantom medicine man to a mocking shrill. A blue landing light tumbled off the roof, fell into the trees, and cracked in half as it hit the ground.

CRACK

Another hit. The right fielder ran backward to follow a high fly and fell over. The ball ricocheted off his leg and rolled toward Collins. He bent down to retrieve it. The grass blurred from green to gray to orange.

Blood slammed into his skull. He closed his eyes and heaved the ball with all his strength. Then opened them to follow the ball as it soared into a shifting gray cloud. Watching this nebulous form change shape brought tears down his face, salt to his lips.

The gray cloud faded into a yellow radiance, a brilliance encircling a form, with shafts of colored light like the reflections of an eye in a head in a halo. His eyes narrowed. They pierced through the cloud, layer beyond layer, as though he were teasing apart mesentery. Deeper and deeper he pried into the matter. Outlines shifted. More tissues undulated in a fuzziness. It became nearly human. Nearly alive again. . . . "There is no heart for Sergeant Back Again!"

". . . Collins. Collins," said Nieland, shaking Collins by the arm. "That's more like it. Heat got you out there. It does that sometimes. Time to slip an I.V. on you now. A bit of sugar and H-two-O. You know the routine. Five percent dextrose. Just lie back and relax now. O.K.? There. I'll be right next door. My office adjoins this room, if you need me," he said quietly. "And then we'll talk about this blackout."

Collins regained consciousness in a cool, softly lit room. Pale-blue curtains were pulled across the window behind his head. The bars were silhouetted through the material and reflected on the ceiling.

He recalled the isolation unit two floors above. There the window was too high up the wall for you to see anything. In the iso bin there

101

was a small white toilet with a curtain for a screen. But the aides could see the toilet through the tiny window in the door. On the floor was wall-to-wall carpeting measuring about eight feet by ten. A wicker chair in the corner. And a small mattress. There was no metal, no doorknobs or fastenings. It was quiet. So quiet that Collins heard only his own breathing. After a while he thought he was the only thing left alive, nearly alive, floating vague and formless in some unfamiliar cell of soiled thought. He remembered the time when he first caught a glimpse of his face in the shallow washbowl.

He was shocked at meeting another person in his room eye to eye. Then he recognized it as his own face and laughed until he recalled the visage of a decomposing VC lying face up in a swamp in the Delta. Most of his face had turned to mud, but Collins fleshed out the contour of a head.

He turned now, trying to look out the window, radiant with sunlight, but his arm taped to the I.V. board restrained him. Collins felt himself to be an ecesic organism, transported from a bloody jungle to the subtle maneuvers of his own struggle for survival.

"What happened? . . . That's a question for a drowning man. But the pact. The pact. Maybe Pollard's right: we need a reason to go home again."

Collins envisioned the Professor standing straight and tall in a coat and tie, lecturing on Asian history. The classroom and the bright-eyed students begin to revolve. The Professor is mortified by this and tries to stop the confusion, until he, too, is pulled into the vertiginousness. And then the Professor emerges alone, in fatigues, floating on his back and fighting the current, struggling with all his might against a mighty stream. His fatigues are ripped from his body and he disappears under the foaming suck of swirling water. He's suddenly tossed up for a moment, crying out something in Vietnamese, only to drown again, his corpse thrown down the current like the others.

"How are you doing now?" asked Nieland, looking in on Collins.

"How far along am I?"

"Oh, I think we can send you back up to the ward in another hour or so."

Nieland closed the connecting door behind him as he returned to his office. Shuffling papers, drawers opened and shut, then Collins heard a voice, but not the psychiatrist's. It began to speak abruptly, garbled at first, the volume rising and falling: ". . . regarding his condition . . . evacuated Saigon 3 February. Request received from Major T. L. Penderspot, Fort Sam BAMC, 12 March. Report by Sergeant Eugene Ross. . . ."

Then the strange voice stopped. More papers were jostled. The impact of a stapler. And a loud knock on the outer door to Nieland's office.

"Edward, come in, please. Right on time. Here, sit down. Yes. Lieutenant Cummings spoke to your wife a short time ago and Carol—it's Carol, isn't it?—was overjoyed to hear that she can see you soon. And I'm hopeful that all will run smoothly this afternoon so you can be dropped to the ground floor according to schedule."

"I don't kn now what to exp p pect now. I mean I I've changed. We've changed. I wo wonder wh what we'll do now."

"Well, you—"

"And I know ow we've chch chan ged."

"O.K. But this is a very real everyday sort of problem. And because you can now consider this, isn't that indicative that you've already made substantial progress? You're only twenty-three. You've been married just over four years. You've been in the service two years and three months. Eight months in Nam and two and a half right here. Correct? Well, sure, things have changed, for you especially. You've begun to take control of things and be responsible for your own actions and decisions. You've often told me you want to go back to school when you get out. That's taking affirmative action. You have a new chance to do those things now. But you've got to show the board that you're aware, that you care, and that you're trying. And you know that as much as I would like to help you all the way, I constitute only one vote out of five.

"And, Eddie," he continued in a lowered voice, "I don't have to tell you—you've been here long enough to know what happens to those who aren't able to walk out of here on their own. They rot in some VA asylum and it's NCB—No Coming Back. But remember, Eddie, how far you've come, and especially your work with Captain Peters in the language lab. That's significant progress.

"I know what you're really worried about. The unknown of what's out there and if you'll be able to cope with it. The fear. Another breakdown, more aphasia, the nightmares, the guilt of killing something innocent, and—"

"I I sssaid."

"Wait a minute, Eddie. These are the facts. Facts. When you

snapped in the field, there were numerous causes. We already know what the major causes were; we've been over that many times. But finally there comes a time to put even all that behind you and get on with the business of living—for better or for worse. I don't mean that you could ever turn your back on the past and pretend it never happened, no, but rather to accept it and build from there."

"I I undersssstand that. I know wwwhat you mean. But I don't feel llllike the sssame perss s person. Iss because of the ss stuttering. Why does it still happen?"

"I've gone over that with Captain Peters and I trust his findings. In fact, I based my whole approach to your problem on his early diagnosis. He feels that since your reflexes, your vocabulary, your grammar, and, most important, your phrasing and intonation, are all in fine working order, the problem is really your unclear attitude as to whether you want to participate in the real world and to what degree. What Peters has been trying to prove is that there is absolutely nothing wrong with you organically. The skull fracture you received on the field had no effect on your nervous system. Dr. Penderspot originally assumed that there was a lesion or pressure spot affecting your speech centers in the brain. That assumption proved false. In essence, you stutter because some protective device in you wants you to stutter. Why? Well, I feel that the conscious impediments to your normal articulation—your speech—remove you slightly . . . well, they excuse you from the responsibilities and pressures of being normal in the cold, cruel world. Peters said that you stutter much more when direct demands are put upon you, or when something causes you to associate with past experiences. The stuttering permits you to bridge back and forth between the regressive infantile retreat and the more dominant part of you, which is mature, normal, and healthy. Is all that clear?"

"Yes, it is. I sssee.   But even www when I try to control it it dd d doesn't w wo work."

"Well, that's probably because you're overconscious of it. I've heard you talk to other patients and even to me with absolute ease."

"I know."

"O.K. Now, Eddie, I want you to hear this tape recording. It's going to take you back to—ah—let's see: to the night of February 2. We've been through some of this before. Now you'll hear your buddy, Ross, give his own account of what happened to you that night. Remember, Eddie, that I couldn't possibly have played it for you until now. You simply wouldn't have accepted it, and chances are that it would have driven you deeper into withdrawal. So deep that maybe you'd never have come out again. I think you'll understand what I've been trying to do after you hear this. If you want me to stop it at any time, just say so. O.K.?"

"O.K."

"Here goes. . . ."

". . . was the mission. Sergeant Sailor and I had served over sixty tricks together."

"All right, Sergeant, let's hear your observations."

"Yes, sir. Well, the perimeter had to be established in the night. This was pretty unusual and very difficult for us. Pitch black, with a high wind. Even if your buddy was five feet from you . . . well, you were alone. You'd have to shout to be heard and then listen through the wind for a reply. It was so damned dark at times. We were all pretty spooked. Recon had established a VC outpost at five to seven hundred meters. We moved up in alternating flanks, carefully controlled so we wouldn't shoot each other in the back, like what had happened last week in HoBo. Remember?

"Then there was this clearing. And there was lots of debris around, you could feel it underfoot. Like walking through a dump after it had been 'dozed for the day. Heaps of stuff all around. We halted, crouched, and waited.

"The rains finally came. They'd been threatening for days. The rains and the high, gusty winds had made everyone nervous and jumpy. Then the signal came down the line: Recon by fire after the looie fires Primo commencing at either end of flank working toward center. We waited, we waited soaking wet, the trees to our rear thrashing about and leaves flying around.

"Sailor was to my left, the last man out at the extreme left flank. A burst of tracers from the center cut through the darkness and sheets of rain. Sailor got up off the ground, squatted, and ripped. A few seconds later, the whole battalion on line had opened up. A second stream of tracers and we ceased, except for the usual H-'n'-I rips.

"The night grew wilder, or maybe we just got jumpier and kind of frightened. Half the province knew where we were now and what we were up to, our location and strength. I was thinking about that when I suddenly felt this cold hand on my own and jumped back. It was Sailor, belly-crawled in from the periphery.

"An ugly, dirty orange glow flickered through the dense clouds streaming overhead. It blew harder and harder; then branches started blowing across us, sometimes hitting us from behind like your back was being clawed at by some monster.

" 'I'd rather face this fuckin' storm head-on than have my back to it,' said Eddie. 'Christ, it's wild. Who the hell thought this up?'

" 'Well, who do you think?' I coughed out a laugh. 'The I-'n'-I boys back there playing cards and just gettin' ready to turn in for a nice rest—who the hell else?' or something like that.

"By now we were really soaked and shivering. And then came the second round of tracers and we opened up again, but only for a short burst. No return. No noise—as if we could have heard anything anyway, sir. Word came down to advance the left flank fifty meters. We moved out, very slowly, and pulled toward the axis. Eddie and I stayed very tight. We didn't go all the way out—Christ, with the whole other flank with their muzzles at our back? We hit the ground and—weird—it was warm!

" 'What the hell is this?' I remember saying as Eddie pushed back some debris and there were glowing coals in the ground, smoldering.

" 'Look at this!' yelled Eddie.

" 'Cover that shit up, you idiot. You wanna get us killed?' I said.

"Eddie covered the glowing earth. Like we were standing on this thin crust over Hell, and the ground was goddamn hot.

" 'But this was supposed to be a virgin take,' he said, panicky. 'Supposed to be all secret, supposed to be that no one had ever been this far to the west before, no one was supposed to be even near Cambodia.'

"And then it was obvious, sir. A village must have been burned out and apparently covered with earth to make it look, by night at least, that nothing but an open field of some sort was there. You could faintly smell gasoline.

" 'There were hootches here not more than a few hours ago. The Cong knows the whole damn thing,' I said to Eddie. He nodded his head in agreement.

"And then another burst of tracer and then—it was odd—only sporadic firing here and there. So the others felt their asses grow warm too, I thought to myself, and nobody's gonna be fool enough to give their positions away this close.

"And then all hell broke loose. We were surrounded to the right

106

and center. The VC were obviously there for some time. Sappers were trying to break the right flank. Eddie and I pulled back toward the center. We were running crouched over and suddenly Eddie just disappeared. I lay flat and called out—but no use. And then a white illuminary went up and it seemed that the whole sky was convulsed in one huge lightning bolt. The high winds made it flicker and tumble, the clouds covered it for a few seconds, and the rain made it kinda throb. But it was bright for a second in the wind and I rolled on my side to see if I could see Eddie. I could just catch a glimpse of someone—no doubt Eddie, I thought—come running out of the scrub very fast and fall over something on the ground which seemed to jump or twitch, or something strange. It went black again, but from that same place I heard Eddie scream something, followed by a long sixteen burst and then some sporadic bursts. The VC, of course, began pumping it into that area and I was pinned.

"And that was it, sir. We moved against Charlie, broke part of his main force, and they dispersed—disappeared. As soon as I could, I made my way back to the outskirts of what had been a hamlet at co-ord 186-43—right about here, sir—and there I found him—Eddie—in the gray light. Just before dawn. It was really strange. I was tired and wet and was tromping throught all this crap: pottery, a cane, little mounds of rice, and cloth, and shit. I saw the limb of a kid, I suppose, sticking out of the ground. I mean, Christ, it was a sloshy, shitting, stinking mess. And we'd lost about half the initial force. It sucked.

"And then when I lifted my eyes, there was this really incredible patch of green, low-cut brush, full of dew and glistening. It was like a little untouched mound. And there was Eddie. Partly naked, covered with all kinds of crap. His face was black and bloody. And his arm was around the head of this damn water buffalo—like this. The buffalo had been blown to hell, with gore strewn all over the place in bright, shiny red—I mean really blown apart. It was on its side, its belly faced to the right of where our line had first been. That is, the buff had his belly exposed toward the VC flank and had taken all their lead. But its back, along the spine, had been ripped up in a few neat lines. And Eddie was laying out flat parallel to the buff's back with his hand draped over the carcass's neck and head. It was the strangeness and the color, I guess, the surprise, the clean-looking scene in that light—I guess that's why I didn't puke.

"I knelt down by Eddie's head and carefully rolled him back. He was still alive, but he sure looked bad. He began groaning in these long groans—'OOOOhhhh nnnnoooo'—like that, over and over again. I tried to talk to him, but he was in a stupor. A lineman came over and called for a stretch. I tried to move Eddie, but he clung to the buff. Suddenly, off to the rear, the weird scene was shattered by forty-five rounds and a few sixteen rips. They were shootin' the prisoners and the VC wounded. That startled Eddie into a frightened sort of behavior. He went into this convulsion and twitched. And then wrapped his arms even tighter around the buff's neck and moaned. Stripes of flesh uncovered by rivulets of rain made him look like he'd been squeezed up out of the earth.

" 'Eddie, Eddie.' He looked up at me almost suspiciously. 'Eddie,' I said calmly, 'it's all over now. It's all over. Now, come on, Eddie, there's no point in this. Everything's O.K.'

"His face grew a sickly white, and he looked like a little child. And he stuttered, in a whisper—I had to bend over to hear him:

" 'But does *everything*—must it all—does everything—must everything be touched?' and he stared blankly at that goddamn bull and yanked at it like an overstuffed animal that he was too little to set back on its feet. I mean, it was weird. The medic and I looked at each other and I knew we were thinking the same thing, although neither of us would have ever said anything there. But Eddie's remark hit home in a strange way.

"I don't know, sir—you asked me to describe it as I felt it. I know it sounds kinda funny, but I'm tellin' you how it felt. It was like Eddie had reminded us of who we really were, or had been, and it hurt. Goddamn it, sir, I would never have mentioned any of this to anyone, but it was cruel, and sickening."

"And then what, Sergeant?"

"Well, sir, I grabbed Eddie by the arm and he kept moaning, 'OOOOhhhh nnnnoooo.' And I said, 'Eddie, come on now,' and the medic took one arm and I had to twist Eddie's arm off the buff, and we dragged him onto the stretcher. And he like snapped out of it for a second and extended his arms like he wanted to embrace that gory animal once more. And then he fell back on the stretcher. And that was it. He just moaned and cried and never seemed to regain consciousness. And I helped them put him on the medevac and that's the last I saw of him."

108

"O.K., Sergeant. Thank you very much. I'll send this tape right off. . . . This is Colonel Regins—"

"Sir, excuse me, but do you know anything about him?"

"Only that he's in the States, in Texas, at the mental hospital there. The shrinks RQ'ed for close-up information and what I think you just reported should present a fine picture."

"Yes, sir, I hope so. . . . You know, it must have been that buff he fell over and Eddie thinking it was a VC or something must have ripped it up the back, and then he probably realized what it was. Saved his life, I bet."

"Yes, Sergeant. Thank you. This is Colonel Re . . ."

Nieland stopped the voices on the tape recorder, leaving Collins breathless, his muscles tense in expectation of some secret revelation about to be made in the next room. But the revelation did not take place in Nieland's office: rather, it was Collins who felt himself undergoing a sensational transformation. He was feeling again. He felt Sailor crying in the next room as his own eyes filled with tears. He knew then that he was a casualty himself.

". . . just part of what's to be faced, Eddie. That's just part of it," said Nieland slowly. "Look at it, Eddie. You're at a point now where we can talk about these things, don't you see? You have your choice now. Most of these men in here—these ghosts of men—have no choice; at least, not the choice you have. You fought for your country—now to hell with the country. Fight for yourself.

"O.K., Eddie. When we meet upstairs, you're gonna be on your own. I'll play the tape, they'll ask you the usual questions. Just keep cool, calm, and collected."

CHAPTER **10**

". . . morning and get up! Good morning and get up! Today is Saturday, 23 May 1970. The wind is out of the southeast at five to ten mph. The temperature at Lackland is seventy-two degrees. Good morning and *get up!*

"This morning is linen exchange and general police and scrub. Strip your bunks. And the pillowcases. But *not* the bedspread. GI the tops of your bedstands. Got it? Good morning and *get up!*

"Let's go. Let's go. Chop-chop. Good morning and *get the hell outa bed!* Rodriguez and Alexander, gather up the linen and stack it in front of the control room. Pollard and Williams, issue two sheets and *one*—got that, Captain, *one*—pillowcase to each of your compatriots. And, men," Hinckley continued in his snotty whine, "think about what you're doing. O.K.? Remember that you have to be able to get into them after you make 'em. So no Chinese boxes this time. O.K.?

"Parker, you mop that half of the barracks, and Wright, you do the other half. The rest of you *line up* for watering *after* you've made your bunks and policed your areas. Specialist Barrett will see that you are watered and Specialist Minor will assist your shaving. Those of you on Thorazine: Alexander, Baker, Cochran, Courtman, Forsyth, Jameson, Kimmell, McCafferty, Mitchell, Stockton, Summerlin, Tylee, and Wells—oh, yes, and Millsaps. Remember, don't drink any water while you're being watered.

"O.K. Let's go. R 'n' R is terminated. Lieutenant Cummings will have the EST roster ready after watering. And, gentlemen, we have an inspection this A.M. from Brooke headquarters. So make it good. . . ."

After they had finished struggling to make their bunks, a large detachment of patients assembled by the main door. Minor, the new NP specialist, had the ward roster. Barrett was standing next to him, reading each patient's name off the list and then pointing him out, to familiarize Minor with the ward residents. As Barrett pointed to each ex-soldier, Minor peered out of the glass box with sleepy brown eyes. His mustache vibrated on his protruding lips. It looked as if he was sneering at the patients, but the truth was that he was frightened to death. Minor visibly spooked when Colonel McCafferty, "recovered" from his recent treatment, pissed his pants. The other patients formed a circle around the confused "lifer" and began shouting.

"War's still going on," said the Professor, as he sauntered over to Collins, who was standing to one side of the control station. The yellow lines running the length of the ward created the illusion that they were standing on a highway. Suddenly something squirmed onto the surface of the far end of the room. Parker was back there, jabbing his mop against the side of the creature's face and then whacking it in the ribs. An echo flashed through Collins's mind— the sound of a grunt beating a mama-san with his rifle butt.

"Do you know Gator's story?" asked the Professor, who was watching the scene. "His real name is—or was—Allan Gilliland. We served together, for a time, in the Fifth Battalion, Sixtieth Infantry. Ha! Ridiculous nonsense. He was out on an S 'n' D maneuver one morning during the height of the monsoon season. Just southeast of the Michelin rubber plantation in Dau Tieng. Know the area? He was a self-appointed point man, nicknamed Crazy Legs because he trampled through minefields and never hit one. He was working arm in arm with a Kit Carson. They were fired on. The squad hit the ground and elbowed their way to safety behind those weird ficus trees. It was a VC hit-and-run ambush situation. As I recall, only the scout was killed and the radioman shot up. But when the team regrouped after a while, and found the scout and attended the

RTO, Gilliland had failed to surface from out of the brush. A quick search was ordered, and he was found—uncovered—still crawling, a sort of horizontal brachiation, you know, slowly, through a thick marsh. His head swinging from side to side like this—like a lizard —as he slithered through the slime and mud. The search party was bewildered—I mean, precisely trapped between tears of horror and hilarity, to use a phrase once put to me—as the monster covered with mud and slime made his way slowly onward toward Cambodia."

The Professor's head was still swinging back and forth as he finished talking, when suddenly he snapped out of his calm and reflective state and charged into the middle of the ward.

"Chronic newtation," the Professor pronounced over the undulating form. "Classic case of deformation of character, wouldn't you say? Ha ha, ha ha. And here we can see—ah, yes, just use your primal imagination—a vestige, the missing link! Here unchained for our observation. Hahahahaha. Oh, yes, brilliant! Here's how we came about, boys—one if by tree, two if by sea. Get 'em, Gator. Get the Cong!

"The forest primeval. By the shores of Gitche Gumee. Crawl on, devoted servant! Please add here"—the Professor pointed at the ceiling, to the imaginary heaven—"a little C-H-O-N. And a zap! A zap of juice!" His voice grew angry. "Doctor! Doctor! If you shock the shit out of him, you just might get him to swing in the trees. Zap-zap-zap-zap! Straighten up! Throw back your shoulders! Throw out your chest! Pull in that gut! Evolve yourself, my boy."

A spark of recognition reflected in Gilliland's eyes. He twisted his body to raise himself up on his elbows. He swung his head from side to side in pain.

"For Christ's sake! Why don't you knock it off for once, Pollard. Get over by the door now!" shouted Hinckley. "Why don't you go read your book, or do something constructive for a change?"

Heads swung back to the door. Turner, his eyes as big as silver dollars, said, "We're goin' out. Hey, we're gettin' out!" And so they did. Like a herd of goats, they bumbled into a large, tiled room. The lavatory looked like an operating room laid out for surgery. Towels, electric razors, disinfectant, toothbrushes, plastic cups, bars of soap, combs, and containers of mouthwash were arranged in rank-and-file order.

The patients were divided into four groups. The first to be "wa-

112

tered," or showered; the second for shaving; the third for "dispensing with bodily demands"; and the fourth for oral hygiene. "Rotate. Let's hurry it up. . . . Come on, Tylee, flush it. There's plenty more where that came from. Rotate!" The patients did their best to slow down the process, since besides eating, this was the only "normal" routine they knew. "Rotate." The Professor moved toward the oral-care line, sleeving tears from his eyes. He was an ashen white. "Rotate."

Then an issue of pajamas and striped robes, and into the medication line-up. Lieutenant Cummings's face beamed from behind the drug caddy. And Hinckley was smiling too, with his pitcher of water and his paper cups. He scrutinized each patient's Adam's apple to ensure that the pills had been swallowed, that the patient hadn't faked taking them, spit them out, or concealed them in his cheeks. Hinckley always caught a few. The Professor refused to accept anything. "No, Lieutenant. You take them. I've had enough. It's all over. No more." Surprisingly, she didn't argue with him. Even Hinckley remained silent and handed the cup of water he had poured for the Professor to Parker. Collins got his flat blue pills with "SK&F" in white lettering.

"Chow," pronounced Hinckley, standing in front of the main door. The patients lined up for breakfast, except those who were singled out by Cummings for ECT. As she read off the names, Collins leaned over to Williams and asked him what "ECT" meant.

"Why, man, you don't know? That's the zapper. You know—the blitz of the brain. Wow! Shock therapy, man. Stay away from that shit. If you ever end up with wires in your head, forget it. You aren't coming back nohow. You go in the nonreturnable bin."

Three aides escorted the others down to the mess hall. They looked out on the volleyball nets swaying in the breeze, the pavement wet from last night's rain. The clean and orderly surroundings created a secure feeling. Everything was being attended to; ordinary people were going about their work, people who had no involvement in the war and little interest in it.

The smell of oatmeal and coffee drew the patients into a long line next to the trays. The three specialists assisted those men too spaced out to handle their trays or maneuver them from counter to table. Some patients turned pale at the sight of food. Thorazine burps contaminated the air.

But the half-dozen old ladies behind the steaming glass were very patient. They smiled and joked about their hairnets. Nothing disturbed their mechanical routine, not even the remarks made by the patients. "Hey, do you know who escaped from here last night? No? Well, it's a secret, but I'll tell you. A psychotic named Dick Nixon —he jumped the fence. Yeah, that's right!" "What ya doing tonight? . . . Good. I'll meet ya in the morgue at eight o'clock. Hey. Don't get me wrong. I ain't no weirdo like these other stiffs." "You remind me of my mother. Can I call you Elsie?" And an outrageous barrage of catcalls.

They never batted an eye, these old ladies. They kept nodding yes to everything, smiling.

The women liked Rodriguez. He smiled and twirled a few times and took his food like a child opening a birthday present. He never said a word, but all the ladies had grown attached to him. They filled his plate with more food than they gave any of the others. The lady doling out the toast took pains to see that his was hot but not burned. Her name was Miss Simms and she checked both sides. And Miss Chupete, a Chicano like Rodriguez, handed him an orange juice from the farthest corner of the ice-filled tray. She had saved the coldest one for him, and she stirred it before setting it on his tray. She smiled and said, "How's my little spinning top today?"

Millsaps, who had spent more time in isolation than any other patient currently on the third-floor ward, retained a violent contempt of anyone around him who revealed the slightest sense of happiness or pleasure. His dark, beady eyes were set close together under his wiry red eyebrows, giving him a menacing air. Rodriguez moved away from the counter with an unsuspecting, happy smile, which attracted Millsaps like a buzzard to carrion. His mouth closed in a twisted, evil little grin as he put his foot out into the aisle and tried to trip Rodriguez.

But Franklin, who had taken an immediate dislike to the puny redhead with the predatory eyes, had seen Millsaps extend his leg in Rodriguez's path. He jumped up from his chair, dashed over to Millsaps, and crushed his foot by jumping on it with all his weight. As Millsaps writhed in pain, the huge Franklin remained balanced on his ankle and calmly said:

"You do that again, sapper, an' I'll break both your legs. Assholes like you got my buddies killed by playin' games. You wanna play these games, you little red worm, you play 'em with me an' no one

114

else. I got boo-coo tricks too, fuckface, like putting this here fist right through your head. Don't forget that, jerkoff."

He stepped off Millsaps's foot and headed for the tray of plastic silverware. Rodriguez, who had paused to watch the amusing scene, seemed very impressed with Franklin's gymnastic finesse: balancing two hundred and forty pounds on the point of an ankle bone. He understood nothing of what had happened, nor why Franklin said what he had said, but Rodriguez knew he had found a kindred soul in the universe.

Collins sat with the Professor and Hinckley, who were discussing the probable fate of an officer who was recently dropped to the ground floor, soon to be discharged. Collins began eating his scrambled eggs and looked up at the two as they continued talking. But Hinckley grew silent and ignored the Professor's comments.

"We were just discussing a patient here," said Pollard, addressing Collins. "Hinckley and I have known him for some time, although under very different circumstances. They had him committed here for his war crimes, hoping that he could dodge a term in prison. I was just asking Hinckley if he thought Stan would get a Dishonorable 215 or a 215A, or whether the JAG office was going to deem him mentally competent to stand trial. I'm sure that's doubtful now, wouldn't you agree?" he asked, turning to Hinckley.

"Yes," replied Hinckley uneasily. So they ate in silence, staring at the other patients or gazing out at the volleyball court.

"What are you thinking about?" asked Pollard, looking over at Collins.

"What time is it?"

"Oh, let's see. It's about six fifty-five," Hinckley volunteered.

"Yes," said Collins. "I was thinking that if it was seven o'clock here then it would be about eight o'clock back East. Correct? . . . I was thinking about my father. He's probably just finishing his eggs too, and he'll be racing to make a tee-off time. Today is Saturday."

Nothing more was said. Hinckley began humming a few bars from Glen Campbell's "Galveston," but was abruptly silenced by the Professor's comment: "Are you crazy, Hinckley, or is it just my imagination?"

Doctors' rounds are not made on the weekends. But *la group* goes on according to schedule whether anyone has anything to say or not. So they sat in an arc in front of Lieutenant Cummings, dozing or lost in their own meanderings.

Questions, the same questions asked during previous sessions, were repeated again: "Why can't we get any mail?" "When can we send letters?" "When can I go back to Nam and get me some gooks?" "Why can't I have a newspaper?" "Are we winning this week, or the VC?" "Where do you get laid around here?"

"Yeah, how come we gots to sit around all day lookin' at each other? Where the hell is the chicks at?"

Slowly a conversation of sorts formed. Few of the verbalized thoughts were completed, overridden as they were by clusters of outbursts focusing on women, or Nam, or both simultaneously.

The exchange became more antagonistic until Wright, who had never spoken in the group therapy sessions, took up a remark made by Williams about "how they turned you on so much you wanted to kill 'em."

"Yeah, yup. Damn it all, Williams. Roger on that," began Wright, so seriously that he was comical.

"Yup. Boy, you're right on to it. Jesus, don't they look just like dolls? Not like real humans at all. Just gook Raggedy Anns. And woe to you, brother, God help you if one of 'em gets to you—I mean, the one that really turns you on. . . . Too many contradictions. Hard to take. Hot stuff, right?

"Here's this doll working her way down the road, right?" Wright stared intently at the space between his hands as he sculptured a woman in midair. "Looks real fine, real fine. Thin. Black almond eyes. Nice tan body. Firm little tits, their nipples showing through her shirt, right? Right! Long black hair put up on her head with a bone pin. And hips. Oh, and legs! Everything in dyn-o-mite proportion. And a tailor-made ass. Great. Right? Roger!"

In the brief pause came catcalls and whistles. Imaginations began coloring Wright's erotic outline as a few of the less sedated patients grew erect in their chairs.

"Yeah! Nice, huh? You can dig it, right? And then she walks by you and you can see them soft thighs as her gown opens a crack. You can see 'em perfect as she goes by, round and tight. Right?"

Legs uncrossed and recrossed as some of the others turned their chairs to watch Wright unfold his sensual beauty. Bathrobes were pulled tighter across in front. The Professor smiled and nodded his head, as if to say, Keep going, Wright, keep going.

116

"And she'll walk by you and you know! you know you can get it
—uh?—and how good that'd feel. To hell with the goddamn gonor-
rhea. And nothing's in your way. But boy, has she got you by the
balls. And then, as your eyes are devouring those fine legs and ass
moving gracefully on down, and you know how nice that'd be—
right?—you've felt your body and you decide to follow her . . . she
stops. Why? And so you stop. Mmmmm. And then you get, like,
self-conscious—uh?—'cause maybe she's on to you moving in back
of her and maybe she's gonna let you catch up, and boy, you can
feel it coming! And then—"

"Oh, yeah. Oh, yeah. Do me. Do me," shouted Millsaps, sliding
back and forth in his chair, his eyes closed.

"And then—*pazoom*—the whammy! She pulls up her gown and
squats. Shits right there on the side of the road. A little pile of turds,
one turd laid over the other."

The whistles changed to boos and hisses.

"And then . . . and then," he said, raising his voice, "she takes
some paper or something outa her sack and wipes her ass. Or maybe
she doesn't. Like nothing ever happened. And all you got is an ache
down here—right? That, and this little pile of shit in front of you.
Groovy, uh?"

"Ahhh! You fuckin' jerkoff," cried out Millsaps.

He took one step toward Wright before he caught Franklin in the
corner of his eye as he, too, stood up.

"There's a lady in the room, shithead," said Franklin, barely able
to control himself. "Now sit down and shut your face or I'll turn you
back into a pile of shit." The Professor grinned from ear to ear.

"O.K. O.K.," said Wright, rising to his feet. He held his palm over
his head like a traffic cop. "I know. I know. But then you think so
they're a different culture and all that. You know, the Hanoi High
lecture. But goddamn it, it's a sacrilege no matter how you cut it.
Yeah? The beauty and the beast, O.K.? The woman and the pig, uh?
You can't help feeling this rancid disgust. A seed of contempt is
born there for women," continued Wright assertively. "For the
whole goddamn race, for that matter. For their womanhood in
general. That's part of the infection. Yeah, like where the germ of
the atrocities began. Yeah. Like the things I did over there. Your
respect and attraction to women is turned into this love-hate thing.
You know, like those dolls that wet themselves. I mean, that's O.K.
But a doll that shits herself. Woe. That's too much.

"I mean, what about Johnny Greenhorn Grunt, who's just come over and he's gonna stay clean-in-the-green and above it all, right? Yeah, you know what happens to the dude with a full clip whipping 'round his Mattel, the guy who hasn't been laid for months. God-damn dangerous dude. Trigger happy. He'll let go at anything."

"Mr. Wright. Mr. Wright," interrupted Lieutenant Cummings, raising a blue pencil. But Wright was off and running.

"So then you get that street shit, right? 'Hey, GI. GI, you want pussy? You want hole show? You want bang-bang, GI? You want . . .' Shit. O.K., so I've been around. Who hasn't? But Jesus Christ, if we're supposed to be the Police Force of the World and all that crap, just think of all the fourteen-year-olds screwed by us guys, the women raped and carved up. The whole thing's a buncha shit. Just like the turds that chick dropped in the road. That's real, isn't it? The higher the climb, the further the fall. Yeah?"

"Look unto the rock whence ye were hewn and to the hole of the pit whence ye were digged," inserted the Professor, but Wright didn't seem to hear him.

"Yeah. And their males—ha ha—absurd. Little mincing puppies. Emasculated paddy-stompers. I watched one father—breeder—just outside of Da Nang telling his son how to pimp out his sister, that the kid must get the Big Yen 'cause she wasn't getting enough for her snatch and lollipop blow jobs. I mean, shit, I'd just as soon rip up that asshole as a VC any day. And I have. Blow his fucking head right off. . . . What the hell are we supposed to be getting our asses shot off for!" he screamed out angrily. "We're out there ripping up Charlie Cong—right?—and we're getting wasted so the dude can make a shitload off his twelve-year-old? Christ, too much.

"And one of my buddies' mottoes was: 'Frighten 'em. Fuck 'em. Frag 'em. Forget 'em.' Man, I hope all the troopers coming back can forget 'em, 'cause if they can't they're gonna be breeding them-selves, infecting everyone over here with some incurable sickness. You follow? Yeah. Like a disease that eats away in his mind, all covered up, hidden. And then *whammo*—what he thought he left behind he's carried with him. Brother. And I think—"

"Mr. Wright! Mr. Wright!" Lieutenant Cummings broke in excit-edly.

"Yeah?"

"You used the words 'contradiction,' 'disease,' 'infecting,' and"—she peeked at her notes—"and 'sickness.' "

118

"So what?" snapped Wright, irritated with the interruption.

"I, for one, didn't quite follow you. You weren't referring to a tropical disease, were you?" she asked, trying to draw him out for the benefit of the other patients.

"Hell, no, Lieutenant," he said, growing impatient. "I'm talking about the kind of sickness you get by seeing and hearing and doing things that make your mind puke, not just your stomach. By being part of something you know inside is wrong. If you go doing things like killing people and you're not sure what you're doing is right, then you're playing Russian roulette with your sanity. And that's for life. . . ." Wright stopped and took a deep breath.

"Look, Lieutenant," he resumed, more calmly. "I didn't see much combat myself. I mostly worked in an operations chart room, computing how many leaves I could knock off a tree. But I knew these two guys real well—MPs who worked the north side of Saigon. They'd drive around at night and grab those little brats, those twelve-year-old pimps, and beat the shit out of 'em. Yeah. Like they were obsessed with getting rid of some disease, but they were getting infected themselves. They'd beat the brats unconscious, even killed a couple of 'em, and then they'd call an ambulance . . . so no one would think they'd done it, you know, like they'd just come upon these half-dead kids. And they hated those MPs, man, they scared the hell outa those kids. But there they'd be again a few days later, going after the buck just the same. And come on, their shithead breeders put 'em up to it, probably counted every penny, and wouldn't feed the kids unless they netted a hundred bucks a day.

"Now, what do you think those MPs are gonna be like when they get Stateside? Uh? How are they gonna explain themselves? How are they gonna look at kids back here? . . . We all brought home an infection. It'll be around for a long time. Ha. Just take a good look around this room," he said sadly. "Just look in the mirror."

Cummings did look around the room and was stunned at how pained and angry the faces in her group had become. She tried for a more positive topic:

"And now that you're back, Mr. Wright? Don't you feel relieved to be out of Vietnam?"

"When I got off the transport at Lackland," he began again, in a distant voice, "I couldn't even look at my wife. They let me see her for a few minutes. You know, a macadam reunion after sixteen months, and I couldn't even look at her. I had carried these images in my mind, see, in front of my eyes, yeah, like snapshots. Click-click, Kodak time. Right? And I couldn't shake them. They were like superimposed over her. All I saw was what I'd been seeing for so long. I saw her pulling up her skirt and shitting on the runway, or squatting to go through the garbage, or screwing for all the dudes in town, stashing up the money under her mattress. I couldn't shake it. Still can't. 'Cause maybe the possibility, given another time and place, is there for all women. And we for them. And I knew it. . . ."

It had become dangerously quiet in the room as Wright's voice blended with the hum of the air conditioner. Lieutenant Cummings felt the volatile tension as she tried to establish eye contact with just one patient—any one of them. No one looked up from the floor, except the Professor, who sat smiling at Lieutenant Cummings. She knew enough not to tangle with him. She decided that the best option was for her to take the lead and reestablish clinical parameters by explaining the purpose of group therapy. But her textbook words only made Wright angry.

"Yeah, I know. The open confessional. I took a few semesters of psychology. But you're wrong, Lieutenant. Because it's my problem. Not yours or yours or yours. It's all mine, to love, honor, and cherish till death do us . . . Right? You got it. I got to work this thing out for myself. The shrink says it's my guilt for my things with women over there, that I project—I think that's what he called it —my sickness onto my wife out of guilt. But it's not that simple, Lieutenant. Ask anyone here."

"Let me ask you this," she said, struggling to keep the discussion away from Vietnam and women. "Why did you share your experiences and feelings with the group now? What was it that prompted you to speak out today?" She smiled and brought her pencil down on her notebook.

"Yeah. That's right, Lieutenant. You better write this down, uh? . . . For one thing, I've decided to try and make some sense out of all this. Out of what happened to me. So maybe I can explain some of it. It's a promise I made."

"The pact, Collins. See. The pact. He's doing it," the Professor whispered in Collins's ear.

"And for another thing, boredom. We're sitting here jam-packed in, smelling each other's BO, and no one really says anything. And no one's gonna say much about themselves, particularly stranger to stranger."

"But you're not strangers, are you?" said Cummings, hopeful of pulling the group together here and now. Her face had a pretty red glow to it as she looked intently at Wright.

"Most of you have been through much the same thing. You probably have more in common than most groups of human beings," she encouraged sincerely. But somehow she struck Collins as too naïve to be able to know what she was doing, to understand the risks she was running by sitting so seductively in front of eighteen horny veterans.

"Yeah, sickening, isn't it. Quite a distinction," said Wright bitterly. "Maybe that's it. Maybe it's the commonness . . . the by-product of the Vietnam Extravaganza. And here we're reduced to —shit. So many cripples, behind bars, belittled by the Army, by ourselves, by the country we fought for. Right? And we freaked out. Well, we got what we deserved. Uh? Maybe we freaked out 'cause maybe we're still human."

"I wouldn't count on it," interjected the Professor.

Wright ignored his comment. "And so you expect us, 'cause we're sitting in front of you, to deal with ourselves openly and honestly. Come on, Lieutenant. What the hell do you expect? I don't care who you are. You open yourself up just a crack, drop your guard for a minute in here, or over there, and you're done for. That's right! Even you, Lieutenant. We look at you and you're a fool if you don't know—just know!—what's going through our heads. You know? But no one's gonna talk about it, except for a rare mention like this. You couldn't handle that yourself, Lieutenant. Right? And you expect us to expose our ugly shit problems? Don't be a fool."

"Bravo! Bravo!" shouted the Professor, leaping up from his chair. "Bravo! Bravo!" he repeated, clapping his hands at Wright's performance. He walked over toward Wright to congratulate him.

Corporal Hassley, who was no different on this, his eighty-fourth day of rehabilitation, than when he was admitted to Chambers Pavilion, rose unsteadily to his feet and dropped into a crouch. He extended his arms and suddenly began to shout in a barrage of different voices:

"Zebra Six. This is Bravo Black Dog. M-60 man's flipped out. I've got flames in the C-6 compartment. Rounds cookin' off. We're goin' down Co-ord A 44-60-510. Eleven twenty-six hours. Repeat: ACS at co-ord A 44-60-510. One unconscious. One wounded. One dead. One over the hill. This chopper's been croaked. Come back, Zebra Six.

"Bravo Black Dog. This is Zebra Six. Roger on that co-ord: Alpha double-four six-zip five-one-zip. Slip your ship to Alpha double-four five-eight five-zip-niner if you can. Come back, Black Dog. Bravo Black Dog. . . . Come back, Bravo Black Dog. . . . Charlie Red Fox, can you make a visual on Bravo Black Dog?

"Zebra Six. This is your Charlie Red Fox. Bravo Black Dog is on a skid going in for scrap at co-ord Alpha double-four five-niner five-zip-niner. We're closing in on VC at three-one-zip.

"Rusty Lion Four. This is Zebra Six. Commence your sweep. . . . Come back, Charlie Red Fox. . . .

"I got 'em, Ricky! I got them fuckers, Ricky. I got 'em for ya, boy! I got 'em."

Hassley was still screaming "I got 'em" at the top of his lungs, with his hands locked around the grips of his M-60 machine gun. His body shook rhythmically, absorbing the recoil. He ran full force, head on into the wall behind Lieutenant Cummings.

BLAM

He rebounded, swayed on his feet, and collapsed to the floor. There was a jagged gash across his forehead, blood streamed from his nose, and a broken tooth was embedded in his upper lip. Laid out cold.

"Oh, shit. Here goes. . . ."

"Now look what you've done!" screamed Wright at Pollard. "For Christ's sake!"

The Professor stood stunned halfway across the room. His torso and head faced Hassley, but his feet still pointed at Wright. His body looked as if it were being pulled in different directions. Then, as he moved toward Hassley, he stumbled and fell to the floor beside the unconscious corporal.

"I know. I know what I've done," he cried out, staring into Hassley's face. Pollard tried to speak again, but the only sounds he made were groans.

Lieutenant Cummings ran out of the room, leaving a trail of notes. Rodriguez sat in his chair, staring down at the ex-M-60 gunner. Blood ran from his forehead and mouth as Rodriguez brought his contorted face closer and closer to the wounds—so extreme was the Spinning Top's sense of another's lifelessness. Alexander wrapped his hands around the back of a chair and began to raise it over his head just as Hinckley dashed into the room, yelling orders to Minor:

". . . Central Control. STAT for any available MDs and PNs. STAT —Ward NP-6. Call the ER at Brooke. Use the white phone—0626. Get an ambulance!"

He spun around and very calmly said to Cummings, "Maybe you better move your session into the barracks while we attend to Hassley here."

Blood oozed from the corporal's scalp as Hinckley rotated his head. A line of glistening fascia parted his hair. As the crimson pool clotted, Collins felt the nausea again. A paralytic repetition of the same scene, same look, same feelings . . . the same sickness. Not the blood. Not the flesh.

"The sameness is the real sickness," he said.

Collins looked down at Captain Pollard, who was trying to talk to Corporal Hassley, M-60 man of gunship Bravo Black Dog. Collins felt it swell up. Coming out again. The feelings he had so carefully buried in the tomb of his soul. Now erupting. Again. Up and out. Graves quivering. Crosses tumbled askew off mounds of fresh earth laden with flowers. Coming back—up, out of the ground.

"But you're dead! You're dead!" he shouted.

They had been deactivated. He had done that well. Or so he thought.

"First, turn the head of the tension screw one quarter turn. No more than that. Second, place your hand on the fourth rib of the shaft. Third, depress the projecting trip-arm. Now this, gentlemen, is the heart of the Claymore mine."

"Condemn every living thing."

"Shut up, Collins! Now just shut up and get outa here! Move!" shouted Hinckley, pointing at the doorway. "Move!"

"It's all backing up again, like a seething sewer," he cried.

"Move," screamed Hinckley, about to go for Collins.

The faces and their exposed anatomy began to recede as Collins swayed into the long barracks. Four soldiers were huddled in a circle, loudly singing phrases from the "Ballad of the Green Berets."

"Fighting soldiers from the States . . .
These are men, America's best . . .

123

The brave men of the Green Berets.
Put silver wings on my son's chest."

The solos became grotesque improvisations of the song, with plays on "deranged Rangers," "kill a Commie for Christ," and "FTA all the way." Other patients joined in, mimicking old battlefield songs. The choruses resounded louder and louder. The gray marble structure seemed to shake as the well-known lyrics echoed through the building and across the court below. The tunes resurrected mutual pasts of boot camp and battlefield.

Collins wandered onto the deck. He looked at the three cantilevered decks directly across from his own, filled with patients from the other wards. They were staring across the court to the barred windows of 3-E. On the top two decks stood men in blue bathrobes. But the patients on the ground floor were wearing jeans and shorts. A few were holding tennis rackets, with towels around their necks. Their eyes widened in amazement, swept into the echoing remains of a past they were trying to forget.

"Airborne, Airborne, have you heard?
We're gonna jump from them big-ass birds.

"Went to Hanoi and took a course,
Came to Saigon to cop some horse.
Killed some Cong and got the clap,
Came back home but wanna go back.
All the frogs in the pond sing *reupp, reupp, reupp*
Ho Ho Ho-Chi-Minh
Did you think that you-could-win?

"Someone told me we were wrong,
But Uncle Sam said *Kill them Cong!*
Draft board man said It won't be long
Till you'll be singin' this song.

"Ho Ho Ho-Chi-Minh
Did you think that you-would-win?
Kill them Cong and get-their-kin.
Ho Ho Ho-Chi-Minh."

Collins watched the stunned expressions of the first-floorers. A few covered their ears with their hands, which reminded him of his own reaction that night when Pollard first proposed the pact; others

124

turned away and went back inside. The distance between the adjoining wings of the hospital seemed to increase as the asphalt court below became a deep chasm separating two states of being: those who had made it, and were about to go home; and those who might spend the rest of their lives in a VA mental ward. Gaps spread between the floors of the hospital, isolating one ward from the other, the patients set adrift, scattered in iron cages on a crimson sea choked with the bodies of young Americans.

> "Marched and jumped and did our drills
> So we'd be ready to score them kills.
> Captain Cool said Take that hill!
> But killin' Charlie takes a lot of skill.

> "Ho Ho Ho-Chi-Minh
> Did you think that you-could-win?
> Grab that gr'ade and pull-that-pin.
> Ho Ho Ho-Chi-Minh.

> "We crawled and ran to kill them Reds,
> An' fired-up all our lead:
> Sergeant Sam got shot in the head—
> We took that hill, though most are dead.

> "Ho Ho Ho-Chi-Minh
> Did you know that you-would-win?
> Doctor doctor, come-here-quick
> This ol' morphine 'bout to make me sick."

Collins raised his watering eyes to the blue sky, but his escape was blocked by the roofline. The cripples in their steel braces were drawn to the edge of the sun deck by the military medley. No obscenities were shouted, and nothing was tossed down from the roof. They were paralyzed again: shot through the ear by songs they hadn't heard since Nam.

The singing finally ceased. The screech of a solitary cicada fell through the quiet air. Collins closed his eyes and leaned into the fence. He poked his fingers through the links of chain as his knees buckled.

"You know," came the voice of the Professor from behind, "there isn't time for all this anymore. We've run out. The ninety-day endurance test asks too much of us."

125

He stopped speaking. The sun shone down from the east, burning off the misty haze. A breeze carried the smell of roses and freshly cut grass through the steel mesh. The giant magnolias swayed, their shiny leaves sparkling through the fog. Commands exchanged between runners and the pilot of a skinship echoed in the court. When the voices ceased and the chopper had banked off the roof, the Professor resumed.

"All existence is a tightrope. It's too delicate, though, don't you see? Too precarious. But we fabricated it and we must—"

"Fabricated what?" asked Collins.

"Ah, the myths, Collins. The myths we make of ourselves, of our world, which we so desperately hold on to at all costs. We acclaim the rights of the individual. We uphold the Christian ideal. We uphold the Brotherhood of Man. . . . We live by our myths, so we must die by them. And you don't have to be a corpse to be dead.

"But these myths, our myths, are the threads which hold our civilization together. Without them we would be nothing but animals. Those fine strands of belief spun in our consciousness are reflected in our flag, our sense of principles, our very souls. A culture is woven of these threads: a civilization becomes a bundle, a life line. It's there to save you if you can only say: I believe. But it's just too frail time and time again.

"And I sliced through one of those threads holding Hassley together!" stated the Professor vehemently. "It was an accident! A simple association: 'Bravo!' And snap! He *thought* he was getting better again. That he would soon go home. He was beginning to *believe* again. . . . What a barrage of impulses rocketed twelve thousand miles in that instant when I forced him to fly that last mission again. To fly into the wall with his gunship.

"What Wright said is true: I can't evade his indictment. Games, he said. Yes, it's a game now. Collins, I am a game. I can't differentiate between the actor and the act anymore: man and machine. One what I feel I should be, the other what I know I am. Both are me." He laughed for a while and then, moving closer, said:

"My time here, Collins, is nearly spent. They gave me ninety days to put my image back together again. Put the images back together again, Collins, if you can. Do it up like a high school yearbook. Pictures and sayings on glossy paper. . . ."

They glanced at the red-and-white van as it sped from the shipping dock beneath them.

126

"This is Major Penderspot. Get those gates open!" The voice came over the loudspeaker. The van wailed down the access road with its lights flashing, headed for the OR at Brooke. The Professor shook his head and was quiet for a while, as if bowing in prayer. Then he looked up.

"The disease I brought back wasn't the sort that Wright was talking about. Not that overt. Mine is substrate L for Ludicrous. It's the knowledge that there is no such thing as capital T truth. There are only masses of little truths, which can be contradictory, mutually exclusive, or can even obliterate each other.

"While at Berkeley, I ran across a book by the man who masterminded the defeat of the French forces at Dien Bien Phu. General Vo Nguyen Giap. The material is partially borrowed from Hitler, de Gaulle, and Che Guevara. . . . Be sure this goes into our yearbook, Collins. . . . But more interesting is this Giap himself. He was born just north of the present DMZ, up in Quang Binh province, in the village of An Xa, I think in 1912. I might be off a year or two—it's been a while now. But he was schooled at the Lycée Nationale in Hué. A bit ironic—or perhaps just coincidental?—that both Ngo Dinh Diem and, yes, Ho Chi Minh attended there too. Although Giap himself didn't meet Ho Chi Minh personally until 1941, at the Eighth Indochinese Communist Party meeting. Even more remarkable than the fact that these three attended the same school was the arrest of Giap in the fall of 1930 by the French Colonial Police. Giap was leading a student demonstration protesting the French-supervised militia troops. The French-led troops halted the peasant march—six thousand farmers who descended on the city of Nghia Hanh. Remarkable because it was to be Giap's own crack division, the Three-twenty-fifth, that was to crush another peasant revolt twenty-six years later in the very same city. The farmers were protesting the same issues—the arbitrary and harsh land-reform measures—this time imposed not by the French but by Hanoi. Add up the 'truths' in that one for yourself. That's one reason I went to OCS. Why I went into Intelligence. Interesting man, General Giap. A study in paradox.

"Another reason. I was a Kennedy kid. Believed, I thought, in what his goals for the world were. Believed that America had a greater share in—and a greater responsibility for—what the development of the world was to be. Follow? Even in the face of the war protests, in which I, too, participated, I understood both sides. But

127

underneath all the elaborate arguments for and against the war, something was missing. Nothing connected. Both factions had merely taken the mind of modern man and sliced it in half. Neither party had the whole consciousness any longer; all they had was the part that matched up with their Domino Theory or the give-peace-a-chance proposition: mutually exclusive. But the twentieth-century American can comprehend and feel both! No wonder, then, the whole thing was a botch—and a new being was created, the *Homo fissi.*"

"The what?" said Collins, turning to face Pollard.

"Who is he?" Pollard smiled. His face relaxed. He had found a possible student. "Don't you recognize yourself? . . . He's us. All of us. Anyone living in the past few years. . . . You still don't see, do you?"

Collins shook his head. "I would like to understand."

"It's simple. Think about it. It begins with that tendency we develop almost as soon as we have our five senses. That emotional, nearly instinctual predisposition toward living things. Some things we allow to live, encourage to live; others we feel obliged to kill— spiders, flies, rats, sharks. You know. I've come to define that tendency in every human being as unconscious selection. You understand? Later, with some maturity, comes a bizarre offshoot—neurotic selection, in which man either teaches himself or learns to select, to single out one particular living thing, and begins to kill or destroy that one living species. Like the Jews in Nazi Germany, the Indians and blacks in the United States, the Vietcong in Indo-Asia. And then comes that peculiar but common battlefield phenomenon —psychotic selection, in which the human has finally lost all ability to distinguish one living thing from another and begins, sporadically at first, killing *every living thing in sight,* his hatred for life is so intense. But it's still a selection of what's out there, since he rarely actually murders himself, at least not directly.

"We all go through the first stage. Anyone in the services, whether he fires a rifle, drops bombs, or lobs shells in from off the coast, knows the second. And some soldiers—many, in fact—have lived in the third plane. Colonel McCafferty has been there. Williams witnessed it. I read about it in an I-2 report—a routine Intelligence investigation. McCafferty had been the XO for operations in the Iron Triangle. He had lost a great number of men . . . for a lot of reasons, but some of the responsibility was his. The day prior to

128

his flip-out he had lost over half of his armored personnel carriers and most of the troops in them—seasoned men too. The tension between the command and the troops was apparently at the kindling point, perhaps beyond. The next morning, McCafferty called for a formation of his regiments. He walked out of his CP, looked into the faces of his men during inspection, pulled out his forty-five, and emptied the clip point-blank into the regiment before he was seized. Killed four men outright. Williams was in McCafferty's company, in formation that morning. Now Williams has amnesia. He can't remember anything else about his tour, except for McCafferty's freak-out.

"Far more common, though, are the field manias: suddenly you're shooting everything that moves, especially in the FFZs. Women, children, old men, animals—everything except your own kind . . . usually. But that's certainly different from the sure kill of a Vietminh. You see the difference?"

Collins nodded cautiously.

"Then . . . then comes the part I know best," continued the Professor, observing the beginning of a volleyball game down on the court. "The sadistic selections: that specific choice—somehow it is *always* conscious, I believe—to bring pain to another living thing by torturing it. Pulling the wings off an insect, or twisting the fingernails off a suspected VC sympathizer: that's localized sadistic selection.

"Generalized sadistic selection is . . . well, it's very much what Wright was talking about—where someone perpetrates a sadistic act on another living thing, which generates some vicarious pleasure to those who either participate, observe, or are later told about the incident. Wright, I think, was talking about what happens afterwards. I'm talking about how the bacteria come alive. At the minimal level, though, generalized sadistic selection is like stopping to look at the victims of an automobile accident smeared out on the highway. At the other extreme are the people like me, who although they never performed localized sadism on another person, nevertheless witnessed it. I saw more of the bestial, perverted reality of humanity as an Intelligence officer than five battalions see in their entire combat tours." The Professor rubbed his eyes, and then ran his hands through his hair. The two men watched the aides down below breaking up a fistfight on the volleyball court.

"How is it that I could condone with my silence the incredible defiling of humanity by carrying back the information that came in screams and cries from those tortured souls, opening the avenues for more killing, more atrocities, like a disease-laden spore? You might say that I saved many lives, but not the way you saved them. Oh, no. You worked with the finished product after I had helped to put them through the meat grinder. I just spread the germ.

"What happened? And why all of a sudden did my system completely stop functioning? Guilt? Of course, but that word, like "civilized," or "patriotic," or "heroic," means absolutely nothing. Ask one hundred people the meanings of those labels and you'll get a hundred different possibilities—maybe not in thought, but certainly in action.

"We romance our preconceptions, our ideals and values—we say we look for Truth, for Reality—but all we really do is put ourselves out there to run after, to have an affair with. And unless we understand that, we are our own fools, the guards of our own prison house. Like a caterpillar in a cocoon, if you don't break out of your own damnable doubt, if you can't finally say, I believe in life in *any* form, then you'll just rot in your own dirty shell. And there, Collins, is my portrait. I have gangrene of the brain."

The Professor laughed suddenly. "Put that in the yearbook too."

They looked each other squarely in the eyes for the first time since they had met forty-seven days earlier.

"I'm thinking about it," Collins said.

The Professor smiled and leaned back into the chain-link fence. It looked as though he had fallen into a deep sleep, like a prisoner on the rack who knows that death is the only comfort. Then he turned slowly and began to walk off the deck, stopped, and returned. He grasped Collins firmly on the shoulder: "Take care of yourself, my friend."

A genuine smile broke out across the Professor's face. Collins realized that he had grown to like Pollard very much.

130

CHAPTER 11

In through the heavy steel doors they marched, to face a warm golden hue beaming out from behind the chaplain as he stood smiling in front of the altar. Another week had passed: here was the place to put your finger on time. Not that it mattered much, but ninety days is, after all, one day short of thirteen weeks.

They sat in the oak pews facing the climbing sun as it gleamed through an arched stained-glass window on which Our Savior spread His arms beseechingly to envelop a field of tiny pure-white sheep. Some looked up from their peaceful grazing, ruminating with an air of disinterest on the size of this Man lately sprung up in their pasture. Above His head, above the flaming halo, were the words "Come Unto Me" in translucent script. Below that was the chaplain, standing on the red carpeting that floated under the base of the altar. On a sharply pressed white altar cloth, the letters IHS in blue hung under the crucifix. Below that, the Saints and Sinners of Bedlam.

They were dazzled at first, rubbing their eyes with both hands, squinting and yawning in a chorus of echoing "Aahhh"s.

"Looks like a fucking recruiting poster, don't it?" Franklin blurted out. " 'Follow me,' you saps." He yawned, pointing at the glowing Savior.

The chaplain was young; his face was round but strong and at the same time kindly. He was doing his best to assert his composure, fearing the worst might happen, as it had two weeks before.

"Good morning, men. And welcome to the chapel, general services, here at Fort Sam. My name is Chaplain Ready, and I'm taking Chaplain Stevens's place for today's services."

"Yeah, he couldn't hack the scene, now could he!" said Williams, looking victorious.

Chaplain Ready clearly tried to ignore the remark. He began to read from Scripture in a tone that lacked the usual confidence of the pulpit.

". . . in His holy temple: let all the earth keep silence before Him. I was glad when they said unto me we will go into the House of the Lord. . . ."

Faintly in the background came the grunts and tweets of somber music, rising and falling in brief phrases. On either side of the altar, against the communion railing, were two narrow RCA speakers, on each of which a tiny golden dog perched before the horn of an old phonograph. He tilted his head to one side in silent concentration. The organ music was prerecorded. Wires with bands of black tape wormed their way up the side of the podium.

It grew warm in the chapel, the brilliant sunlight heating the audience in a flood of mellow colors. Collins sat next to Williams, who was waking up with a long, rigid yawn, his arms thrown up straight over his head like a referee signaling from the field.

"This is more like it, now. Ah, yes, Sunday in the chapel. How quaint. If only these goddamn seats had cushions, uh? You know, I never missed a church day in my life when I lived at home. And when the snow was too deep to make it into town, Dad and brother and I would build a huge fire in the kitchen and we'd have our meeting there, just us people alone. That was when we had the farm in Wisconsin. Sometimes that damn snow'd be fifteen or twenty feet deep. . . ."

". . . Let us listen closely to the words of Saint Peter as he said: 'Dearly beloved, I beseech you as strangers and pilgrims, to abstain from all fleshly lusts, wh . . .' "

"Hey, Wright," shouted out Williams, "you listening to this good stuff?"

" '. . . your conversation honest among the Gentiles, that whereas . . .' "

"Gott mit uns," said the Professor under his breath, staring in-

132

to the swirling grain of the oak pew, stained dark from sweaty palms.

"Ah, shut the hell up, will you? What the hell you trying to say anyway?"

" '... free, and not using your liberty as a cloak of maliciousness, but as the servants of God. Honor all men, love the ...' "

The snores of those pilgrims who never fully regained consciousness in the migration from ward to chapel droned on. On Sundays, the dosage of drugs is reduced to permit a one-day breathing spell.

"Can't get your religion all doped up, now can you?" said Williams as he scanned the lethargic congregation.

Groans and coughs, then a joke and muffled laughter drowned out the chaplain's words. The confluence of loud or peculiar snores interfered with his concentration. He raised his eyes from the text to scan the noisy but sedate congregation. There was a curious look on his face just then, as though he had momentarily misplaced the importance of his mission and wished to leave the room for a few minutes to see if he could come up with it again.

Williams folded his arms across his chest and straightened up against the backrest. He chuckled to himself and said, "Now then, this could be downright entertaining."

"And with these words," began the chaplain as he closed the book with gold page markers. But he paused again in stepping toward the podium, so that the Bible hung suspended between his body and the lectern as though he were reluctant to give it up. He drew in a deep breath and turned to face his congregation. His voice grew louder with each word, until he was almost shouting:

"With these words of Peter, I would like, for us, this morning, to consider, the nature, of his message, to the congregation, thoughtfully, and calmly, men."

"He's not gonna have to worry about that, now is he?"

"I would like, to read, a few more Psalms, and also undertake, a consideration, of a so-called pagan book: Homer's *Odyssey.*"

"Are you putting me on?" came a voice from the back row.

"First, let's think for a moment: why does Peter refer to us as 'strangers' and 'pilgrims'?"

"Let's not!" bellowed Williams.

Chaplain Ready glared at Williams. The silence between the chaplain's question and his impending answer pulled some patients out of their uneasy narcosis. The dopey muttering increased. A few

133

men shifted their positions, tried to sit up, or readjusted their heads on their arms, stretched out along the backs of the pews in front of them. Some of them perhaps would never again wake up completely.

"Well," resumed the chaplain, a bit more reserved now, "we are all strangers and pilgrims, mere wanderers on this earth. We are set adrift at birth to roam through the beauties and torments of this life, to enjoy peace and to suffer great storms. Not only must our bodies and minds endure, but our souls as well. And I don't mean endure as mere existence. I mean endurance with a sense of responsibility to ourselves, and to God. We must be mindful of our most important course through life.

"But"—the chaplain paused for more emphasis—"but where are we headed? Where, I ask you, is the final harbor of the soul?"—now pointing firmly at this lethargic crew. "Where should our hearts and minds always be striving for?"

"Oh, no," sighed the Professor. "Oh, no," he repeated in a whisper. "Not . . . about home? Here we sit in this shop for defective parts and he's—I know he's going to wheel and deal the Holy Homeland." The Professor's eyes came to rest blankly again, lost in the swirl of the darkened grain.

"Where," said Chaplain Ready, his finger aimed at the ceiling with its fake beams, "where is our true home? Our true home, men, is know—"

"In da grave, man," cried Alexander from the second row, struggling under the weight of his medication, squinting, his body twisted between the pews. His lips were trembling, he panted through his nose; rocking back and forth, he was trying to climb up on the bench. He couldn't coordinate his feet.

The chaplain was standing there in his arrested pose, his mouth having just formed the last syllable. The gap in his expression pleaded for some kind soul to walk up and close his mouth lest he evaporate altogether. His eyes opened wider in the horror of watching Alexander come painfully back to life. His mouth still ajar, the chaplain turned his head to look at Hinckley for guidance. Chaplain Ready stared dumfounded at the creature with the ebony hands locked over the backrest of the pew.

"Hang on tight. Here we go again," whispered Williams.

Alexander was gazing with fixed eyes . . . not at the chaplain, but into the golden blaze of the stained-glass window.

Chaplain Ready broke his own intense gaze in a great exhaling of breath which seemed almost to deflate him. He put his hand on the communion railing for support.

"What the fuck's the matter with this asshole?" shouted Franklin with disgust. "What's this bullshit anyway?" He turned to face in Hinckley's direction and yelled across the room: "Hey. Hey, Hinckley! Let's get the hell outa here. Huh? Come on."

A great hissing sound came from the specialist in response to Franklin's demand: "Sssssshhh. Quiet over there."

Chaplain Ready seemed more composed after this show of authority. He took his notes in hand, committed to going on with his service.

"Yes," he asserted with conviction, "you're right. Surely, it is in the grave. Our corporeal resting place is in the grave: the home of all flesh and blood." Chaplain Ready stepped out from behind the podium again, leaving his notes behind.

"But Death is more appropriate to those who are living, not—"

"Now what the hell's that supposed to mean?" interjected Franklin.

"—to the living, not to those who have already surrendered, or to those who are running away from life, or those who have already given up living by refusing to enter into the world. Living"—he paused again—"living is more than existing in this hospital. All will pass. And that, men, is what I'd really like us to think about this morning. Let's not concentrate on the grave right now. Let's think about the living: life is for the living, the passionate spirit in man. And let us think, too, on our heavenly seat prepared for us in God's House. And—"

"Hey, Chaplain, I thought that's where we were," howled Franklin in a spasm of laughter, slapping his thigh. His eyes jerked from side to side to solicit an enthusiastic response to his joke.

All he heard when he stopped laughing were the usual snores and a few squeaks of a clarinet from the speakers. The rest were listening to the chaplain. He was gaining.

"Let us listen to the words of David in prayer. Let us pray."

And their adolescent conditioning tripped the knee rests as many parishioners slid off the benches. The noise of the rests hitting the floor aroused the more distant pilgrims. Williams and Franklin, sneering and rebellious at being under the chaplain's command, finally submitted:

"You stupid son of a bitch—that thing landed on my fuckin' toe."

"Lord, let me know my end, and what is in the measure of my days; let me know how fleeting my life is! Surely every man stands as a mere breath! Surely every man goes about as a shadow! Surely for naught are they in turmoil: man heaps up, and yet knows not who will gather! . . .

"And now, men, let us rise and think about our present condition. Let us—"

"What condition, uh, Chaplain? What . . ."

"Franklin. Relax, will you, please, just relax. Please?" said the Professor, on his knees.

"Many of you will probably recall the *Odyssey* from high school or college. Well, the *Odyssey* is a book that is more than just a story of ancient adventures. It's a tale of the living, for the living to read and understand. And there's one section of the book which I think is especially important for us to consider this morning.

"Do you recall the scene—the incident—when Odysseus, the captain of the ship, brings his men to the land of the lotus-eaters?"

"Yeah. That's right. The lotus-eaters. O.K.!" bellowed Wright, leaning forward. He cradled his face in his palms and stared at the chaplain.

Chaplain Ready surged on with the thrust of his delivery. He looked briefly at his notes, pushed them aside, and maneuvered out from behind the lectern as though he no longer needed the protection. He moved forward, down off the podium. He pointed out into the congregation and asked the conscious to hoist up those who had fallen asleep along the knee rests.

Collins leaned over to help the Professor—who wasn't asleep but was dazed and distant—up off his knees. He had been staring into the back of the pew.

"Yes, yes, yes, yes," he muttered with the irritation. He rubbed his eyes as he shifted from knee rest to bench.

"What's the use. What's the use of any of this, Collins?" But he wasn't asking a question. He was affirming something he had concluded long ago.

". . . is what sort of land this was and what it meant to the crew. And let's think about those men who wandered away from the ship and what became of them. . . ."

"Yeah, man, they all got stoned," announced Wright, captivated by the chaplain's interpretation.

"Yes, that's right. They did get stoned. But why: I mean, what was it they were really doing to themselves? You remember their arduous voyage, and the grueling trials and tribulations they had to endure. Their sadness, their tortures. And then they came to this strange, weird land, an island of peace and tranquillity—a sanctuary —surrounded by a merciless, relentless waste of water. But in this land it seemed always to be a peaceful, soft afternoon. There was no work to do, no labors to perform, no suffering, no war, no hunger, no evil.

"But the men who wandered away from their ship . . . these are the ones for us to think about. For we are all wanderers, and sometimes we, too, wander too far afield of *Our* Captain, Our Lord Jesus Christ. But even more than that, those men wandered away from themselves, walked off the job, forgot their duty to Odysseus and their mission. . . ."

The tape of organ music ended, and the loose end slapped from inside the lectern. That broke the chaplain's momentum. He bounced over to the podium and dropped out of sight.

"Must be a standard Army issue," said Wright.

The swelling of snores began to fill the ears of those still awake. Even Wright lost interest, and picked at the loose threads hanging along the frayed edges of his bathrobe.

Chaplain Ready reappeared, his face flushed. He was nervous again and remained anchored behind the podium. The organ music ground on in long swells.

"Now then, men," he resumed, after conferring with his notes— but he had lost the connection to what little consciousness was available. It was as if they had just this minute sat down.

"Yes, men, we are all travelers making for home. But, men, I ask you again, *where* is our *true* home? Our true home is with—"

"Is six feet under! Like the man said. Don't you know yet that's all there is, Chaplain? Uh?" Master Sergeant Parker, one of the more restrained patients in Collins's ward, had suddenly begun shouting. His booming voice echoed in the large room with the fake-beamed ceiling. "You don't know shit, Chaplain!"

The peaceful dreamers were waking up again. They rubbed their eyes and squinted at Parker. Hinckley was on his feet.

Chaplain Ready had been stalled just as he was getting up steam to push on. He drew in a long, deep breath and waited, puffed up. Sweat stained his collar a light gray.

"You been over there, Chaplain? Uh? You been through that hellhole, boy?" demanded Parker.

The chaplain's face turned beet red. Finally he exhaled in a rush of breath that trailed off into a sigh. He raised his arms and embraced the lectern. He reached into the podium and brought a glass of water to his lips. His head twitched, spilling water down the front of his vestments. The water ran onto his notes. He mopped up the mess with his sleeve. He prepared to speak once again. But nothing came forth.

"I was glad when they said unto me, 'You're goin' into the loony bin, my boy,' " Williams whispered.

"What's Parker's problem?" asked Collins, pointing to the forty-one-year-old master sergeant.

"Ah, he's just probably feelin' his oats," replied Williams. "Didn't you hear Hinckley bid him farewell this mornin' when he read off the roster? Well, it's Parker's last day on our ward. He's getting dropped to the second floor tomorrow after rounds. . . . He'll get outa here."

Collins could see the side of Parker's face as the sergeant studied Chaplain Ready. The lines running from the corner of his eye met in a dramatic crow's-foot which looked like an old scar. And the corner of his mouth was deeply etched from the weight of skin hanging along his jaw like a jowl. But Parker wasn't fat at all. If anything, he was emaciated. Because of his age and the lack of exercise, though, his muscles had lost their tone.

Chaplain Ready walked to the center of the platform and stood in front of the crucifix. The candle flame flickered. He had forgotten to cross himself. He glanced at Hinckley and then stepped off the podium. Chaplain Ready walked down the center aisle toward the steel doors, as if to leave this place forever. That's what had happened to Stevens, more or less. The first Sunday after Easter was his last—his final—sermon to the men of Chambers Pavilion. He cracked, finally, gray-haired old man that he was. They shipped him to some distant room in a dark corner at Walter Reed. He had made a serious mistake: had pretended too long that God is good, that the world is beautiful, that we are our brothers' keepers, that wars are fought only by heathens in Godforsaken lands. Stanley Jones had tried to strangle him.

Chaplain Ready didn't walk out, though. He stopped and went up to Parker, to face him eye to eye. Parker had his fists wrapped around the top of the pew, the veins and tendons like spans of taut rope.

"No," said Chaplain Ready after a tense pause. "No," he repeated, "I've never been over there. I've never been in combat. I've never even sighted down the barrel of an M-16. But I'll tell you this," he went on thoughtfully. "There are times I wish I had. And you know what I'm driving at. Then at least . . ."

"Then at least what?" Parker sneered. "Who the hell do you think you are, boy? What do you think you're trying to tell us? What could you possibly tell us? What do you know about duty and turning your back on yourself—you ever done that? You haven't even killed anyone. What could you know about answering to God? What do you know about dying? You just let all those words run off your lips like you had diarrhea. Yeah, Chaplain, shit! What do you even know about living, all safe and secure in your little plastic chapel?"

"Well, I'll tell you. . . ."

"You won't tell me anything, pansy preacher."

"Now just a minute. You asked me, so I'll tell you."

"Tell me what?" Parker screamed so loud that the chaplain cringed, but he held his footing. He was determined.

Ready went on. "I've been on the other side of the stick. I've done the covering up. I buried 'em in plastic bags inside aluminum boxes, some so battered from overuse they had holes in the tops. I was the fence between the corpse and his parents, between the corpse and his wife. The stiff and his grave. That's all I've done for the past eighteen months—straight, full time. One time I was so out of it that I forgot to pick up a handful of dirt. And when I said 'Ashes to ashes, dust to dust' and threw out my hand over the grave—air, just air. Yes, I know the meaninglessness. Empty words and gestures. The whole shit process. And then I look at you, the likes of you, and you're no better off than the carcasses rotting in their soft caskets."

The chaplain and Parker both lowered their eyes and stared at the vacant seat beneath them. Parker sighed, and shook his head.

"You know what our chaplain—Pasowski, yeah, Chaplain Pasowski—I'll never forget him. You know what he said to my company, the morning before our first S 'n' D assignment—it was a Zippo run. He said, 'Men. Let's clear the air and get one thing straight right from the start. There's two sides to this coin,' he said, waving the Bible in front of us. 'There's the Old Testament, and the New. This,' he said, holding up the book by its inside pages, 'is the New Testament.'

"And you know what he did, Chaplain, you know what he did? He slammed the Bible down on his knee and ripped out the New Testament. Tore 'em out and threw them into the dirt. Kicked 'em under a row of benches.

" 'I suggest you live by the old rules, men. You'll live a lot longer. Remember this: Do unto others before they do unto you. Remember that on the third day *you* ain't gonna rise from the dead! Remember that the trigger finger is quicker than the eye, is quicker than the head. Don't think too much or you won't be thinking at all. Got it? Good luck! You'll need it.'

"You got that, Chaplain? Uh? You see what he was doing? He was trying to save lives—*our lives*, Chaplain. In one minute he talked right through all this church shit. And you know, Chaplain, he told it like it is. And you know what? I did as he said, and he was right. So don't go givin' me all your shit about God and pilgrims, and all that crap about going home. We got our home—and it's six feet under, not six light-years above us. Got that yet, Chaplain? I did unto others and I did it damn well. That's why I'm still here."

"Boy, you said it," whispered Wright, shaking his head in feigned seriousness. "If this keeps up, yip, I'm gonna volunteer to go back up into iso. Yip, that's right. Yeah, maybe I'll even re-up to get out of this zoo. Always wanted to fly gunship. Yeah, that's what I'll do. Right. The war's still on, isn't it?"

"Well, if it's too late to catch this one, you can make the next," answered Williams in his monotone.

Parker slammed back down into his seat with such force that he set the others rocking back and forth the length of the bench.

"Hey, man, I had guard duty last night," moaned some sleeper jostled into a second's speech between snores.

Parker folded his arms across his chest. He slammed his feet down on the knee rest with all his might: "Goddamn it! Goddamn it! Shit!" The men sitting in the pew ahead of him were rocking now, hit by a heavy swell. Both pews rocked, squeaking in unison. Parker slammed his feet down on the knee rest once again. This time it snapped, as though a good-sized timber had let go.

The chapel was quiet. All opened eyes were on the chaplain.

140

"I'll tell you something else," resumed the chaplain. "What's your name?"

"Parker—Master Sergeant Parker. What the hell difference does it make to you anyway, Chaplain?"

"Well, Parker, believe it or not, I would have told your company the same thing if I'd been in that chaplain's shoes. The same damn thing. I've thought a lot about that. I mean, how I would handle something like that if I had to . . . what I'd say. I thought about it when I buried my brother four months ago. He got it in Bien Hoa. He was high—stoned—a real pot head, they told me. And you, Parker . . . ? I wish I had told him what your chaplain told you, rather than 'God be with you, brother,' my last words to him as he shipped from Frisco. Shit. Right? Parker?"

"Yeah, but you—"

"Wait, let me finish, Parker. I would have said, 'Get the Cong before he gets you,' if you were over there now. But you're here now. You're not in Nam anymore, you're in Texas. But you're not home yet. Not really. And what I'm trying to get at is just that. You're not home, and you're going to have to fight to get back home, to get out of this halfway house, this prison, this . . . I'll tell you ano—"

"No, Chaplain, I'll tell you! Your error, Chaplain—you stupid fuck —is that even if we could go home, how many men—if that's what you call them—would want to go back?

"Look, Chaplain, there is—there really is a thin line out there. Step across it, Chaplain, and you might as well have stepped on an M-70. You come back, maybe, but you sure as shit don't come back right. You're maimed, one way or the other, and who wants to be a fuckin' lame duck the rest of their lives. Maybe you don't really want to come home at all, 'cause you're sick. Maybe your instinct for life is pulverized, uh, Chaplain? What's your thinking on that?"

"Yes, Parker, I tried to imagine what—"

"Well, don't bother!" retorted Parker. "Don't bother yourself!" Parker smashed the broken knee rest with his foot. A large splinter trailing a piece of upholstery rocketed through the air, just missing Chaplain Ready's red face.

"I tried," persisted the chaplain, "to imagine what it would be like to come back here, to a mental hospital, instead of stepping off a plane in my home town. And that's when I thought of the lotus-eaters—"

"Shit-eaters, Chaplain, like you. You fuckin' fairies."

"—how easy it would be to forget what we really have: how you might get so submerged in your own memories—"

"Well, forget it, Chaplain. Your wares are obsolete here. You're not gonna sell any tickets for a passage home on *your* boat. Go back to the suburbs—they'll buy your trip. Fuck off, Chaplain," Parker said, turning his head in disgust, as though the chaplain had a bad smell about him. "Leave us alone."

Alexander began mumbling. His eyes closed, he was smiling into the radiant beams of red, yellow, and green. Then he put his feet up on the bench and swayed from side to side, arms wrapped around his ankles. His voice grew louder, deep and mellow. Softly he began singing words, his face taut. The pitch of his song rose and fell in waves of melody as he swayed back and forth.

"Hummm, yeah, O-o-o Lord, gonna go now, O Lord, gonna go an' lay dis ol' body down. Gonna put this ol' tired body down. Hummm, yeah, O Lord. Been risin' up each day too long now, O-o-o Lord; and dat sun ain't so warm now, O Lord. O-o-o Lord, gonna go now, O Lord, Gonna go and lay my body down. Hummm. . . ."

"Christ," whispered Williams. "If my mother was here she'd be bawling by now. She cried a lot in church. All the old ladies did. Never missed a chance to turn on her faucet. Wonder why she just didn't dry up like an old prune."

Chaplain Ready walked back up the aisle and faced the patients from in front of the altar. Alexander's humming floated through the still air.

"Let not your hearts be troubled, believe in God, believe also in me. . . . In my Father's house are many rooms; if it were not so, would I have told you that I go to prepare a place for . . ."

". . . gonna walk through dem fields once more, O Lord, 'fore I go an' lay dis body down. . . ."

". . . dead bodies shall live, their bodies shall rise. O dwellers in the dust, wake and sing for joy. For the dew is the dew of light and on the land of shadows thou wilt not let it fall down."

The Professor squirmed in his seat like a kid waiting to piss. His body was drawn so far forward that he nearly plummeted off the edge of the bench. Collins put his arm across the Professor's chest and pushed him back into his seat. Pollard stared dead ahead as he said:

"Come, my children, enter your chambers, and shut your doors

142

behind you; hide yourselves for a little while, until the wrath is past."

"Ah, shit—him too, huh?" squawked Williams, tucking his hands under his thighs.

Alexander's humming was contagious. A number of others in the congregation joined the lead soloist. Chaplain Ready stepped off the podium and began talking to a patient in the front row.

Suddenly Millsaps jumped to his feet. "What we gonna do? Let him turn this into a nigger's church?" He was pointing at Alexander, who ignored the antagonist. But not Franklin, whose hatred for Millsaps had already led them to violence. He jumped over Wright, raced around to the back row, and slugged Millsaps in the face. And again, and again, until Millsaps's body hung limply over a backrest.

"Take. Drink," said Collins as he watched the carpeting absorb the blood pouring from Millsaps's nose.

"Clever, Collins. Sick, but clever," sighed Pollard.

"Man, that's two down in one day," said Williams in his monotone. "Franklin's sure to get the zapper for that one. He won a ticket to never-never-land."

Hinckley and Minor pawed through the crowd. Minor ran into the corridor. Other specialists bounded through the doors. Hinckley ground his forearm into Franklin's throat. Franklin shook his head in pain.

They lifted Millsaps. Blood ran from his temple. His feet scraped two dark lines in the carpet as they dragged him through the doors and disappeared.

Hinckley handcuffed Franklin and threw him against the wall.

"All right! On-your-feet! Let's go. The party's over. Wake up! On-your-feet! Line up! Move!"

They wormed their way from behind the pews and gathered in a straggling line in the main aisle. Chaplain Ready shook the patients who were drowned in sleep.

Wright looked once more at the arched window of Our Savior: Come Unto Me.

Chaplain Ready blessed the backs of the somnambulant lotus-eaters.

". . . of the Holy Ghost be with us all evermore. Amen."

CHAPTER **12**

Dr. Nieland knew that the anonymous letters in Collins's file were written by Collins. They were curious pieces, written in a jerky, bent script. But each letter had a distinctive style and its own vision of a wounded personality in the process of death or reconstruction. And out of the three dozen letters—or "forgeries," as Dr. Nieland called them—there was one in particular to which he always returned when reviewing Collins's case:

The field sensors are working against us, because of their sophisticated talents and the idiotic monitoring from Thai Command. They heard me all right. They work just fine. Someone saw me as a white blip-blip on a gray screen. The next thing I knew was this radar-guided U.S. artillery shell hit my squad. Called a smart shell. It blew my right foot off. Imagine that . . . I—a U.S. regular—fingered by a transistor made in Japan concealed in a plastic plant molded by Rubbermaid, and the whole lousy contraption marketed by Honeywell.

It was . . . well, I don't know what kind of a bush it was, but some GI had planted it there right along the trail. It heard me!—and the SOB blew my goddamn foot off. So now we got another enemy to deal with, and he's without a proper brain. Now we never really see him because . . . well, because it isn't human, for one thing! Or is he? They call this assassin EARS —that means Electronic Assisted Range Sensor. He belongs to the species CAIN—that's short for Computer Assisted Intelligence Network. And it's a hell of a big family they got, spawned by crossing a Honeywell transmitter with a Sylvania sensor. Quite a sadistic clan. One of the hybrids is Electronic Infrared Engager—called EIE on the field. It can see in the dark. But let me tell you this—if you meet him on the trail, remember he doesn't know the difference between a cow and a man, and keep in mind, too, that he's been programmed not to know why or what he kills. And is he good at it! You can take my word.

Anyway, the surgeons here at the 40th Field are doing a real fine job on me. I was certain I'd lose my whole leg, but they saved most of it. When I told them that some kind of rubber plant zapped me, they sent the shrink over. That was a good laugh. You should have been here! Now, I think that Honeywell should make other things, like parts of the body. I think they owe me a new foot. So I can walk again. Wouldn't you agree?

As Dr. Nieland finished this letter, he felt a frustration and light-headedness, as though he were being led into an intricate puzzle by an evasive narrator. He concentrated again on the adjectives, pronouns, and anagrams. It was clear that the modifiers bequeathed human qualities to inhuman gadgets.

"And yet 'saw me as a white blip-blip on a gray screen' works in the opposite direction—backward," said the doctor aloud. "Here the protoplasm is electronically reduced to something so specifically unhuman, so deprived of an identity, that it ceases to be recognized as man."

The doctor underscored those constructions which indicated this breach of faithfulness. The insanity is right here in our language, he thought, as he swung in his chair to watch the pines and palms swaying in the breeze.

"But they're not swaying!" he stated, irritated by his own propensity to misstate the activity. "The trees are being swayed by the wind. . . . This is absurd." It seemed absurd because it seemed so simple, a commonplace in perception and language so fundamental to consciousness that to debate the active or passive quality seemed a sophomoric undertaking. And yet Dr. Nieland realized that his patient was functioning on just that level: the delicate buffer between *me* and *it* had been eradicated. How to reinstate that space in one's thoughts and speech? Insist that a "limb" be called a branch unless it is an arm or leg; talk of the center of a city rather than its "heart"; refer to the "mouth" of a river as the opening . . .?

"Ridiculous and stupid!" muttered the doctor aloud. "Absolutely ridiculous. . . . Sophistication. A liberal sophistication, to level the

enemy to something less than human in the mind of the soldier. . . ."

Dr. Nieland turned back to his desk and selected a gray transcri-
ber disk from his files. He switched on the dictation machine and
stood up to stare out the window:

This emerging pattern of syndromes derives from a *cultural* neurosis.
Indeed, the veterans who consciously recognize that they had a hand in
marring the idealistic notion of the Family of Man suffer from an acute
neurosis born of the fifties and nurtured by the liberalism of the sixties.
These men—in varying stages of disintegration—form the majority of our
psychiatric communities. And as they witnessed—or participated in—the
wholesale destruction of another race, they experienced the mutilation of
their own personal, psychological identities as reflected in the dismemberment of an alien culture.

To comprehend the unprecendented rise in service-related mental disorders resulting either directly or indirectly from the conflict in Vietnam
as evidence of a neurosis pervasive within our culture is perhaps one way
to understand why the returning veteran is so difficult to diagnose and
nearly impossible to treat by conventional therapeutic methods. Why?
Because we are not treating merely an individual with psychological problems; we are treating—and unsuccessfully, I might add—an entire country,
a population fighting among itself.

If each soldier represents the impress of his country's values and beliefs,
then we may measure the stability, the depth of ascription and conviction,
and the efficacy of those values and beliefs during three critical phases of
a soldier's career: initiation (basic training), performance (active duty), and
assimilation (his ability to reintegrate himself with his society when he
becomes a civilian again).

If we scrutinize the first phase, it is obvious that the sophisticated initiation into contemporary warfare is by methodically reducing the enemy to
something less than human in the psyche of the soldier. In effect, he is
conditioned through the pejorative vocabulary and crude gestures of the
training staff to neutralize and then liquidate the species at hand. But
according to reports from the major training bases, it has been very difficult
to create a spontaneous killer instinct directed against the North Vietnamese. The reasons for this—

Dr. Nieland stopped the Dictaphone and advanced the disk:

—servations on Collins, Specialist Andrew B., RA 1111-8686.
This patient was indoctrinated according to the rudimentary psychologi-
cal predispositions toward the North Vietnamese while in basic training at
Fort Dix. During this early stage of preparation, the patient, either con-

146

sciously or unconsciously, initiated an overreaction against the *reductio humanitas* propaganda. The first phase of this distortion commenced with a deliberate shifting of animate qualities over to inanimate matter. The earliest indications of this *projectio anima* are documented in the patient's personal notebooks, written by him during basic training. Gradually, all things, whether living or nonliving, whether animal, vegetable, or mineral, were raised to the position of humankind, thereby confounding what is the natural ability to distinguish a lower form of life from the higher. This unquestionably psychotic process, perhaps further exacerbated during formal indoctrination, became increasingly pronounced, as evidenced in the patient's use of written language, at which point he became a prisoner of his own unreliable perceptions and semantics. There is, in fact, an overt continuum of acute depersonalization of the patient during this process, reaching its most dramatic psychotic phase while he was actively attached to the Fortieth Field Surgical Hospital.

I consider this patient's state at that time to be most closely defined as step-one psychosis rather than acute psychoneurosis because of the massive deterioration of the person occurring concomitantly with his bizarre propensity to attempt a psychic reanimation of separated pieces of human flesh and even corpses.

Transplantation and relocation of this patient's ego-personality became an obsessive, extensual reduplication of severed limbs and trunks and even a surreptitious assumption of certain alien personalities: i.e., soldiers whom he was engaged in treating in a medical capacity. Because of the magnitude of this extensual phase and the undermining of the foundations of his own personality, this patient further suffers from a series of psychological fragmentations into numerous and conflicting splinter persons who he may very well believe incarnate in living or deceased soldiers who were at one time known to the specialist.

The series of letters included in this patient's medical record further verifies the linear progression of this complex deterioration. The letter beginning—quote—The field sensors are working against us—end quote—was probably written by the patient although he claims to have no memory of doing so. The transgressions from subject to object are repeated throughout all the letters and substantiate my deduction. These letters confirm the range of fragmentation and the severity of the patient's confusion between himself and other, agent and object, and human and nonhuman categories of perception and recognition.

My initial course of treatment will be to assert an antagonistic and hostile pressure on the patient in an effort to flush out and deactivate the more tenuous splinter persons. Hopefully, I should be able to use this patient's perceptual workings and his own distortions of language against him. Once these subordinate counterpersons are made apparent, an effort will be made to help the patient see the more entrenched and traditional aspects of his personality. My choice here is to force him into as many and varied social situations as possible in the anticipation that the incongruity of contradictory personalities will make him feel more than uncomfortable. To institute conventional treatment in this case would be, I believe, tantamount to aiding and abetting the consortium of his fragmented and dislocated personalities. He must be forced to respond to confrontations which are not blatantly clinical. My recommendation is therefore to place him with the floating group and expose him to as many social realities in a nonhospital setting as possible.

Twenty-eight April 1970/End. Case 8686, Andrew B. Collins, CPFSH, MHU/G. W. Nieland, Captain.

"One minute, please," said Nieland when he heard a knock on his door. "Is that you, Collins?"

"Yes, sir."

"I'll be right with you." Nieland cleared his desk and arranged the one other chair in the room besides his own so that it would face both him and the colorful shirt pinned to the wall—Collins's illustration of a right knee reconstruction.

"Come in, Collins. . . . Have a seat."

But before Collins was halfway across the small room, his eyes were following the tibial collateral ligament to the medial epicondyle. He looked over at Nieland, who was standing behind his desk.

"Please, sit down," said Nieland, motioning to the chair. Collins seated himself and then glanced up again at the shirt. He turned his chair so that he could see only Nieland and the sky through the window behind him. The psychiatrist stared at Collins for a moment before beginning. He watched Collins look once again at the shirt pinned to the wall and then turn his head away.

"Memories, Collins, what are they really?" asked Dr. Nieland.

"Moods and scenes you have in your mind's eye."

"Then you can't share them? . . . Can't you reminisce with someone about a mutual past?"

"You can try. But then they're not really memories anymore. Memories are moods and feeling caught in a certain atmosphere that won't come across with words."

"Can memories keep something alive, or resurrect something from the dead?"

"Sure. When you remember, you put something back together again—you bring it to life again. Yes, Dr. Nieland."

148

"Do you think the mind retains a memory of virtually every waking moment of your life?"

"Maybe."

"Well, how about in the case of Andrew B. Collins? Do you remember very much?"

"I suppose as much as anyone else. It's awfully relative."

"Can you control how or when your memories dominate your thoughts or moods? Or do you think they've already influenced your thought process by the time you're aware that you're remembering a past incident?"

"How can you know the difference?"

"Do most people forget more than they remember?"

"I think most people probably try to forget more than they choose to remember. But we all preserve scenes of happy times and places."

"Can you destroy a memory, Collins? I'm asking you. Can *you* obliterate a memory?"

"I don't know what you're getting at. You writing a book or something?"

"Do you have the power to consciously suppress a remembrance? Can you forget, Collins? That's what I'm driving at."

"Sure you can. Look at Jim Holbrook. He's in my ward. He remembers nothing."

"O.K., Collins, let's look at him."

"Well, why ask me? He's your patient, isn't he? . . . All I know about him is that he's got amnesia. Which proves that some chosen few do have the presence of mind to forget. Correct?"

"How about ex-Lieutenant Robert Williams. You know him."

"What about him? You know him better than I do. . . . Williams's is the opposite of Holbrook's amnesia. Williams knows—remembers —only one thing: Colonel McCafferty shooting his own men. In that case his memory keeps him alive to his vengeance, which keeps alive the memory of murder in the mind of Colonel McCafferty."

"Do you believe in the accuracy of Williams's memory?"

"Who knows what to believe in here, Dr. Nieland? . . . What is this anyway, Twenty Questions?"

"Two thousand questions. Maybe you can answer just one?"

"For instance?"

"You, Collins, what do you remember about yourself?"

"Collins, Andrew Baker. Medical Specialist, E-5. RA 1111-8686—"

"You're not a POW."

"I was born in Concord, New Hampshire, in 1945. I grew up in a suburban farmhouse about fifteen miles outside of Concord. My father was—is—an insurance executive who commutes to Boston weekdays and to the golf course on weekends. My mother's maiden name is—"

"Knock it off, Collins. I don't have the time. . . . How did you end up in an isolation cell on the fourth floor of this hospital?"

"Because I was a member of the Fortieth Field Surgical Unit and worked for the ESR."

"Yes, I know. But why would you be committed for that?"

"Because I was court-martialed and cracked up serving my sentence. That's why."

"Tell me about this court-martial."

"You have all that in my record."

"Well," said Nieland, opening one of Collins's notebooks from Vietnam, "I find references to a court-martial in your journals. But there is no entry anywhere of a formal indictment in your military records."

"You're lying, Nieland! There—"

"There's no record of any trial."

"But there is! . . . Then they've pulled the transcript."

"There isn't any. There was no trial."

"There was a trial! They read the charges. Black Eye testified against me. There was a brawl in the chambers. A fistfight. And they tied me down and sent me back to the field hospital. That was my sentence, Dr. Nieland. A major rose from the bench—"

"There wasn't any major, and no bench."

"A major rose from the bench and said: 'It is the opinion of this tribunal that you are guilty of subversion against the Army of the United States of America according to the definition of such offense as set forth in Paragraph 64.3.3c of the *MLP*. We hereby sentence you, Andrew B. Collins, to the Fortieth Field Hospital Division in Bien Hoa. You will serve your sentence not as a member of the surgical staff, but as a patient. For life.' "

"That's the right paragraph, Collins, but there *wasn't any trial, no sentence!* That was your promotion from medic and reassignment to the Fortieth Field as a surgical specialist."

" 'For life, each day, you will receive new wounds, and the wounds from the previous days will never heal. Even as raw flesh

150

you will never lose consciousness. . . . This tribunal stands adjourned. Take him away.' Yes, I remember that as clearly as if it were happening again today. I remember the smug, gray-haired major and his staff of henchmen. And my defense counsel, who was so stunned he never uttered a word in my behalf. . . . Why? Because he was dead. They killed him. And I remember Captain Northcross after the attack—but by then I had my defense and nothing can ever touch me again. Do you understand? Nothing. Ever again."

"O.K., Collins, then how do you explain that the charges of subversion were placed against you—true—but that you were never tried by any court at any time? How do you explain that, in reality, you're still awaiting trial?"

"Don't try to con me, Nieland. I was already found guilty and began serving my sentence."

"Not by military court."

"Who am I to trust now, Nieland? You? The records? Me? My memory? Or the men who were killed because of information leaks in the ESR?"

"How can one person be in two different places at the same time?"

"We've already been through that one. You can be sitting out by the diamond waiting for your ups but really you're sitting on a sandbag outside a bunker smoking dope. Like being in a time machine when the controls go haywire and you can't come out of it with a snap of the fingers."

"Isn't that a function of memory?"

"That's the present reality for some of us. But you forget the difference between a nightmare, a daydream, and regular consciousness. You just don't know which is which anymore. They're all one."

"Yes, Collins, as a state of mind, if it persists, that we call insane. . . . Are you insane, Collins?"

"I thought that's what you were commissioned to find out, Captain. Be thankful you have a secure job."

"If you ever stumble across a sense of humor, Collins, you'll be blown apart at the seams."

"A little smile at the wrong time in the wrong place is a devastating thing, Doctor. I've seen it work! I've watched it creep across a trooper's face when he knows that even his fucking death is ludicrous. 'My death is the punch line to someone else's sick joke,' he seems to be saying, with a broadening grin. Laugh, laugh. I thought I'd cry. And then—"

"Collins, wait a minute. Before you get carried away again. We're not interested in *them,* Andrew. We don't care about their yesterdays. We're interested in *you* today. Got the picture?"

"Well, you're calling the shots."

"You're so goddamn condescending. . . . What do you remember about leaving the Fortieth Field Unit?"

"Leaving? When? Who says I ever left?"

"Or about those thin scars across your face and wrist? On your left wrist, yes. How did that get there?"

"I remember the concertina wire stretched out along the perimeter like a gigantic Slinky. And the razor blades jammed between the strands. They sparkled like diamonds when the lights swept the area. And the gasoline and diesel fuel sitting in polyethylene trenches just in front of the wire. And the command, 'Hit the Fryolator!' And the sweet stench of VC cooking on the vine."

"So?"

"So, Dr. Nieland, I've learned never to look beyond the counter in the mess hall because I know what the metal sign in red and silver letters says on the deep fryer. Yes, I've trained myself not to look. I remember not to look at the sign so I won't remember what it stands for. And I'm no longer aware of why I don't look. There, Dr. Nieland, there is your conscious control over memory; perhaps as conscious as my inability to remember the Fortieth Field Unit those last few days. Does that answer your question about leaving?"

"Your argument reminds me of a Möbius. Warped. Yes, twisted but with a linear continuity. Is that how these sick, absurd letters got written to you? By a warped mind? About electronic sensors and Rubbermaid plants? Or this one about a soldier who could still feel pain, although he was dead? Or this one about a trooper who became untouchable when his chute opened because his feelings remained suspended in the clouds. Or this nonsense about a remote-controlled tank operated by a computer in a command chopper. And—"

"Dr. Nieland. Wait! They're all true. Every one of those letters is true and accurate."

"How do you know? Who wrote them, Collins? And who walked around the camp one morning trying to match someone's foot to someone's body like Prince Charming looking for Cinderella?

While it rotted in the boot? Who, Collins? And who had some grunt's arm come off in his hand? And who, in order to make up for this guilt, drove himself with a masochistic madness to help put things back together again. Things that would never fit together again. And, at this moment, which voice speaks the truth about the past . . . your past? Who, or what, Andrew? And who, Collins, loans *things* qualities only a living human being can possess? Who sees man pitted in the same struggle as all the inanimate elements of nature? There, Collins, these are the charges against you. Charges you have already prepared against yourself. And finally, because you refused to let anything human touch you, your own inhumanness has sentenced you—"

"Stop!"

"—to drown in a sea of guilt over what happened to you and a lot of others in Vietnam."

"Shut up!"

"But no, you washed your hands of it all. Or so you thought. What you really accomplished was to divide your soul between the living and the dead."

"Nieland, I'm warning you. . . ."

"Why, Collins?"

"Just shut up! You don't know what you're saying."

"Oh, is that right? Everything I've been saying is based on your notebooks, and letters, and—"

"Your reading, Nieland."

"And my conversation with Major Hepburn."

"Hepburn?"

"Know him, do you?"

"I . . . I . . ."

"I'll bet you know him pretty well. He was your CO with the Fortieth Field Unit. Correct? You know he's personally responsible for getting you off the field and into MacArthur's Hospital in Tokyo?"

"When . . . when did you talk to him? How?"

"Last night. He was committed here just over a week ago."

"Travis Hepburn? But . . ."

"Memories, Collins, what are they really? Nothing more than vignettes from the past carried into the present. Subjective recollections. Bits and pieces of penetrating feelings and emotions given a life in the mind. They're dead and static except—as you say—for

153

the life you lend them. And far more haunting and insidious than the black-and-white reveries of the family album. And the night-mares, Collins, if they live on through the day, are the memories taking hold of your being. Follow? They come back so intensely that you lose all sense of proportion. The mind is conditioned by external time: never the other way around. And when you talk out loud, apparently speaking for other persons, you become the translator of the dead. They cannot speak the language of this world, but you can—and do, in their behalf. The dead voices consume your living consciousness like parasites; they fester and comprise your very life.

"Do you understand yet that you are untouchable because there is no you—there are only the unnamed Others, their voices in your substance. And you know that if you want to remain untouchable you can do it. You've already proved that. But win their game, Collins, and you'll lose your mind. For good.

"And that soft spot, Andrew, lives in your memory. But it is all tangled up with the others: the wounded, the dead, and the re-stored. Somewhere back there you drew a line through your own mind. You saw only the black and white and lost the tones—the grays. And as more dismembered, blown-apart bodies passed under you, the more fragmented your mind became, until the chasm between life and death grew too—"

"How ingenious of you, Doctor. How very bullshit."

"Working with you is a pleasure, Collins."

"I'll sign up for next semester."

"Now then, Collins," said Nieland abruptly. "Listen carefully. Today is Monday, 25 May. What happens to you in the next two to three weeks will determine where you end up for the next twenty months or twenty years. It's not a question of what happens *to* you. No, it's a question of what *you make* happen. . . . You look per-plexed. Ninety days, Collins, remember?"

"I am perplexed. And I'm scared."

"I'm glad to hear you say that," said the psychiatrist, nodding his head. "I wish more troopers coming back from Nam could admit they're scared. Not about their past, but about their future."

"I know what you're talking about."

"Good. O.K., two weeks from today—that'd be 8 June—you and four other patients from 3-East will be dropped to the second floor. To ward 2-W. You're being dropped as a group experiment. My experiment. To prove that alliances made in this hospital have a

154

positive, rehabilitative effect rather than a detrimental one. So you'll have company.

"Understand two things, though," he continued, leaning over his desk. "First, that a formal diagnosis of your condition will be made on the second floor. And it's this diagnosis which will determine your psychiatric classification when you go before the Board. And second, Andrew, regardless of what happens, I'm behind you, as a human being and as a veteran. In that order. You can come to me. I'm here because I want to help. I have my own hatred and guilt over what's happening in Vietnam. In some ways, Collins, you and I are very much alike. Follow?"

"I think so."

"By the way, your father called again this morning. It's up to you, if, when, and where you want to see him. And remember, Collins, I'm here if you need me. Anytime."

Collins left Nieland's office, numbed by the seriousness of his situation. He was running out of time. It was as if the more aware he became of his past, the more frightened he was of confronting the present. Nieland had told him this might happen and that if it did it might be a sign he was getting better.

"Better than what?" he whispered as he walked downstairs.

Collins felt his face grow warm as he imagined staring down at the polished wingtips. He was dizzy and leaned against the door.

"I'm going to be sick."

"Mother sends her love," his father would say, "and hopes you'll be home soon." He would embrace his son awkwardly.

"I . . . I . . ."

Collins felt that his ears were on fire. He caught himself about to drool.

"I am one of them. Speechless and ashamed. A stranger in my own father's arms. I am one of them. I have so much to say. To explain. I have something to say to you, Dad. . . ."

But though he had thoughts, he couldn't remember any for a minute. They rushed through his mind all at once and paralyzed his vocal cords.

"Your doctor says you're doing very well . . ." his father would begin again, cheerfully. And then a long pause. "How are you, Andy?"

"O.K.," he'd say, with his eyes still on the shoes. His father's last letter had been conciliatory. He wrote that maybe things had changed. Attitudes about duty and manhood. That "whatever happened to you over there doesn't matter over here." But as Collins remembered his father's neatly pressed beige suit, he knew that wasn't true—that there were men in this hospital who could prove how very wrong his father was. At the very least, they could raise a doubt in your mind, Dad, he thought.

Your first glance out the window would be sparked by some primitive revulsion, and then your pity for me, for the son who didn't quite come home after all. At least, not altogether. And then your long stares out over the grounds . . . you'd be afraid for your own sanity, wouldn't you, Dad?

What went wrong? you wanted to ask me. Well, a hell of a lot went wrong. With me, with you, with this country of ours. But you'd never admit that to me. Guess what, Dad: I've forgotten who the enemy is—or was. We destroyed ourselves over there. Not the VC. Think that one through, Dad. And while you're at it, tell me why this is a war, and yet isn't a war. And now you have to deal with this —with me—around the dinner table, on the golf course, at the yacht club. How I disgraced myself because of a "mental frailty."

Because maybe only cowards suffer such ailments. Maybe so. Goldbrickers, you were thinking as you fought the Second World War again in your mind. Guadalcanal. Truk. Okinawa. Ironic, isn't it, Dad. We fought fifteen hundred kilometers apart separated by twenty-five years. I want to tell you how very different this war is.

"Alison graduates next week. Maybe it can be arranged for you to come up to Skidmore somehow. . . ."

"How are the dogs?"

"Ol' Red died two weeks ago. But the pups are in fine shape. . . . Tom was in an automobile accident. He's in Mass General. He's O.K. Two broken legs and . . . Andrew . . . oh, Andy . . ."

And another long stare through the window. "No," you would say to yourself. "No," you'd whisper in your mind, looking through the ivy. "No, the world is still the same," and you sensed you could handle all this, the whimpers and moans, the soldiers without limbs, the crazies. That you could overcome this problem—me. There's so much to say. And you would go to the door, say goodbye, down one flight. You would nod authoritatively to the alert MPs as they swung open the gates for you, down three more steps into twilight unfiltered through the bars, and out, out into that world, your world. Please leave now, Dad.

And you would walk away, listening to the sound of your shoes hitting the pavement sure-footedly. And that would sound good. And you would say quietly, "No, the world is still the same." And for you it would be. Wait! I want to tell you how all this happened. I want to make sense of it so you'll know, so you can know how meaningless it all was, how devious and corrupt. And how we knew that, even from the start. And it broke our spirit, Dad, and with that went our pride, then our will to win. Then our will to live. Do you understand how they all go together? Look, there are good men in this hospital you'd never understand because they're not the smiling troopers stepping off transports across the country. But did you ever look beneath their smiles, Dad, beyond the high school bands, the mothers with Kleenex, the sisters with ribbons in their hair? And this post you're on . . . did you know it's manned by the maimed? That's right, over four thousand of them, who you'd never acknowledge as other people's sons. But you see, Dad, this is a war of reflection, not action.

"Whatever went on over there doesn't matter now. We love you. We want you home," said his father, with tears in his eyes. "Your doctor said I . . . could visit again. If you want me to come . . . Goodbye, Andy." And you would shake my hand and say, "Get well soon, son."

"Goodbye, Dad."

Collins looked out the window and watched his father walk slowly up the sidewalk toward the parking lot. He walked the way he did when a business deal had fallen through and he was trying to figure out what he had done wrong. Then he stopped and looked back through the chain-link fence at Chambers. He put his hands up to cover his face and shook his head. Collins wondered if it would really be that way.

CHAPTER **13**

Following the noon mess on June 8, Collins was "dropped" into the Camp of the Câu Lu'u. The Vietnamese expression meant "political prisoners" or "internment camps," but in Chambers it was used to designate those patients who had been transferred from the closed wards on the fourth and third floors to the open wards on two and one. Of the four levels in Chambers, the second floor is the most critical: you might get "sent up" again, or you just might make it to the first floor. No patient was released back to duty or sent home unless he reached the first floor well before the ninetieth day of his commitment.

By the end of his first week on ward 2-West, and his ninth week in Chambers, Collins no longer gazed out over the grounds looking for some curious event. Conflicts among the inmates came and went as boring commonplaces. And the magazines, TVs, record players, telephones, clocks on the walls . . . somehow they didn't mean much anymore. In fact, as he became acclimated to the much more civilized atmosphere of the second floor, he was increasingly impatient to break out of the tedious routines, the endless conversations about the war and campus demonstrations, and his own sense of stasis—nearly paralysis.

But he knew that his mind had cleared, sometimes briefly, like the sun breaking through clouds on a rainy day, and on two notable occasions for more than a day. Perhaps that was because Nieland had cut his dosage of tranquilizer almost in half, or perhaps the events precipitating his breakdown had receded slightly from his consciousness and so did not impinge as frequently and drastically on the present. He experienced a kind of relief, a freedom of thought, and would not have felt imprisoned by the past if he could only escape from Chambers altogether.

There was also a pensiveness, which had come over Collins since those nights back on the third floor when he would crawl out of bed after lights out and sit under the cart to think. Now he thought while standing on his feet or sitting on the edge of his bunk. And rather than continuing with his anatomical drawings, he began writing, in the notebook requisitioned for him by Dr. Nieland, what he could remember of his past sixty-two days at Chambers. He wished he could recall something more substantial about his stay on the third floor, something more lifelike than disembodied voices fluttering in a web of nebulous bodies.

He wondered, as he looked at the unfamiliar faces surrounding him, if their world would always begin and end in some marsh or leafless forest on the other side of the planet. Time. It will take time on the outside, say the doctors in the corridors and conference rooms—because no one knows just what will happen with this generation of soldiers. Released rehabs from Chambers have already been arrested by the police, who find them night and day roaming wooded parks in combat gear, looking for VC; in a cemetery of a Boston suburb, shooting at gravestones and shouting something about gooks and Chicoms; rappeling down the wall of a building after planting a bomb in a Chink's apartment. It will take a lot of time. The unreality of it all has become a mundane way of life for the veterans on the second-floor wards. For them the past is present, with no future.

Collins has been staring out at the red benches below the window. He's been watching the people who come and go in an endless procession. They're half hidden by the pines and magnolias and screened from the road by the overgrown rosebushes. But from the second floor he can peer into the secluded gardens inhabited by the ninety-day wonders and the amputees playing with their wives, girlfriends, or themselves. They haven't noticed him perched next to the window casement because they're so absorbed in talking and fondling. With a mere glimpse, Collins has learned to tell the difference between a remade cripple and a psycho by two criteria: curiosity and aggression.

The psychos are more withdrawn and cautious and shifty. They don't know whether they like each other. They avoid looking into each other's eyes, as though their souls have been poisoned by something shameful and sinister. A psycho knows he possesses forbidden knowledge. Hence the question: how best to hide it? And yet the psychos seek confession. They search for a certain tone of voice, a soft gesture, a curious but compassionate eye which sees their tormented souls without fear and loathing.

But Collins knows, too, that there is no return to peacetime for the psychos. When they close their eyes it is to watch with amazement the unforgettable acts. Their acts, painted in miniature on the inside of their eyelids. And with them open?—they fear the outsider who might decipher the secret taint of their souls. Every mental patient feels both the rebirth of an inner consciousness and with it the madness of his own self-defeating defenses.

"Collins. I'm gonna tell you just once more. This is the second floor you're on, boy. Not the fourth or the third. Them things you got in your hands is called cards. The game we're playin' is called Hanoi Hearts. Now get your ass down off that window sill and get back here an' play!" shouted Perkins, one of three Green Berets on the second floor. He had introduced himself to Collins and showed him around the ward on the morning of his transfer to 2-West: a baby-faced surfer from Ventura. He had light-brown hair with streaks of blond, and a deep tan which he preserved by spending three hours a day with his Coppertone on a lawn chair. He also jogged and did endless calisthenics every morning before mess call. Collins envied his ease, his sense of self-sufficiency, and his apparently effective conviction that what he had experienced in Vietnam, as brutal and horrible a mind fuck as it was, could be neutralized by his "That's life" attitude.

Collins climbed down from the window sill, reordered his cards, placed the three of spades over Perkins's eight of clubs, and said:

"In the wind are many voices; many voices make great storm in ignorant ears."

What he had done, since spades were the highest "force"—the force of nature—was symbolically to spread fear, confusion, and dissension throughout Perkins's carefully constructed village of peasants. Now it was up to Perkins's partner, Sergeant Grimes: only

160

a heart-diamond pair, representing the union of the forces of emotion and reason, could restore peace and order to Perkins's hamlet.

As Grimes studied his cards, Collins glanced through the window. He saw a cripple trying to climb the tree in front of him. He laughed, having labeled the cripples the comedians of compensation. They arrived at the body shop feeling so sorry for themselves —until their self-pity turned to self-hate as they began taking out their anger on everything and everyone around them. The amputees came on especially hard and fast. They got all worked up talking about their battalion's reunion two months off; or dickered over the number of gooks they'd wasted; laughed over losing their limbs; shot each other with squirt guns in motorized ambushes; and smoked dope in the shade.

Grimes glanced at Wright with a big grin before snapping down the king of hearts and the king of spades.

"Ooooo. Another fuck-up in the Great Wall," muttered Wright. "What is this, Grimes, you want the Tet offensive?"

"A chariot comes. The farmers leave their fields to admire the jade and present their sons. Two chariots come and the Great River will surely turn red with enemy blood. The force of nature flows strong in the veins of brave warriors." Grimes sat back in his chair.

"Quick brown frog, deep pond. Ker-plunk!" said Wright.

"Cut the shit, turkeys. Lay 'em down for the body count. You too, Collins."

Wright and Collins were forced to sacrifice two cards apiece. Luckily, they each had clubs, the lowest suit in the hierarchy—the force of man-made creations.

"Now we bury these suckers with their MIGs." Perkins slid the four cards under the face-down deck, referred to as "God's Trash" or "Genesis," depending on how badly one was losing.

Perkins's next move was a critical one. But as Collins studied his cards, he felt his mind wander back to that afternoon on the third floor when Pollard had explained the mentality of Hanoi Hearts.

"It's an exercise in the Asian thought process," Pollard had said. "That's why it's so challenging to play well: you must realize that the Asian mentality does not construct wispy abstractions the way we do in the West. That doesn't mean they don't think in complex or paradoxical terms; they most certainly do. But their lives, their beliefs, and even their language are concretized in the real object-world because their very words are firmly rooted in the soil of

161

natural phenomena, where movements, change, and conflict exist in the harmonious equipoise of the eternal moment. That's why, when you lay down a card, you paraphrase your motive with a witticism rooted in the ebb and flow of natural events, where permanence and predictability are admissible only inasmuch as Nature is permanent and predictable.

"Of course, we've bastardized the real meaning of Hanoi Hearts. We play it in opposing teams, like cowboys and Indians, the Americans versus the North Vietnamese. Still, it does force us to begin thinking as they do . . . a lesson in the acceptance of mutability, of affiliations limited to field and family, of the meaninglessness of abstraction. The game for me is symbolic of the love-hate relationship I've always had with the Asian civilizations. That's why—"

"Collinsssss!" hissed Perkins. "Are you payin' attention? Now here goes. . . . The young farmer makes a line of stones in his field to separate his crops," began Perkins, dropping the five of clubs over Grimes's pair of hawkish kings, followed by the ten of diamonds: "The old wise one who wandered through many kingdoms returns to teach the farmer. Together they make a great force."

Perkins turned to Collins and said, "You's in Trouble Town, turkey."

Collins moved quickly.

"A farmer in the North hears a strange sound like the voice of his dead wife calling. A kernel of grain has sprouted unattended. He leaves the wall, returns to the good earth." Collins laid down the jack of hearts. "The one deposed from the House of Justice by your bloodthirsty kings returns like a maiden to her father's hearth," he continued as he put down the queen of diamonds, followed by the ace of spades: "Made of dust, this wall so returns. The farmers and soldiers have left. The divided empire is reunited in peace."

"Nice work, Collins," said Wright. "Jack. Queen. Ace. . . . There goes the DMZ. And I've got the king of creation." Wright tossed the king of clubs on the pile.

"Well," said Grimes, "I've got the ace of clubs here, but you Chinks got us again. So much for the Stars 'n' Stripes. . . . Shuffle up, will ya, Collins."

"I'm out for a while. Dixon . . . you want to play?" Collins motioned to one of the onlookers.

"Sure. My great-great-grandpappy rode with General Lee. He

162

an' Sherman together'd waste the gooks," said Dixon, taking Collins's place.

Collins climbed into the window casement above the four troopers at the card table and sat sideways with his knees drawn up to his chest. He leaned his head against the cold marble frame and thought about Captain Pollard again. Nieland hadn't dropped five patients after all: only Collins, Wright, and Alexander. Collins realized for the first time that Dr. Nieland was not omnipotent and that maybe good men—like Pollard—don't ever go home.

As the card game continued, Collins watched a few cripples maneuver through the vines and overgrown rosebushes. Their journey marked the beginning of a common but solitary ritual along the peninsulas of close-cropped grass walkways. Nervous and fidgety, they had come to face the conditions of their bodies with the sobriety of reformed alcoholics. Alone. Solemn figures in weird contraptions navigated silently across the lawns, casting shadows of elongated spinning wheels, enormous rhomboid gearboxes on motorized wheelchairs, and gigantic crutches.

Cicadas rattled and screeched in the swaying branches high above the compound. A few of the cripples meditated in the quiet isolation. Then, slowly, a hand moved to grasp the missing limb replaced by a part, often followed by the momentary shock—the fear and horror confirmed—and then the wretched stare of a man made so grotesque to his own touch that his living flesh writhes in disgust.

In the cool tranquillity of a late Texas afternoon they begin with Step One under the heading "Exercises in Extension" from the *Manual for Individual Reacclimation,* rubbing muscles, twisting appendages, and stretching digits. Then they practice moving their legs and arms. Some examine their parts like a watchmaker, looking for a hint of imperfection in the workmanship. Others stand their substitutes against a tree trunk or rose trellis to study the sculpture with an aesthetic eye: the hand of Ulysses, the foot of Mercury, Apollo's arm, the leg of Achilles—but also with the cold eye of a frightened and unbelieving twenty-year-old American.

One rises cautiously from his chair to contemplate walking a few steps; another picks flowers with the clumsiness of Frankenstein's monster.

163

Legs that buckle, feet that drag, arms that won't extend, hands locked open . . . down they go! Again, and another.

They fall into the rosebushes and across the miniature white picket fences. Some accept the falling and lie there gathering strength and courage for another try; others pound the ground and tear clods of grass or flowers from the earth. The cicadas screech in a mocking crescendo. All fall down.

A cripple leaning against the pump house turns up the volume on his cassette recorder. He moves his leg with both hands, straightens it, and slouches back against the building.

> . . . my light come shining
> from the West out to the East.
> Any day now,
> any way now
> I shall be released.
> They say everything can be replaced.
> They say every distance is not near.
> Yet I remember every face
> of every man who put me here.

Collins has found a new variety of bitterness here on the second floor—a unique sense of letdown and failure. The patients in these wards react to news from the front with scorn and disgust. But they don't know what it is they hate. The very same areas that were such crucial campaigns and costly battles a few months ago have today been lost or surrendered to the VC. How can that be? they ask. Some here have fought to hold those peaks and valleys, which Walter Cronkite says are now VC strongholds. They blame Thieu, Johnson, Nixon; greed, stupidity, corruption; the imperialist war hawks, the silent majority, the peaceniks, the yellow bastards, the Chase Manhattan Bank.

But no one seems to know for sure how all this came to pass. Most know they are losing a war that should never have got out of control; and yet, having fought in it, they find it bitter now to stand on the sidelines helplessly, watching it being lost. And the pervasive atmosphere of the second level is this bitter mystery of having been called upon in the most drastic way one moment, only to be forgotten and discarded the next, like the territory so hard won and so easily given up. Why?

Again, later this evening, another base camp falls. This time on the roller-coaster ridge just a few kilometers north of Hué. A TV reporter steps out from behind a burning half-track with a hand-painted Running Bear insignia blistering off the armor plate. "A paradigm of incompetence and cowardice on the part of the South Vietnamese regulars assigned to this important support base," says the reporter, pushing his thick glasses back up on the bridge of his nose. A wounded Marine flashes by as the camera jerks into tele-photo focus: VC artillery pumping rounds on the woven mesh air-strip. For the past three months, the reporter tells them, this camp has been held "at all costs because of its strategic importance as a defense to the coast." What they see is not a group of stalwart defenders, but the South Vietnamese troops scurrying like beetles from this major base camp secured and operated by Americans for the past two years.

"So *this* is Vietnamization! You just hand everythin' over to the fuckin' enemy!" shouts a patient, leaning toward the TV.

Someone sitting behind Collins bounces a soda can off the picture tube. And another. Soda splashes on the curtains, drips down over a shot of downtown Saigon. A glass smashes against the wall as the camera pans the U.S. embassy.

"Well, well, well. There you see it. See it?" Grimes asks, with a confidence uncommon to most patients on the second floor. He tosses his *Playboy* on the table as a Mobil seascape comes on. "I know my wife an' I are gonna get divorced. Maybe not this month, maybe not in six months. But I know what I feel. You know—like a sixth sense of somethin'—when the handwriting's on the wall. I haven't said a word about it yet. And maybe she knows, and maybe she don't. Doesn't matter now anyway. But I know that I'm dodgin' the truth with her about our marriage. We promised this and we promised that. . . . It's the sort of feeling you try to shove aside. But then every time you begin thinkin' about yourself and your future, the feeling comes back again. Something in your mind.

"And I got that same feelin' over there. I just felt it again. I mean, about why I was doing what I was doing. I just woke up one mornin' and I didn't give a shit anymore—I just didn't care and I knew I was just going through the motions, hoping to get my ass outa there before the whole thing went to hell. You can support a lie so long as the pressure don't get too great. But the pressures did get to be too much—for me at least. I knew the war would end the way it's ending like I know I'm gettin' divorced before I'm divorced.

"Now, you all know I'm the last one to run away from a fight. Dixon's seen me in action. Right, Dixie? And I ain't been brought up to give up, neither. But I ain't no kamikaze, either. I just got to the point where I was sayin' I don't care *that much* anymore. It ain't no Pentagon hocus-pocus either; it's just that the divorce has begun, only no one will say it to anyone's face. But why waste the rest of your life hanging on to somethin' that ain't gonna be worth a shit anyways? So maybe you have to get the shit kicked out of you before you get smartened up enough to admit it just ain't worth it. Forget who's to blame. Just get out. Is that chickening out, or just common sense?"

"Yeah, O.K., Grimes," responded one of the second-floorers in an angry tone, "but how about all the guys who were wasted over there? They could have died for something. Now they'll have died for nothing. Not only that; we're getting our asses wiped by a bunch of fucking gooks. That's a real nice parting shot for the world to see —America with its back to the gooks. We shoulda dropped the goddamn H-bomb months ago. Years ago."

A few heads in the circle bobbed in silent agreement, like moorings on a calm bay.

"What I'm sayin'," answered Grimes, "is this stuff we're watchin' now shouldn't come as such a depressing shock. Didn't the rest of you figure it'd turn out like this? The afternoon I saw this lieutenant stuffin' heroin into a smoke canister, I knew the war to save Vietnam was kaput. I think the best troopers I know—or knew—already sniffed out the worthlessness of it all. Like they had some sixth sense. They knew and accepted the war for the farce it is and so they did it better and smoother than the rest of us.

"But I was slower or something. So for me, I felt like I'd been had the whole time I was in Nam, that's all. More than that, really—I was divided: now that I knew the truth about what was going down, how was I to act? Just go on playing dumb grunt leading more dumb grunts to the happy hunting ground and don't go asking any questions? Say that it's not in my job description to reason why, like the rest of us lifers? Or should I try to convince command that what I knew I knew was right—that I'd figured it out? Well, I tried the last choice and I became one of you. Hello—pleased to meet you."

Grimes was permitted to visit with his wife again the following morning. Collins watched the healthy, handsome, intelligent-look-

166

ing man walk out of the main entrance and head for the pool without water. Grimes had said that he decided to become a career man in the Army shortly after he returned from Korea in 1953. "I got so bored when I got out that I decided to re-up—permanently." Now he was thirty-nine, with a wife and two children, and Vietnam had become synonymous with the biggest change in his life. "What I thought was right and what the Army said was right were the same for the past twenty years. Then I go to Nam and wake up one morning and I knew one of us was wrong."

From his perch on a second-floor window sill, Collins saw Grimes kiss and embrace a tall, thin woman with blond hair and dark-blue shorts. He took her by the hand and led her to a bench by the pool. They sat turned toward each other, talking and smiling in the bright sunshine. They put their arms around each other's shoulders and pulled themselves close together. Then, as Grimes leaned back and began talking, a serious, sad expression came over her face. She in turn became suddenly very animated, with her hands held beseechingly toward her husband as if explaining something over and over again. He turned away, then jumped up from the bench and walked swiftly away. He turned around to face her at a distance and began shouting. She listened intently at first, and then with disbelief. She covered her face with her hands and then carried it to her lap. She shuddered. Grimes shook his head and walked slowly back toward the bench. He pulled the green ribbon out of her hair. Blond, wavy curls spilled over her knees and hid her face. Grimes knelt in front of her, placing his head against hers. He rolled his forehead back and forth along the sides of her concealed face. She shuddered even more. He stood up and looked down at her for a while before turning and heading toward the main entrance to Chambers. She lifted up her face, wet with tears, and walked after him sobbing, shouting his name. He disappeared into the hospital.

"From affection to estrangement in twenty minutes," muttered Collins as he jumped down off the window sill to join the other patients already gathered for discussion group. As he approached the day room, he saw the form of Dr. Penderspot leaving the ward. Collins took a seat between Alexander and Perkins.

Dr. Benjamin Goldfarb, the most recent addition to the staff at Chambers, was moderating.

". . . and you say you feel you were no different than any other twenty-year-old when you were shipped over there," said Goldfarb to a patient Collins had never seen before.

"Yeah. I looked the same, talked the same, dressed like 'em, laughed at the same stupid jokes with 'em. You know, no difference really."

"Who's that guy?" Collins whispered in Perkins's ear.

"Name's Prout. Corporal Rodney Prout. He was dropped from this ward to floor one the day before you dropped in here. Pender-spot just brought him up and had a few words with Goldfarb. The turkey's in Trouble Town. You get sent back up from floor one and you might as well take what's left of your brain and put it out with the rest of the garbage."

"I'm not sure I understand you yet. . . . And so your question to the group is what?" asked Goldfarb.

"I'm not asking them anything," responded Prout angrily. "I'm telling you I don't see why I'm here and the rest of us million vets are back home."

"Maybe it has something to do with your attitude," suggested Goldfarb, sticking his finger into his thin black mustache. "Perhaps one of your buddies here could point out to you that you still have a very bad attitude toward Asians."

Half the patients slid off their chairs and fell to the floor in fits of laughter. Wright tried to repeat Goldfarb's last sentence, but he was laughing too hard. He turned red, trying to catch his breath in gasps:

". . . bad attitude toward Asians," he finally managed to say.

Goldfarb was red too, but he wasn't laughing.

"No," shouted Dixon from the floor, wiping tears from his cheeks. "Prout . . . he . . . Christ, Prout loves the fuckin' gooks. We all do!"

And another round of hysteria swept over the group. It was the first time Collins could recall laughing like this in a long time. He chuckled along with the rest of the patients until he saw Grimes walking toward the day room. He had tears in his eyes too. Collins noticed that Grimes had tied the green ribbon he had undone from his wife's hair through a buttonhole in his shirt. The laughter ceased abruptly as Grimes sat down at one end of the semicircle.

"Yeah, Doctor, we love the gooks," said Prout bitterly. His eyes were riveted to Goldfarb's. "It's your mind we gotta get right. 'Cause you couldn't have said that to me if you knew anything and knew what you were talkin' about." Prout was so angry that the words burst from his mouth in spurts of saliva. He rose slowly from his chair and aimed his finger at Goldfarb.

"I'm gonna tell you something about them and us. About all of us. And you better believe me or you're gonna get yourself beat to shit going 'round here sayin' things like that. You understand?"

Goldfarb's thin little hands trembled in his lap. He crossed his legs over them.

"He's scared shitless," whispered Wright, leaning across Perkins.

"He should be, for saying that," Collins whispered back. "But who can ever really understand just what happened—over there, or in here?"

"It's like what we were saying that night with Pollard. Remember, about the pact?"

"Yes, I remember," replied Collins quietly.

". . . and then I'd be lookin' at them. Asians, like you said. And I'd think: I'm a human being. And they're supposedly humans. But they're not! You understand now, Doctor? They're rats. Nothin' but rats. And I used to shoot rats back in the dump in Ohio, where I come from. It was no different then, and no different in Nam. No different really."

"No different," repeated Goldfarb.

"I'll tell ya why. I wasn't in much action after the first few months. I spent most of my tour at Base Camp Blueballs, and I'd be drivin' this deuce, you see, runnin' garbage from Blueballs to the dumpin' area. You know, from the mess hall to the dump. An' it would be crawlin' with these dirty disease-carryin' gookkids crawlin' in an' outa the rotten stinkin' garbage. You see now? Christ, it turned my stomach just to see them. 'Cause the base camp joes fed these same gookkids plenty of chow every day. Good chow. Stateside chow. An' then these gookkids'd show up at the dump. They'd see me dumpin' the mornin's slop an' come crawlin' over to the back of the lift, their sick'nin' faces smilin', maggots on their necks, smilin' for the slop to run outa the drums and pour over 'em like a shower of shit, an' they'd cup their hands an' rub it on 'em smilin' and drinkin' the shit smilin'. Mind you, smilin'!" he shouted, smashing his fists together. "An' they'd sing out, 'Campbell's Campbell's mmmmmmm good. Campbell's Campbell's mmmmmmm good,' over an' over an' over again. Every mornin'. . . . Rats!" he yelled. "Rats!"

"Rats," agreed Goldfarb, nodding his head.

"Rats," Prout repeated.

"And you remembered shooting rats in the dump back in Ohio and so you—"

"No. Not at first," Prout interrupted, pointing to his head with its whitewall haircut. "Not right away. . . . I mean, I know the difference between right an' wrong. I tried to stop myself. I tried to feel sorry for 'em. But day after day after day. The joes at the base camp gave 'em clothes, food, even money an' toys. I tried to think it through, but I couldn't feel nothin' for these gookkids. Just animals. Less than fuckin' animals!"

"He's right," said Grimes, twirling the green ribbon around his finger. "You just plain stop feeling." A few of the others nodded in agreement.

"I couldn't feel anything either after a while," mumbled Collins. He thought he had said it so quietly that no one overheard him.

"Me needer," echoed Alexander, who sat with his eyes closed next to Collins. Goose bumps ran up Collins's spine.

". . . one of these rats reminded me of somethin' special. He had the face of the perfect gookkid. Ya know what I mean? If the gooks had *Life* magazine, this gookkid' w'd be on the cover. And the headline would read, 'The Real Victims of Nam,' or some such garbage. And one mornin' I jumped off the back of the tailgate and landed with all my weight on this gookkid's head. Crushed it. It went *pop!* Like stepping on an egg. And this shit ran out of his eyes an' ears. It didn't look any different than the garbage I'd been pouring off that tailgate for months. No different really."

"And so you jumped on this kid's head in the dump?" Goldfarb had turned white.

"This turkey was in this ward for three weeks and I never heard any of this," Perkins whispered to Collins.

"It felt weird, man!" Prout shouted out defensively. "Don't go gettin' me wrong now. Sure it felt strange. But I felt much better just the same. Much better. So the next mornin' I brought my Mattel out of the cab an' began pickin' off these rats—these smilin' gookkids—one at a time. Pinggg. Pinggg. . . . Ping. Yeah, I shot these rats in the dump and then cranked up the Caterpillar an' plowed 'em under. They rotted with the rest of the shit. You can change ice to water, but shit is shit."

"Shit . . ." repeated Goldfarb.

Prout came out of his confessional trance long enough to realize that a dozen vets were listening to him. It shocked him to find that he wasn't alone in the dumping area at Base Camp Blueballs.

"Yeah," he said, looking back at Goldfarb, "shit. You're gettin' your mind right." Prout sat down and stared at the floor. Goldfarb took a long breath and sighed. He changed his position in his chair.

"And—ah—you buried them with your bulldozer?"

"Yeah," Prout answered without looking up. "And then some prick, some colonel flying in the area, saw me through his field glasses and landed his chopper right in the fuckin' dump. Right in the dump!" he shouted. "An' held me there till Security from the base could get over to pick me up. And I ended up in here. But why just me?" he screamed. "Plenty of grunts wasted gooks who weren't dressed in black pajamas an' carryin' a rifle. Gooks are gooks. That's all I can tell you."

A silence fell over the discussion group until a distinguished-looking man with graying sideburns rose to his feet. He reminded Collins of his own father, and in his mind he transformed this rather cool, stately patient into a tweedy corporate executive.

"He is right, of course, Captain Goldfarb. He is correct," said Major Clifford Olson, recently relieved of his position with Operations Command–First Air Cavalry, to become senior patient of ward 2-W. "Anyone who spent any time over there could have done what Calley did. Whether *he* actually did it or not doesn't matter. My Lai is a drop in the bucket. . . . It happens because we believe that all lives are sacred and everyone's equal and has the same given rights as anyone else. That's poor thinking. And if they're not equal, we *make* them equal—by deceiving ourselves. And when we get ourselves deceived, we set out to deceive the world. . . . Until our bluff gets called and we got to put *our bodies* on the line. You get poor performance. Rights? Equality? Democracy? You earn your rights. You pay big for equality, if there is such a thing. . . . Do you understand what I'm saying?"

"You're talking about the U.S.," responded Goldfarb quickly.

"Yes, the Western countries. But especially the States. The ones that put theories ahead of reality. An army's for war, not for games. This country's experimenting with hundreds of thousands of lives on the notion that this Vietnamization claptrap will work. It won't work. Take it from me. And the same country that's outraged over Calley—prosecutes him for war crimes—hems 'n' haws over Kent

State. Can you imagine? Guardsmen wasting our own kids on a campus in Ohio in the 1970s. And the politicians saying, basically, that the kids got what they deserved. That's a very poor performance. These colors may not run, but they sure as hell bleed. Here, and over there. Prout is right, though, Captain. You have my word on it. As an officer and a gentleman. The Asians are rats. All of 'em. Gooks, Chinks, VC, Chicoms—"

"An' niggers," pronounced Alexander from the other end of the semicircle. "I want dat boy down de end to say gooks, Chinks, an' niggers. Now, boy, you's say dat for you ol' Uncle Tom here." Alexander got up from his chair and walked with a slouched-over, bouncing gait past Dr. Goldfarb. As he approached Major Olson, Alexander snapped his fingers with each step. Goldfarb seemed determined to intervene this time. He shuffled his feet. He opened his mouth. And he stuck his finger into his mustache.

"Now, we's bin privledge to hear dis stiff in hiz whidt coat get his ed-u-ca-shun. So now I's gonna done ed-u-cate you, boy, 'bout niggers an' other types. Now"—he continued standing in front of the major—"you's says after me: Gooks. Chinks. An' niggers."

"Why?"

"Now don't go an' mess wid da teacher, boy. Jus' do like I says."

"Gooks. Chinks. . . . Niggers."

"Wow! Put your ear ta dat re-si-tashun. We got us one smardt whidty. Now you gets da real ed-u-ca-shun. Us niggers bin in dis same po-sishun some two hundred years an' we ain't seen no release. You done give Sambo a right—da right to be kilt jus' like any ol' papa-san. We gonna go an' lay dis here body down like we's bin doin' fo' years. Shootin' rats in da rubbish is like goin' coon huntin'. Sho'nuf seems da same to me, oh yeah."

"Why the hell are you telling this to me?" demanded Major Olson.

"'Cause this ain't no game." Alexander put his thick black finger against the major's graying temple as though he were holding a gun to his head.

"'Cause it's best that you know your enemy when you see him," stated Alexander with an abrupt change from his usual dialect. "Not like it was over there, where everyone looked the same and your yellow buddy one day is your slant-eyed enemy the next. Oh, no. 'Cause when I get outa here, I ain't gonna go back to our wooden shack in Alabama. Oh, no; not this boy. 'Cause when you see me

172

again, if you ever do, I just might be burnin' *your* house, shootin' *your* kids, or rapin' *your* wife. 'Cause, buddy, the war ain't over, an' I'll play the game an' be cool till I get out. 'Cause all that good stuff I learned in Nam I'm gonna be puttin' to use in Dee-troit, in Neeww-York, in Dee-Cee. 'Cause me an' a lot of other boogies in Nam already got us a little pact together, 'bout what we're gonna do when we come back to the States. 'Cause we ain't gonna be boppin' on de block no'mor an' jive-talkin' with whitey 'bout jobs, an' pay, an' de po-leece bustin' our teeth. Das right, brudder. Das de truth. Ain't gonna be no 'mor jive-talkin' with de King's En-glosh. We gonna be some black mutter-fuckers out der on de street an' no 'mor whitey gonna slap me upside de head. Oh, no, brudder. Dis war's just begun fo' *you,* an' you best not forget that.

"Now ain't dat de darndest truth yo' little ol' pink pig's ears dun ever heard? Oh, Lordy, gonna be some cum-bustion. Oh-eee!" Alex-ander laughed, rolling his eyes and slapping his knees like a bongo player. "Oh-eee, yes. . . . Now den, Mister In-ter-loc-utor," he said, looking around at Goldfarb, "what's de dif'rence between a gook, a Chink, an' a nigger?"

The psychiatrist shrugged his shoulders.

"Dat's right! You gots it! Like da man jus' finish sayin', no dif-rence. No dif'rence ad all."

Alexander performed a ten-second tap dance in front of the semi-circle. He exaggerated his smile so that his teeth shone in a bizarre grin while he crossed his legs and twirled an imaginary cane. He looked like a vaudeville actor until he dropped suddenly onto one knee and machine-gunned the audience. He left the room, snap-ping his fingers to his favorite spiritual: "Oh, operator, gimme Jesus on da line." The two other black members of the discussion group chuckled and walked out, followed by the other patients, who went into the barracks.

Wright headed for the Ping-Pong table on the deck. Collins walked the length of the sleeping quarters and climbed up into his favorite window casement. He felt the warm weight of the sun streaming through the glass, crisscrossed with thin strands of wire. Rhythmic respirations from a napping trooper mingled in Collins's mind with particles of dust undulating in the shafts of sunlight. The minute pieces seemed strangely sensitive as they bobbed and twirled in floating circles of effortless confusion. Some flew off in jerky spasms as though controlled by an invisible puppeteer. Others

173

danced slowly in a widening descent and settled on the card table beneath him.

He was more weak and listless this morning than he had been at the end of his tour with the surgical unit. The accumulation of incidents and recollections fell over his thoughts like a heavy quilt. He slouched down in the casement and wondered about Captain Pollard, one floor above him. His eyes closed and his pale hand dropped limply off his knee. His head fell against his shoulder.

"I, too, must make some sense of this nonsense," he muttered cynically. "Ha. Ha. Ha. That would *be* insanity."

He recalled the half-dozen pages he had written in his notebook during the past five days. As the passages echoed in his mind, he grew increasingly frustrated with his inability to convey the reality of Chambers and portray its inhabitants. What he had written to date, he decided angrily, was a banal hodgepodge of incongruous and inarticulate one-liners: this patient did this in Nam, this patient said this about the gooks, this patient freaked out because . . .

Collins suddenly sat bolt upright, awakened by the revelation that his inability to make some sense of this nonsense was his own: his failure to make sense of himself.

"I missed it," he said, looking down the length of the ward. He jumped from the window sill and walked swiftly to his bedstand. He opened the drawer and took out his notebook.

"I missed it," he began writing. "These are living people, men, not just veterans and patients. And Chambers is merely another mental hospital. That's all it is. And Vietnam? . . . Vietnam is the catalyst, not the symptom, not the entire cause.

"I see their heads, their bodies, and hear what they say. That's the mistake. I see now. Pollard said 'sense,' to make some sense of the nonsense. But he meant more than just some act of the intellect. He meant in the primitive sense too. The senses. The feelings. Make some sense of the nonsense.

"If you want people *out there* to understand how all this happened, you're going to have to put them *in here*, right inside Chambers. You're going to have to make them sense it, feel it in themselves, in their bones first. Then, maybe, they'll comprehend it in their brain."

174

CHAPTER 14

The bus swung slowly away from the asphalt walkway leading from the hospital, passed the pool without water, surrounded by cripples basking in the sun, rounded the corner by the Fourth Army photo lab, and stopped facing the monolithic clock tower in the old quadrangle. Near the top was a light-gray stone tablet inscribed: "IN PEACE, PREPARE FOR WAR." Some famous soldiers had passed through this post: Ord, Wood, Robert E. Lee, Pershing, Theodore Roosevelt, and Dwight Eisenhower, who met Mamie Doud at the OC in 1916. They lived just down the block, at 688-B Infantry Post Road. Statues of these men sat in the tower wall.

Gilliland slumped forward in his seat, pulled a knob of bubble gum off the back of a cushion, and popped it into his mouth. The bus turned left and headed into San Antonio.

What a distinguished group had been assembled for this outing: Specialist Minor, Sergeants Gilliland, Millsaps, Turner, and Tylee, and Colonel McCafferty from the third floor; Sergeants Wright, Franklin, and Alexander, Corporal Rodriguez, Ranger Perkins, Master Sergeant Grimes, Lieutenant Williams, Specialist Collins, and Major Olson from the second-floor wards; and Sergeant Sailor and Master Sergeant Perkins from the first level; but the majority of the sixty-eight patients on the bus were nameless ninety-day-wonder rehabs from the first level.

The bus had been loaded by floor and ward beginning with the more "reconditioned" psychos, who were assigned seats at the back. Collins, Wright, and Alexander sat together just forward of the center. They talked and joked along with the others from the first and second floors while they waited for the patients from the third floor to be boarded. Collins and Wright had been expecting Pollard to join them, but when the aides loaded the last third-floorer, the Professor hadn't appeared. Then, after a fifteen-minute delay, Captain Pollard emerged through the main doors, with Nieland on one side and Hinckley on the other, holding the Professor by his left arm. Nieland spoke to Pollard outside the bus, and then the psychiatrist walked back into the hospital. Hinckley and Pollard climbed aboard. Collins and Wright had waved and called the Professor's name as he took his seat behind the driver, but he did not acknowledge either of them.

"Where we goin'?" shouted Millsaps for the tenth time.

No one answered, until Hinckley turned around and assured the psychos that they were in for a "copacetic trip."

"What the hell's up with Pollard?" asked Wright, frowning at Collins.

"I don't know. They must be restraining him now. See that gauze on his wrist?"

"Yeah, right. I do see it," replied Wright. "Shit, he looks like a stiff from the iso bins on the fourth floor. He musta heard us yelling to him. Right? What's up?"

"I don't know, damn it. He's on a twenty-one-day extension. Nieland got him more time. Remember?"

"Yeah. Yeah. Right. . . . But something's wrong with him."

"Let's try to hook up with him when we get to wherever we're going."

"O.K. Right."

On the right side of the bus from Chambers, a bus full of Brownies waited for the light to change. Some were pointing, laughing at "those men in pajamas," others flashed the peace sign. What did they mean? The pack mothers were puzzled.

"What are them?" asked Franklin sarcastically as he pointed at the girls. "You Wacs in trainin' to be dykes?"

The olive-green transport rounded the corner and passed the Davey Crockett Hotel, crept past sidewalks and intersections packed with tourists in madras shirts and walking shorts. Nikon.

176

Instamatic. Young families attached hand-to-hand wound their way snakelike between parking meters and halted traffic, wove in wide circles around the groups of quiet Chicanos meandering aimlessly under wide straw hats. A coonskin cap lay flattened in the road like a gutless furry animal. Polaroid. Canon. They had come to look at History, at the site of the Lone Star State's conception. Hasselblad. Leicaflex.

"Climb up on the bench next to Mommy. Hold Jane's hand. . . . Look at me."

Click.

"Memories. What are they really, Collins?" he said aloud. But when Collins heard his own voice, he realized that those were Nieland's words and not the distant voices of dead and dying troopers speaking through his vocal cords. At first he was shocked with this realization, and then relieved to know that he could at least discriminate which voice belonged to whom.

"Hey, Collins, what the hell are you waitin' for? You wanna sit on the bus for two hours talking to yourself or come get some culture?" asked Hinckley, about to step off the bus. The driver smiled and shook his head, removing his cap. He curled over the wheel, laughing.

"Yes, two scoops of culture with jimmies, please," said Collins, moving out of his seat.

"Come on, will ya?"

The driver cracked up. "Let me outa here. I'll be at the bar, Specialist, right over there, when you're ready to take these . . . these whatever they are back to the post. . . . Whew. Let me by."

Kids pointed and laughed, cameras clicked, some parents jeered and pulled their children under their arms as the column of sickly-white ex-soldiers made their way toward the stone façade. Franklin smiled and flipped the bird while Wright graded the women according to the size of their tits. "Mmm, tasty." Rodriguez extended his arms in a slow twirl. The Professor read aloud from *Moby Dick*, with his bandaged hand raised in the air. Sailor walked straight ahead, fingers curled into his palm, fly open, a few curly hairs poking out. Alexander, humming a few bars from his favorite gospel hymn, held up a fist clenched so tight that his veins and muscles leaped out from wrist to neck. Williams passed out olive-green pencils stamped "PROPERTY US ARMY" to the kids and puzzled parents, saying, "Here. Take two.

They forgot to put the lead in some." Colonel McCafferty was moaning up front.

Plainclothesmen with Mace pistols were closing the Alamo to the public. Two jeeps filled with MPs drove up on the grass. They were clearing the old fort, the museum, and the long barracks in order that these ex-soldiers might visit the shrine without embarrassing or molesting the tourists.

They had arrived too early, Hinckley said, and had best be quiet and stay together "until the perimeters are secured." O.K. O.K. But a perverse spirit rose among them as they entered the cool, dimly lit quarters of San Antonio de Valero. Collins looked down at a plaque embedded in the stone floor as he crossed the threshold:

> On this spot, January 4, 1937,
> Bones of Four Unknown Persons
> Unearthed, Reinterred May 11, 1937

"Fresh air for four months. . . . Spanish, Mexican, American, or Indian?"

"What's that, Collins?"

"Whose earth?"

"What?"

"Leftovers. You're standing on them." He pointed at the bronze plaque embedded in a concrete rectangle cut into the floor.

"They're down for the second time. They won't feel—"

"Hey! Collins and Wright. Knock it off!" ordered Hinckley from across the mission. He had just emerged through a door, walking a stooped-over woman slowly across the floor. She took little shuffling steps with the aid of a cane in her right hand. Hinckley walked bent over in order to talk in her tiny ear. They spoke quietly, she looking down or straight ahead, smiling, and pointing her cane with every few steps at the various antique furnishings and paintings. When they reached a long mahogany counter, she nodded to Hinckley, thanking him for the escort. Once behind the counter, she turned and faced the assembly.

"Now," began Hinckley in his most authoritative manner, "I want all of you to quiet down and pay attention. We have a special treat in store for us on this outing. . . . This is Mrs. Abigail Mayfield, the hon—"

"Dickenson Mayfield. Abigail Dickenson Mayfield," she interrupted, her head tilted toward the ceiling.

178

"Yes. Yes. Pardon me. This is Mrs. Abigail Dickenson Mayfield," resumed Hinckley. He wiped his forehead with a two-by-two gauze. "Mrs. Mayfield is the honorary curator of the Alamo. Her son is General Stratton Mayfield, over on the post."

"Yeah. The asshole."

"Now, if you give Mrs. Mayfield your undivided attention, you'll learn a lot about this place, and men like Bowie and Crockett and the others. After she's finished, you rehabs from the first level will take the rest of you patients around the area. . . . Oh—ah—Jacobson, keep an eye on the man to your left. Yeah. His name's Gilliland," said the specialist, pointing at the Gator, who was standing hunched over apelike, drooling, his hands dangling around his knees.

When Hinckley stepped aside and retreated to a darkened recess in the wall, the old matron was standing under a concentrated beam of light from the ceiling. She was wearing a yellow print calico dress—tiny yellow roses on thin green stems—with red-and-white trim along the hem. The fabric was puffed up at the top of her shoulders. White lace encircled her neck. She raised her thin hand and pushed the curved combs firmly into her white hair. A few wispy strands hung from her woven bun like the tattered remnants of an antebellum wedding veil. Her powdered face, with rouge blemishes on each cheek—one higher than the other—teetered and tottered on her neck. And a weird, high-pitched whistle came from her quivering lips with each exhalation of breath.

Her whole body synchronized itself into an abrupt spasm as she opened her mouth to speak the first words:

"Amen . . . the strength to . . . Amen. Good afternoon, gentlemen. On behalf of the San Antonio Rehistorical and Development Association and the Daughters of Texas Independence, I would like to welcome. Welcome ya'all to the birthnest of the Lone Star State. Which is Texas, in eighteen . . ."

Her voice had grown louder as she mentioned the "Daughters"; and by the time she reached "the Lone Star State," she held her head high, back straight and stiff, and her brown eyes twinkled with the gleam of a young woman's. The guards leaned into dark corners, their arms folded high across their chests.

"As ya'all know," she resumed with a more pronounced Southern drawl, "this is the famous Alamo mission, where a group of one hundred and approximately eighty-two men met their destiny one afternoon. Their destiny was their death, their immortality, and the founding of this great State. Brave men from the length and breadth. Came here in February in the Year of Our Lord Jesus Christ eighteen hundred and thirty-six. They came to provide. To protect. The helpless American families against the Mexican dictator, His Excellency General Antonio López de Santa Anna, President of the Republic of Mexico. And they came to win the Province of Texas for America. On this very earth beneath your shoes, the famous Congressionalman from Tennessee, Colonel David Crockett, whose portrait hangs about me to the right—

> "I leave this rule, for others when I am dead
> Be always sure you are right, then go, a head—

was shot through the head defeating the southeast palisade. The painting in the center there, above my head, is the Southern gentleman from Red Banks, South Carolina. William Barret Travis, from Red Banks, South Carolina. Commander of the Alamo. He met with death a few hundred yards from there. Where ya'all's standing. Over on the north wall. And James Bowie, the celebrated explorer and adventurer, was brutally murdered in his bedclothes. That was in the third chamber over in the Long Barracks. His portrait, painted here by the gentleman painter James Donleavy, to your right.

"Over there," she began after a short, shaky pause, "by the stairwell which once led to the artillery on the ceiling, is a charming sketch of Susannah Dickenson. She was my great-grandmother. Susannah, and her daughter Almeron Dickenson from Pennsylvania, Tennessee, and Travis's darky, Jim. These were the ones to leave the Alamo alive. The only ones to leave out of two hundred children, women, and men.

"And there— Young man! Do not expose yourself to a lady. Mr. Hinckley! Mr. Hinckley!" shouted out Abigail, raising her cane at Sailor.

"II did didid didn't know."

"Never mind, sir! Excuse yourself this body and repair your thing to the gentlemen's lounge in the southeast corner of the fosse. . . . Jamie Burnham, please remove this man to fosse," she said to the tall guard leaning against the arched door. The first-floorers shook their heads. The rest of the patients suppressed their laughter until Franklin broke out in a resounding laugh that echoed throughout the stone shrine.

180

". . . outa you, Franklin, and you can go sit on the bus. That's it! One more, from anybody, and you'll all sit on the bus," shouted Hinckley. "Now, that's it, men. I've made myself perfectly clear." He spoke with Mrs. Mayfield for a moment and stepped back into his corner. Her whistle came faster as Sailor was ushered past with his hands in his crotch.

"Hey, mate, don't beat it. Eat it."

Mrs. Mayfield's head vibrated.

In the confusion, Collins and Wright jockeyed through the mob toward Captain Pollard.

"You need a stroboscope to keep her still," the Professor muttered to no one, waving his fingers in front of his eyes.

"Pollard! Pollard!" whispered Wright, as he and Collins came up to him. Pollard looked blankly at each of them.

"Collins. . . . And Wright. Wright. . . . And Collins." He squinted at them.

"What in God's name is with you?" asked Wright.

"I? I, Wright? I have crossed to the other side. But I can see into the distant future, should you wish prophecy. Yet when things draw near, or happen, I perceive nothing of them. Except what others, like you, bring me, I have no news of those who are alive. The past is as dead to me as I am to myself."

His speech and appearance reminded Collins of the first American POW he had seen when he was attached to the First Air Cavalry. The POW, Corporal Winegaard, had been tortured by the VC for three days before he escaped and made his way back to the American encampment. He would have been shot by a grunt if a greenhorn lieutenant in the forward LP hadn't heard him moaning the words to "Hey Jude" as he stumbled through the brush.

"But what'ave they done to you, uh? What happened to your hand?" demanded Wright, touching Pollard's arm.

"Collins Wright Pollard! Be quiet!" shouted Hinckley.

Captain Pollard looked up at Mrs. Mayfield.

"But there was a great deal more to this engorgement than most people realize. In the 1830's—and remember that our Civil War was less than thirty years in the future—there were questions of manifest dignity, slavery, state sovereignty, social contact, and profiteering.

"In Virginia, Judge Upshur of Virginia—afterwards he became Secretary of State under President Tyler—remarked at the state convention in Virginia in 1829. He said, 'If Texas should be obtained, which be strongly desired, it would raise the price of slaves, and be a great advantage to the slaveholders of the State.' Now, as ya'all know, Red Banks, South Carolina, was a breeding state. And influential men, such as Judge Upshur of Virginia, were anxious to see the Province of Texas become a new slave state to further the demand of their stable commodity. Which is slaves, of course."

"Oh, op-or-a-tor. Gimme Martin on da line," sang out Alexander, staring up at the ceiling. "Gimme me Mista Martin Luther King on da line. You done hear what dis whidt woman's sayin', my man?"

"Quiet! Silence! We'll have not talking in the tanks." The old woman's voice echoed in the dark. She raised her cane and shook it threateningly.

"Ya'all 'ill have plenty of time to talk when we tour the grounds. . . . Behin' ya'all, on the wall, is the flag of the Lone Star State. But ya'all remember—"

"What! It's the same as the fuckin' gooks' flag," shouted Franklin, placing his hands against the sides of his head in disbelief. "What's goin' on here? For Christ's—"

"Now, that's the last time I'm gonna tolerable any more outbursts from ya'all. If ya'all can't act like gentlemen act, then ya'all can't expect to be treated like gentlemen."

Franklin stood fixated beneath the flag. His eyes roamed the surface for some bit of evidence to justify this coincidence. The background was divided into two horizontal bands of color: red across the top half and blue on the bottom. A large, cream-colored star with five points sat in the center. Feet shuffled, throats were cleared, Gilliland slipped to the floor, "Red is the color of my true love's land," pronounced the Professor, hand over heart.

"Charlie's infiltrated the Alamo," shouted Franklin.

Mrs. Mayfield beat the countertop with her cane. "Order! Order! Order in the court! Remember that this was not the flag which the defenders of the Alamo fought under! And below our flag is a plaque which contains the proclamation delivered by General Taylor to the Mexican peasants. No. No. You don't have to go over there. It reads as follows: 'Your gob'ment is in the hands of tyrants and usurpers. They have abolished your state gob'ments; they have overthrown your Fed'ral Constitution; they have deprived ya'all of your rights of suffrage, destroyed the liberty of the press, despoiled ya'all of your arms, and reduced ya'all to a state of absolute dependence upon the power of a military dictator. We come to overthrow the tyrants who have destroyed your liberties, but we come to make no war upon the people of Mexico, nor upon any form of free gob'ment they may choose for themselves.' "

". . . nhưng tụi tao không đến đây để gây chiến tranh với người Việt Nam hay để chống lại một chính quyền tự do mà chúng tao lựa chọn cho người Việt Nam," came a voice from a nameless face in the crowd.

"Sự suy nghĩ của mày cũng bị méo mó như đầu óc của mày, đồng chí ạ!" fired back the Professor bitterly.

"Mày muốn nói con gà hay quả trứng, hở Mày!" responded the first-floorer, raising his voice and turning toward Captain Pollard.

"Tụi bay chơi chữ đã nhiều quá rồi nên không còn chút gì để đưa lòng tin vào cả," stated the Professor, patting his ass officiously.

"Ê, coi chừng đó ông bạn," sneered the ninety-day wonder as he pushed his way through the cluster of patients. "Tao đã phải ngồi ở đường Tự Do uống cả một chai rượu burbon mỗi ngày để tìm ra là chữ bắt nguồn từ chữ rồi để đem đi đốt. Từ thuở khai thiên lập địa đã có Chữ, va Chữ đó là Láo Toét."

"So what's your problem?" demanded the first-floorer, switching to English. He shoved the Professor in the chest. *Moby Dick* fell open on the stone floor between the two patients.

"You grab the tall one in blue jeans and I'll take the one in the robe," Hinckley ordered one of the guards as he stepped between the adversaries. The guard took the first-floorer by the wrists from behind and yanked him backward. The other patients, who had already taken sides, grumbled about "police brutality" and the "right to fight."

Hinckley bent over and picked up the book, replaced the jacket, and handed it to the Professor.

"Now listen, Pollard," said the specialist. He took Pollard by the arm. "I don't know what was going on between you two, and at this point I really don't care. All I know is that there are only two NP specialists here, and I need all the help I can get. It's a tricky situation and . . . well, you know the story. O.K., Professor?"

Pollard sighed and nodded.

Hinckley stood in front of him and stared into his eyes. "Come on, Pollard," he whispered sadly, "don't do this to yourself." The spotlight shining down from above accentuated the dark circles under Hinckley's eyes and the worn, expressionless face of the Professor.

"Collins. And you, Wright. Stay with Pollard, O.K.? He's had a rough time, and he's on some heavy meds," said Hinckley. He looked at the guard who had seized the first-floorer. "Get him outa here. Give him to the MPs outside," ordered Hinckley.

"What was that all about?" asked Wright.

"What was what all about?" said Pollard.

"That argument you had in Chink talk."

"He was . . . He was drawing attention to the contradiction inherent in General Taylor's proclamation to the Mexicans. It was the same proclamation, he was saying, which we delivered to the Vietnamese. But you see," continued Pollard coldly, "I know him. He worked for the ESR. Didn't you recognize him, Collins?" Pollard laughed.

Collins made no reply and turned his eyes toward Mrs. Mayfield.

". . . ya'all can see the small band of Americans who fought in the Alamo actually touched off the Mexican-American war. There were terendous fractions in this country over the issues and our gob'ment secretly supporting a war down here in another country. . . .

"The parchment in the frame is an address from Mr. Giles, Congressionalman from Maryland. He said, and I quote ad verbatum: 'We must march from Texas straight to the Pacific Ocean, and be bounded by its roaring wave. It is the destiny of the white race, it is the destiny of the Anglo-Saxton race; and if they fail to perform, they will not come up to that high position which Providence, in His mighty Gob'ment, has assigned them.' "

"Tell that to Chairman Mao," came a voice in the assembly.

"Now, we call that divine right of manifest destiny. And it can be applied anywhere. So ya'all can see what a trying and difficult situation these two hundred brave men forced when Santa Anna attacked with his source of twenty-five hundred trained troops. And on that night before Santa Anna laid siege to the Alamo, Colonel Travis wrote: 'To the People of Texas and all Americans in the World: I will never surrender or repeat. I call on ya'all in the name of Liberty, of Patriotism and everything dear to the American character, to come to our aid, with all dispatch. If this call is neglected, I am determined to remain myself as long as possible and die like a soldier who never forgets what is due to his own honor and that of his country. Victory or Death. P.S. The Lord is on our side.' "

"*Gott mit uns,*" whispered the Professor.

"Now then, Mr. Hinckley will redress you before we break and tour the rest of the landmark. Of particular interest is the famous Long Barracks. And do stop across the street and see the monument just on the other side of the circle out front. If ya'all have any questions, I shall be glad to answer them. Answer them, if I can. My name is Abigail Dickenson Mayfield, and on behalf of the Daughters, I hope my brief introduction to the fort has been illuminary. Thank you, gentlemen, and do come again. Welcome to Texas. Do come again. Good evening."

"Thank you! Thank you very much, Mrs. Mayfield," said Hinckley above the light applause. "Outstanding." Her beaming smile danced in midair to the beat of her cane as it rattled along the base of the cabinet. The specialist helped her to a chair.

"O.K. All you first-floorers who met with Dr. Penderspot this morning, you know the gig. Right? One on three. Any problems you can't handle, you got the blue caps on the inside of the walls, and the red hats on the outside. When you hear the whistle, fall in at the statue in the middle of the circle. . . . Ah, Jacobson, you take Gilliland back to— Jacobson! Where the hell's Gilliland? Where's Gilliland!"

They turned up the Gator as Pollard, Wright, Collins, and their chaperon approached the outer grounds. He was lying on his stomach in one of the shallow, man-made moats just beyond the entrance to the trinket shop. The narrow, stone-lined trenches surrounding the buildings were stocked with oversized goldfish. He was having lunch when they pulled him out of the mud, and he surfaced grinning, with a fish in his hand.

"Quite a gourmet, this one. The Oriental suggestion . . ." muttered the Professor as they entered the Long Barracks behind the Alamo.

They looked in on an exhibit of Bowie lying in bed, attended by his faithful subordinate, William Travis. Caught between the catalogue of federal and state grants blaring from one speaker and the cries and groans of dying men emanating from another, Travis seemed to assume a peculiar expression. The Professor tapped his finger against the glass partition, pointing to Bowie.

"Tell me, Wright," he said, staring at the still life, "what is Bowie suffering from?"

"A deep-rooted fear of matches, or intense sunlight. Maybe distemper?"

"And the colonel from Red Banks, South Carolina?"

"A broken home. No doubt about it."

"Ah ha, my good man, you are a man of the mind. Does he remind you of anyone in particular?"

"Nah, just another lifer stiff."

"Observe how the sculptor carved the corners of his mouth. . . ."

"Yeah, a sorta half-assed sneer there."

"Precisely. Well, that, gentlemen, is what I maintain we all wore on the day of our admittance to the *casa gris. Comistas?* I was shaving one morning," continued the Professor, covering one side of his face with his hand, "and half my face was hiding in lather; but in the other half I saw that same expression as worn by the good colonel from Red Banks. And—horrors!—I couldn't change it! The harder I tried to alter the lines of my face, the more entrenched became the sneer. But the shock, the real shock, was that as I peered deeper into the mirror, every face around me had a trace of that sneer. Every one of them! I wanted to slit my throat.

"And there is fear and guilt, gentlemen," shouted the Professor as he pointed at the wax manikins. "Those are the faces of fear and guilt turned in upon itself in the twist of a lip, a signature on a document, a finger on the trigger. The sneer is that last mask in the theater of madness: it won't wash off. And that's what the sculptor caught. If we are insane, gentlemen, there is our common lineage. Ah ha. Yes. Yes. Yes! Hail to the Chief!" And he fell to the floor.

"You see?" said the Professor out of the corner of his mouth as he held his latest expression. "There's the sneer," he insisted, pointing to his face. He grasped Collins's hand and pulled himself up off the stone floor.

The chaperon from the first-floor ward shook his head in convulsions of laughter. "Fantastic!. . . . Fantastic! When's the next performance?"

"Just hop the eight-ten transport to Tan Son Nhut, sonny," replied Pollard. Wright put both hands in front of himself and leaned into the wall, laughing so hard that tears spattered on the stones.

The four patients stumbled, laughing, into the fourth chamber, which was considerably darker than the others. The relics and display cases were dusty and disheveled. Wright flicked the wall switches, but only one small bulb went on. Two long glass-topped cases along both walls contained silver scabbards, regimental insignias and epaulets, diaries and letters written in Spanish, with English translations to one side. On the wall was a bronze plaque which read:

> This exhibit donated by the Republic of Mexico and maintained by the San Antonio Historical Association.

A series of faded maps depicting the sequence of territorial boundaries hung on the center wall. Treaties, agreements, and letters of state were mounted in columns around the maps.

"What a goddamn fiasco," said Wright. "Hey, look at this thing!" In the case facing the entrance to the Mexican chamber was a minute reconstruction of the deployment of forces and the lines of attack engineered by General Santa Anna. The siege strategy was marked with numbers in the sand which corresponded with numbered entries in the general's field book. Wright scanned a letter written by Colonel José Batres, Santa Anna's private aide-de-camp, and then read the translation out loud:

> "By the time we had finally reached the walls of the Mission—especially those of rank—we knew that the Americans inside that Fortress were insane, hungry for the Land, mad for Martyrdom, and destined for Immortality. But destined in a way which we would never have anticipated: To create such Legendary, Monumental heroes out of such a band of Uncivilized, Barbaric frauds—who had no more business fighting on Mexican Soil than we would have had waging war from the Meeting House in Philadelphia—was totally beyond the Comprehension of all the Officers. We were fighting—engaged under General Santa Anna, our President—to protect and defend our Motherland, not in conquest for their Territories or States. Later, at San Jacinto, we were bewildered to hear such summons to Rage as, 'Remember the Alamo,' or 'For Fannin,' or 'God Is on Our Side.'
>
> "I do not understand. I was twenty-two then. I now am nearly in my Forty-Sixth Year, and I still do not understand the Americans. As the sun rises, so it sets. As the Americans have spilled Mexican Blood on Mexican Soil, so they will continue to Shed the Blood of Others on Others' Soil. It is their legacy. America is the Trojan Horse come back to life again.
>
> "I am now old. But it is with Clear Eyes I look with the World's Seeing to the Americans. They celebrate the raising of their Flag streaming in Red Blood over the White of Flesh. So may They forever Know Themselves by It."

When the whistle blew, they left the Long Barracks and walked along the brick paths. Mounds of bleached wood chips encircled the

187

bandaged trunks of gnarled trees. Blistered branches supported bulbous bean pods of green and brown. Hairy palm trunks with spongy moss spilling out of their huge scales crowded the reddish wall of the south parapet, smothered in broadleaf, blue ivy. Puddles of water, which had accumulated during a momentary cloudburst, rose up in swaying eddies of mist.

Collins inhaled deeper and faster, hoping to lift himself above the heavy air and the swollen clusters of ferns that choked the paths. When he reached the arched footbridge spanning a section of the steaming moat, he stopped, stunned by a vague recollection of MacArthur's Hospital in Tokyo.

He leaned against the wooden railing and put his hand, wrist up, on a post. He stared at the minute scar and then at the green water below. Strange, almost human-like forms were strangled by lily pads. Buzzing insects crawled feverishly among the flowers. A fly landed on his hand. He was faint and nauseated.

"Make him fly again, Captain. . . . Behold. What a thing of work is man."

Sick and suffocated, he thought of swimming. But the bodies floating under the bridge turned the water red. He thought of falling into the cold air and swaying in the shade of a parachute. Then running through an orchard in Vermont. Suddenly North-cross's face was in front of him. Collins looked down at his scar again. Blood seemed to run from his wrist, along the railing and into the moat under the footbridge.

"Hey, Collins!" yelled Wright from the other side of the bridge. "Forget it, man. It's not the damn Brooklyn Bridge, ya know. Right? Besides, there isn't enough water to even drown in. Come on." Wright crossed over and slid his arm under Collins's shoulder.

"Just a minute," mumbled Collins. He peered into the water. "I spilled my own blood over there," he said faintly.

"Come on, man." Wright jerked his arm. "Pollard and the ninety-day wonder are waitin'." Wright supported Collins as the two patients walked slowly across the bridge.

"It was Northcross who found me," whispered Collins. When he raised his eyes, the landscape blurred into tones of gray and green. The other patients crossing the lawn melted into the steaming vapors. Distant voices, detached words and phrases, garbled remarks about Saigon and Tokyo, carried across the grounds. Dying echoes, even though a few forms passed close by, on the other side of the hedge. Patches of sunlight sparkled on the wet grass beneath the trees and squat clusters of magnolias. Through the mists, human silhouettes bled into pastel shades like an impressionistic watercolor.

Suddenly the words of a song congealed in a chorus:

"So he packed his gear an' his trusty gun,
An' lit out grinnin' to follow the sun.
Davy, Davy Crockett, leadin' the pioneer!

"I don't want to go back," said Collins.
"What's that?"
"I don't want to go back."
"We're not. We're leavin' for the post in a few minutes."

Wright had grown increasingly nervous. Somehow he never expected to see Collins freak out. But now that it was happening, Wright felt a sudden resurgence of his own inner strength, a sense of control, which he had forgotten since his commitment to Chambers. He wondered where it had been all this time, and why he hadn't noticed that he had lost it.

Wright stared at the lush grass as he guided Collins toward the exit of the historical site. For a second, the grounds were superimposed with the plastic coordinate grids he had used in plotting defoliation assignments in Vietnam. It was painstaking work, carving up the countryside into neat square kilometers earmarked for extinction, compensating for the wind and the rain, the age and dilution of the chemicals, and the carelessness of the Pissers—the choppers that dispensed the anti-chlorophylloid spray at five hundred liters per minute. For six months Wright's only job was to turn anything green to brown, and from brown to black. It amused him at first to think he could change the seasons at will.

Then one morning, as he scanned the landscape where the DMZ intersects the Cambodian border to verify the chlorotic effectiveness of the last sortie, he decided that "cooking" a few hundred kilometers at a time was a waste of time and money. He changed the focus of his binoculars for maximum range and slowly turned three hundred sixty degrees.

The following morning, Wright saw to it that every Pisser and all the remaining drums of Agent Orange were in the air by 0900 hours. That day his unit sprayed 4,000 square kilometers of forest, 2,000 square kilometers of waterways, 3,800 square kilometers of rice and soybean fields, 2,200 square kilometers of cultivated land, one Marine patrol, a Rangers camp carefully concealed in the dense foliage of a mountainside, and eight populated villages. The mission was a success according to Wright's calculations: he and his unit had accomplished in one day what would have taken 291 by the usual inefficient and wasteful means. At the end of the day he was ready to come back home. He went Stateside all right, but not home.

Collins stopped a few feet from the Professor, who was standing with the first-floor chaperon.

"I'm not going back."

"I told him we weren't goin' back to the Alamo," explained Wright, relieved to share the responsibility for Collins.

"I don't want to go back to Chambers. I want to go home."

"Well, now, Collins," began the Professor, putting his arm around Collins's neck and nodding to Wright that he'd take over, "you know that word doesn't exist in *our* dictionary. . . ."

Collins looked at the Professor's bandaged wrist, and then at his own wrist.

". . . by now that we don't use that word. Because we're home and we're not home. So the word is self-canceling and simply—"

"What did you do to your wrist?"

"So you and the rest of us are homeless. You must think of yourself as a war orphan. Yes, it's the best way, really. And not only that, but—"

"Tell me the truth: did you slit your wrist?"

"And not only that, but it would be absolutely correct to describe yourself in such a term. Wouldn't you agree, Wright?"

"Right. Absolutely correct." Wright was looking at Pollard's wrist. He saw the crimson patch inside the webbing.

"Home is not a place after all. It's merely a state of mind, Collins. Horace once—"

"You tried to kill yourself, didn't you, Pollard," said Collins, trying to look into the Professor's eyes. But Pollard turned his head away.

"Horace once said that a house represents a state of being, and the furniture reflects that being's state of mind. . . . Yes, Collins," continued Pollard quietly, "I tried to kill myself. Twice. . . . So if anyone asks you, 'Where's home?' you just tell them you're an MIA, or a war orphan, and that they've taken you in over at the *casa gris,*

190

where you wander up and down the hallways thinking of ways to kill yourself. See?"

Pollard smiled, patted Collins on the back, and set out for the circle in front of the Alamo, where the bus was parked.

"Now then, gentlemen, what has the San Antonio Historical Association chosen to erect with their federal grant for our further edification and amusement?" The Professor extended his arm toward a statue with a slight bow.

"Why, it's another monumental myth rendered by none other than that celebrated sculptor Pompeo Coppini—straight from Vesuvius, I've heard it said in polite circles," he announced, reading the sculptor's signature on a bronze plaque.

A massive wall of marble rose up out of the manicured shrubs and rows of flowers in the circle. A woman of proud origin, standing forty feet tall, had been carved out of the stone. She was crowned with a headpiece like the Statue of Liberty's. She meditated between a lonely star to her left and a galaxy of smaller stars on the right. Beneath her torso was inscribed:

> In memory of the heroes who sacrificed their lives at the Alamo, March 6, 1836, in the defense of Texas. They chose never to surrender nor retreat.

"The whole show's kinda pathetic, isn't it," Wright confirmed.

"Reminds me of that gigantic statue of a grunt with a Mattel they put up in downtown Saigon," said the first-floor chaperon. "It was—"

"Yes, we all know it," interrupted the Professor.

"The GVN made such a spectacle of appreciation to the U.S. when they put that fuckin' thing up," the chaperon persisted. "I found out later that we bought it for 'em."

"Yeah, like everything else. So what's new," stated Wright, supporting the Professor's efforts to discourage the ninety-day wonder from talking.

"Well, I was thinkin' that—"

"Well, think to yourself," ordered Captain Pollard. "We're concerned here with the efficacy of self-aggrandizement, not with papier-mâché effigies, which can *only* be understood as self-mocking edifices to this country's most egotistical and absurd efforts. *Comprende, amigo?*"

The Professor glanced up at the life-sized soldiers who fought Santa Anna. Of the dozen or so men chiseled from the stone, only the names of Travis and Crockett were carved beneath the two most prominent figures in the foreground.

"I wonder why Pompous whatever-his-name-is—I wonder why he placed these statues with their backs to the Alamo," asked Wright. He pointed at the mission and then back to the legendary heroes of Texas.

"Now, that is a provocative question! . . . And if I may, permit me to answer it by suggesting that artists are compassionate by nature. Only a sadist would choose to immortalize a man—bring him back to life in the minds of the living—and force the poor resurrected soul to forever look upon the travesty of his own acts. . . . How is Judas portrayed by Leonardo? Although the traitor felt no shame or guilt in his own lifetime, the compassionate artist turned his subject's head away from the object of his treachery, his sin, and his sickness. I propose the following: that our sculptor, Pompeo, knew what he was doing when he put the Mission of Madness behind the backs of these misguided men.

"But of course, it is with the understanding that we stupid mortals who look upon these heartless creations as our clan will stand in awe of the demagogues and be forever misled.

"I really should apply for tenure when I get out." Pollard concluded with a mocking laugh, which echoed off the Alamo. They passed to the third face of the monument, which was also pitched steeply upward. The scenes were depicted in a vertical triptych. At the base was an inscription:

> From the fire that burned their bodies
> Rose the Eternal Spirit of sublime sacrifice
> which gave birth to an Empire State.

Flames emanating from a torch spread up from the inscription. Embroiled in the conflagration were the figures of two naked men crouched or fallen one over the other, consumed in the inferno. From their burning bodies, and mingled with the flames, emerged a man soaring upward, his eyes searching the clouds, with arms raised beseechingly toward the heavens.

"So—*werf ich den Brand in Walhalls prangende Burg,* " the Professor muttered slowly. His arm was raised in a Nazi salute.

"What in hell does that mean, Pollard?" asked Wright.

"Well, literally, it means 'So I throw the torch into Valhalla's magnificent mountain.' But it really means the end of an illusion which cannot be acknowledged in this life. . . . A miscarriage, if you will." Captain Pollard stepped off the curb behind the chaperon. They headed for the olive-green bus with one white star painted on the side.

"Any complications, MacAndrews?" asked Hinckley of the ninety-day wonder as the patients piled into the vehicle.

"Who the hell can tell? . . . They're here, aren't they? Isn't that enough?"

CHAPTER

When the patients had returned from their outing and were signed back into their wards, the second-floorers who had remained behind were sitting in the day room arguing about the fighting in Cambodia. The *CBS Evening News* was screening the footage of an ARVN raid along the Ho Chi Minh Trail. Somewhere between the concussions of mortar rounds and "Swiss steak/mushroom gravy/-peppers" written under "MENU" on the blackboard, Collins lost his appetite again.

Since his relocation to the Camp of the Cau Luu he had developed an obsessive craving for day-by-day news from the front lines. The delicacies served up by the media were very fresh—at most, only forty-eight hours old. Once his hunger for news was satisfied, then the pleasing anticipation of meat and potatoes was metabolically canceled. He could stomach either the newsreels or tuna casserole with green beans, but never one within a few hours of the other.

When the ward was fed prior to the news, Collins would sit on the couch in front of the color TV with the sensation of having overeaten. He imagined an invisible I.V. tube running from the TV into his stomach. Then he would stand over the toilet and make his offering to the gods of War.

And when they ate following the newscast, like tonight, all he had

194

to hear was: "And that's the way it is. Thursday, June 18, 1970," and he began salivating . . . until the nausea worked its way up from his stomach. He could satiate one craving, but never both. Either way, he went hungry.

At about eight-thirty that evening, the floor supervisor of ward 2-W called Collins out of a Ping-Pong tournament. There was an order from Dr. Nieland that he was to attend the "evening's social events in Building Six." Collins joined the line of other patients named on the P.M. roster. The electronic door buzzed and they marched down the stairs to the basement of Chambers, passed the Broca-Wernicke Center, wove around the shock stalls, and came to the guarded elevators at the base of Building Six. They climbed to the fifth floor.

Building Six is the most most curious facility on the grounds of Fort Sam Houston because of the variety of patients it houses and the manner of their incarceration. The troopers occupying the building were called the Good, the Bad, and the Had, and sometimes the Lobotomized Legionnaires.

The "Sixes" is situated about four hundred meters to the west of Chambers. It was built in 1967 and opened in 1969 as an experimental combat-related psychosis center—both in design and in therapeutic mode—with private baths in private rooms, where men and women come and go, talking of Madame Nhu. But there was something sadistic in its layout: the floors were divided like layers in a cake, plain sections alternating with plush, rich ones, boasting walnut walls and polished oak furniture, where the odor of perfume and alcohol mingled with the scent of wool from the maroon carpeting.

Veterans assigned to the odd-numbered floors had been passed by the board and were waiting for orders of transfer to another base —to resume their Army careers. A few patients were cleared from Building Six every week to return to active duty in Vietnam.

The quarters on floors one, three, and five were the finest on the post and their residents were displayed as shining examples of the Army's success with mental rehabilitation. But the patients on the even-numbered floors were confined in small, ordinary hospital rooms. These men either were judged too unsound to begin serving a criminal sentence in a federal prison, or were waiting to be locked away in one of two hundred VA insane asylums across the country. Their crimes ranged from assassinating American diplomats and

195

officers, to skinning Vietnamese women and selling their dried hides to private collectors in the U.S. and Europe, to spying for the VC and the Chinese. They sat for months handcuffed in their tiny cubicles, listening to the clatter of pool balls, the thud of beer mugs, laughter and giggles, squeaking bedsprings, and the voices of men and women above them.

It was rumored that the neurosurgical mistakes were also hidden away on the even-numbered floors. A patient originally assigned as a medic to the Brooke OR (before cracking up) told of the mysterious disappearance of troopers who had sustained—or were inflicted with—brain damage. They usually arrived semicomatose, he said, and the surgeons "would cut up their brains like wheels of cheese. . . . We called the seventh floor at Brooke the Vegetable Garden, because the post-op failures were tucked in rows of soft beds, where they did just that—vegetated. Or died. But the worst monstrosities were wheeled to the basement in the early A.M. and put on an ambulance with an M.D. and an MP. All I know is that those meat wagons always took the road toward Chambers. So you tell me . . . they must have been transplanted somewhere in Building Six. . . ."

The patients selected from the second floor of Chambers stood in a dark corner of the large cocktail lounge on the fifth floor, waiting for the social. Two regulation-size pool tables sat in the center of the room. Hanging lamps illuminated their green surfaces. Squares of chalk were positioned at the corners, attached to the tables with string. Across from the entrance, along the far wall, backgammon boards lay open on wide shelves with semicircular niches carved out on either side for the players. Two oak tables were surrounded by men in summer dress uniforms and neatly pressed fatigues. They sat talking and joking with their female friends. Drinks were served by a black waiter in a white waistcoat, who waited patiently for the rehabs as they tossed dice to see who would sign for the round. No money crossed the table. They were neat, clean, well tanned and relaxed. The guests from 2-W stared dumbly at them: except for a whisper and raised eyes, the regulars ignored the psychos from Chambers completely. But it was understood—everyone in the room shared a common heritage . . . a small matter of Chambers Pavilion reflected in the mirror over the bar.

An aide in dark blue escorted them into another large room: a combination bar and dance floor. Young women in pastel skirts and madras blouses sat among thirty or forty ninety-day wonders from the first-floor wards. The women, Grimes explained as he watched them in the mirrors, were either first-term Air Force nurses or students majoring in psychology, imported from San Antonio State College.

"Any one of the nurses will give you a hand job in the latrine. But the chicks from that suitcase college? . . . They write notes about you on the cocktail napkins and stuff them in their purses," he said, grinning into his Coke.

"You know, the Army's amazing, if you think about it. One way or another, they give you whatever they *think* you might need, *whatever*—even if you don't really need it. The deal is that you really didn't need it until they put it in front of you. And then they got you hooked . . . 'cause then you need it. Very clever, this Army.

"You remember that whorehouse the 409th built in Bien Hoa? What an . . ."

Collins caught the eye of a girl who was staring at him in the mirror. She sat with a rehab in a booth along the wall. Collins glanced down at his ginger ale and twirled the ice, shaved into perfect disks. He looked up, and their eyes met again. An aide dimmed the lights in the lounge and flipped on the spots over the dance floor. Up came the jukebox just to the point of distortion. Collins looked back into the mirror and watched the girl join her rehab for a dance. He looked into his own pale face and sunken blue eyes.

"God, have we aged," he muttered.

"Collins, you been listenin' to me or falling in love with that blonde that just got up to dance? Uh? Never mind. I gotta whiz anyways."

After Grimes left, Collins imagined getting ready to go out on a date. He stared at himself in the mirror above the bar while he took a long, hot shower, shaved, rubbed deodorant under his arms. He had a great tan. He slid into his best white pants, then his belt with the large brass buckle, dark-blue socks, shined his shoes with a towel, brushed his teeth, patted on some aftershave lotion. He combed his hair, put on a starched yellow shirt and a tie, then his dark-blue sports jacket (with the gold buttons). He looked in the mirror and straightened his imaginary tie, drawing the knot firmly against his collar.

"Any vanity is a kind of sanity. . . . Yeah, it keeps the ego looking out for itself."

His eyes followed the girl as she returned to the booth. She held the rehab's hand under the table. Collins remembered a whore he'd known in Saigon. He thought he might have been in love with her. But the love sprang from guilt and the guilt came with his civilization: predator turned prey in one crummy night. She said that Americans smelled like rotting water buffalo. She said the GIs she'd known back in the sixties were men: they arrived, enjoyed themselves, paid, and left. But the ones who came to her in the last year or so were different: they didn't want to leave, or they wanted to leave in the middle. They held on to her and sometimes cried like children. The recent ones didn't understand the rules of the game, she said. And they either came so drunk it was a waste, or too sober to lose themselves, even for a moment. And they refused to pay, or paid too much. A few came back to marry her, she said, and take her to America, the supreme insult: her mother's and her mother's mother's placentas were buried on the banks of the Red River.

"A gin 'n' tonic with a slice of lime, honey," said a woman to the bartender. She was in her mid thirties and wore a long cocktail dress.

"Sorry, ma'am, no booze served at this bar. I think you want the one by the elevators."

"What'sa matter with this one?" she asked, looking down the length of the bar.

"This one's for the . . . This is a special party for special people." The bartender grinned and glanced over at Collins. The woman walked to the opposite end of the counter. She turned around and scanned the room, looking for something special.

"What'd he mean by that, honey?" she said, walking back toward Collins.

"He was trying to give you a compliment."

"A compliment? By refusing to pour me a drink?"

"It's nothing personal, I'm sure," he replied.

"Nothing personal? Everyone has a drink in their hands, honey, even you."

"But like the man said, it's a special party for special people."

"What is this, some kinda fraternity or special club thing?" She was getting irritable.

"That's it. A special club."

"Well, what kind?" she demanded, leaning over Collins. She smelled like wall-to-wall carpeting and decaying lilacs.

"Well . . . ?"

"It's embarrassing, this special club."

"Listen, honey, ya hang around this post long enough and nothing's embarrassing."

He turned and looked her squarely in the eyes. "We're all war orphans. All the men in this room are war orphans."

"War orphans!" She studied the dance floor and stared at the couples in the booths along the walls. "War orphans? You mean all the guys out there lost their parents while they were on tour?"

"Not exactly."

"Well, an orphan means the person's lost *something.*"

"That's right. Their houses all burned down."

"Oh. Oh, how awful. I see. Then they're just homeless soldiers."

"No, they're orphans," he corrected her.

"But an orphan's someone who's lost *someone.*"

"And there you have it! And that's why it's such a special party."

"But I—"

"Irma! What the hell are you doin' in *here?* I've looked all over the goddamn place for you," shouted an odd-numbered rehab as he approached her, followed by a corpsman.

"Well, Eddie, you took so long, and the music . . ."

"How the hell did you get in here anyway?"

"I just walked."

"Do you know what these people are?" he said, raising his voice.

"Yeah, Eddie, they're all war orphans."

"War orphans! War orphans. . . . Christ, Irma, you're far out!" He laughed and hit the corpsman, who was smiling, on the chest. "Did ya hear that? . . . War orphans. Irma, these are the kooks from over the hill."

"The gooks?"

"No. No. . . . Kooks, gooks—what the hell's the difference? Yeah, the gooks. . . . Come on, let's go. You're far out, Irma. Jesus, I wish . . ."

"You know her?" asked Grimes, climbing back up on his stool as the threesome left.

"No. I never saw her before."

"Looked to me like you was cuttin' in on that dude's piece."

"Me? Get off it. I couldn't cut in on my own shadow."

"Well, Collins, she seemed pretty interested in you, ol' boy. What were ya talking about?"

"War orphans," he said.

"War orphans! . . . War orphans? Tens of thousands. Hundreds of thousands. What'd she wanna do, adopt one or somethin'?"

"She already has."

"Yeah?"

"Her rehab."

"Hey, that's pretty good, Collins. I'll remember that one." Grimes chuckled and then stood up. "I'm gonna see if I can get me a piece of that good stuff. I got horns growin' outa my navel. See ya in a bit. . . . War orphans. Yeah, a room full of war orphans. . . ."

Collins asked for a root beer and turned his stool to face the dancers. Two thirds of the patients were working up a sweat under the spotlights. He glanced at the booth and saw that the blond girl was sitting alone. A different rehab came up to her and asked for a dance. She smiled and shook her head. Then she began writing something on a piece of paper. She got up and walked toward the bar. Collins swiveled his stool, rested his elbows on the counter, and watched her in the mirror.

"Hi."

Collins nodded and turned Grimes's vacant stool toward his own.

"My name is Ginger."

"I'm Andrew. Andy Collins. . . . Let me guess: you're in your junior year at San Antonio State and you're majoring in psychology."

"Me? No. Where did you come up with that line?"

"Well, you're not a nurse, are you?"

"No. . . . Do I look like the nurse type?"

"They're wearing disguises these days, you know," he said, trying for a less than insulting recovery.

"You're right about me being a junior. But I'm at Ohio State, and my major's poli sci."

"How amusing. . . . And just how did you end up at this party?"

"How come everyone asks me that question? . . . Well, it's simple. My father was admitted to the hospital here; I finished exams two weeks ago; and my mother and I came down from Ohio to be with him." She concentrated on drawing circles with the water on the bar. "But they won't let me see him. And—I don't know—I guess his doctor thought the party would break the boredom, you know. He said these men might be a little peculiar because they're in a mental hospital. I guess he figured I was together enough to handle it, though, or else he wouldn't have suggested it in the first place. Anyway, it's been interesting so far. Better than watching TV with my mother." She drew circles.

"Why did you come over and sit with me?"

"'Cause I wanted to and I thought you wanted me to. O.K.?"

"I haven't spoken to someone from the straight world in a long time. It's a funny feeling, that's all. So . . ."

"You're acting fine—so far." She winked.

"How long have you known the guy you were sitting with over there?"

"Oh, let me see," she replied, checking her watch. "Two hours and twenty-six minutes."

"You seemed to get along pretty well for a two-hour-and-twenty-six-minute acquaintance."

"Well . . . You have been watching me most of the evening, haven't you? He was depressed about something and I thought I'd lend him a warm hand. Wouldn't you?"

"In my next life."

"Bitter, uh?"

"No, just tired."

"You should get out more often. Sorry. . . ."

"Did you take notes about him?"

"Notes? . . . Oh, you mean the letter I was writing. Since I can't see my father, I thought I'd write to him. But it's hard to know what to say. I mean, I don't even know what happened to him, except he's exhausted and needs a lot of rest and quiet. I guess that excludes me, for the time being. . . . Do you dance?"

"Not in my current classification."

"What difference does that make?"

"Perhaps none to you. . . . You see, I'm considered normal over in Chambers. But in here I feel very out of place."

"You mean you think you're the most abnormal person in this room?" A smirk crossed her face.

"You could see it that way, though I'd rather you didn't. Being here is enough of a stigma."

"It's nothing to be ashamed of. Some people handle stress in different ways. Anyone would flip out in certain—"

"That's enough. Save it for your father—I mean, I know what you're saying, and it's true if you're on the outside looking in."

"How long have you been in this hospital?"

"Seventy-two days."

"When will you get out?"

"It depends upon what you mean by out. Almost everyone admitted is turned out in ninety days. After that, some go back to duty, some go to prison, some to VA hospitals, and a few go back . . . and a few just get out. Is your father in Chambers Pavilion?"

"Yes. He's been there for about four weeks. He's a doctor. He was a doctor in Korea, and then joined a surgical group in Cleveland when he got out. And then, during a break from school, he told us he had volunteered to run a hospital in Vietnam and that the Army had accepted his offer. He left the States in January of '68. . . . I don't know—I mean, as I think back now, he certainly was strange last Christmas. He slept most of the days, and just walked alone in the woods at night. It was really cold last winter, and he'd be out from midnight till dawn. He hardly said anything to us, except about football games and the snow. My mother was pretty stoic about the whole thing. They put her on Valium when he left. She's still on them. You know, Mother's Little Helpers? It's true. Now all she does is pop pills and eat TV dinners. . . . Oh, well, he's back now and things'll work out, I hope."

"Where is he in the hospital. What floor?"

"On the fourth, in a private room."

"In a private room? Must be a *very* private room."

"Say, are you sure you don't want to dance? Come on—why not? You haven't anything to lose." Collins stopped dancing after a few minutes. He was getting dizzy.

"Too much excitement for one day? Really, you should get out more often." She smiled and looped her arm through his as they navigated through the mob.

Suddenly, a loud scream. Her fingernails dug into his skin. One of the rehabs had spooked while receiving cake and punch from an old Red Cross lady. He reeled back from the cart, screamed again, threw the cake and punch in the air, and fell on the dance floor.

"What's happening to him?"

"Hot flashes. They can't be helped." Collins leaned against the wall.

A glob of chocolate cake with white icing dropped from the

ceiling and landed on one of the girls. She shrieked and swept the thing out of her hair. A few others wiped punch off their faces and arms as they backed away from the fallen trooper. He crawled on his stomach, clawing at the parquet squares. "I can't reach him. Christ, help me. I can't reach him. Come on, you guys, give me a hand. *I can't reach him!* He's stuck on the pungies. I can't reach him. . . . I can't reach him. . . . I can't . . ."

Two corpsmen dragged him off the floor. An aide in blue dress held up his hands to quiet the crowd. Someone turned down the jukebox.

"O.K., folks," said the picture of confidence. "Nothing to get all excited about. We all have one too many once in a while."

The crowd laughed and hopped back on the dance floor, demanding music.

"What'll happen to him?" she asked.

"He'll get sent up, probably."

"Sent up?"

"He'll get bounced back up a floor. It might cost him a day, a week, maybe the rest of his life."

"What, for one freak-out? Ridiculous."

"Who knows?" he said. "The board may decide it's one too many. The Army doesn't like to take responsibility, except for defeating the enemy. They won't risk an incident by releasing him unless they're sure he can handle himself on the outside. That's the purpose of this sock hop. It's like a test ground."

"Are you feeling better now?" They walked toward the bar.

"Yes, somewhat."

"What happens to all these people when the party's over?"

"At the stroke of midnight, the coach turns into a pumpkin and behold! We become neurotics, schizophrenics, psychotics, and catatonics again and slip off to never-never-land. But under lock and key, of course."

When the music stopped and the lights went up, Collins watched the girls gathering in one corner.

"I'd like to see you again sometime. Here's my phone number. I'm staying with my mother in the guesthouse." She wrote her number on a slip of paper and flipped it on the bar.

"Good night."

Collins ordered another root beer. Yes, he felt better. But then he thought of the ones whose lives had been left behind—the wasted—who would never go to another party, hear music, or feel a warm hand in theirs.

"They'd be enraged at our childishness, if they could be here now. . . . Did I write those letters? But it's what they would have said if they could have."

Collins looked down at the piece of paper on the bar:

Ginger Hepburn
Room 312
-0979

CHAPTER 16

At first just muffled, quiet conversation: a question from one voice, an answer from a second party, and then a summation by a third voice. The last person to speak in this trialogue was Nieland, whose voice had become loud and abrupt.

The Professor appeared through oak doors embossed with a white caduceus encircled by the words:

**4th ARMY MEDICAL REVIEW BOARD–PSYCHIATRIC
MEDICAL RECEIVING, HOLDING, PLACEMENT
GEN. DESMOND. M.D.**

Pollard tried to unravel the gauze bandage on his wrist.

"Leave it alone, Captain," whispered Hinckley. He took the Professor by the arm.

"Does it really matter now?" he replied. He was shocked to see Collins sitting on a bench in the antechamber. Slowly Pollard walked up to his friend. A book—the same book—dropped from under his arm and slammed to the floor. Collins picked it up and handed it to him. Pollard never moved a muscle.

The door to the judges' chambers slammed shut.

"Bastards," muttered Dr. Nieland, shaking his head. His face was red; dark circles outlined the armpits and collar of his uniform blouse.

"Sorry, Pollard. I'll appeal it again this week. . . . You're up next, Collins. I have to step out for a moment to cool down. Sit tight." He headed for the water cooler at the far corner.

"What happened?" asked Collins, looking from Pollard to Hinckley.

"It didn't—"

"Watch out for Lacersis, the one on the riser in the middle." Captain Pollard turned and looked out the window. A few below-the-knee amputees were playing badminton. The Professor pointed toward the pool without water.

"See that, Collins?"

"The pool?"

"No, just beyond that."

"Building Six."

"And beyond that?" he said.

"I don't know what's beyond that."

"Neither do I, Andrew, but that's where my ticket reads: Beyond."

"They refused him an extension this time," interjected Hinckley, "and he's well past the ninety-day cutoff. Not very copacetic, really."

"And you know, I still believe what I did ultimately had to be done. But that's not good enough for them now. What was right is now wrong, and what is wrong is best forgotten, so another someone in another somewhere can make the same mistake again. Otherwise, just imagine how dull life would be!" He began laughing. "And so it is *comme il faut* that I should be shut away lest I spill the secrets. Sentenced to a sea of stagnant idleness, blind, boundless, mute, and motionless." He laughed again as his eyes scanned Building Six.

"Something out there. They said there was something out there. But they're wrong. You're wrong!" he screamed, running at the tall oak doors. He stopped in front of them, at attention, and whispered through the crack where the double doors met:

"Vacancy absorbing space and fixedness without a place. To hell with you. The catalogue of chameleons is complete! I need not see or hear from you again!"

"Come on now, Pollard. Here's your book. Come on," said Hinckley. There were tears in his eyes. He pulled the Professor away from the door and headed him down the corridor.

206

"Keep it in mind, Collins. Keep us all in mind." He laughed over his shoulder. *"Auf Wiedersehen. Gott weiss wann. . . .* Remember the pact, my friend."

"We'll get you a review," said Nieland from the water cooler. "Remember the—"

The elevator doors closed behind Hinckley and the Professor. Dr. Nieland looked down the empty corridor and crushed a paper cup in his fist.

"O.K., Collins. Wait here for a minute until we're ready for you. How do you feel?"

"What's going to happen to Pollard?"

"I honestly don't know. But look, Collins. This boarding is serious business. You know that. You see what they've done to Pollard? If there was ever a time for you to take yourself seriously, that time is now. O.K., let's go."

"Good morning, Collins. Sit down. I'm General Desmond. This is Major Porta, in charge of military investigations; and Major Sanderson here, who heads our disability claims division. And you know Major Penderspot and, of course, Captain Nieland.

"Before we begin, let me mention that the corporal sitting in the corner is the stenographer. Since your case involves court-martial charges, I'll remind you that you have the same rights as you would if you were still on active duty. That means that you have the right *not* to answer any questions which you may feel are incriminating. This is not a court-martial proceeding, but I advise you to remember that what you say here will be forwarded to the criminal office. Is that clear?"

"Yes."

"Yes, sir."

"Yes, sir."

"One last thing. We are not here to punish you for something you may have done. But we are charged with determining the facts which led to your incarceration, and assessing the degree of mental impairment incurred—if any—while on active duty. Major Porta will open the inquiry."

"Who was Black Eye?" he asked, leaning across the counter.

"A contact."

"Between who and what?"

"The ESR and the media offices in Saigon. Primarily CBS."

"When did you meet him?"

207

"I don't recall exactly."

"Where did you meet him?"

"At a bar. On Tu Do Street, during my transfer to the Fortieth Field Surgical Hospital."

"What was his position at that time?"

"He was part Vietnamese and part French by birth—an ARVN interpreter assigned to Communications Intelligence—when I knew him, at any rate."

"Who arranged the meeting between you and him?"

"A member of the ESR."

"Who?"

"I . . . I don't care to answer that."

Major Porta leaned back in his chair and pulled a file off the shelf. "How about Lieutenant James Fitzsimmons?"

"I won't answer that question either."

"Very well. Do you have that, Corporal? Did you willfully gather and transmit information which you knew to be classified and, in some cases, secret?"

"I did."

"For how long?"

"Eight months. Closer to nine, I guess."

"That would be between . . . May 1969 and February 1970?"

"Yes."

"What was the nature of this information which passed through your hands?"

"Verifications—count and cause—of VC deaths. That was my assignment. And to uncover the circumstances of torture, injury, murder, and accounts of missing civilians."

"Did you ever have any direct contact with the VC?"

"No. Except for a few injured *chieu hoi* I treated."

"Were you familiar with Operation Early Bird?"

"Yes. The last week in July. Southwest of the DMZ."

"Did you enter a report, to Black Eye, a couple of days prior to the commencement of that operation?"

"As I recall, yes, I did."

"Was there any mention of a VC officer by the name of Vinh Diem?"

"I honestly don't remember. There was a lot going on the end of that month. . . . Was he a major from a training cadre who was captured and committed suicide?"

"Right. Did you file that report?"

"Yes. That's right, I did."

"Did you know your information was leaked to the VC just before that assault? And that Intelligence was going to exchange a stand-in for Diem through a VC agent in return for a pilot who had information we needed to launch the assault? Did you know that because the gooks knew Diem was dead, we ended up getting massacred in that engagement?"

"No. I found out later that there had been leaks in the organization."

"How did you learn about CAIN—the secret Computer Assisted Intelligence Network?"

It went on like this with Major Porta for just over an hour. He ended his interrogation by asking:

"Do you feel you're guilty of subversion against the American forces in Vietnam?" And then: "Did you know that the ESR was directly responsible for at least eighteen to twenty-two hundred American casualties from the period April 1969 to April 1970?"

Collins answered "No" to both questions. Major Porta looked him squarely in the eyes with a puzzled expression.

"Collins," he said, removing his glasses. "People like yourself confuse me. Confuse me very much. Did it occur to you and your associates that the ESR was creating the casualties which you later treated? Why did Vietnam get to be such a special, confusing war? Vietnam is like any other war. Fifty years ago, you'd have been tried and hung a traitor. How are allegiances so split in people like you? Why can't you serve and get it over with, like the thousands of other men in uniform? Why . . . I'm finished, General."

Major Porta and General Desmond whispered back and forth, nodding at each other's comments. Penderspot watched the cripples playing badminton while Dr. Nieland wrote on a legal pad.

On the wall behind the board officers stood three standards, bearing the flags of Texas, the United States, and the Fourth Army. Above the center staff was a large caduceus, about three feet in diameter. Inside the circumference were four scenes from the field, each with a corpsman in action depicting "The Courage and Professionalism of the Army Medical Corps." The scene, in relief, positioned at one o'clock showed a surgeon from the Civil War standing against a horse-drawn Union ambulance. He pointed with urgency at a Confederate soldier who had been left outside the circle of

209

wounded, presumably to die untreated. The doctor had halted a medic with a stretcher: "WE DISTINGUISH AMONG WOUNDS, NOT UNIFORMS. BRING THAT MAN HERE!"

"Collins. . . . Collins!" shouted Major Sanderson.

"Yes, sir."

"What I have to ask you and what you answer will help us determine your psychological profile, both prior to your commitment and your present status. In addition, you can provide us with information which will call for your immediate separation from the service—assuming the pending criminal charges are successfully waived—or conclude that further psychiatric treatment is in order. Do you understand?"

"Yes, sir."

"Very well. Your records show that you've never been under the care of a psychiatrist, and weren't hospitalized for a mental disorder while you were a civilian. Is that accurate?"

"Yes."

"Then why did you choose to develop a problem in the Army?"

"What problem?"

Major Sanderson glanced briefly at Dr. Nieland, who met his eyes, and then turned back to Collins.

"Do you know why you're in this hospital?" he resumed.

"Yes, I think so."

"Why?"

"Because I thought I was doing something constructive, but I was fooling myself the whole time. What I felt was serious somehow became a joke. And what I helped to put back together kept falling apart. I don't think I understood what I was doing, or why; I don't think so."

"What's this Sergeant Back Again stuff?"

"I don't know anyone by that name."

"You wrote about him in this notebook," asserted Major Sanderson. "This one here, dated 14 December. It says, 'Sergeant Back Again has come back again. Why did you have to come back again Sergeant Back Again? Why did . . . ' and so on. Well?"

Collins could feel Nieland's eyes piercing through him.

"Sergeant Back Again was a corporal when I first knew him. He was one of the first I treated at the Fortieth Field. A frag in the neck. We fixed him up and put him on the E-vac to Tokyo. He said he had nine lives and that America could have one. That this was the one.

Why did he have to come back again? The corporal had returned a sergeant. Sergeant Back Again had miscalculated. They didn't send him home, did they? And he ran out of lives, didn't he? We should have done a messier job. . . . Did you volunteer for a second tour? 'Yes,' I said, choking on my own blood. The corpsman leaned down over my face to hear me better. They worked on my chest," continued Collins, whispering, his face contorted in pain. " 'I came back 'cause my buddies are still here.' . . . The corpsman said I must have a minus IQ, and I tried to laugh, but I couldn't breathe too good. . . . 'It's hot in here.' . . . And then he asked me if I had an identical twin with the same name and serial number who was a corporal. And I told him no, that I was a corporal when they first stitched me up. 'Don't you remember! Don't you remember me! I've come back a sergeant, with a Purple Heart. Wanna see it?' . . . And they strapped a mask over my face and the corpsman said, What heart? But I couldn't talk after that. And they—"

"I see. I see," interrupted Major Sanderson. He glanced over at Dr. Nieland with an irritated expression, as if to say, Don't you think his boarding is a bit premature, Doctor?

"Did Sergeant Back Again die?" resumed Sanderson.

"Who?"

"This sergeant who was a corporal when you treated him the first time. . . . Did this Sergeant Back Again die?"

"Yes, he came back to die. Half his chest was blown away."

"And did you blame anyone or anything for this man's death?"

"Whose?"

"This Sergeant Back Again. Did you blame anything or anyone for his death?"

"Everyone and everything. I still do. Mostly, now, I blame the body for being so vulnerable. The senses for being so slow. And the brain for being so stupid to waste the whole organism. And the Army for insisting that it be so. And myself for having had anything to do with it."

"Did you attempt suicide?"

"I'm not certain. But from what I can gather, it seems likely."

"Well, you did. Do you feel the Army owes you any compensation for your sickness?"

"What sickness?"

"I'll ask you again: Do you feel the Army owes you any compensation for your injuries?"

"What injuries?"

Major Sanderson ran his hand through his hair and then closed the file. He looked at Dr. Nieland for a moment and then back to Collins.

"What would you do if you were released from this hospital right now?"

"There is something I *have* to do."

"What's that?"

"I'm not sure yet. . . ."

Major Sanderson looked briefly at Major Porta. The three board officers leaned together in a huddle. They nodded and exchanged papers.

At four o'clock was a scene from World War I, with a medic running through a hail of enemy fire to reach a fallen comrade. The wounded man's hand was raised in the distance, beneath a shattered tree. Above the blasted branches was inscribed: "NO MAN SHALL DIE BECAUSE I FALTERED."

At eight o'clock was a medic about to jump from a transport flying over an island marked "Guadalcanal." The corpsman was carved in profile, looking back at the faces of a fireteam hooked to the static line. He knows he will see them again, as casualties, within a few minutes. The caption was covered by a fold in the American flag.

The last was a tableau from either Korea or Vietnam. It portrayed a squadron of medics standing at attention and listening to a captain. The training officer was pointing at the outline of a body covered with an American flag. He said: "WHEN A SOLDIER FALLS, HE FALLS ON YOUR CONSCIENCE. TELL ME HE WAS DEAD BEFORE YOU REACHED HIM, NOT AFTER."

". . . to his feet. . . . Are you with us, Collins? O.K. On your feet," ordered the general. "We have reached a tentative decision. It is the opinion of this tribunal that the two counts of subversion be taken under advisement on medical grounds. Further, it is our decision not to grant Captain Nieland's request for an expeditious release from Chambers Pavilion at this time; and you will not be released until we are convinced of your stability and the certainty of your recovery.

"We do grant Captain Nieland's request that you be permitted sign-out privileges, limited to one four-hour pass every two days, but that you must be on post between 1000 and 2200 hours. If you break any hospital rule or create problems, you will be dispatched to Building Six—to an even floor. You will be transferred to the first floor of Chambers, pending Captain Nieland's acceptance of our decisions and provision. . . . Captain Nieland?"

Dr. Nieland glanced down at his legal pad while rising to his feet.

"I request permission to petition for extensions, if necessary," responded the psychiatrist.

"Denied." The general leaned back in his swivel chair.

"I request that my petition for an expeditious discharge be reviewed within forty-eight hours."

"Denied."

"I request that this patient's personal notebooks, letters, and—"

"Denied."

"I insist that this patient be provided with legal counsel in light of your decision not to drop the charges of subversion at this time."

"Denied."

"On what grounds?" challenged Dr. Nieland.

"The charges of subversion are pending. The Judge Advocate General's office will not provide counsel until a new warrant for his arrest has been issued," answered Major Porta.

"But *you* can request counsel on his behalf at this time," retorted Dr. Nieland.

"But I won't. And that's that, Captain." Major Porta leaned back in his chair with his hands behind his head.

"I request—"

"Look, Captain," interrupted the general. "Do you want your patient dropped to the first floor or not?"

"Of course I do. But this ap—"

"Captain. For the last time, do you accept the decision of this tribunal or not?"

"Yes, yes . . . yes, sir." Dr. Nieland was halfway across the room.

"Dismissed," said General Desmond, rising from the bench. "Collins?"

"Sir."

"Play it cool, soldier."

The boarding had been strangely anticlimactic for Collins. Aside from being nervous, he felt as though he hadn't really been in that room in front of those men. Nieland greeted him on the second floor as he was packing up his toothbrush and mail.

"Well," said the weary psychiatrist, "I think we're about out of

213

the woods, Collins. At least we know where we are."

Sergeant Gibbons, the first-floor attendant, walked Collins down to the ground floor, ward 1-E.

"We don't baby ya here like they do in the detention floors. There's washing machines in the basement. Use 'em. Here's a key to your razor. If ya wanna slit your wrists, do it in the shower stall, uh? Chow's at 0645, 1300, and 1830 hours till we rotate. If ya wanna go on a hunger strike or anythin', let me know ahead of time. Saves me headaches with the brass."

Gibbons took Collins's fingerprints, read the rules relevant to first-floor conduct, issued him a plain set of fatigues and boots— "You're still in the fuckin' Army, ya know"—and signed his pass.

"Here, sign on this here line." He pointed to the Patient Transfer & Pass Roster. On the line above his was the nearly illegible signature of Jackson Pollard, Capt. His abbreviated rank had been crossed out.

"What's the matter? Forget your name already? . . . Finish the roster, will ya, Collins?"

Under the heading "Destination," as of 1620, was printed: "Room 612, Build. Six, North Ward, Single, Sixth Floor, Pollard. To be dispatched by MPHD escort."

"O.K. This here is a four-hour, call-in pass. That means you gotta call this here number every hour right on the stroke. If ya miss the gong by five minutes, we'll be out ta git ya. And we ain't never come back empty-handed yet."

Captain Pollard had been signed out for Building Six at 1744 by the MPs. Collins had missed him by an hour.

"God, what does this mean?"

"It means don't screw up. You still a meathead, Collins? The zapper get to you? Let's get your mind right this time. Ya gotta call this here number every hour you're off this here floor. And ya gotta sign in on this here sheet before 2200 hours. That's ten o'clock, in case ya forgot how to tell time. You remember how to use a phone, don't ya? You know, like this black thing on the desk with the wires. Good. Well, there's three dimes taped to the back of this here pass. See, ya use 'em at 1900—at seven, eight, and nine o'clock. Your calls go in to the medication supervisor on this here floor. Got it? . . . Good. Sign here, too. That's to O.K. the ten bucks we took outa your pay. And no booze. . . ." He passed Collins a ten-dollar bill and put him on the bus for San Antonio.

214

CHAPTER **17**

Forty minutes later, Collins climbed off the bus two blocks from the Alamo and walked through the crowds on the streets as though he had someplace to get to in a hurry. When he crossed over the San Antonio River for the fourth time, he stopped, caught his breath, and decided to follow behind a group of tourists who were descending the stone steps leading to the banks.

"Excuse me, do you have the time?" Collins asked a man in a suit coming up the stairs from the river.

"It's six fifty-seven."

"Is there a pay phone close by?"

"Yep. Turn around and go to the rear entrance of the first building on your right. That's the Safari Club. There's a pay phone right outside."

Collins made the call to the medication supervisor and started back down the stairs. The stone steps were bounded by white-blossomed magnolias and terra-cotta ridgework. Ornate Christian crosses had been pressed into the orange bricks. On the second landing of the spiral stairs sat red and white azaleas in pottery planters. The odor of flowers and ripe fruit mingled with a heavy, musky smell rising up from the river.

A fine rain had begun falling. The leaves sparkled beneath amber street lamps. It was more like a thick fog, and as moisture gathered on the leaves, heavy droplets spattered under the trees.

Down below, level with the water, it was calm and clean. The bus driver called it the Paseo del Rio—Walkway Along the River. It ran parallel to the San Antonio River for about three miles, on both sides. Small shops with wrought-iron gates displayed Mexican tapestries, pottery, and expensive leather boots. Restaurants opened onto the river. White tablecloths, with candles burning among the china and crystal, seemed to glide in midair. Three Chicanos emerged from the mist, carrying trays with food aboard two wide launches. Polite couples in summer suits and wispy formal dresses were boarding the boats for dinner on the river. When the parties were seated, the first launch swung around and turned upstream. First a single guitar, and then two guitars accompanied by Spanish voices, carried across the water from an open-air bar. The lobby and second-floor dining room of a hotel reflected in orange fragments on the river's surface.

Hepburn had once commented, shortly after Collins began his tour with the Fortieth Field, that the "world is a hospital. Every day we play medicine man to some, and patient for others. The roles," he said, "oscillate with person, place, and situation."

Later, after they'd worked together for two months, he said, "The world's a hospital, and a second-rate one at that. We hurt some, and heal others. We do it innocently, we do it knowingly. The problem with this mess," he went on to say, "is that nothing's innocent. Not a move. Everything that happens here is intentional. Maybe hidden in some dark motive or some such bullshit. But it's there. I'm sick of it. The intentional. The only way to cover it up at this end is to bury it. This fucking war. And no way to turn it around."

Collins remembered that night after the napalm case had been dressed and tented, they walked down the hill, past the sentry at the perimeter, and sat on the bank of a narrow river. The yellow moon flickered across the ripples in shooting lines. Collins had changed into new-issue fatigues because of the bugs and dampness. But even then it was cold. So cold that the cigarette in his hand danced like a firefly. The cool night breeze chilled them into a listless exhaustion. Hepburn said he couldn't understand why they continued to pour so much of themselves into such "hopeless approximations"—his phrase for the wounded, or their work on them. That "the men who slave over the wasted are eventually wasted themselves. Drained to emptiness," he muttered, working his hand into his back pocket.

Hepburn rolled on his side and pulled out a thin leather case with a shiny top. He twisted off the cap, took a swig, and passed it over. The vodka burned down Collins's throat. When that was finished Hepburn left for more.

Collins, dazed by the sudden break from duties in the surgical hootches, felt as though he were dreaming. Can it really be, he wondered, that I'm sitting here on the banks of this river in Vietnam not more than four hundred meters from the six stainless-steel tables? These trees . . . they must be alive, they must be growing. And those are birds I hear singing in the night, aren't they? And the moon is really out, and there, yes, there are stars. Can it be that there are fish in this river?

He stood up slowly and walked to the edge of the river to wash his face. He knelt down and cupped his hands in the cold water. He thought he saw something, something large and gangly, floating just under the surface. He tilted his head and looked again at the mysterious shape pulled along by the current. It rolled back and forth, like a log. Then he saw another one a little farther out. And another upstream. And another. Then it hit him: they were bodies. Whole bodies, and bits and pieces too. They were floating just under the surface in what seemed like an eternal stream. Hundreds. Thousands. . . . Horrified, he rubbed his eyes in disbelief. He tried to move, to stand up, to crawl away from the river, but his body was frozen. He squeezed his arm with his hand. There was no sensation. No feeling.

He heard something moving in the brush behind him and slowly rose to his feet.

"What are you looking for, Collins, enemy fish?" said Hepburn, sitting down unsteadily.

"I don't know. Something to hold on to. Something to bring it back together. Magic glue. Something like that, I guess."

Hepburn laughed and took a long swallow from a pint bottle. "Magic glue? If it exists, it exists in your mind, in your imagination." He passed the bottle.

"No; maybe later on," Collins said, declining.

The major stared into the water and then put the bottle to his lips and drained it. He tossed the empty bottle in the river: it bobbed, and then sank.

"Collins, I'm having trouble with this stuff. Yeah, the booze, and it's getting worse. I keep praying the war will end yesterday, and then today, and then tomorrow. But it doesn't look like it will. Will it? No, not a chance. Disgraced and broken, that's why I can't quit now. The hospital, that is. And I can't get myself off this shit either. I couldn't live with myself, walking out now. And I can't live knowing what the stuff's doing to my skull. My judgment and precision are going down the drain. It's getting to me."

He threw sticks and stones into the stream. And then a shell casing, an empty pack of cigarettes, a spent 16 clip. He pulled another pint of vodka out of his breast pocket.

"I told Sidney Northcross about it yesterday or the day before. I don't remember, exactly. But he already knew. Stuck, you see. To go in either direction would . . . ah. Well, you know too. I want you and Sid to take over more work for a short while. Work as a touch-'n'-go team. You work together like a single mind. I have to recede for a bit, for a little bit. For a while. I have to. No one else, Andy. You and Sid are the only ones. I don't want anyone else to know. Not a soul to know about this."

He stood up and pushed his hands into his pockets. For a moment, Collins thought the major was going to leap into the river. He swayed back and forth.

"Want some more of this . . . glue?" Hepburn put the half-empty bottle on Collins's lap.

"It's not *really* serious yet," he said, turning for the path that led back to the hospital. "But I can't really trust myself like I used to. Not for a bit. Maybe it'll recede. . . . Take your time out here. Thurston and Esplaier are over the cloth now, finishing up the afternoon's odds and ends. And I . . . Well. O.K., Andy. . . ."

He stumbled through the underbrush. Collins heard the sentry challenge him for the password—which he couldn't remember without a few hints. It was raining hard by the time Collins finished off the Smirnoff's.

When he got back to the dugout and stripped, the dye from his new fatigues had bled into his skin. From neck to ankle, and it wouldn't come off. "Gangrene has finally set in," he muttered to himself, falling on his cot. "A very contagious condition, sir, unseen in medical history till now. Gangrene by osmosis."

"Dying?" asked Northcross, looking across the table at Collins's arms the next morning.

"No, just stained," he replied.

It was more than a week before the coloration disappeared. "Collins?"

Someone—no, more than one were calling his name. The voice came from behind, and echoed under the arched footbridge just ahead. "The catalogue of chameleons is complete," a voice said from across the water, in front of the El Mansion Hotel.

"Captain Pollard, is that you?" But there was only a woman sitting under a lamp. "Pollard. Pollard!" A couple stopped and stepped back into a recess in the gardens. They waited for the soldier in fatigues but without any insignias or rank to pass. Collins stopped and asked them for directions to Kangaroo Court.

Sergeant Pierson had been shot through both eyes. The bullet had shattered the left zygomatic crest between the first and second quadrants of the orbital. Through the left eye, then the nasals, the right eye at ninety degrees, and exited at two-seventy. Preliminary cosmetics and tie off the optic nerves.

Corporal Liebert begged for someone to finish him off. He knew he was a zombie. Some did. But there wasn't much for the team to finish. "Who's got the honors this time?" asked Esplaier. "High card?" Liebert smiled when Collins clamped off the I.V.s and shut down the O_2 respirator. The smile lived on even after the body snatchers took him off to the deep-freeze an hour later.

"Memories. What are they really, Collins? The dead sucking life from the living? . . . Did you kill anyone over there, Specialist?" . . . Yes, and no.

Then, near the end, Hepburn whispered across the trooper they'd just put under: "It's gone beyond anything human." They lost him too. The suction couldn't keep up with the hemorrhaging. He went fast. Captain Carson—the Sandman—began disconnecting the regulators. "The problem is," said the anesthesiologist, holding the inhalator up to his face, "that I gas them too late to be of any use. We're going about this the wrong way. They should take a whiff when they land here. . . . Instant siestas, anyone?"

"Andy Collins!" Ginger came out from behind an umbrella table. "You would have walked right past. That's it. The Court. Remember?" She pulled up her sleeve and looked at her watch. "Nearly an hour late. You're not very reliable. . . . This is my brother, Peter, and his friend, Michael Burrows."

Michael was wearing the Medical Training Corps graduation insignia on his dress uniform.

"The river is eternal and endless. Crisscrossed in layers of tissue, it flows crimson into the soil," he whispered to himself.

They shook hands across the table. Peter ordered another pitcher of beer and a fourth mug.

"Excellent beer. And at the perfect temperature." He leaned back in his chair and folded his arms across his chest.

"Ginger tells me you're in that same hospital as my father."

"Yes, but he's on the fourth floor and I'm on the first. There's a difference."

"There must be a lot of soldiers in that place." He wiped the foam from his red beard.

"About three-fifty, including the cripples in the wings and on the fourth floor."

"You mean the crippled are in with the mentally ill?"

"No," replied Collins, "they're segregated from the rest of us. The body shops at Beach—the big reconstructive complex just down from Brooke—got so overcrowded that they had to put the overflow in Chambers."

"You haven't, by any long shot, run into my father in there, have you?"

"No."

Peter turned and looked at his sister. "We were with his shrink today. . . . What was his name? Needling? Or . . ."

"Nieland," she said.

"Yes, that's it. Do you know of him?"

"He's my doctor too." Collins drank the last of the beer in his mug.

"You mean you both have the same shrink?"

"You're right. . . . What time is it?"

Collins stopped a waiter to order another pitcher of beer on his way to the phone. The inside of Kangaroo Court was crowded with tourists and a new cycle of recruits in Air Force uniforms from Lackland as well as regulars from Fort Sam. They drank and smiled as they sang along with a guitarist doing a slow version of "Don't Let Me Down."

"What branch were you in?" asked Michael before Collins had sat down again.

"Same as you."

"You had an MOS 90?"

"A 90, 91, 91a, and 901."

"You had a . . . bad time of it, I assume." Peter spoke matter-of-factly.

"Nothing out of the ordinary. It was confusing and wearisome, that's all. You don't realize the extent until you're removed from it. Everyone goes through that. Like being in shock: anyone can see that's your condition but you."

"What unit were you with?" pressed Michael eagerly.

"With a group in Pleiku, and then in Bien Hoa."

"That'd be the Sixth Surgical. Or even the Fortieth Field Surgical Hospital, your father's unit!"

"You forgot the Ninth." Collins took another long draught. He felt his face turning red with the lie.

"I'm being shipped out next Tuesday, but I don't have unit assignment yet. I'll probably end up being a line medic, but that's O.K. too. It's better than being point, or airborne," he offered, looking for agreement. "I enlisted, you know. And—"

"Yeah, Michael's really proud of his 'choice,' " interrupted Peter. "He hasn't figured out yet that *anyone* who's part of the military-industrial complex, *including* my father, is both a victim and a criminal. He thinks if he plays Dr. Kildare, he'll be a good, clean, conscientious corpse himself. What did you say the expected life of a medic on the front lines was? Something like three minutes. Michael's so gung-ho on—"

Michael slammed his glass on the table. "You're not goin' to start that rap again, are you? You and the rest of the college punks. Too bad the gooks don't do a commando hit on Penn State. Then you'd shit. You'd be singing a different tune. Somebody's got to fight, even if you and your students won't. Right, Andy?"

"It doesn't matter either way."

"It does matter," they shouted in unison. Peter and Michael stared at each other and continued arguing.

Collins opened the menu. On the inside cover was an oval etching of the presiding kangaroo. He was bewigged and black-robed, with gavel in hand, peering down on the courtroom. The judge's bench was identified as "Star Chamber." A motley jury of kangaroos pointed thumbs down at another kangaroo. He was shouting back

221

at the jury. Under the drawing was a brief description: "Actually, the expression Kangaroo Court is a mock or sham court, usually set up by inmates of a prison, to try fellow prisoners for violating the 'code.' " Collins folded the document and shoved it in his pocket. Somehow it would find its way under the door of Room 612, Building Six.

"O.K., Collins," said the medication supervisor at the other end of the phone. "You better be on the nine o'clock bus so you can sign in before ten. This is your first pass, isn't it? . . . Well, when you come past the MPs on the main entrance, show the pass and open the door on your right, just past the control desk. That's where you sign in. Better not miss that bus. . . . Roger on that, at the corner of Crockett and Travis. Where are you now? . . . Great place! No booze —the Stelazine's still active in your system. O.K.? Just play it by the numbers. No Gomer Pyle shit."

Collins returned to the table while Peter was discussing Major Hepburn's visit home last Christmas. He mentioned his father's withdrawn and peculiar habits, how he slept during the day and vanished by night. A bottle of liquor under the front seat of the car, cheap porno novels in his shirt drawer, and an unfinished poem written on the hospital's stationery.

"It spooked me so much I ended up memorizing it. It ran something like: 'The Wall of China, the Maginot Line, set there for the making in the mind of man. Ethereal in thought, lethal in life to the men driven mad by a Chink in the reeds, or a view from above. Walk tall and proud over this line. . . .' "

Other voices were getting louder in Collins's mind. He drank more beer to quiet them—their cries and curses—nearly all of them wasted. They got even louder.

Collins said good night to Peter, Michael, and Ginger. The two young men gave Collins an odd look as he began walking down the Paseo del Rio. Ginger caught up with him. They walked to the footbridge spanning the river. He teetered up the incline and stopped at the crest of the arch to steady himself. A dinner barge with candles flickering in the mist passed underneath. He could hear someone talking loudly and then a resounding laugh.

"Just another sick joke."

Ginger leaned against the railing and looked at the river. "What were you thinking when you said that?"

"What?"

222

"About the sick joke."

"Oh, nothing, really. . . . Just how far apart we've all become over this whole thing."

"You mean the war."

"Yes."

"Don't mind Peter. He's as upset and confused about my father as I am. It's really pathetic. He's such a dedicated . . ."

And then he saw them, clearly. Faces, bodiless limbs, limbless bodies, floated swiftly under the surface. They churned and rolled for as far as he could see upriver. Their words funneled down into one turbulent stream of sound. Lips moved, eyes blinked, fingers felt for something to grasp. They groaned and spoke. Bled. Died. And came alive again.

"Are you all right?"

"It's the beer and the drugs. How disgusting." Collins had vomited over the bridge.

"We'll get you back to the hospital."

"No. Not yet. I'll be all right. I just want to clean up."

Collins came out of the men's room and they resumed walking along the river. They crossed to the other side. It was raining now. The floating dinner boats headed for cover.

"Andy, don't walk so fast. I can't keep up and I'm getting soaked. Look, I'm not going to hassle you, but . . . I mean, I don't think you should be running around in this condition. You know? I mean, it's crazy." She jumped in front of him and lifted her drenched hair off her face. "Let's sit down for a minute."

They sat on a stone wall tucked under a large cypress. The wall was part of the old, open-air amphitheater he had read about in a pamphlet on the bus. Rough stone seats were set into the bank facing the river. And the actors, calling themselves Teatro de Brusso, performed below on the wide sidewalk. The wind blew papers and branches down the aisles from above. Flashes of blue lightning illuminated the stage. Three drunken regulars were weaving up the walkway, arm in arm, singing the airborne training song. A burst of thunder, the crash of a broken bottle, and "Johnny-no-balls, have you heard, we're gonna jump from them big-assed birds." Collins bolted.

"Andy!" He heard the quick splashes of her sneakers behind him.

"Andy! An . . . dy!"

Faster. Two three four. Hep, two three four.

He was cold and wet when he opened his eyes deep in a gray forest. The sun wasn't quite up, but a murky light shone behind the cypress and pine. Long sweeps of moss hung like spiderwebs suspended from limb to limb. A musty, rotting smell came up from the earth. Pockets of dense mist floated in layers above a swollen stream. He was lost somewhere deep in a Texas bayou. "This land felt of a bad omen," he could hear Mrs. Mayfield say; Moses Austin's "viable Utopia," she called it.

An animal resembling a Gila monster crawled out from under a stump. It sprang at a large butterfly. A wing fell to the ground. It ate that too. The monster changed from a reddish brown to bright green as it slithered onto a patch of moss.

The catalogue of chameleons is complete, he thought. No, not quite, Captain, not quite. The corporal has come back a sergeant. He left alive and came back dead. I'll put Sergeant Back Again in the catalogue. Do it up like a high school yearbook, Professor, with smiling pictures and stupid sayings. And Hepburn with his poem, in with the literati. We could find a match for the foot I found in a boot. And the shoulder that fits the arm that came off in my hand. Give it an idea of unity—that way they can't accuse us of spilling the secret. We can work in reverse: pick up the pieces and give them the illusion of unity. That's better than the other. Things come apart, you know. And it kills a lot of people to have to admit that. Bodies bleed, friendships dissolve, marriages are liquidated, eyes water. It really kills them to say they just didn't believe they'd ever come apart over the whole thing. By bits and pieces. We could do it like a jigsaw puzzle.

And a wide-angle shot of the *casa gris* with the roses in bloom. Have the pool filled, and arrange the cripples in deck chairs. But even then, it might look phony, you know, only hopeless approximations. It might not add up to the same sum we think it would. And you're right, we'd only have the black-and-white and not the thing itself. So we should start off with the fly from the Café Delaronge, and dedicate the catalogue to the brown dog in the ditch. Have Chaplain Ready throw air instead of ashes. "The grave is greater than the sum of the parts"—use that for his caption. And maybe one of you, Professor, with your arm around the woman you were to fall in love with in Thailand.

Collins was crying when he leaned over the bank for a drink. The water was turbulent. It swept splotches off the bottom clean, exposing the red clay bed. Small stones and twigs whirled across the bottom. They etched shapes: some jagged and sawtoothed, others graceful and soft. A hand without fingers, an eye and a socket, lips on an opened mouth, appeared to move on the clay.

"Don't tell the secret! Don't let anyone know the truth!"

He moved upstream a few meters to a place where the water was calmer. There was a clear spot under the water where a tree had fallen across the river. He saw the reflection of his own face again, shimmering clearly on the surface. There were outlines of other people beneath his face, and where the anatomies were defined, he dredged up the clay. It took him a long time to shape them, from two- into three-dimensional organs. He made a foot for the trooper who was sniffed out by the Rubbermaid plant. An ear for Ron Courtland. A new hand for the M-60 man in the recovery hootch. Eyes and nose for Sergeant Pierson so he can see again. New fingers for the master sergeant from the motor pool. An arm for Captain Sarkofsky. A head—for general use—for the Unknown. And a new heart for Sergeant Back Again. He piled them on two mounds of moss and stepped back to examine his work.

"The body shop'd be jealous as hell!"

The sun had burned off the haze. Thin waves of steam evaporated from the collection resting on the moss. It was high noon, with some shade, but no shadows, when he finished assembling the man of many parts and laid him to rest by the river. He was a young American, just another someone in another somewhere, washed up by a river in Vietnam, or Texas.

"So may we forever know ourselves by you."

Collins covered the clay corpse with his fatigue shirt and walked out of the woods.

"And after all this time . . ."

"Chambers Pavilion. Sergeant Lieder speaking."

"Yes. Captain Nieland, please."

"Who's calling?"

"Andrew Collins."

"Collins! Where the hell are you, man?"

"I don't know. Just get me Nieland."

"Collins, is that you?" screamed Dr. Nieland.

"Yes." Collins held the receiver away from his ear.

"Damn. Do you have any idea what's been going on here since

ten o'clock last night? Damn. Half of security is searching for you. Nice goin'. . . . Christ, where are you?"

"I don't know. Out on some backwoods road. There's—"

"Are you all right?"

"I'm all right now. There was something I had to do and now it's done. It's over."

"Yeah, Collins. Tell that to General Desmond for me. Now where in hell are you?"

"In a phone booth on a dirt road. There's a sign ahead. It says Considine's Crossing."

"Considine's Crossing! Where the Christ . . . Sergeant Lieder. You ever heard of Considine's Crossing?"

"Yes, sir. I used to go fishing out thata way," Collins overheard Lieder say.

"O.K. Call security and have them take you out there to pick up this patient. Collins! Collins! You there?"

"Yes."

"I want you to count backward by ones from a thousand. Go ahead, Collins: nine hundred ninety-nine . . ."

"Nine hundred ninety-eight. Nine hundred ninety . . ."

Nieland was waiting at the emergency bay when Collins arrived with Lieder. He watched his patient with more than just professional sadness. As he looked at Collins—his disheveled light-brown hair, the boyish lines of his muddy face, his clear blue eyes—Nieland grew angry. Walking toward him was another casualty of the war. Another botched life, a wasted career, a meaningless end. For Nieland it meant another failure: but of what, he was still unsure.

As Collins approached the incline ramp, Nieland noticed that he was smiling. It was a relaxed, happy expression on Collins's face and Nieland saw a buoyancy in his stride that he knew wasn't there the day before. It was also unusual for Sergeant Lieder to be involved in a conversation with a psycho. Yet they walked together like classmates discussing a particularly provocative lecture. Had it not been for Lieder's being dressed in white, and Collins half undressed and covered with mud, Nieland would have felt more at ease.

The sadness and anger gave way to curiosity: What in God's name is going on with these two? he asked himself. He knew Lieder well, and the man spoke only with the cripples.

226

"He's all yours, Captain," said Lieder as he saluted.

"Thank you, Sergeant. You did a fine job."

"Thank you, sir. Anytime. It was a pleasure, believe me. See ya 'round, Collins."

"Well, Collins. . . . You recall how Steve McQueen finished up *The Great Escape?*"

"But I wasn't trying to escape," pleaded Collins. "Just the opposite. I came back on—"

"Save it!" snapped Nieland, taking his patient by the arm. "You can talk all you want later. I'm putting you in isolation for the day."

"You're what!" screamed Collins, tearing his arm from Nieland's grasp.

"Don't get rattled! Jesus. What the hell do you expect me to do? Do you realize what you've done to your chances of walking away from this hospital *for good?* . . . Do you realize that all the gains you've made—we've made—over the past two months were obliterated by the past twelve hours?"

Nothing more was said between patient and doctor as they rode the elevator up to the fourth floor.

"Collins," said the psychiatrist before locking the cell door, "I don't know what happened to you last night. And maybe when you tell me I'll understand. But now we have to play it according to the book. You violated the conditions. If I didn't take some action which the board construes as punitive, then they'd nail you and me to the wall. I'm sorry, but you've deprived me of any say in the matter. We'll go over all this tomorrow."

When the bolt was thrown, Collins glanced at the walls, the narrow window slit, the wicker chair, the mattress on the floor, and the mud he had tracked in across the blue carpeting. He cringed when he realized that he had spent a week in this very same room two and a half months before. He wondered if Nieland had put him back in this room on purpose.

"My God," he muttered. "It's true. It's all true. Pollard was right. He was right the whole time! . . . God. . . ."

Collins was awake when Nieland walked into his cell at five o'-clock the next morning. He handed his patient a glass of orange juice and said, "Come on. Let's get out of here." Collins—juice in hand—followed Nieland through the dark corridors to his office.

"Here. Here's a clean uniform. Use my shoeshine kit for your boots. It's in that closet. There's a shower through that door. You need to get cleaned up."

Collins, more suspicious than grateful at being out of isolation so early, thought that this might well be the end. He was about to be transferred to a VA loony bin.

"Fine," said Nieland as he looked up at Collins, clean and neatly dressed. "That'll do just fine." He was nervously gathering up his files and stuffing cassettes into his pockets.

"Here. You carry this. We'll catch breakfast in the staff mess hall."

After breakfast, Collins, with Nieland's portable tape recorder slung over his shoulder, walked quickly with the doctor through the basement tunnel to the elevators for Building Six. When the doors closed and Nieland had pushed "6," he turned to Collins.

"I'm taking you on rounds this morning. Say nothing. Just operate the recorder. When we walk into a room, push down 'Record.' When we walk out, push 'Stop.' Think you can handle that assignment?"

Collins nodded.

"Remember. Under no circumstances are you to say a word."

Captain Nieland didn't begin with the name at the head of his list. Instead he walked to the end of the sixth-floor corridor and opened door number 612. Collins's first thought was of the menu from Kangaroo Court, which he had left in his trousers in Nieland's office. But as the door swung open, he wanted to run back to isolation.

Captain Pollard was kneeling on the floor with his back against the bedframe. His arms were held above his head by leather restraints locked to the bedpost. The sheets were twisted around his body like a cocoon. He looked like someone on a torture rack. As Nieland approached him, he opened his eyes wider and mumbled in Vietnamese to an imaginary someone, for whom he answered in a different voice.

"Well, well," said Nieland. "You studying to be Houdini's successor, Pollard?" Nieland knelt in front of the Professor and looked back up at Collins.

"Specialist. . . . Specialist!"

"Sir?"

"I didn't hear that button go down."

"Sorry, sir," said Collins, coming out of his daze long enough to push "Record."

Nieland unwrapped the Professor and removed his restraints.

228

Pollard's hands, above the bandages, were blue from lack of circulation. He continued with his imaginary dialogue and stared into the wall. Nieland helped him up onto the bed.

Pollard suddenly turned to face Nieland.

"Now," he said in a hoarse voice, "I ordered you yesterday to see that these prisoners who are marked up from the interrogation were executed by dawn. The sun is up and I'm still alive. Why, Sergeant? Why?"

Nieland tried to initiate a conversation with Pollard for over half an hour, but the patient spoke only Vietnamese or nonsensical English phrases. Except at one point, when he looked squarely at Collins for the first time and said:

"Now do you understand why you have to come to your senses?"

Collins was so shocked by the meaning of the Professor's remark that he almost called out to Nieland that it was all an act, that the Professor was just playing a game, that he was perfectly sane, and that this was just his way of punishing himself. But as Collins got closer, he saw that Nieland had unwrapped the bandages and was examining not one old scar on the Professor's wrist, but two new lacerations, on both wrists, which ran up the radial arteries. Collins turned his head and walked back toward the door.

After Nieland had re-dressed the wounds, he stood the Professor on his feet and handcuffed him behind his back. Nieland put his arm on Pollard's shoulder.

"See you in . . ." But the doctor never finished his phrase. He just shook his head and signaled for Collins to leave. Collins watched the Professor whispering into a crack which ran down the wall.

"Come on, Collins. That's all there is in here." As Nieland was locking the door, an aide came along the hall.

"I told you never, never to leave Pollard in that room alone. If I ever find out that he's been left unattended, I'll have you court-martialed so severely you'll be slitting your wrists. Jerk. That order is written for every shift. Obey it."

It was ten o'clock when they returned to Nieland's office. Collins, depressed and exhausted by the rounds through Building Six, slouched into the chair in front of Nieland's desk.

"Seen enough? Or do you want to accompany me on rounds through the VA hospital in Austin? That's even worse."

"I've seen enough."

"O.K. Now let's get down to business."

"What business?"

"Push the 'Record' button down and tell me what happened to you in the past thirty-six hours."

Nieland listened to Collins's explanation with a skeptical, clinical ear at first. But as Collins revealed what had occurred along the stream, Nieland was amazed. When the tape recorder in Collins's lap beeped, he didn't stop his patient's story to change tapes. He pushed the button on his Dictaphone.

As Collins was describing the anatomical parts he had constructed and for whom each organ was created, Nieland rose from behind his desk. He glanced at Collins's drawing of the knee reconstruction on the shirt pinned to the wall, and walked to the window. When Collins finished speaking, Nieland remained staring down at the men from the third-floor wards playing softball.

"Did it ever occur to you, Collins," he said, with his back to the patient, "while you were assembling this . . . this Universal Soldier, that you were putting yourself back together?"

"What do you mean?"

"I mean this: you disintegrated piece by piece, organ by organ, right along with all those casualties you helped treat over there. You might as well have been wounded yourself. Not once. Hundreds of times. As you once said to me," he continued, turning to face Collins, "you were sentenced to the Fortieth Surgical Hospital as a casualty, not a staff member. Correct?"

"Yes. And that's just how it felt. Nobody died right. I mean, they didn't die a good death. A complete death. . . . Do you know what I mean?"

"Go on."

"Nobody died knowing what they were dying for. There wasn't any purpose to it, and they knew it. That's what was so horrible. And the ones maimed and missing limbs, they just couldn't really accept it. Because they weren't sure what they were doing in Nam in the first place. And then to lose an arm, or legs . . . That's why there's such hatred in the cripples. And they couldn't even come back to a grateful homeland. Just wasted."

"And so . . . Let me see if I have this right, Collins. So you couldn't accept it because they couldn't: that there, right in front of your eyes, were Americans just like you, as bright and idealistic as you —and there they were, laid out, wasted, dying, dead, for nothing. And since they were dying for nothing, your efforts to help save or restore them amounted to the same thing. Nothing. Then the ulti-mate straw—straws: your activities in the ESR, Sergeant Back Again, and then the arm that was re-severed in the VC assault on the support base attached to the field hospital. And your spirit snapped, and then your sanity. . . . Yes? . . . No?"

Collins nodded yes.

"So in order to survive this absurd waste which you were power-less to control, you created fictitious lives and even futures for the soldiers who died or were critically wounded."

"Then you knew. You know, then."

"Know what?"

"That the letters are real."

"Yes," answered Nieland cautiously as he sat down, "but I really didn't understand just how real they were until I listened to Hep-burn's mumbling and spoke to Northcross. By 'real' you mean fac-tual, and that you wrote them. . . ."

"Yes." Collins closed his eyes and lowered his head.

"All rather macabre, isn't it, Collins? But don't you see, now that these facts are coming to light, that there's a method to your mad-ness. A logic. Don't you see that the soldier you made of clay is the logical, tangible conclusion to your fictitious letters? That this clay effigy was the sum total of all the Americans killed or wounded in Vietnam: your yearbook, or catalogue, as you just said?"

Collins nodded.

"But as these others—the real soldiers—expired one by one, a piece of you died with them. You had to sacrifice part of yourself to resurrect them from the grave. Finally, you were nearly forced to join them when you tried to kill yourself. The fiction, you see, and the responsibility to those men to keep them alive—it grew too great. Am I making sense to you?"

"Yes. Yes."

"O.K. What's important about yesterday is that you created a tangible, composite American—Albeit a very dead soldier, for whom you made parts of the body and organs out of a lifeless substance. But when you covered him with *your* Army shirt, you were saying: I, too, was a soldier, and the soldiers in me have died with him. And as you said, then you laid him to rest. You walked out of those woods *out of uniform.* Correct? . . . You returned yourself to a civilian by stripping your military identity. No wonder you seemed happy when you came back with Lieder."

231

"I did." Suddenly, he began to sob. "But the voices came back again last night. I thought it was over. I thought it was over!"

"Well," said Nieland reassuringly, "all this didn't happen in one night; you can't expect it to go away in one night."

"What happens to me now?"

"Well, today is the twenty-second of June. You've been in Chambers for about . . ."

"For seventy-six days. And nights. Except last night."

"O.K. Then we've got thirteen days to get you out of here. But I can't board you until July 2."

"But what happens to me?"

Dr. Nieland sighed as he stood up and walked from behind his desk to sit in the chair next to Collins.

"I used to be able to predict the futures of men brought before that board. But when they reversed my case on Pollard, I swore I'd never play fortune teller again. In my opinion, they destroyed Pollard. So I'm not going to say—"

"When will you see him again?"

"Pollard? In my official capacity, probably never again after this morning. The board assigned Penderspot to him after the argument I had with them for another extension."

Collins's expression changed.

"What? What's the matter?"

"It's just that Pollard said that whatever happened, don't let Penderspot near him. He said Penderspot couldn't tell the difference between a Babinski reflex and Korsakoff's syndrome."

Nieland chuckled. "That's Pollard through and through. Babinski and Korsakoff's." His laughter increased as he tried to repeat the phrase in Pollard's academic tone of voice.

So there they sat, captain and ex-specialist, doctor and patient, laughing together while Pollard proposed to a Thai woman as he mumbled Vietnamese into a crack on the wall. While Perkins lost another Tet of Hanoi Hearts. And another five thousand Allied troops crossed the border into Cambodia.

CHAPTER **18**

Collins slept peacefully for the next four nights. Except for vivid dreams of the Fortieth Field Surgical Hospital, he wasn't plagued by nightmares and voices. But no matter how much he slept, he awoke exhausted.

On the fifth night, Collins was visited by two people in one form: the face and voice of Captain Jackson Pollard set in the body of the clay soldier. It rose up like a monster from a grave and walked in front of the Alamo, this earthen veteran in fatigues, asking people where he could find Specialist Andrew B. Collins. The passers-by pointed to Chambers. And the thing walked into the first-floor ward and said to Collins: You. You must do it. You made a pact.

When Collins awoke that morning he knew it was far from over. He didn't need Nieland to interpret the ghastly visitor. But, he reminded himself while sitting in the mess hall, he had promised Pollard nothing. In fact, Collins's only thought was to get out in one piece. That was as far as he could project. . . . All bets were off until the boarding of July 2.

After breakfast he intended to stroll out to the picnic tables under the pines. But as he began walking across the softball field he became absorbed in his thoughts and wandered aimlessly: in and out of the rose gardens, then down beyond the pool without water, then along the north fence and into a dark magnolia grove. He realized, when he looked up and saw that there was no path through the grove, that he had walked down a narrowing peninsula of grass which wound back on itself behind the picnic area. He knew he had walked in a wide circle, but he couldn't figure out where he was. There wasn't a fence in front of him, no warning signs that he was within twenty meters of the barricades: the path simply stopped.

Collins turned around and looked back down the grass path. I've walked completely around Chambers without ever seeing the building, or hearing any voices. Is that possible? he asked himself.

He moved his head to the left. There it was: rolling lawns, manicured gardens with bright flowers, the control station perched above the volleyball court, the birdbath outside the main entrance, and the wide gray hospital with a chopper pad on the roof. Framed by the trees and gardens, it reminded him of a painting by Turner. . . . Mists, a pond instead of the pool, a few cows on the softball diamond. He laughed and knew it was time to go back.

As he came toward the side entrance to the first floor, he noticed a young woman sitting on a bench with an old man in the restricted —No Visitors Allowed—area. Her head was bowed and her chestnut hair covered the side of her face. She was oddly dressed, though, he thought, in a plaid skirt and a white turtleneck.

He was nearly inside the ward when she spotted him. She looked happy and sad at once when he looked back.

"Andy," she said again, rising from the bench. He avoided her eyes.

"I found out you were back in the hospital. But no one would tell me what happened to you. How are you?" She smiled and walked toward him.

He let the door to the ward swing shut. He really wasn't up to seeing her again. Not after what had happened. As she came closer, he could hear her in her soggy sneakers, chasing after him through the darkness like a harpy.

"I want you to meet my father." She motioned toward the man on the bench. "He's not feeling at all well."

Collins scrutinized the shriveled face.

"Your father?"

"Yes, my father," she repeated, as she watched Collins turn white. He stared down at a man who had aged twenty years since Collins last saw him. "That's . . . " he stammered in disbelief.

She turned away and knelt in front of her father: "Daddy.

Daddy." She shook him. He tried to lift his head. "Father, this is Andy Collins. Andy Col—" She broke off and looked up at Collins. She saw the tears in his eyes.

"You're Specialist Collins!" she cried out.

Hepburn, aroused at hearing "Specialist Collins" outside his own mind, resumed his role as triage chief and directed the nape case to Colonel Shied and the head would to Northcross.

"Oh, my God!" She swung herself off the ground and collapsed on the bench. "You're the one he babbles about," she said, as if answering a question she hadn't thought of asking until this moment. "Then you do know him. And *you know* what happened to him. But why did you lie to me, and Michael, and my brother, the other night?"

Collins felt his face flush. He stared at the ground and thought of the evening when Pollard first proposed the pact and he pulled his pillow over his head. "It won't work, Collins, I've tried it. There's no escape."

"I . . . I couldn't deal with it. The connection. It's too close. The questions I can't answer. Don't you see?" He held out his hands defensively.

Major Hepburn began speaking again. Collins realized that he was repeating the names of the surgical staff from the field hospital, always in the same order, and ending the list with "Ah, hopeless approximations." Collins's own roll of the dead and maimed began to echo through his mind like a memorial service. But the reality of yet another casualty, slumped on a bench not more than six feet away, suddenly shattered the peace he had made in the forest.

"Sergeant Back Again has come back again," he said aloud. "This time as a major."

"What are you talking about?" Ginger asked.

Collins sighed and sat down on the bench. "He fulfilled his own prophecy," he said. "The men working over the wasted are eventually wasted themselves. That's what your father said."

"But he's used to working with sick and injured people. He has, all his life. I don't understand what you mean."

"There's a difference," responded Collins slowly, "between sickness, injury, and the wasted. And he knew what was happening to him—to all of us—as it was happening. I see that now. We play physician for some and patient for others. The world's a hospital. But the difference, he said, was that everything that happens in

Nam is intentional. The men we treated weren't just wounded and sick. No, they were wasted. See? Wasted. Caught in a moral crossfire. Used by this country, by the Vietnamese, by themselves. There is no rationale. There is no way to make sense out of the senseless. You either accept it or go insane trying to answer the whys, by being committed to the question by the question. That's why this hospital is so crowded. Because if you—"

"Magic glue," blurted out Hepburn. He began laughing in such a hideous wail that the cicadas rattled and screeched frenziedly above the threesome on the red bench.

Collins looked at the crazed expression on the face of his commanding officer. His ashen pallor and gray stubble against a background of red and white roses gave him a funereal appearance. Collins struggled to find words to explain how desperately he wished to perform a last rite over her father, how Collins yearned to list him with the dead laid to rest under his fatigue shirt by a stream near Considine's Crossing. But those words never came: Hepburn, like Collins, Pollard, and Wright, had survived—at least, they were still alive.

"None of us will ever really come home again. There is no coming back when your beliefs are destroyed, your soul shattered. We are war orphans, as a friend of mine once said."

"So am I."

Collins looked inquisitively at Ginger.

"I'm a war orphan too," she repeated. "I've lost a father. I mean, this is not the man I've known for twenty years."

Collins was about to say that you can be an orphan to yourself. But as the meaning of Ginger's statement beckoned his empathy, it occurred to him that there was a bond between the veterans and their families which went beyond the battlefield. He realized then that the possibility of making some sense of the non sense was not the futile plea of a madman.

A chopper swooped over the baseball field and landed on the roof. Ginger turned and straightened the collar on her father's bathrobe. Collins rose from the bench and began to walk away.

"Where are you going?" called out Ginger over the noise of the helicopter.

"I'll be right back."

Collins rounded the corner of Chambers and looked out at Building Six. He scanned the sixth floor and counted down twelve win-

236

dows. He imagined Captain Pollard talking to himself in Vietnamese with his hands lashed to the bedposts. Collins held up his own hands as if comparing their two states of impairment.

Forty-eight hours after his boarding, as he sat overlooking the San Antonio River from Kangaroo Court, he began to write about himself and Pollard and Captain Nieland.